"Moves along at a breakneck pace. . . . The whole thing works and works well."

Philadelphia Inquirer

"A fine brew of courage and corruption, with a last-minute twist that will leave you dizzy!"

Cosmopolitan

"An exciting, beautifully crafted novel of intrigue."
John Godey
Author of *The Taking of Pelham One Two Three*

"Add James Mills to your list of 'must read' authors."

Pittsburgh Press

THE TRUTH ABOUT PETER HARLEY

Also by James Mills
Published by Ballantine Books:

ON THE EDGE

THE TRUTH ABOUT PETER HARLEY

JAMES MILLS

BALLANTINE BOOKS • NEW YORK

Library of Congress Catalog Card Number: 79-10654

ISBN   0-345-29005-4

This edition published by arrangement with E. P. Dutton

Manufactured in the United States of America

First Ballantine Books Edition: May 1983

Notes

Could I be sure that it would cause no embarrassment to list by name the people who helped me with my research for this novel, I would do so with delight. But since the circumstances of those to whom I am most indebted may be inconsistent with public acknowledgment, I must thank them in the only way certain to do no damage: anonymously.

Also I want to emphasize that this story is entirely a work of fiction. None of the characters ever existed. Tony Deniset, though he narrates the story, does not resemble myself; nor do any of the other characters portray individuals I have ever met or heard of. Any reader who imagines that any character or event in this story depicts a real person or event is mistaken.

J.M.

Contents

Bangkok

1

PETER HARLEY was raised by the state, adopted by a madwoman, recruited as a government assassin. He fell in love, pursued enemies, sheltered friends, and today is alive or not depending on whom you think it wise to trust. I trust he's alive, because I like him and because faith is more reliable than fact. The last I saw of him, he was in a missionary's house on the run from other American agents and a squad of Marine embassy guards. The last I heard of him, he had been attacked with flamethrowers on a small island in the Andaman Sea 175 miles from Burma. And the last I *believe* of him, he and the madwoman and a thirteen-year-old Thai girl were roaring past Tiffany's on the back of a Honda motorcycle. But that takes some preparation.

My name is Tony Deniset. The story begins last winter. My wife had just been killed in a skiing accident, during the first vacation we ever took together, and I had returned to New York to move out of our apartment. Her death was a catastrophe that went beyond grief. It left me enraged, bitter, and tormented by the possibility that I myself had helped to bring it about. Then, a week after I arrived back in New York, sixteen shopping days before Christmas, I was fired from my job as articles editor of a monthly magazine, which I won't name here. Not content to have betrayed me, but wishing to be thanked for it as well, my superiors gave me a contract to write six articles the following year for a combined fee only slightly less than my annual salary.

I was, therefore, looking for a story to do, an escape, something that would take me far from New York, take me in fact to the world's most distant, crumbling edge—and if that edge should suddenly sheer off into oblivion while I was there, so much the better.

You see how melodramatic and self-pitying I was. I needed a cure.

I had read a story in the *New York Times* about narcotics agents the American government had sent to Southeast Asia to find and cut the columns of smugglers streaming like army ants from the mountains of Burma and Thailand to Malaysia, Singapore, and the West. Opium and jade came out, rice and guns went in, loaded on the backs of hundreds of mules, escorted through the ancient Shan states by private mountain armies, earth-brown warriors fighting bandits, insurgents, and the assembled forces of other jungle fiefdoms. The Americans were there only to stop the opium, the embassy said, but governments in Rangoon, Bangkok, and Kuala Lumpur worried about more important things, about rice and guns and revolution. Opium was the barter that financed war: one *choi* bought one M-16, and as a unit of exchange was more stable than the Swiss franc.

I decided to find one of these agents—some milk-fed young American, I assumed, with too little experience and too many morals, sitting astride that trail of contraband, growing more and more nervous and uncertain, frustration corrupting his courage. I wanted to talk with him, watch him, adhere to him, and discover what would be his end.

So I went off in search of something promised by the *New York Times* and my own naïveté. Reality proved more complex, of course, and what began as an idea for a magazine article grew finally into something more.

2

IN WASHINGTON they took me to lunch, two New York Italians in three-piece suits and an American Indian in a turtleneck. The Indian was only five feet five but he had a barrel chest and arms that stretched the wool of his sweater.

When he took off his coat the sweater pulled up and I saw a revolver in the waistband at the small of his back.

One of the Italians, a thin man with a bony face and a Clark Gable mustache, said, "Where is it exactly you want to go?"

I said, "Where are the Americans most active?"

They considered that for a few moments—all of them, it seemed to me, having the same thought. Finally the thin Italian looked at the Indian. The Indian's name was Frank. He grinned, a shy crinkling around the eyes.

"That would be Thailand," he said. "The Burmese don't like other countries poking around in their business. The Malaysians aren't too happy about it either."

"But in Thailand?"

"The Thais let us do pretty much what we want. They have a problem with Communist insurgents, some of whom get money from the drug traffic. They hope that when we take out a trafficker it means less money for the insurgents."

"So you have agents in Thailand who are pretty active."

"Yes."

"How close can I get to them?"

The Italians looked nervously at Frank.

"Well," Frank said, grinning again, "I guess you can get about as close as you want."

I had come to these men with the recommendation of Senator John Ehrlich, chairman of the Subcommittee on Foreign Policy Research and Development. He had roomed with my brother at Yale, was an usher at my wedding, and had said that if I wanted to write about American drug agents in Southeast Asia he'd see to it I got cooperation.

"As long as they don't have any complaints and you're not disturbing their operations." The other Italian said that. He was older than the thin one, somewhere in his mid-fifties, and wanted to be sure he got his reluctance on the record.

A waiter arrived with spaghetti and clam sauce and a bottle of wine.

The thin Italian, pretending cooperation, said to Frank, "What about Songkhla?"

"Yeah," Frank said. "We've just sent a man down there. It's in the south near the border, an old smuggling town. Everyone carries guns, shoot-outs in the street, that sort of thing." He filled my glass. "That's what you're looking for?"

"Maybe. Why'd you send a man down?"

No one answered.

"I mean, will he be there permanently?"

"We hope so," Frank said. The others kept their eyes on the tablecloth.

Frank appeared amused at his colleagues' caution. "We have a target there," he said.

"What do you mean? A trafficker?"

Before Frank could answer, the older man, the reluctant one, said, "It's a routine operation. The Bangkok office has many operations going all the time and we don't place any more emphasis on one than the others."

Frank ignored that speech. "For what you want to do—that's hang around with some agents, right?"

"Right." I wished I could have talked with Frank alone.

"Then I'd suggest you start in Bangkok. That's your best bet. Talk to our people there and get an idea what's happening and what you think might interest you."

"I'd like to do that."

"We'll send a cable. You won't have any problems. The senator has weight."

I liked Frank for his lack of discretion. The Italians looked scared.

3

I FIRST SAW Peter Harley a week later at a Christmas party in the American embassy in Bangkok. Even his enemies never turned down a chance to drink with him. I realized later that everyone, women especially, was in a rush to know him while he was still around, to claim their fair share of stories to tell. Something about him told them he would not be around long, and they knew that when he was dead prestige would accrue to those who could claim a close acquaintance with him.

But though everyone wanted to know about him, listen to him, not everyone actually liked him. He provoked fear, guilt, envy, anger. His closest friend, his adopted partner, was a Thai lieutenant named Jaran Varunsara. And Lieutenant Jaran was disliked by other Thais for much the same reasons the Americans disliked Harley. "They were made for each other." Everyone agreed to that.

I had been invited to the party during a visit my first day in Bangkok to the Drug Enforcement Administration's regional director, a man named George Valdez. His office was in an annex next to the three-story white colonial embassy building itself, separated from the street by a wall and guarded gate, surrounded by lawns, a fountain, and topiary shrubs in the shape of elephants and peacocks.

Valdez was short, thickly built, originally from Uruguay I learned later, and, sitting behind a large desk in a corner office, he told me he had been cabled from Washington by one of the men who took me to lunch. "You want to meet some agents, sort of follow them around, do I have it right?"

I told him he did.

"What sort of agents?"

He wasn't the kind of man who could successfully hide impatience. He was busy and I was another problem. He wished Washington would leave him alone.

"The most active," I said.

"Well, look," he said, trying to find some way to get rid of me, "why don't you come to this party tonight. We're having a Christmas party. You can meet a lot of the people."

So I went to the party. Desks were covered with paper cups and bottles. Wastebaskets were filled with ice. Valdez took me by the arm and hauled me around and introduced me to a Thai colonel who *wai*ed me politely—his palms joined, fingertips raised to the chin. (The higher the hands are raised, the greater the respect shown. Later I was to see hands raised all the way to the top of the head, by monks in prayer and by a heroin addict begging drugs from a dealer.) The colonel smiled pleasantly at everything I said, although, it turned out, he understood no English. Before long, Valdez was pulled away by a man in a beard and I found myself alone. I felt awkward and out of place, the only man in the room not engaged in conversation. I was suddenly sorry I had come to Thailand. I was dependent on these strangers—diplomats, agents, government bureaucrats. If for some reason they failed to cooperate with me, if they simply ignored me, what the hell would I do? Go back to the men who fired me and confess another failure? I was at the mercy of uninterested strangers ten thousand miles from home. Or maybe the ten thousand miles didn't have anything to do with it. The Thais in the embassy room—bowing, smiling, pretending to understand English—looked as uncomfortable as I was, foreigners too.

I was watching the crowd when an older woman, perhaps the wife of some senior officer in the embassy, paused as she walked past me. She said, "The ones in suits are FSOs and the others are narcotics agents." I asked her what an FSO was. She said, "Foreign Service officer," and walked away. She must have been reading my mind. The party looked like the strained get-together of two opposing football teams. I wondered, in fact, if it had been given to encourage closer relations between the rival players. If so, it was failing. Very few suits were talking to very few sport shirts. Maybe because the sport shirts concealed guns and that made the suits nervous, or jealous. I thought I could locate the center of this anxiety in the person of a girl, about twenty-five, standing against a set of filing cabinets. Her familiarity with passing FSOs identified her as one of them, but she was talking with, or at, a good-looking young man in a safari jacket.

The girl was very pretty, but a bit cocky, perhaps unintentionally so. She had shoulder-length brown hair, a slender expressive face, and thin lips that never did less than smile in the time I watched her. She looked rich. She was wearing a black dress, old and not quite right at this party, but one that obviously had been fashionable at some earlier time and place. It was letting everyone know, whether she planned it that way or not, that the other place had been nicer than this one and its people nicer than the people here. For some reason, possibly connected with the perversity that made her wear that dress, she had placed a black beauty mark, the width of a pencil eraser, on her right cheek about an inch in front of the earlobe.

The agent she was speaking to was in his early thirties, dark-haired, well tanned, quite a bit taller than she. At first he seemed relaxed and happy, looking at her eyes and smiling, but then I noticed that the empty paper cup in his hand was crushed and mangled. As he listened to the girl his fingers quietly tore holes in the cup. An older man in a suit joined them, and the agent, as if suddenly remembering someone he needed to talk to, excused himself with smiles and a nod, and hurried off. When he was on the other side of the filing cabinets, out of sight of the girl, he stopped, adrift for a moment, his smile gone, his fingers punching and tearing at the cup. He was next to a window, standing in the sun, and he looked out absently at a group of guests talking and laughing on the lawn.

In a moment he was approached by a woman in slacks, and again he stood listening, smiling, ripping and mangling. He seemed trapped, as if he had just dropped in unwillingly from some other world and was doing his best, despite disturbing preoccupations, to be polite to the natives. I wondered what could be so important that it held him in that room, among those people.

"Let me introduce you." Valdez had returned and was gripping my arm.

"Is he one of your agents?" I said.

"Yes, but he's not what you want, believe me. He's here temporarily, based in New York. I'd like to get him permanently but I doubt if I can swing it."

When Valdez and I walked up, the woman in slacks looked embarrassed, said she had to find her husband, and disappeared.

The agent's name was Peter Harley. His face broke into a smile and he said, "You're the guy who's writing the article."

I looked at Valdez. "Word gets around."

"I want him to meet Jaran," Valdez said, as if we had been discussing that possibility. I had never heard of Jaran and asked who he was.

"The only honest cop in Thailand," Harley said immediately.

"Have you seen him?" Valdez said.

"He's working. I don't think he'll be able to make it."

"See me before you leave," Valdez said to Harley and walked off toward one of the desks covered with bottles.

"What kind of article are you writing?" Harley said.

"I don't know yet. How long have you been in Bangkok?"

"A few months, off and on. I come and go. Are you going to travel around any while you're here?"

"I hope so. Who's Jaran?"

Harley looked down at his hands, noticed the remains of the cup, and tossed it into a wastebasket.

"No matter what you do while you're here," he said, "don't leave without meeting Jaran. Don't waste time with the bullshitting thieves. Jaran is it. Look out for the guys with the gold chains and Rolexes.''

''Where can I find him?''

''We're doing something tomorrow, but maybe the day after— where are you staying?''

''The Siam Intercontinental.''

''I'll talk to him and call you.''

''Fine.''

I had noticed, several yards away, a man about fifty-five years old who was staring at me. I tried to ignore him, but from the corner of my eye I could see that he continued to peer, as if he had unpleasant business with me and wanted to size me up before making his approach. Harley and I went on talking, and before long I began to suspect that it might, in fact, be my proximity to Harley that drew the starer's interest. Perhaps in the severity of his scrutiny there was a touch of something like jealousy. I was becoming a little uncomfortable when the girl in the black dress walked up and handed Harley a paper cup with a drink in it.

''Would you like a drink?'' she said to me.

''No, thanks.''

Harley introduced us. Her name was Sandra Gilchrist.

''What do you do here?'' I said, turning my back to the starer.

''I work for the embassy, in the political section. You're writing a magazine article.''

''Yes,'' I said. ''Everyone seems to know that.''

I saw now, with surprise, that the spot on her cheek was not a beauty mark at all, but a mole. I wondered why she had not had it removed. The longer I stood there, watching her and listening to her, the more certain I became that she kept the mole as a gesture of defiance. There was an independence, almost an arrogance, in her smile and laughter. She was not going to give up even that small, ugly part of herself for the sake of public opinion.

After several minutes she turned to Harley, and her eyes looked as if she was willing to join him against the world.

''Tell him about the dog,'' she said.

Harley pretended not to hear her. ''Excuse me a moment. I've got to see Valdez.''

''What about the dog?'' I said when Harley had left, and glanced quickly over my shoulder to see if the starer was still there. He was not. I looked carefully around the room but the man had disappeared. I did not see him again that day.

"Oh, it's just a little story about Peter," Sandra said, "but it was a sensation around here, it almost got him sent back. And it shows how things work."

"What happened?"

"Well, you've seen all the horrible diseased dogs in Bangkok . . ."

"Yes." That morning getting into a taxi I had had to step over a hairless, emaciated animal with a broken leg and a thick tumor growing from its neck.

"The Thais, being Buddhists, won't do anything about them. They think dogs are the reincarnation of people who lived wicked lives, and anyway it's not the Buddhist style to intervene, you just go along easily and don't rock the boat. So they have no compassion at all for these dogs. They think a *farang*'s crazy for having—"

"A *farang*?"

"Roundeye. Westerner. They think we're crazy if we have a dog in the house for a pet. Well, Peter was driving behind a bus and the bus hit a dog, ran over its hindquarters, and the dog was lying there in the street, still alive, yelping and howling. People were standing around just watching the poor thing die. Peter got out of his car and shot it in the head. You'd have thought he'd shot the king."

"Why?"

"Governments don't like foreign agents firing off guns in the streets. And certainly not in Thailand just to put some suffering dog out of its misery. There was a terrible stink. Peter had to leave the country for a month. If he hadn't been in the middle of an operation he'd have been PNG'ed."

"What's PNG'ed?"

"Persona non grata. Kicked out."

"Oh, yes."

An older man walked up and, with a friendly nod to me, put his arm around Sandra.

"Everything all right, Sandra? You look very excited."

"This is Tony Deniset, Fred. Fred Stewart."

We shook hands.

"It's just that thing about the dog. I was telling Mr. Deniset."

He laughed. "I wish you'd forget about that."

She put her arm around his waist and squeezed. He had a tanned, strong face that looked as if it had been through a lot. His suit jacket, perfectly cut, fit the way I had always wished mine would fit. He was much older than Sandra, in his mid-fifties, but nevertheless, watching them together, I wondered if they might not be more than friends. I decided to leave them alone and find Harley.

He was speaking Thai with three uniformed Thai officers. He had just told a joke and the Thais were roaring with laughter. When he saw me he excused himself from the group and said, "I see you met the station chief."

"The man with Sandra?"

"Yes."

"I never met a CIA man before. He seems like a nice guy."

"Yeah, he is."

"I've been thinking," I said. "You said you were doing something with Jaran tomorrow. Is there any chance I could go along?"

"Do you know what it is?"

"No. But whatever it is, it'd be a chance for me to get to know you and Jaran, just be around and watch and listen. That's all I'm here for."

"Valdez might not like it. I'd be delighted to have you along and Jaran probably would be too, but they're a little hinky around here, overcautious, everyone has to cover his ass. I'll see what I can do."

I had started to notice something peculiar about Harley's speech. He had a way of using words or phrases ("delighted to have you along") that didn't quite fit with some of his other expressions ("bullshitting thieves," "cover his ass"). I had had a rather foppish editor once who slipped "fuck" and "shit" into his sentences so the office girls wouldn't think he was queer, and I'd known cops who stayed up nights reading Roget and Bartlett. But the mixture seemed to come naturally to Harley.

I let him go back to the Thais and spent some time wandering around with a drink in my hand. When the party started thinning out, I looked for Valdez but didn't see him. Then I realized that Harley and the station chief had left too, and I was surprised to see Sandra still there, talking with a couple of young men in suits.

She called to me. "Getting down to the hard core."

I smiled back and she came over. "What are you doing next?"

"What do you mean?" I said.

"We're going out for some dinner, if you'd like to join us."

"I'd like to very much."

She said she'd get her bag and we'd all meet at the door.

Ten minutes later there was no one at the door but me. She came out of the ladies' room, walking quickly, took my arm, and said, "The others can't make it. Wives."

4

I FOLLOWED HER out to the parking lot. She unlocked the driver's door of a red Volvo, then removed the key and stood back. She did not open the door. Had she seen something in the car that frightened her? I leaned over and stared through the window.

"Could we get in?" she said.

"I'm sorry. I thought you'd seen something." Feeling like a fool, I opened the door for her.

At the gate a Thai guard lowered his newspaper, glanced at the car, but did not bother to stand. Out on Wireless Road the breeze through the car's open window was fresh and smelled of jasmine.

Sandra took a deep breath. "Isn't that heaven? It's from the ambassador's garden."

We turned left into the heavy traffic of Phloenjit Road and immediately the car filled with dust and exhaust fumes. She maneuvered the Volvo behind a bus, and we followed it, tailgating, cowering in the noisy onslaught of trucks, cars, three-wheeled *samlors*, and swarms of darting motorcycles.

"I'm afraid I'll never get used to Bangkok traffic," she said, leaning forward, her slender fingers clutching the wheel.

It was dark now, and the lights from the traffic and the neon signs of bars and restaurants reflected off her dark hair. When a sudden shaft of light from a turning taxi struck her eyes, their expression was determined. It seemed important to her that she master Bangkok traffic, that she subdue it.

The bus we were behind had so many people hanging on the side that it seemed in danger of falling over. Even the driver was hunched onto the edge of his seat, his left arm and shoulder sticking out the window.

"How can he drive like that?" I said.

"All the bus drivers sit like that. They squeeze onto half the seat so Buddha can come and sit next to them." Then she added, "Sometimes people are in a terrific hurry in this country, and sometimes you can't get them to move at all."

Phloenjit Road turned into Rama-I Road and we were headed toward the Siam Intercontinental Hotel. Since I had had my last two meals there I felt like going somewhere else.

When we pulled into the hotel drive and got out of the car, I said, "Is there someplace around here besides the hotel? I'd rather—"

She laughed. "You don't think I'd take you to your hotel for dinner your first night in Bangkok. Or any other night."

She took my arm and led me to the curb of Rama-I Road. We were in the middle of the block, and between us and the other side were four lanes of menacing free-for-all traffic.

"Are you proposing to walk through that?" I said.

She gripped my arm and pushed close to me. "Just stick with me."

Thirty seconds later we were on the other side, having left behind a wake of screaming drivers, skidding tires, blaring horns.

"Do you do that a lot?" I asked.

"It's the Buddhist way of life. If you're killed it doesn't matter because you'll be reincarnated. In Thailand one lives like that. You'll see."

We were in front of a movie theater. High-pitched atonal singing screeched from speakers over the ticket booth.

"Come on," she said, "I want you to meet someone."

We walked briskly past liquor stores and coffee shops to a small dim street behind the theater. We turned into it and after a few steps it narrowed to an alley. People sprawled in the darkness, glancing up at us as we passed. An old man squatted between two straw baskets, one containing an iron brazier, the other filled with stubby, thumb-sized bananas. Charcoal embers glowed inside the brazier, and his bananas roasted on the top. Ahead I could see a flickering blue neon tube. As we approached, the tube turned out to be attached with metal rods to the top of a bicycle. The front of the bicycle had been converted into a mobile kitchen: a large stainless-steel box containing two charcoal braziers, pots of steaming liquid, piles of squid, small fish, noodles, bits of raw meat, spices, and a battery for the neon. A folding metal table and five stools had been set up in the glow of the blue light. Two bare-chested Thai men in shorts sat at the table eating from bowls. Beyond them the alley changed to dirt and disappeared into a forbidding gloom and what seemed to be a settlement of shacks. I was contemplating the dinner we might have at this table, and just exactly what Sandra was trying to prove, when she said, "Here we are," and pushed open a door at the side of the alley.

I followed her in and pulled the door closed. The room was crammed with fifteen tables, and all of them occupied by Thai families. Sandra ignored the stares and sudden silence and moved with proprietary confidence toward another door at the back. We walked through it into a small parlor with two empty round tables. In an instant an enormously fat dark woman exploded through a curtained opening at the back of the room, arms outstretched, black hair streaming in disarray around her laughing Asian face, her voice shrieking delight. She and Sandra hugged, and the woman swept us to a table and yelled in the direction of the curtain. A young boy came out with a plate of peanuts and ginger and crisp fried meat strips (pig intestines, I discovered later). After that, there was no looking back. For two hours food came at us in waves: soups, fish, chicken, meat, salads, most of it heavily spiced and blazing with peppers.

"Do you own this place, or what?" I said.

"Beatrice is an old friend of the embassy," she said. "She likes Americans. She even has rooms upstairs she lets us use."

"Sounds lively," I said.

"Not for that, just for resting or if someone can't find a place for the night."

She laughed and tossed her hair. She was a happy little girl who loved to show off the clever things she had learned playing with grown-ups. Already she had thrown PNG and *farang* at me and I had obediently requested clarification. Now she tossed out Thaimac, Jusmag, DCM, and other bits of embassy arcana. I ignored the bait until she said she couldn't understand why Harley had wanted to be a drug agent instead of a "feeb."

"What's a feeb?"

"FBI. That's what the agents call them."

She dropped names, places, and phrases. Though she knew I had been in Thailand only one day, she asked if I had met the wife of the Norwegian first secretary. When she talked about a trip to Chiang Mai she said she had been "up-country." She had two more years "in-country." She had spent a weekend in "KL."

She was a dedicated, self-propelling gossip (bad news division) with abundant information on embassy accidents, firings, miscarriages, adulteries, and runaway children. Since I did not at the moment feel like suffering the sorrows of strangers, and since I half-believed she was making it all up anyway, I nodded and yes-ed and really-ed and turned my attention to the food. Beatrice had brought out a cone-shaped object made of tin, its top flattened, its sides punched with holes, the bottom turned up to form an inch-wide circular trough. Hot coals burned inside. Beatrice put strips of lettuce in the trough, a lump of fat on the top and small pieces of marinated beef over the holes in the side. Everything sizzled. The fat dripped down into the meat, the meat juice mixed with fat dripped into the trough, and the lettuce simmered. With chopsticks we picked off the bits of cooked meat, added them to the braised lettuce, and ate.

When Sandra's mouth was full, I said, "Have you known Peter Harley for a long time?"

She chewed and swallowed. "I knew you'd ask me about him. Not long. Just three months."

"What made you so sure I'd ask about him?"

"Because you're writing something, and everyone's always so fascinated by him."

"Except you?"

"Me too, but maybe not as much as the others. He's interesting, but he's not all that unusual. He just does things sometimes that other people wouldn't do."

"Like shooting the dog."

"Yes, and other things. He's a foundling, did you know that?"

"No, I didn't."

"He was left at a hospital in New York when he was three days old."

"Really?"

"Some woman adopted him and brought him up."

"Where'd he go to school?"

"NYU."

"How old was he when he was adopted?"

"I don't know exactly."

I offered her more of the beef.

"It depresses him when he talks about it. It worries him not knowing anything about his parents, where he really comes from, what his background is."

I remembered Harley's troubled expression by the window at the Christmas party. Something was disturbing him all right, but I didn't think it was anything as distant as his birth.

"He's obsessed by the idea of relatives," she said. "He says not having any makes him feel as if he's floating. When he reads about an accident he goes right to the list of next of kin, all the fathers and mothers and aunts and uncles. He's like a poor man who's obsessed with money. He told me he wishes he had just one cousin, some hundredth cousin a hundred times removed, even an old drunk in the street. Just a thread. You understand?"

I would have preferred hearing these things from Harley.

"How does he like Bangkok?" I said.

"He doesn't. He wants to get back to New York. He's afraid they'll try to keep him here even though they promised it was only temporary. The big difference between him and the other embassy people is that they're staying, they're assigned here for two or three years, they're developing their careers—that's what they're really interested in, their careers—so they don't trust this guy who's just thinking about his job, doing what he has to do to get back home."

"What is it he has to do?"

"You'd have to ask him that."

She glanced up from her plate, and her eyes, just for a moment, had an honest intensity as arresting as the stare of the man at the party. She added, "But I'll tell you this, for your own good. Two weeks ago Peter got in his car and found four cobras asleep on the floor of the back seat. And the car was locked."

I was startled. Was that why she had wanted *me* to open the door of her car?

"Who did it?"

"Harley has a one-on-one thing with a trafficker here— sort of I'll-get-you-before-you-get-me. Everyone knows about it. You can even put down a bet at the embassy. The sentimental money's on Harley, but the realists are going the other way."

"What's the name of the trafficker?"

She considered that for a moment. "I'll tell you because you'll hear it anyway. Lichai. His name's Lichai."

I filed the name in my memory, and we ate silently for a minute. Then I said, "Harley told me he comes and goes. Does he ever go to Songkhla?"

"Why do you ask that?"

"Some agents I saw in Washington said it was where I ought to go. Lots of action, they said. Like the Wild West."

"Well, they were right. Bandits and smugglers and CTs."

"What are CTs?"

"Communist terrorists. I'll give you an example about Songkhla. Last year an American drug agent went down on a case, undercover, almost no one knew he was there, and after he'd been there six hours the consulate was warned that if he wasn't out of town by sundown he'd be shot."

"Dodge City."

"But he stayed anyway, and the next morning an informant he was working with was found dead on the consulate lawn with a machete in his neck. He had a note in his pocket saying the agent would be on the lawn the next morning. So then the agent left."

"I guess."

"Last month they sent down another drug agent to set up a permanent office."

"How's he doing?" I remembered that the men who took me to lunch in Washington had mentioned sending an agent to Songkhla.

"He's alive. I don't really know much about it. They don't confide in the typists."

"You're not a typist."

"Almost. I type up reports for the head of the political section, and every once in a very long while I get to change a word or two. I spent four years at Vassar and what I do is type."

"Where are you from?"

"Beverly Hills. My father's an actor. You never heard of him. He hasn't worked for fifteen years."

"What do you think of Peter?" I said.

"I like him. He's a well-intentioned guy who woke up one morning to find himself in Thailand with a diplomatic passport, diplomatic immunity, and a lot of peculiar friends and enemies."

"He seems to speak fluent Thai."

"He does. That hasn't won him any friends either."

"Why not?"

"Because most of the Americans in the embassy spent six to ten months at FSI, the Foreign Service Institute, where they teach you the language before you come over. Only most people don't learn much. It's very difficult. Harley was only there three months, but he worked. And when he got here he wouldn't speak English to any Thais, even the one's who'd been to school in the States and spoke it perfectly. If they wanted to talk to Harley, they had to talk Thai. So he learned it. He speaks it better than anyone else in the embassy. Some people think it's not right to be that conscientious—it's bad taste, if you know what I mean."

"I think I do. And what about you, what about Sandra Gilchrist?"

"My Thai stinks."

"That's not what I meant."

"I told you about me. What about Tony Deniset?"

"What about him?"

"Are you married?"

"I was."

"Any children?"

"No."

"That's lucky."

"Why?"

"Children of divorced parents get fucked around."

"I'm not divorced. My wife died."

"Oh, I'm sorry. How?" Not too sorry to ask.

"In a skiing accident."

"Where?"

"Klosters."

"I'm sorry."

"Are your parents divorced?"

"Yes."

"Did you get fucked around?"

"I think maybe I did."

"Well, maybe it's better to have divorced parents than none at all."

"That's what Peter says."

"So that's you, me, and Peter," I said. "Who've we left out?"

She put half a large prawn in her mouth, and let a tear of butter roll down her chin. She left it there for a moment, smiling with her mouth full. Then she raised her napkin and wiped away the butter. "Can't think of anyone."

"Fred Stewart. The man you introduced me to at the party? What's his story?"

"What do you mean, *story?*"

"What's he like? He's the only CIA station chief I ever met."

"I really couldn't tell you."

"Is he married?"

"I haven't any idea."

"It must be difficult in this country, for a girl like you, living alone. Someone so attractive."

She tensed at that and poured tea into our cups. She didn't answer.

When we left the restaurant the mobile kitchen was gone—bicycle, neon, table, stools, everything had been cleared out, leaving the alley in almost total darkness. Sandra took my hand and stepped out confidently, quickly, her legs swishing the fabric of her skirt. She was very much in charge. We dodged across Rama-I Road again and when we got to her car she ignored it and walked with me into the hotel. I thought, Is she seeing me home? Do I look that helpless? I got my key at the desk and turned around to see her standing at a door leading out to the swimming pool and the ground-floor rooms.

I walked up behind her and she took hold of my hand and lifted it to see the number on the key. She pushed open the door. "Your room's down this way."

"You open hotel doors but not car doors."

"I didn't know you then."

At the pool a dozen Thai musicians were playing Glenn Miller for a group of Americans in green and orange aloha shirts.

I opened the door to my room and she walked in and went straight to the open sliding glass door that gave onto the pool. She slid it closed.

"The music's so loud. How will you sleep?"

"I'll manage."

"There's a zoo out there. Did you know that?"

I walked up behind her but did not touch her.

"No, I didn't," I said.

"They have peacocks. Have you ever heard a peacock? They sound like screaming women. It's bloodcurdling."

Then she turned and moved against me and looked up at my face. In the dim light from the pool her expression appeared serious, frightened—much *too* frightened. I tried not to smile. She had put herself into a role having to do with mysterious lands, dangerous men, romantic encounters. She was playing games with the CIA station chief, and now a writer had showed up and that might be good for some additional fantasy. She reminded me of another meretricious, rich little American girl I'd know who lived in Paris and thought she was adventurous because she didn't own any underwear. She wore her boyfriend's. Before you could take her to bed, you had to remove the boyfriend's shorts.

I stepped back into the center of the room.

"You're right," she said, misinterpreting my withdrawal. "It's too dangerous."

"Dangerous?"

"Forget it. You must think I'm crazy. I'm sorry."

"I don't think—"

"Let's not talk about it anymore. I've got to get out of here."

She was headed for the door. I took her hand.

"Let go. You were wrong at dinner."

"I don't understand."

"I know you don't. You said I live alone. I don't. I live with Peter."

"With Peter Harley?"

"How many Peters do you know? Good night."

She walked out and closed the door.

I sat down slowly on the bed and waited for my heart to stop pounding. After a moment I whispered, "Close, Tony. Very, very close."

In half an hour the band stopped playing and the pool lights went out. I lay down dressed on the bed. Then the peacocks started. They really did sound like women screaming.

5

AT 2 A.M. the phone rang.

"Tony Deniset?"

"Yes."

"This is Peter Harley."

I sat up in bed, opened my eyes as wide as I could, and tried to get fully awake. Maybe she'd lied and told him I made a pass. Maybe she'd even told him she'd slept with me.

"I'm with Lieutenant Jaran. It'd be a good time for you to meet him if you still want to." I heard a horn honk. He was in an outdoor booth. He sounded as if it weren't 2 A.M. at all, as if he'd have been very surprised to learn I was in bed asleep.

"Sure. Of course. I want to very much."

Harley picked me up five minutes later in a brown Toyota with dark-tinted windows.

"Is this yours?" I asked, weighing the possibility of a cobra under the seat.

"No, it belongs to the embassy. They all have these dark windows—fine during the day because you can see out and no one else can see in. Only at night you're blinded."

"Did you talk to Valdez about my coming along?"

"I decided the hell with Valdez. If you want to come and Jaran and I want you that's our business."

He turned left into Rama-I Road. Through the dark windows it was impossible to see anything but headlights, and since many of the cars weren't using headlights, I was nervous. Harley seemed not to notice. We had gone only a couple of hundred yards when he swung the car to the right through a gate in a wire fence. A large wooden building with a few lighted windows was ahead of us. He turned right again and stopped in front of a smaller building, completely dark.

We walked up some steps and Harley pushed open the door. He said something in Thai to a young man sitting in the dark at a desk. The man grunted and we walked past desks and chairs to a small office. The door was open. A man was inside talking Thai on a telephone. The only light came through the window from the street.

The man hung up the phone and said in English, "Hello, Peter."

He was tall for a Thai, slender, about thirty-five years old.

"Jaran, this is Tony Deniset."

The man stepped forward and shook my hand. "Peter was telling me about you," he said. His voice was high-pitched but strong and straight-forward. No nonsense. "He said you're a very good writer."

"I've heard a lot about you too," I said.

"You always sit around in the fucking dark, Jaran?" Peter said. "You hiding from your creditors, or what?"

Jaran looked at me. "Someone threw a grenade at one of my men last week." His voice carried a note of apology, as if it'd been his fault. "My wife says I'm paranoid, but I don't like the idea of people knowing when we're in here at night."

"You ready?" Peter said.

Jaran called to the man Peter had spoken to coming in, then opened a drawer in his desk. He took out bundles of money, hundred-baht notes fastened with rubber bands, and packed them neatly inside an attaché case on the desk.

Four men came into Jaran's office, opened a side door to a storeroom and brought out a wooden case. Without speaking they opened it and removed an M-16 rifle.

Jaran stuck an automatic in his belt and filled a leather pouch with bullets.

"Ready," he said to Peter. "Let's go."

We walked out to the driveway, Jaran carrying the attaché case and a small black walkie-talkie.

Peter, Jaran, and I got in Peter's car. The four men with the M-16 climbed into a black Fiat behind us.

We drove out into Phloenjit Road. Peter and Jaran spoke in

Thai for a moment and then Peter, turning to me in the backseat, not seeming to care too much about steering the car, said, "I don't really know what sort of things interest you, so anything you want to know just feel free to ask."

"Well, for openers," I said, "what the hell are we doing?"

Peter laughed. "How much do you know already?"

"I don't know anything."

Peter looked at Jaran. Jaran stared silently out the front window.

"Well right now we're headed for Thonburi. We're meeting someone there. I'll try to give you a very fast version of what's really a long story. Jaran?"

"I'll just listen," Jaran said.

"About a year ago, an American soldier—" He stopped. A faint voice came over the walkie-talkie. Jaran rolled down his window and stuck the radio's antenna out of the car. The voice came in louder then and as Jaran answered it Harley let the car slow down. He pulled over to the curb and stopped. He spoke in Thai to Jaran, and then said to me, "Jaran's men in the car behind us think they've got a tail."

He spoke again with Jaran.

"We'll just sit here a moment and see if they pass," Harley said.

In a moment a green panel truck speeded past and was soon out of sight.

"The sergeant's a little jumpy this morning," Jaran said.

"No, no," Harley said. "He's right." He twisted his head toward me. "Did you see the sergeant back there at the unit? The fat guy who looks like he couldn't walk downstairs without falling on his ass? He's the toughest fucker you ever met."

We crossed a bridge over the Chao Phraya River. I could make out a bare electric bulb on the back of a rice barge.

On the other side of the bridge the streets were almost deserted.

"This is Thonburi," Jaran said. "It's mostly an industrial area. And a high-crime area too. You could hire a professional killer here for a hundred dollars."

"So, as I was saying," Harley said, "about a year ago an American soldier gave us something about a man in Thailand named Lichai who was supposed to be very big with a group of Communist insurgents. He was controlling about a thousand CTs down south and he was paying them with profits from the heroin traffic. Communist terrorists, that is. This solider had never heard of Lichai before, but the name meant a lot to the embassy and the Thai government. He owned a lot of businesses, he'd been a member of parliament, he knew everyone, he had plenty of muscle. If Lichai was making his money and influence available to the CTs, then Lichai had to go. This soldier's Intel said Lichai was shipping heroin to the States in the personal effects of returning American soldiers. Then about the same time—''

Jaran interrupted Harley with a few words of Thai and we made a left turn into a deserted, darkened side street. Harley put on the parking lights and we drove about a block and slowed down at the doorway of a shop with an iron grille across the front. The back door opened suddenly and a very thin, raggedly dressed Thai slid in next to me and slammed the door and we speeded up again and made another turn. When we were back on the main road Harley put the headlights back on and Jaran turned around in his seat and faced the Thai. The Thai raised his joined hands to his forehead and nodded his head. Jaran's hands went perfunctorily to his chin. He and the Thai spoke. Then Jaran turned back to the front and the Thai relaxed. He was wearing a short-sleeved dark shirt and as lights flashed into the car I saw dragon tattoos up both forearms. His four upper front teeth were gold. He never looked at me, never gave any indication he even knew I was there.

In five minutes we had left Thonburi and were in the country.

Jaran said to me, ''You could stay on this road and go all the way to Penang, Kuala Lumpur, and Singapore.''

''Let's do it,'' Harley said. ''Tell Valdez to stuff this shit and we'll spend a week on the beach. Damn, I wish I was at Don Muang Airport right now, sitting around waiting for Pan Am 2 to New York. You got a beautiful country here, Jaran, but I'll take New York.''

After five minutes Harley said, ''Anywhere here?''

''Just a little farther,'' Jaran said.

We pulled off the highway onto a narrow dirt road and turned off the lights and stopped. The other car had pulled up behind us and one of the men got out. He was young, no more than nineteen, and had a peculiar, elongated face with a large nose and immense dark eyes. He was wearing tight jeans, a red crocheted vest, and green skullcap. He looked like a clown, a pleasant clown.

We all got out and Harley opened the trunk of his car and reached in for a roll of adhesive tape and a white nylon belt, four inches wide, with pockets along the front and two dangling wires. He said something and the man with the tattoos and gold teeth unbuttoned his sport shirt and held it open. Harley put the belt around the man's waist, secured it firmly in front, then ran the wires up the man's chest and taped the ends in place, one above each nipple. He showed the man a small switch at the front of the belt. Then Harley pushed the belt down behind the man's waistband and rebuttoned the shirt.

Jaran and I and the young man from the other car watched. When Harley was finished we got back in the cars and returned to the main road.

No one spoke so I said to Harley, "What's that thing around his waist?"

"It's a Kel, a radio microphone. He's going for a visit in a minute and we want to hear what gets said. I'll tell you about it when he's out of the car. Take a look at this building up ahead when we pass it."

We drove by a large low wooden building fifty yards in from the highway. A sign by the road said, "Asian Garment Export."

A couple of hundred yards past it we stopped and backed into another dirt road. The following car passed us, made a U-turn and returned toward the building.

"They'll park on the other side heading back toward town," Harley said.

A voice came over Jaran's radio.

Harley spoke with the tattooed man and he got out and walked back toward the building. Then Harley lifted a panel between the two front seats and switched on a radio. We heard static.

"You probably saw me showing him the off-on switch," Harley said to me. "I told him to turn it on just before he goes inside. But really the switch is a phony. It's on all the time anyway. So if he decides to give us up to his friends and leaves the switch off while he tells them he's wired, we'll hear that."

Harley and Jaran sat quietly staring into the darkness in the direction of the garment factory. I waited until I thought I wouldn't be interrupting anything and said, "What's he going to do?"

"Well, the Thai government and some people in Washington got very heated up about the idea of this Lichai financing the CTs. Jaran's men tracked nine kilos of heroin all over Bangkok for half a day until the car it was in drove onto an army base. The guards wouldn't let Jaran follow it in. When he finally got permission to go on the base the next day, no one there had seen that car or heard of it or knew anything about it. The car didn't exist. Jaran checked the license number and it was registered to a leasing company, signed out to a business supply house owned by Lichai. The commander of the base is part owner of one of Lichai's hotels. He never paid for the share. It was a gift. One of his sons went to the same school in Switzerland Lichai's daughter went to. He's a friend of the family. He's also a very good friend of the minister of defense whose wife is on the board of directors of the Asia Banking Corporation, which Lichai owns. She's *also* president of the Bangkok Community Drive, a charity to which Lichai contributed two million baht last year. Get the picture?"

"I'm beginning to."

"Lichai has a way of doing favors for people with power. In a bribe-oriented country like Thailand, that's not hard if you have the money. He's made himself the kind of man who'd be very appealing to anyone thinking about overthrowing the government. He has a lot of well-placed friends, like that base commander for example, he can subvert, betray, blackmail, whatever. If there's a Communist takeover in Thailand, Lichai will be among those in back of it and definitely among those on top when it's over. He's seen to that."

Jaran had listened to all this silently, offering no corrections.

A small light flickered out on the road. "Bicycle," Harley said, and then went on. "So the American and Thai drug agents here went to work on this American soldier who gave us the first tip and eventually they got to another soldier and he gave up his Thai boss, a man right under Lichai, and I came over from New York as an undercover and made two three-kilo buys off this boss. So finally I got pretty tight with him, the Thai the soldier gave us, and I told him that if we were going to do any more business I'd have to talk to Lichai himself, who maybe should go to the States and meet my people because by this time there was a lot of money involved. But the guy got hinky on me and said he didn't want to make the contact with Lichai, that if anything went wrong it'd be his ass. We figured, well, what the hell, we don't care, if he's scared of trouble, we'll give him a shot of real trouble and see if he doesn't get cooperative. So we arranged for him to get busted on something else, and he was in Klong Prem jail, in the dark cells, and you can stay there eighty-three days before the prosecutor has to bring formal charges. That's a long time in that rat hole. So it's eighty days and we think he's about to turn, and then bingo, the prosecutor dimed us out. Lichai must have smelled something, got worried about his number two man in the hole that long, so he had someone get to the prosecutor's office and they let him go. Like that. They made up some phony story about how he was already in longer than the eighty-three days and they had to let him go. The next we knew we had Intel he was in Burma, and then one of Jaran's stools up north said he was in Mai Sai, on the border. So there I was with my ass shattered. I'd been here almost three fuckin' months, and spent thirty thousand dollars of government money, for all of which we had absolutely nothing. What we're doing out in the dark at 3:30 A.M. right now is picking up the pieces.''

When Harley began this long explanation he had been sitting straight up in the seat, talking fast. But as he continued, he relaxed, the sound of his voice diminished, and his words took on a private, introspective tone of almost hopeless resignation. The final words, *picking up the pieces*, were spoken so softly that I could hardly understand them. Harley by then was down behind the wheel, slouching so low only the top of his head was visible from the backseat. When he had finished no one said anything. For several minutes we sat in the darkness, hearing only radio static and the roar of passing trucks.

Jaran said, ''We still have a chance to salvage something. The man who was in the backseat with you works for a gang in Thonburi. He says they have a shipment of opium coming down from Mai Sai tonight to that garment company. My stool in the north says Lichai's number two man, the guy they let out of jail, is shipping something down from the north this week. So maybe it's the same. We hope it's the same. If it is we might be able to follow it south and make a connection with Lichai, get the case going again.''

"What's this stool going to do now?" I asked.

Jaran said, "He's going in to talk to someone from the gang he works for and tell them he's got a buyer—that'll be me—and see if one of them will meet me now. If he agrees I'll get a look at him and maybe I'll recognize him. I'll show him the flash roll, the money in the case here, and maybe I can con him into letting me meet someone else. Maybe they'll even make a sale to me. But mostly it's for the Intel—to see who they are."

"What if he recognizes you?"

Jaran had been running a hand over the top of his head, flattening the hair. His hand came down and his soft, hoarse laugh sounded like a large dog settling down for a nap. "Then we've got a problem. But I've got good men with me. I don't know how many they've got in that factory this morning, but they'd better have an army."

"Jaran's got the best cops in Thailand," Harley said.

"You have to be careful with your men," Jaran said. "They see a lot of corruption. But if you spend time and listen to them and eat with them and sleep with them and find out what's on their minds and help them a little you learn who you can trust and then when you have to do something they don't run away, they're ready to stand up in front of the bullets with you."

"Why is this stool helping you?"

"He just got out of jail a couple of months ago for a murder he did for the gang and he says they've cheated him out of some money and he's broke. If he helps us I can get him a little money. But maybe he's setting us up. Maybe they want to rip off the flash roll or kill us or try to find out what we're doing. Who knows? You have to get out and take chances. You can't sit home and wait for the phone to ring."

"Like MNU," Harley said. "That's the Metropolitan Narcotics Unit. They sweep up little street dealers."

Jaran laughed again. "That's what I tell the colonel, my boss. I don't want eggs, I want chickens."

"What he's afraid of," Harley said, "is maybe you'll get to the farmers."

"Yes, maybe."

Harley adjusted the squelch on the radio and the static stopped. We sat in silence again. Fog was thickening in the moonlight over the open fields.

I had one more question. "What's it mean, 'dimed you out'?"

Harley said, "Dimed you out, dropped a dime—like into a pay phone, to call someone and give you up, betray you."

A burst of static exploded from the car radio and again Harley adjusted the squelch. We heard background noises from the stool's Kel and then a Thai voice. Another voice answered. Harley and Jaran bent their heads over the speaker. We heard more noises, possibly a door slamming, then more voices, then silence.

"They're going to get someone," Harley said.

We waited. More voices.

"They're bringing tea."

Background sounds. Then nothing but static.

"The fuckin' Kel's gone off," Harley said. "These fucking damned things never work."

Jaran spoke into his walkie-talkie and a voice from the other car answered.

We waited two or three minutes and then the static dropped and the Kel started working again and we heard voices. Harley said, "They're talking it over."

The conversation went back and forth for several minutes, then stopped. Finally one of the voices spoke again, faintly, as if from another part of the room.

"What'd he say?" Harley asked.

Jaran shook his head.

The same voice spoke again, much clearer this time, as if the speaker had moved directly in front of the stool. He was talking fast and the words came from the radio in shouts.

Harley's hand jumped to the ignition key and the car started. Jaran spoke into the walkie-talkie. I leaned over the back of the front seat to get nearer the radio and saw that Jaran's automatic was in his lap.

The shouts were still coming from the radio. Harley switched on the parking lights and we shot across the highway and turned back toward the factory. Jaran was talking on his radio. We pulled up behind the other car and it began to move slowly ahead of us. Conversation from the Kel grew stronger as we approached the factory. We heard loud background noises and a slamming sound. In a moment a dark figure was beside our car and Harley reached back and opened the door. The stool jumped in beside me, breathing hard. Jaran spoke into his radio and the car ahead speeded up. We followed and were soon moving rapidly down the highway well past the factory.

Jaran turned in his seat to listen to the stool, who was talking as fast as he could between deep breaths.

Harley said, ''Fuck!''

We drove back to Bangkok and parked in the drive by what I now knew was called the Police Narcotics Unit. Jaran, Harley, the stool, and I went into Jaran's office and closed the door. Harley removed the Kel from the stool's waist. In a moment the thin man in the red vest came in with chopsticks and several plastic bags tied at the top with string. We opened the bags and ate—vegetables and curried pork and curried chicken, all of it spiced hot enough to scald a Mexican.

Harley closed the window curtains and turned on a dim light. Jaran's office proved to be even smaller than it had appeared before. Filing cabinets covered one wall and the floor around the two straight wooden chairs was cluttered with walkie-talkies connected to battery chargers plugged in the wall. There were only three chairs and Jaran remained standing, insisting that I sit at his desk. A snapshot of a woman and three children was under the glass cover, beside another photograph of opium bags stacked on a pier next to a trawler. A fly swatter lay among scattered papers and there was also a bottle of Quink ink and a cracked glass full of pencils.

Jaran and Harley asked questions and the stool answered. Harley picked an empty metal cigar tube off the floor and bent and twisted it as he talked. He leaned toward the stool, his shoulders hunched, head down, looking on a line straight into the stool's eyes. I have never seen anyone give another person as much attention as he was giving that stool. He appeared to be listening to him not only with his ears but with his eyes as well. He never interrupted, and if the stool interrupted him, Harley immediately stopped talking and insisted that the stool continue. There was nothing resigned or hopeless about him now.

Finally the interrogation stopped and Harley sat silently in his chair bending and twisting the cigar tube. He started to ask something else of the stool, then stopped in mid-sentence and shook his head. He said to Jaran, ''Looks like we wait.''

''No other way, Peter.''

''If the scumbags are taking the stuff south, they've got a

lab around Hatyai. They're not going to risk driving a truck full of opium into Malaysia."

Harley looked at me. "They execute you in Malaysia."

I nodded, but he had already turned back to Jaran.

"On the other hand," Harley said, "it could all be bull-shit. This bastard here and all his friends could be pissing in our pocket."

"I'll try to talk to Lichai tomorrow," Jaran said. "He'll be at the Sports Club for the races. If he's heard what happened tonight maybe he'll be nervous."

Harley said, "This guy here could get dead, you know? They've gotta be worried about what he saw."

Jaran was stroking the top of his head again. He took his hand away and examined the fingers. Then he opened a drawer in his desk and replaced the bundles of bills from his attaché case. "If they know he's stooling we could all be dead."

Harley stood up and stretched. "Pessimism, pessimism, pessimism." He looked at me and smiled. "Maybe we'll all be reincarnated as Chinese dope dealers, rich as hell, broads up the ass."

Jaran grinned and handed two hundred-baht notes to the stool. The stool *wai*ed us all and left.

"Sufficient unto the day . . ." Harley said. "Let's get some sleep."

Outside, an emaciated dog lay spread-eagled on the cool grass beneath a flame tree. Harley and I got in his car and pulled out into Rama-I Road. I asked him what had happened.

"The stool says he saw about forty M-16s in the factory and there was a guy there he thinks was a CT. He says his friend in the gang was angry as hell that he'd seen the guns. Really gave him hell. He's afraid they might kill him. There've been a lot of reports about CT saboteurs infiltrating Bangkok. Last week there was an explosion in a police station in Thonburi and a bomb scare at Pan Am. The government says there's about a thousand saboteurs already in the city and more coming. Some of them are probably getting money from Lichai. So the stool thinks he's got a lot to worry about, and probably he has. He says the people in the factory are defi-nitely expecting an opium truck from the north but he doesn't know when. From here it goes south. He's sure of that. They've probably got a number four lab around Hatyai, that's—"

"What's number four?"

"Heroin."

An almost empty bus cut in front of us and slowed down. Harley spun the wheel and we passed it.

"Maniacs. Yeah, it's heroin. There's number three and number four. Four's the pure stuff, the white powder you see in New York. Hatyai's a smuggling and CT center near the Malaysian border. Everything going to Malaysia by road or train passes through Hatyai. If it's contraband the CTs get a cut. The important thing to Jaran and me right now is that if this opium coming down is really Lichai's, then those guys in the factory work for Lichai and the guns are Lichai's and he'll hear about what our stool saw. He'll be very upset about that."

It was just after 5 A.M. and we drove past orange-robed Buddhist monks in the streets with their begging bowls, collecting scraps of food.

"In Washington I had lunch with some agents and they mentioned a target down south, in Songkhla. Is that Lichai? They said they'd sent an agent down there."

"They told you that? What else did they tell you?"

"Nothing. One of them just used the word 'target,' and I was wondering tonight if it was Lichai."

Yeah, it's Lichai all right. The agent's still down there."

Harley squirmed in the seat, as if he were sitting on a rock.

"How's he doing?"

"Well, not too good. Have you heard the name Samak yet, from anyone?"

"No."

"He's the chief of police in Songkhla Province, where Hatyai is, and he is a mean, vicious, thieving son of a bitch. Another agent went down there once and one of his stools ended up with a machete stuck through his neck. That was Colonel Samak's way of saying hi. He works for Lichai. He's Lichai's protection down there. Lichai owns him. That's one reason why I'm still up here, trying to develop something against Lichai in Bangkok instead of the south. He doesn't quite *own* Bangkok yet. Once you get down south you're really on his turf."

"If you want Lichai you have to get Samak first?"

"Exactly. You got it. And no one wants a machete in the neck."

Harley squirmed again, then reached back and removed a revolver from a holster at the small of his back.

"Jaran said he'll see Lichai at the Sports Club?"

"Right," Harley said. "The Royal Bangkok Sports Club. After what our stool saw today, Jaran wants to talk to him at the club and see how he acts, needle him a little, see what develops. He's usually there for the races on Saturday. He likes the races. The Chinese love to gamble."

"I thought he was Thai."

"He changed his name. He came here thirty years ago and all he had was a rice bowl. His name was Lee. He changed it to Lichai and went into business. That pisses Jaran off—the way the Chinese work like hell and grab up everything while the Thais are busy having fun. Jaran's an exception. He works like a Chinaman. He works too fucking much."

"Why too much?"

An old woman in a wide-brimmed cane hat shaped like a lampshade stepped off the curb in front of us, and Harley braked to a stop. She began to inch her way across the street, waving a stick feebly above her head. Harley watched her, but did not stop talking.

"It's not good for his health. One of these days someone's gonna cancel his ticket. He knows it, too. He's on the target range every Tuesday morning and he's a helluva shot. At seven yards he gets a five-second group in the heart."

The woman was bent almost double, her face the color of teak.

"Next time you see him," Harley went on, watching the woman, "take a close look at the back of his neck. He busted a guy and told him to take his hand out of his pocket. The hand came out with a grenade. The guy killed himself, and Jaran caught a fragment that damned near cut his spinal column. . . . She can hardly fucking walk."

The woman was almost to the middle of the street and had stopped to rest, leaning on the stick. She looked as if she might be there all day. Harley seemed in no hurry to go around her.

"Jaran really makes me nervous," he said, relaxing in the seat. "Whenever I'm around him I keep expecting loud noises. If he was a thief like the others he'd be a colonel. The Americans developed a case against a big trafficker once and Jaran went along to make the arrest. You know what the guy said to Jaran? He said, 'Lieutenant, you are a stupid man. If you had made a phone call to me I would have given you a hundred thousand dollars.' They're scared shitless of him because he's so honest. He doesn't care who pops up in front of him—if you're wrong, man, he'll nail you."

The woman was moving again, waving the stick over her head, crossing the oncoming lane. A truck was approaching about two blocks away. Harley drove forward fifty feet, spun the wheel, made a U-turn, and stopped again in front of the woman, blocking the truck.

"That prosecutor who let Lichai's man go, who I told you about? Jaran took the story to the newspaper and he put the heat on and the guy got fired. You've got to understand—that just *never* happens in Thailand. You don't rock the boat, you just—"

The truck had stopped behind us, honking its horn. Harley paid no attention.

"—keep the status quo and build up Buddhist merit points for the next life. Jaran scares them. He really does. He's a good fuckin' shit."

The woman reached the curb, and the truck honked wildly.

"I hope she never tries that in the rush hour," Harley said, making another U-turn to head us toward the hotel again. She had never looked right or left and probably had never even seen our car.

"If I wanted to hang around with Jaran for a few days," I said, taking my mind off the woman and Harley's matter-of-fact protective maneuvers, "do you think he'd mind?"

"No, I don't think he would. He'd love it. He knows you're writing a magazine article and he'd want you to get things right. I'll tell you, Tony, there are so damned few people around here, Americans *or* Thais, who really give a shit. I think he'd welcome you, I really do. I can ask him if you want."

"Maybe I'll just walk in on him and see what he says."

We stopped at the entrance to the hotel.

"So you don't know exactly when the opium shipment's coming down," I said.

"No. Probably in the next few days. The stool couldn't find out. Everyone bullshits everyone else. Confusion's a tool of the trade."

6

I THINK JARAN paid periodic visits to the Royal Bangkok Sports Club for no other purpose than to see the men whose wealth and position placed them safely beyond his legal reach. After several weeks of sitting up all night in parked cars, driving with a gun in his lap, worrying about the safety of his family, slogging through garbage-strewn slums in pursuit of minor dealers who knew nothing of where the heroin came from or where the money went, he began to lose sight of his real prey. Then he returned to the Sports Club where like a hunter in a game preserve he could study the powerful giants who were too clever to present themselves for a shot in the open.

I'd called Jaran and he'd agreed to take me with him to the club. He parked his Fiat on the roof of the garage and we walked over to the railed edge and looked down on the Sports Club complex. It was immense. The racetrack, surrounded by grass, the infield cropped fine as a putting green, blazed in the sun. Sunbathers lounged in chairs at the side of an Olympic-size swimming pool. Tennis players filled six grass courts. We left the roof and entered the main building, passing beneath a portrait of the king and queen and through a corridor lined with trophies.

We selected lunch from a buffet table (also Olympic-size, one side covered with Western dishes, the other with Thai) and took a table beneath a portrait of King Rama-III, founder of the club. Jaran told me half the members were foreigners, half were Thai. The waiting list was endless. Jaran, the eldest son of a member— his father, dead now, had been a doctor and professor at Thammasat University—was a member automatically.

After lunch we strolled out to a terrace in the sun where men and women watched horses parading on the track. Occasionally Jaran indicated someone who had just drifted out from the dining room, program in hand, and provided a swift, concise background of the man's family, business, politics, and criminal record.

Others were watching us. Men noticed Jaran, nodded to him, and pretended to study the horses. He concealed a smile behind his program and said, "They think you're an American spy and that I've brought you here to identify them."

It was this day on the terrace of the Sports Club that I first thought I understood something of the unity in Thailand of family, money, politics, insurgency, and crime. In America one tends to view these elements as basically distinct, though occasionally intersecting. In Thailand they are indivisible.

"For example, Lichai," Jaran said, leading me to a deserted area at the far end of the terrace. "He came here a long time ago from China, made a lot of money, married the daughter of an American tin merchant, and now he's one of the most influential men in Thailand."

We leaned on the railing, watching the horses. Jaran had studied criminal justice at Berkeley and spent a year in a special program with the Los Angeles Police Department. His English had the crisp, formal correctness of a language studied and read for years in school before a visit abroad produced oral fluency.

"Lichai has worked very hard," Jaran said, turning toward me in a way that gave him a view of the rest of the terrace. "The Chinese say money has the sweetest smell. They'll carry shit and garbage if they have to and they don't care because they say the money smells so sweet. The Thai is always, 'Oh, let's have a party, we'll have a party,' and the Chinaman is out making money. Lichai has done very well. He's what you would call socially prominent. He owns—"

Jaran stopped talking and turned to see what it was on the track that had suddenly diverted my attention. A girl in her early twenties, dressed in white trousers and blouse, jet black hair falling to the small of her back, had come onto the track with a horse and trainer. She was talking up to the jockey, arguing about something.

"You'll probably see her later in the bar," Jaran said. "Right now listen to me. This is important."

"I'm sorry," I said. "You were telling me what Lichai owns."

"He owns three hotels, a brewery, a department store, a

big travel agency, I don't know how many smaller businesses, and a couple of racehorses.''

"Racehorses?"

A rather sly smile had crossed his face.

"What are his colors?" I said, suspicious.

"Blue and gold."

The jockey talking to the girl was wearing blue and gold
silks.

Before I could ask about the girl, Jaran said, "I always bet
on Lichai's horses.''

"Why?"

"Because for me it's a sure thing. If the horse wins I make
a few baht, and if it loses I have the satisfaction of knowing
Lichai lost too.''

I laughed.

"You should see his home, Tony. We'll drive by it some-
time. It's a palace. He built it when he became a member of
parliament. Now he's trying to get his seat back. He finances
his campaign, as he financed his other operations, with drug
money. It's not only a way of financing the campaign—he
gets a lot of his political power through his criminal contacts.
He's like a giant onion— you peel off the layer of money and
you find drugs, peel off the drugs and you find politics, peel
off the politics and you find insurgency, peel off that you find
guns, peel off that you find money again, peel off—''

"I think I understand," I said.

The trainer pulled the girl to one side and the jockey
walked the horse slowly up the track.

"Are you waiting for me to guess that that's Lichai's
daughter?'' I said.

"You'll meet her later in the bar. Let's take a look around
before we go in there. Maybe we can find her father.''

We left the terrace, walked down some stairs, and Jaran led
me on a tour of a huge gymnasium, indoor badminton courts,
billiard rooms, karate gym, and card rooms. We ended up in
a softly lighted, oak-paneled bar adjoining the terrace, and
installed ourselves in leather chairs by a small round table
more or less isolated in a corner opposite the bar. We ordered
gins and tonic, and Jaran continued with his work, spotting
the wildlife.

At one large table in the center of the room five or six men
were going over race programs and exchanging fistfuls of
money.

"They're making book," Jaran said. "It's illegal to bet anywhere except at the windows, but they don't worry because one of them's a police colonel."

A very short, round little man with an ingratiating smile slid off his barstool and came to our table. Jaran returned the man's *wai* but did not stand and did not introduce us. They spoke in Thai and the man returned to his stool.

"He was trying to find out as discreetly as possible why I came here," Jaran said. "I told him I came to make money on the horses. If you want to know how Lichai got hooked up with the Communists in the first place he could tell you."

"Why him?"

"He was the initial contact. You see how friendly he was to me just now? But really he would like to boil me in oil. Go ahead and watch him. You can't hurt his feelings because he doesn't have any. He will pretend not to notice. Get a good look while I tell you what happened."

The man had his back to the bar, facing the tables. He seemed to know everyone who came through the door.

"A little radical left party decided to run a candidate for parliament," Jaran went on. "They needed money, and since Lichai owned a lot of businesses they went to see him. When I say 'they,' I mean that man who was just here talking to me. He was a waiter then in a Chinese restaurant, so you see how good communism has been to him. He told Lichai—he and one or two other men with him—that if Lichai didn't give them money they'd make trouble for him, threaten his customers and employees, blow things up, that sort of thing. But Lichai surprised them. He said of *course* he'd give them money, all the money they wanted, and a lot of other assistance too, under one condition— that he be the candidate. Well, they couldn't believe it. They never dreamed they'd be that lucky. They said okay, and he ran and won. After that he picked up a lot of Communist friends. They really went after him. And vice versa."

A tall slender Chinese man, one of the few in the bar wearing a suit and tie, approached our table and bowed elegantly to Jaran. They exchanged a few words and the man left.

"In the old days, before I got this job, that man and I used to come here often to play tennis. I was ranked seventh and he was sixth. Now I don't have the time but we are still good friends." Almost as an afterthought, he added, "He's from

Special Branch, Thai counterintelligence. I told him about the guns. He's probably here for the same reason we are, looking for Lichai.''

One of the gamblers at the round table twisted in his chair, trying to get comfortable, then removed a revolver from his pocket and laid it in his lap. The man next to him, glancing at Jaran, took the gun and put it in his own pocket.

I said, "How sure are you the opium we were waiting for last night is Lichai's?" I was trying to keep an eye on the fat Communist, the man from Special Branch, the table of gamblers, and at the same time get as much information as possible out of Jaran.

"If it goes south, I'll be very sure. The southern labs are all around Hatyai and Songkhla and that's Lichai's stronghold. He has a house there, solid connections with the provincial police, and he supports the CTs. I'm certain of that. And so is the embassy.''

I had noticed that Peter and Jaran referred frequently to "the embassy" when clearly they meant something more precise.

I said, "Harley told me Lichai owns the chief of police down there, Colonel Samak."

"That's right. He does. And Samak is a very dangerous man. He's a sadist. It's just like Lichai to have that kind of man to do his dirty work for him down there. Lichai is very clever at selecting subordinates.''

"Do you agree with what Peter said about Lichai being behind a Communist takeover if it comes?"

"Yes, I do," he said thoughtfully, taking a slow sip of his gin and tonic. "He won't necessarily be the leader of it, but he'll be one of the top people, one of the people an outside government would use.''

The girl I had seen on the track, Lichai's daughter, walked into the room, and Jaran's eyes followed her as she went to the bar and settled on a stool.

"I've seen Lichai many times, informally, and listened to him," Jaran continued, still watching the girl. "I know him. I've been through the Special Branch files on him. He doesn't really care about money, not for the things it can buy him. He wants power. He wants to control people's lives."

His eyes left the girl and he took another sip of his drink. "Let me give you an example. He owns the only child whorehouse in Bangkok. He pays fortunes in bribes to keep it open, and I imagine he does so only because it gives him an opportunity to buy people, actually to purchase individual human beings for cash. He has little girls—nine, ten, eleven years old—in there whom he has bought from their parents in the slums and in the mountains. Sometimes I even suspect that the real reason he deals in heroin and opium is not for the money but for the number of people it allows him to corrupt. Politicians, police, military men—people who take his favors, his money, do what he wants, and then realize too late that they're his slaves, that one word from him and they're destroyed.''

Jaran paused for a minute, calm and relaxed. I had been more aroused listening to his words than he had been speaking them. He was a pragmatic man, more practiced than I at accepting the limits of reality.

"Excuse me a moment," he said abruptly. "I'll be right back."

I assumed he had gone to the men's room, but in three minutes he returned with two twenty-baht parimutuel tickets for the next race. He gave me one.

"Lichai's horse?" I said.

He nodded. "Of course. Are you going to write something about Peter?"

"I don't know. Maybe."

"I would like to see something good happen to Peter." He put his ticket on the table and covered it with an ashtray. It did not seem to occur to him that what I wrote might not be good for Peter. He knew a lot about criminals and insurgents, but not much about journalists.

"Why is that?" I said.

"I feel sorry for him. He works so hard, and he'll never . . .''

Jaran shook his head.

"Never what?"

Lichai's daughter waved to the table of gamblers.

"Succeed."

"What do you mean?"

"He's trying to do his job, to get Lichai, to make a dent in the heroin traffic and the insurgency. He thinks he can make a difference. He thinks he can fight off all the idiots at the embassy and all the corruption in this country and accomplish something. He can't.''

"Can you?"

One of the gamblers waved back. Jaran watched from the corner of an eye.

"Maybe not. I'm a realist and I know that it may not be possible to save my country. Even if we stop Lichai there are surely others like him. But I have to *believe* it's possible." He turned to face me squarely, giving me all his attention. "I *must* believe it, no matter what the facts are. I'm a Thai. This is *my* country. If I fail I won't just lose my job or go back to the States to another assignment. I'll lose everything. If I'm not dead, then I'll be in the jungle with those men you met last night. I have fifty thousand baht saved in cash to send my family to the States, and I'll go into the jungle. But Peter is here as part of a job. He has no absolute *need* to be here, no moral commitment, no family, it's not his country. He hates it here and I don't blame him. He wants to be home. But the embassy won't let him go. He feels he has to finish what he started, and they manipulate him."

"But he came over voluntarily."

Jaran, who had been very deferential with me, raised his glass and put it down with a sudden look of anger. "Yes, but they'll keep using him. He's going to get killed."

I said nothing. The Communist pulled a barstool over to Lichai's daughter.

"Peter overextends," Jaran continued, adjusting his position to give him a better view of the bar. "Take his Thai. His Thai isn't anywhere near as good as he thinks it is. But he doesn't know that and he barges in when he shouldn't and makes terrible, very embarrassing mistakes. Thais maybe aren't so quick as an American to show their disapproval. So he keeps right on going, honestly believing that he speaks almost perfectly, overextending his ability with the language, and it's just that overextension that often ends up, incredibly, getting him understood. Whereas if he had any idea how bad his Thai is he wouldn't speak it at all and he'd get nowhere. So you have to pity him and admire him at the same time, and sometimes you get very angry with him."

"Why pity him?"

"Because it's not only the language. That's just an example. He's like that with everything, with the way he works. Look at him—he's not so strong, you know. That wiry body, he hardly even has a beard. Sometimes you almost think he's a child. The women love it. Two weeks ago I saw him at a reception at the American ambassador's and he had a kind of

charm. I think it was involuntary, but he was like a diplomat.
He was using words I'd never heard him use before and he
wasn't saying 'fuck' constantly, he wasn't even saying things
like 'That'll knock your socks off,' and 'You'd better believe
it,' expressions he usually can't do without. I'd never seen
him like that. The women were hanging on him, all those old
ladies. I thought it was particularly funny because I'd been
with him that afternoon in a room at the Oriental Hotel and an
American dealer had pulled a gun and Harley very coolly
stood up, walked across the room, kicked the man in the
balls, and took the gun. And all these women thought he was
such a sweet little gentleman. People want to see one side and
that's the only side they see.''

''So he's not really such a child then, if he knows how to
take guns away from people.''

Jaran thought about that. ''No, but he's vulnerable.''

''Why?''

''Because he doesn't understand how many different kinds
of fights he's in, and all the different kinds of weapons there
are. Like with his bosses at the embassy. They have all the
cards—*all* the cards. He thinks he fights with them and gets
his own way. But they just manipulate him.''

''He'd probably disagree with that.''

''I'm sure he would.''

Jaran was silent for a moment, drawing vertical lines in the
condensation on his glass. ''I like him very much. He doesn't
talk with his mouth. His behavior speaks. He's the only one
of them I'd work with. So I hate to think what's going to
happen to him.''

He surprised me then with a sudden smile. ''He keeps his
bosses in a perpetual state of fury.''

''So they don't manipulate him *that* well.''

''Well enough. But they pay a penalty. He despises them
and they know it, and more than that—this is what makes
them so mad, I think—they know that he's right to despise
them. They care only about their careers, and about enjoying
their time in Asia. One thing you have to give Peter, he's got
more courage and guts than all of them together and he *gives*
a shit, he has a sense of what's *right*, and he doesn't care a
damn for his career.''

The Communist and Lichai's daughter had turned on their
stools and were facing us. They whispered to each other,
smiled, whispered some more, giggled, obviously having a

joke at our expense. Jaran seemed not to notice. He was quiet as if running some story over in his mind, and then with a loud snort of contempt he said, "Do you know what they said to him once, one of his bosses at the embassy? Peter told me he'd just arrived, had been in Bangkok two days, and Valdez called him into his office and said, 'I want to give you a piece of advice I give to every man who comes over here.' And Harley asked what it was, and Valdez said, 'Never make the mistake of thinking you're in Thailand.' "

Jaran laughed, the soft, hoarse growl again.

"So of course Peter said, 'What do you mean? I *am* in Thailand.' And Valdez said, 'Harley, stubbornness like that can get you into a lot of trouble.' Harley was mystified. But I know what Valdez meant. I've seen a lot of Americans here who believe the same thing. They're *not* in Thailand. They're still in the States. They're afraid to come out of that American bubble they live in. It can be very dangerous to start living and thinking the way Thais think and live."

"You said Harley's going to be killed. What makes you so sure?"

"Because when Harley gets to Hatyai he'll *be* in Thailand, and he's not prepared for it. None of the tricks he learned on the street in New York will be enough there. He'll be on his own. He'll be isolated. We have a saying in Thailand, 'Before you hunt tigers make sure you have a tree house.' Harley won't have a tree house. Something will hurt him—the air, the trees, the people. Whatever it is, it will be something that could not have happened in New York."

"I remember," I said, "when I first saw Peter at the Christmas party at the embassy, he looked—"

Jaran wasn't listening. He didn't need my opinions about Harley. He had turned toward the bar, and Lichai's daughter caught his eye. She smiled brightly, got up from the stool, and came over to our table.

Jaran introduced me and she sat down. She was even prettier close up than at a distance. Her name was Miki.

"I'm sorry I was staring at you," she said to me. "Some idiot at the bar was saying very silly things and I couldn't help laughing at him."

"That's all right," I said, forgiving her instantly, happy then to have had her stare at me as long as she liked.

"Daddy's not coming today," she said to Jaran with a

confidence that made it clear she knew why Jaran was there. "He was out late last night and was still in bed when I left."

The races had blended well. Her face was narrow, the chin strong, and when she turned to me to ask politely how long I had been in Thailand, her large dark eyes were bright and direct, with a childlike readiness to engage my own.

Jaran ignored her remark about her father and asked if she had money on the next race. She said she had bet "a few baht," and they opened their programs and discussed the horses and jockeys. I stayed out of the conversation, happy that I knew nothing of the subject and could be a spectator. Her mouth was particularly appealing, not a prim Western mouth, not round and full either. It was simultaneously elegant and flashy, too delicate to be Western, too unrestrained to be wholly Asian. It did a lot of smiling.

Three young Thai men came in from the terrace, waved to Miki, shouted something in Thai, and sat at a table on the other side of the room. Jaran took my ticket from me, placed it over his own, and tore them in two. All smiles, he deposited the halves in the ashtray.

Miki said, "If you were going to bet, you should have talked to me. I had the winner."

"That wasn't very loyal," Jaran said, still smiling. "You should have bet on your father's horse."

"Oh," she said, laughing as playfully and simply as a child, "you ought not to think of loyalty when you gamble."

She stood and said, "Shall I tell Daddy I saw you?"

"Only if you like. It isn't necessary."

"Anyway," she said, smiling at me, "I'll come back in a few minutes if you're still here. I just have to say hello to some friends."

She and Jaran *wai*ed each other and she shook hands with me, then joined the three young Thais across the bar.

"Not bad," I said.

"I'm sorry that I won't be able to introduce you to Lichai," Jaran said. "But do you see what I mean about coming here? Isn't it interesting to know that he was up late last night? There must have been quite a battle when they told him someone saw the guns."

"She's a very beautiful girl," I said.

Jaran looked at my face and smiled. "I would not get too interested if I were you," he said.

"Why?"

"She has a very tough boyfriend."

"A trafficker?" It had seemed to me that afternoon that everyone Jaran spoke of was a trafficker.

"No. He's a countryman of yours. Peter Harley."

He leaned well back into the soft leather of the chair, taking pleasure from my surprise.

"You're joking," I said.

"That may be another reason why Peter has problems at the embassy."

"What do you mean?"

"Peter seems to be very attractive to women. When he first came here there was a girl at the embassy, in the political section, who was going out with the station chief—"

"Sandra Gilchrist."

"You know about that. So I'm not telling secrets. She left the station chief and now she lives with Peter. I'm not sure that made him any friends at the embassy."

"I met him, the station chief, two nights ago. Fred Stewart. He seemed like a nice guy."

"He is a nice guy. He's not like the others."

He stopped. He didn't want to go on.

"So what about this girl, then—Miki?" I asked.

By now she had left her three friends and was at the table with the gamblers. Jaran watched as they leaned toward her, listening.

"She's telling them what she learned from her father's trainer and jockeys. If you want to make some money I suggest you ask her for a tip."

We watched for a few moments and I said, "What do you know about her?"

"She's only twenty-two, but she's been around. Maybe you guessed that. She went to school in Switzerland and the States and she knows a lot of people. I'm sure Harley would tell you about her himself if you asked him. He talks to me all the time about her. He talks too much about her. It was my fault. I hadn't played tennis in over a year and Peter wanted to play so I brought him over here and we played a set. Then I had to leave, but the court had been reserved for another hour and he wanted to stay and Miki was there hitting balls by herself, so I introduced them. The next thing I knew he'd taken her to lunch, and then to dinner."

"What did Sandra say about that?"

"She doesn't know. If she knew she'd explode. She's an

American. She's not a Thai. Anyway, Sandra's not the real problem. The problem is Lichai. If he had any idea—'' Jaran picked a lemon seed from the edge of his glass and held it on his finger. "If he had *that* much of an idea, it would be very, very bad. You see what I mean about Peter overextending himself? He's reckless sometimes.''

"That sounds almost unbelievable to me,'' I said. "That he would do that. What would happen if the embassy found out?''

"That's just it,'' Jaran said. "I think they know. If I hadn't introduced Peter and Miki myself I'd say the embassy had set it up. It's nice for them, isn't it? Having a man actually going out with the daughter of a Class-A violator and prime political target? How could they hope for anything so nice? Peter says I'm crazy. He swears they don't know. He says if they knew they would *not* like it, that they'd have shipped him out in a second.''

"Since he wants to leave so badly, maybe he should let them find out.'' I said it in jest, but Jaran thought I was serious.

"He'd never do that. He's too determined to finish his job. No matter what he says, he won't leave before he has his hands on Lichai. They'd have to fill him full of Pentothal and take him away on a stretcher.''

That last remark came out so naturally I almost suspected Jaran of once having had a part in such an abduction.

7

THE DAY after I met Miki, Harley was attacked. It was Sunday and he called me at the hotel to say that he and Sandra Gilchrist, "the girl we were talking to at the party,'' were going to take a boat ride through some of Bangkok's canals and would I like to join them.

I accepted.

Most Americans attached to the embassy lived in apartment complexes or in large modern concrete houses. Harley lived in ''an upper-class shack.'' The phrase was Sandra's, and it was apt. The house was perhaps fifteen or twenty years old, completely of teak, one-story, erected on stilts at the edge of a narrow klong, or canal. The rooms were open, airy, furnished with little more than mosquito-netted beds, a few teak cabinets, a dining table, chairs, and two well-upholstered sofas. Shelves along one wall of the main room were filled with books. As I stood examining the titles Harley came up behind me and said, ''Yes, the beast reads.''

We sat in the almost empty room and a barefooted Thai woman brought iced grapefruit juice. I heard another servant in the kitchen and saw a gardener on his hands and knees outside by the klong.

Sandra saw me looking around and said, ''We have more servants than furniture.'' Considering the short length of time since she had switched to Harley from the station chief, the word ''we'' seemed unjustifiably proprietary. Like her mole, it proclaimed a sense of security perhaps more longed for than felt.

Harley said, ''Some German tobacco dealer had the house before me and when he left he took all the furniture and none of the servants. They were here when I moved in and I couldn't throw them out.''

''You didn't try very hard,'' Sandra said.

''I like them.''

''You don't know anything about gardening anyway.'' It was a retreat.

I guessed that Harley's books, clothes, and an old, badly scarred Sony one-piece record player, visible on top of one of the cabinets, were his only possessions and that he took them with him wherever he went, even on temporary assignments to Southeast Asia. Simply to have something to say, and because I thought he was the sort of man who would prize personal mobility, an absence of encumbering objects, I said, ''Peter, I'll bet the only things you own in the world are those books, your hi-fi, and the clothes on your back.''

''And his gun,'' Sandra added quickly.

Her tone suggested disapproval, not so much of the gun as of the job that required it. Yet I was certain it was partly the job, and the gun itself, that had attracted her.

They were an interesting pair. Sandra moved about the

room, instructing the maid, putting records on the changer, with a proud, mistressy air that convinced me it was she who had taken the intiative. She had decided to move in, and Harley, perhaps at first hardly even noticing, had not objected. Once there, however, she had made herself as indispensable as the roof. He was overcome. Gracefully, expertly she performed the role of hostess, gliding among the chairs and tables, in and out of doors, chatting, passing things. Harley watched with something close to devotion, entirely absorbed by the sight of her.

Watching them, I thought of my wife. In the two years we were married, we never spent a night apart. We never thought there was the smallest possibility of happiness except with each other. For an instant I went into a trance— Patricia was in the room with us and the world had changed. Then Harley said something, and I was back, pretending not to have heard, afraid that if I spoke my voice would crack.

In the afternoon we toured a small network of narrow klongs in a "longtail boat," a narrow wooden craft powered by a four-cylinder automobile engine whose drive shaft extended like an insect's stinger over the pointed stern. The driver was a friend of Harley's who had taken him on trips before. He eased up through klongs lined with orchids, banana plants, wooden slum shacks, cultivated fields of lettuce and asparagus. Small children splashed in the water, and snakes, large but harmless, basked motionless on the muddy banks.

That evening, with Sandra complaining bitterly at being left behind (as Jaran had pointed out, she was an American, not a Thai), Peter took me for a round of some of Bangkok's bars and nightclubs.

We had a sandwich in a place on Patpong Road called the Brittany—tables, a combo, a girl losing at poker dice to the young bartender, paying off with hundred-baht notes folded into tight little postage stamps. Groups of Thais were having dinner at tables in the back. I remarked to Harley that there was no wine on any of the tables, only whiskey and Cognac.

"Wine's expensive here, also hard liquor's the only drink that'll stand up to the hot spices. It's a big status thing. If you're rich you drink Hennessy, otherwise it's scotch or Mekhong. Some Thai police colonels invited a few American agents to dinner one night and we all sat at a long table with officers and agents at one end and enlisted men at the other end. There were a couple of bottles of Hennessy on our side and Mekhong down with the troops. After about two hours we were all drunk as hell, singing songs, laughing, corporals and colonels all arm-in-arm, one big happy drunken family. But even at the height of all the drunkenness the Mekhong stayed at the enlisted end and the Hennessy stayed with the officers. No one forgot who was entitled to what, and there was no sharing of the booze.''

We left and took a stroll up crowded, noisy, neon-lit Patpong Road. The city of sex was suffering an unprecedented attack of coyness. The bar girls and go-go dancers, naked a few days earlier, were wearing bikinis. Owners said it was the cops cracking down, which meant that certain public officials were demanding higher bribes. In one nightclub, with seats arranged around an elevated platform as at a prizefight, determined customers sat over warm beer wondering if the three uniformed cops dozing in the back would ever leave and allow the young lady, now dancing sleepily, to remove her clothes and perform the cigarette trick that had won her international fame. She had dyed her hair blond, everywhere, and in exploitation of what some people considered the country's two major commodities, sex and drugs, she was billed as ''The Golden Triangle.''

With no better place to sit and drink, Harley and I settled at the bar and ordered scotch.

"Jaran's upset," Harley said.

"Why?"

"Not really upset. He called early this morning and said he thought he might have been too indiscreet telling you about Miki and me."

"He just mentioned that you knew her."

"That's about all, too. I just know her. I haven't slept with her."

He turned on the stool and gazed absently up the bar.

"She's a very sexy girl," I said.

"Yeah. But I'm living with Sandra. I feel guilty seeing her, even though I haven't done anything."

"It's none of my business," I said, "but Sandra seems like the kind of girl who can take care of herself."

"I'm not so sure of that."

"I'll bet the station chief is."

He looked at me sharply, then smiled. The dim light behind the bar caught the fuzz on his almost beardless face.

"Yeah," he said. "Maybe."

"You're from New York?" I said.

"Yes. Manhattan. You?"

"I was born in Baltimore but I've lived in New York since I was six."

"Sandra said she told you I was a foundling."

"Yes, she did." So she had mentioned we had dinner together. It didn't seem to bother him.

"She likes to talk," he said.

"How old were you?"

"Three days. That's a guess. A woman called St. Clare's Hospital and told them to look around near the front steps. I was wrapped in a newspaper."

I didn't know what to say.

"Later I spent a year going through hospital and probation records but I couldn't find anything. All I know about my parents now is that at least one of them had a familiarity with the *Journal-American*—which, if you remember that paper, isn't much of a recommendation."

I sat there silently, happy for the dim light. I had the impression there weren't too many people in Bangkok Harley liked to talk to. He didn't seem to be close to any of the other agents. As far as I knew, his only friends were Jaran, Sandra, and Miki.

After a couple of minutes Harley said, "I saw an interesting cable today."

"What was it?"

"The agent down in Songkhla, who they mentioned to you in Washington?"

"Yes?"

"His name's Tom Niekro. He thinks maybe he's found a stool. A girl."

"A girl?"

"A child, really. He says she looked about thirteen years old. She's a whore. She said she wanted to talk and then she disappeared and he hasn't been able to find her again."

He stopped talking. I wanted to encourage him to go on, but wasn't sure I ought to. Finally I said, "A thirteen-year-old whore . . ."

"Yeah. Doesn't sound too hopeful, does it. But I can't see too many adults down there having the guts to step forward."

He fell silent again. Then he said, "You look for a little wedge, Tony, anything you can get, something to slip into

Lichai's defenses. You have to tell yourself it'll work and really believe it'll work and go all out with it. Of course you hope for something a little more promising than a child. The trouble is that Niekro's got other problems down there. Like trying to stay alive. He's got his family with him.''

"Does he have children?"

"Yeah. A baby boy. I might have to go down soon myself."

At three o'clock the cops were still there and the management gave up and shut down for the night. We drove to an alley off Silom Road for a nightcap at what Harley said used to be the dirtiest, raunchiest bar in Bangkok, a title not easily won. A toothless old woman at the door seized our hands and dragged us into a murky cavern with light reflecting from two puddles on the concrete floor. When my eyes adjusted to the gloom I made out a girl sitting at the bar playing with what looked like a kitten. The woman yelled at the girl and she came over with her kitten and, holding it in one hand, unbuttoned my shirt and ran its fur over my chest. As I pulled back I caught a close look at the animal and saw that it was not a kitten at all but a large rat. I jumped about a mile and ran back out to the street. Harley came after me. At the corner he grabbed my arm and pulled me to a stop. He was laughing so hard he couldn't walk. After a couple of minutes we started back down the empty street toward the car. We had taken no more than a half-dozen steps when Harley, walking beside me along the curb, was suddenly grabbed from behind. I turned quickly and saw three men lift him from the sidewalk and heave him ten feet through the air into the middle of the street. When he landed he didn't move. One of the men walked over and kicked him two or three times in the back, then took careful aim and kicked him once more in the face. Then he came over to me and said in a calm, not unfriendly voice, "Tell him not see girl." He was very large for a Thai, over six feet, and had a small downward-pointing dagger tattooed in the center of his forehead.

They walked off up the street and I went to Harley and bent over him and touched his shoulder. He looked at me and said something I couldn't understand.

I said, "How are you? Are you all right?"

"You okay, Tony?" He mumbled the words and pushed himself up on one elbow. The side of his face was puffed.

"I'm fine. Can you get up?"

"We'll go back in the bar, okay? We didn't have a drink."

"We'd better go to a hospital."

"I'll drive you back to the hotel." He was on his knees now, but the words sounded heavy and had a irrational insistence to them.

"Where are you, Peter?"

"Thailand, right? I'm in Thailand."

I decided to stop talking and get him to the car. "Come on." I pulled at his arm.

"You okay, Tony?"

"I'm fine, Peter, let's go. Come on."

"Yeah. Right. You're the boss, Tony. You okay?"

He let me drive but wouldn't go to a hospital. He insisted I return to the hotel. "I'm fine, man. I'm fine."

I parked in the hotel driveway and asked if he wanted to come in and sit down. He said he'd leave the car where it was and take a taxi home. He got out and walked in the direction of the taxi stand, then passed right on by it, down the drive to Rama-I Road, and turned left. I went after him.

"Peter, you said you'd take a taxi."

"I will, I will. Go on inside, Tony, I'm fine. I'm really okay. I'm just gonna take a little walk, think things out, then I'll get a taxi."

It was three-thirty. "I'll go with you."

We walked two blocks and stopped at the statue of Brahma on the corner of Rajadamri Road. The statue, at the center of a shrine, was decorated with broken bits of bright glass. Peter *waied* it, then took a book of matches from his pocket and lighted several joss sticks placed by passersby. We sat on a bench.

"What the hell happened?" he said, his first sign of completely recovered rationality.

I told him what I had seen, including the dagger tattoo. "He said, 'Tell him not see girl.' "

Peter gently touched the side of his face. The puffed area was now badly swollen and discolored. He said, "You ever see a man get beat up before?"

"Not like that."

"Well, you'll never see it done better. Very professional." He drew out the word "very" so that it conveyed a suggestion of admiration as well as disgust.

"What about the man with the tattoo?"

"It protects him from enemies. You see a lot of tattoos. Daggers, snakes, dragons."

"But what he said . . ."

"He got paid to deliver a message and he delivered it. Lichai doesn't like Americans. He particularly wouldn't like one working for the government."

"Will you stop seeing her?"

He touched the bruise on his face, then arched his back and winced. "He gave me a good fucking shot in the back."

"Several."

"What did you ask me?"

"Will you stop seeing Miki?"

"I don't know. I'll have to think about it."

He felt again at the bruise.

"Don't you think you ought to get that looked at?" I said. "You might have had a concussion or something."

"Anytime you've been knocked out you've had a concussion. It's okay. I've had them before. This isn't the first time I've had the shit kicked out of me. Have you ever been beaten up?"

"No."

"I was raised on beatings. The young guys spit on the food so the older ones'd have to give it to us. It was the only way to get anything to eat, but naturally you get knocked around a little for something like that."

"Where was that?"

"At various facilities provided by the state of New York. Most people are raised in homes, I was raised in facilities. The juvenile gulag, you might call it. You learn a lot."

He straightened his back again, winced, then smiled.

"A lot of lessons that would destroy you later, you can learn when you're a kid. You don't know how bad off you are. When I was nine I thought I had it made. I got my own room. I'd been in Goshen for two years and that made me senior man, so when a single room opened up I got it. For about half an hour, I thought I had it made. And then in one second of my life that I will never forget, I grew up. I knew that the reason I had my own room was that I had been there longer than anyone else. And that meant they couldn't find anyone to take me. I was never going to be placed. I was too old. I was permanent. Up till then I'd been drifting along, waiting for judges and probation officers to do something, get me into someone's home. I'd been in some foster homes but I never got along. And now it was over. There wasn't going to *be* any home. It was just *me*. That's when my life picked up,

from that day when they told me I could have my own room
and I knew I was going to have to look out for myself.''

"What happened?''

"After a while I got too old for that particular facility and
they moved me to Juvenile Center, in with the mother-beaters,
sister-rapers, pet-torturers, teacher-incinerators, and so forth.''

Harley did not sound self-pitying. In fact, he appeared to
feel he had come out a winner.

"I was a very good survivor. If abortion had been legal
then like it is now I probably wouldn't be here. In Juvenile
Center I used to think how lucky I was. I used to say to
myself, 'Peter, if you've got this far, you can get *anywhere*.
You could be fucking President!' By the time I was twelve I
had this idea that life was like school. You could drop out
anytime you wanted. But then you ended the possibilities.
Everything would freeze or go backward. You could be comfortable and complacent, but you'd be static. So how far are
you willing to go? The further you go, the greater the risks. I
figured I must be a genuine born winner, so I promised
myself I'd go all the way. Never quit. I'd rather die in the
street knowing what my limits were than be some old man
sitting around comfortable as hell never knowing what he
missed.''

He stopped and watched me for a moment to see if I was
interested in any of this.

"You know,'' he said, "I think a lot of people die, and
their last thought, they think, 'My life! What happened?
Where did it go? Where the hell *was* I?' Like you're eating a
piece of chocolate cake, but all the time your mind is somewhere else and when it's gone you can't even remember the
taste. When I go, I want to *know* what it tasted like.''

He stopped again and relaxed slowly, cautious of his bruised
back, against the wooden slats of the bench.

"I'm telling you everything about me, and I don't know
shit about you.''

I wanted to tell Harley about myself. I wanted to tell him
about my wife. But I was afraid, so I made myself keep
quiet. He was the story, not me.

"What happened after that, when you were twelve?'' I
said.

"A miracle. A fucking miracle. I was adopted by a madwoman. She was the only person in the state of New York
crazy enough to want a twelve-year-old who'd never lived

more than three consecutive months out of captivity. I still
don't know exactly how it happened. She always told me she
just walked into Family Court on Twenty-second Street and
said she wanted a kid and didn't care if it was male, female,
old, young, Jew, Catholic, Protestant, white, black, or polka-
dot. So she got me. Her name was Alice Spillner and she
lived on Barrow Street in the Village and she was wonderfully, beautifully crazy as hell. She thought she had a man living
in the house with her. She talked to him all the time. His
name was Danny and he was a retired cop and she used to
watch TV and discuss all the programs with him. After a
while I talked to him, too, just to make her feel good. We
used to have long conversations, the three of us. She was an
outpatient at St. Vincent's and she had a big German shep-
herd named Sharp I used to take for walks when she was at
her group. I was so fucking happy to be living in a house with
a real person. I was so *proud*."

8

THE NEXT day I went to the embassy to see Harley, and he
wasn't there. I was wandering around the halls, drawing
curious glances from people who weren't sure I ought to be
there, when I heard a voice from an open office.

"Looking for someone?"

I put my head in the door and saw a man about Harley's
age, tall and lanky, standing behind a desk in jeans and a
yellow T-shirt with a drawing of a bicycle and the words
"Put a little fun between your legs." I remembered him from
the Christmas party.

"I'm looking for Peter Harley," I said, "but he doesn't
seem to be around."

He waved an arm. "Come in and have a seat while you
wait. Someone'll lock you up for a spy."

We talked for a while and then the subject got back to

Harley and he told me a peculiar story. He said he'd worked with Harley in New York, when Harley first moved to the Drug Enforcement Administration from the New York police.

"He came to us with a reputation, like he was sharp and tough, but he didn't look it, so we were waiting to see what he had. And he got assigned undercover, posing as front man for a dealer we'd turned in Detroit. Harley was supposed to have come to New York to deliver the cash for four kilos of heroin, 240,000 dollars. The deal was all set up. Harley was just the errand boy. The bad guys made their call and told Harley they'd meet him in the coffee shop of the New Yorker Hotel and to have the money nearby, they're ready to deal. We run the flash roll over, 240,000 dollars in a suitcase, and we put it in a room in the New Yorker. We take another room across the hall for ourselves, six of us. Harley makes the meet in the coffee shop, wearing a Kel, and we listen. There's four of them, all black. They say they've got the stuff upstairs, but they want a look at the money before they'll hand over the shit. Harley says okay and they go up to the room that has the flash roll. We're standing guard across the hall, door un-latched, ready to move if they try to take Harley off. But it's cool. They count the money, close the bag, and start for the elevator with it. We don't know what room these guys are using so the plan is for Harley to let us know. When he gets to the room he says, 'Hey, 2415, I had a broad up the hall here once, in the corner there, terrific piece. Next time I'm in town—' etcetera etcetera, all that shit. So we take off for the twenty-fourth floor. Now, when they show Harley the shit he's supposed to check it with a Marquis [a vial of fluid that changes color when mixed with heroin] and if it's heroin he's supposed to say, 'Yeah, that's really good shit,' and that's the bust signal, we hit the door and take everyone, Harley in-cluded just to make it look good. Well, we lose contact with Harley's Kel when we get in the elevator. That's natural. But when we get out, we don't pick it up again. Something's wrong. The Kel's not working. We figure Harley's in the room now maybe two minutes and any second he's gonna be expecting us and we can't hear anything. We wait down the hall around the corner from the room so they won't see us if they look out, and we don't know what to do. We're just hoping like hell the Kel goes back on. Because Harley's gonna say, 'Yeah, that's really good shit,' and nothing'll happen and the blacks are gonna reach for the money and

Harley's gonna say, 'Oh, man, yeah, that's really great shit,' and still nothing'll happen and the blacks are gonna pick up the bag and Harley'll be screaming, *'Hey, man, that's really terrific shit,'* and when they're headed for the door with the government's 240,000 dollars what the hell is Harley gonna do? If he lets them go and they get in the hallway they'll run for it and we'll have World War III out here, six of us and four of them, some of the good guys gettin' hurt. That's what we're thinking. Then we hear a shot. We run up the hall, hit the door, and you know what we find inside? We find one black on the floor with a neat little .38 caliber hole over his left eye, another guy next to the bed half upside down holding his balls, and another guy standing flat against the wall, trying to get behind the wallpaper. And that's all. No fourth guy. No Harley. No heroin. No money. We look in the bathroom, we look in the closet, we look under the beds. Nothing. Disappearing act, right? None of the guys in the room is saying anything—one's dead and the others're so scared they can't talk. Okay, it's a very hot day, July, and the window is open. Twenty-four floors down. No one wants to look. But we do look. And we don't see anything. No crowds. People walking up and down Thirty-fourth Street, but no crowds. No bodies. There's a ledge there outside, four feet below the window. It's ten inches wide and it runs about ten yards to the building corner, then around the corner where you can't see it anymore. We run down the hall to the other side of the building, banging on doors, and finally someone lets us in and we run to the window and about fifteen yards back up toward the corner, there's Harley, sitting on the ledge, legs dangling over, ankles crossed, smoking a cigarette—like he's just hanging around, waiting for someone to get with it and lend a hand. The fourth black guy is lying flat out on the ledge next to Harley, holding the suitcase with the money, facing me, scared shitless. He sees me and he yells, 'Don't let him push me! He's gonna push me! Don't let him push me!' Harley says, 'You let go of that bag, motherfucker, you're gonna chase it down.' And the guys yells, 'I ain't lettin' go! I ain't lettin' go! Don't let him push me!' So we called the cops and they put lines out and dragged them in.''

I asked what had happened to the heroin.

''It went over the side. We found it in the street, bag broken open, four kilos of heroin run over by cabs and buses. Anyway, that told us all we needed to know about Harley.

After wiping out the three guys who stayed in the room he didn't really *have* to go chasing after the fourth on the ledge. I mean, there wasn't any obligation. But he hadn't even thought about it. He just went—bang, like that. No one in the *world* would have expected that of him. Even if the guy had got away with the money—I mean there are *some* things you're just not required to do, right? Chasing guys on building ledges twenty-four floors up?''

Later that day when Harley showed up at his office, I asked him about this story. He said, ''Oh, you heard that? Well, you know, things get changed a lot when people tell them. The ledge wasn't ten inches, it was about three times that. There wasn't any problem. People just like to make a good story out of it.''

''You didn't consider what would happen if you fell?''

''I knew I wouldn't.''

''How did you know?''

''I just knew.''

Something about his assurance, the complete absence of doubt, his coercion of reality, appealed to me. He was encouraging to be around.

9

WHEN I try to remember what I did the next few days, I find the impressions indistinct, obscured by the distress and violence that followed. I've pulled out my notebooks—thin brown pocket-sized pads stolen from the magazine that fired me—and I find several entries for that first week:

CIA is Aim. I got up at 4 A.M. and drove with a narcotics agent, not Harley, to the beach resort of Pattaya about 145 kilometers south of Bangkok on the east coast of the Gulf of Siam. The agent had a map drawn with pencil on a sheet of Xerox paper pointing out a house that had been rented by an

American drug trafficker. The agent said the map and the information had been given to him by one of the ''aim men.'' When I asked what an aim man was, he said it was an agent for the American Information Mission, which is what CIA is called in Thailand. He said no one ever used the initials CIA and they very rarely even said Aim. Euphemisms included ''the third floor,'' because Aim offices are on the third floor of the embassy, ''the cookie factory,'' for no discernible reason, and ''the ice men,'' also for no known reason. (Even the meaning of the initials was cloudy; someone later told me the A stood for ''Asian.'') The agent said the map was drawn on Xerox paper, like most Aim communications, because it's a universal paper, available throughout the world, almost impossible to trace. We found the house, watched it for five hours, saw nothing and returned to Bangkok.

SuperVel hollow points. The agents use a brand of bullet designed to expand inside the body and make it less likely to penetrate and strike an innocent bystander. Also, perhaps the real reason for their use, an assailant goes down faster with hollow points in him. Thai cops have trouble getting them and they are something of a status symbol. Harley told me, ''If you give a Thai cop a bottle of Hennessy and a box of SuperVels he's your friend for life.''

The heroin broker. Harley took me to see an American drug exporter who makes no bones about what he does but cannot be prosecuted because Thailand has no conspiracy laws. (You've got to catch them with the stuff in hand.) He was twenty-seven, from Brooklyn, tall, lean, sandy-haired, good-looking, and when Harley referred to him as a trafficker he made a face and said, ''Please—I am *not* a trafficker. I am a commodities broker. Some men deal in pork bellies and soybeans, my business is heroin futures. I only handle premium brands, principally Double UO Globe.'' Competing Chinese heroin manufacturers are jealous of their trademarks. Jaran had shown me an empty ''half unit'' (350 grams) bag of Double UO Globe, bearing a picture of two lions with their front paws on a globe. Chinese writing warned: ''Puts Wind in Your Sails—Beware of Substitutes.'' The American had a huge gold ring decorated with a relief of the lions and globe surrounded by small diamonds. He took it off and handed it to me. ''Ugly, isn't it? Horribly ostentatious. But when I'm back in New York I'm going up to Harlem and find the biggest nigger dealer on 117th Street and he's going to give me ten thousand dollars for that ring." Harley said, "If you ever go back to New York you won't make it past Park Row." Park Row is the location of the Federal House of Detention.

The dark cells. Harley told me, "You spend a lot of time trying to see things the way the Thais see them. But they keep surprising you. For example, if you look at the dark cells in Klong Prem prison you wonder how these people can be so barbaric. They're small, pitch-dark, filthy, stinking concrete holes—no light, no air, no toilet, no nothing. Then you go to hit a house full of armed dope traffickers, and the Thai cops stop at the door, ring the bell, wait for someone to come, bow, *wai*, take off their shoes, and go inside. Meanwhile the bad guys are out the back door and halfway to the airport. It's hard to figure out, but you try."

I tried myself, and found Harley at times as difficult to fathom as the Thais. It seemed not enough for Harley that he spoke the language. He wanted to think as the Thais thought, to understand them, and to let them *know* he understood. He wanted to participate. We were on a stakeout with one of Jaran's sergeants, watching a young Thai trafficker (someone had said he worked for Lichai) parked in a van in front of a restaurant in Chinatown. The sergeant, the fat tough man Harley had mentioned the first night I met Jaran, didn't say anything. He was a bit sullen for some reason, possibly because he would have preferred to be working with Thais rather than an American. We were in an embassy sedan and the sergeant, next to Harley in the front passenger seat, was keeping in touch with his office on the car's radio. To conceal the sound and ourselves from passersby, the tinted windows were closed. The unclouded sun had driven the temperature in the car well over a hundred. The air was damp and heavy, smelling of sweat.

We sat in silence for several minutes, watching the trafficker's car, listening to the the radio, and then an unmistakable odor, obscured partially by the smell of sweat, reached me in the backseat. Harley glanced accusingly at the sergeant. The sergeant didn't move. Harley returned his gaze to the street and settled farther into his seat. A moment later the smell intensified. Harley looked innocently out the window.

The sergeant shifted his weight onto his right buttock and again the stink increased. Harley squirmed, strained, and another invisible cloud enveloped us. The heat, the dampness, the sweat, and the stench were now almost unbearable. I was drawing short breaths, holding each until my lungs were bursting, but neither Harley nor the sergeant gave the slightest indication of discomfort. They breathed naturally and stared vacantly at the street.

So far all the wind had been vented silently. Now the sergeant, with a grand rejection of pretense, exploded a fart that rattled the ashtrays. Responding to this escalation, Harley lifted a cheek and filled the air with fetid thunder. The sergeant retaliated. Harley fired again.

Neither man spoke orally or altered his breathing. Both continued to gaze out the window with expressions of bored detachment.

Finally a puff of black smoke shot from the exhaust pipe of the trafficker's car. The trafficker pulled out from the curb and we followed him two blocks until the sergeant was instructed by radio to return to his office. We continued straight, and after another block the sergeant lowered his window. I caught Harley's eye in the rearview mirror and it revealed just the smallest twinkle of triumph.

I rolled my own window down, and when we dropped the sergeant off I got out too and walked up the street, sucking in deep lungfuls of fresh air. Harley came after me.

"Where're you going?" he said, breaking into a grin.

"You guys almost gassed me to death, you know that?"

He was bouncing along beside me, pleased as hell with himself.

"Don't be so cocky," I said. "All you did was beat a Thai in a farting contest."

"*All* I did! Man, the Thais are champs. That guy's probably got a black belt in farting."

You would have thought he'd conquered the country.

10

I HAD BEEN in Bangkok less than a week when I was warned, politely but disturbingly, that my association with Peter Harley might turn out to be dangerous for us both. Harley and I had gone to a Thai court where Harley wanted to listen to the testimony of an arrested American heroin courier. The court building was open, airy, with a veranda on each floor serving as the main hallway between courtrooms. Bats nested in the veranda's high corners.

The American was testifying in a small room with swinging doors, fluorescent lights, and a green overhead fan. The judge— young, serious, competent-looking—sat in front of a pulpit from which the witnesses spoke. The American defendant was sitting on a bench. He was handcuffed. While the judge spoke to the prosecutor, the American slipped one of the handcuffs over his wrist to free both hands so he could draw a diagram for his lawyer. When he had finished he slipped his hand back into the cuff. Harley smiled and whispered to me, "You see how casual things are here. In the States that'd be attempted escape."

Several minutes later I had my right leg crossed over my left knee, and a guard signaled me to put both feet on the floor. My right foot had been pointing in the direction of the judge. In Thailand it is rude to point with your foot, the most unspiritual part of your body, as it is rude to touch another person's head, the residence of his soul. These things are watched over more diligently than the position of a prisoner's handcuffs.

During a recess we ran into Valdez on the veranda. He spoke with Harley while I watched prisoners marching past, nude to the waist, barefoot, each man's ankles joined by a length of chain. The chains, prevented from dragging by a piece of string tied to a center link and held by the prisoner, made a bell-like tinkling that would have been pleasing had you not known its source.

Suddenly Valdez turned from Harley and took me by the arm. He started walking me down the hall, and when I said to Harley, "Are you coming?" Valdez said, "You can see him later. Someone wants to talk to you at the embassy."

Valdez drove me back to the embassy and walked me into the main building. A Marine guard pressed a button that unlocked a steel gate at the bottom of the stairs. I was worried, but when I asked Valdez what was going on he said, "Nothing serious. Someone just wants to talk to you for a minute."

We walked up the stairs, down the brown linoleum-floored hallway to a closed door. Valdez pressed a sequence of buttons next to the door and it snapped open. We walked through a narrow passageway with overhead fluorescent lights, the walls lined with colored maps and charts, and came to another door, this one made of metal. Valdez pressed more buttons and this door sprung open. We entered another passageway, to yet another metal door, painted a light shade of green, guarded by a uniformed marine. While Valdez talked to the marine, I tried to memorize the stenciled writing on the door:

> THIS ENTRANCE IS SECURE AGAINST
> SURREPTITIOUS ENTRY: FOUR MAN-HOURS
> FLAME: TEN MAN-MINUTES
> EXPLOSIVES: THREE MAN-MINUTES

The marine opened the door and Valdez turned to me and said, "Drop by when you're finished."

I stepped through the door and it closed behind me. I was in a closet-sized room with a crew-cut man about twenty years old, dressed in dark trousers and a fiery red sport jacket. "Would you raise your arms please, sir?"

I raised my arms and he frisked me. "Are you carrying any metallic objects?"

"No. Some keys."

"May I have them, please?"

I gave him my keys.

He opened a door, opposite the one I had come in, and I found myself inside a large rectangular room whose floors, walls, and ceiling consisted of one single bubble of transparent plastic. Through the plastic I saw an outer wall that could have been concrete. The plastic room had been set inside a concrete vault.

The only furniture in the room was a conference table and several chairs, also made of transparent plastic.

A man in late middle age was sitting at the table, leaning back in his chair, legs crossed, reading a book and smoking. An attaché case was on the table in front of him. When he looked up I realized that he was the man who had stared at me so persistently at the Christmas party. My apprehension increased. He stubbed out the cigarette in a large cut-glass ashtray, put the book, a paperback, in his jacket pocket, and stood and shook my hand. He pointed to a chair and said his name was Bryan Knowles. I sat down. He was short and slender, with a sharp angular face, a nose like a knife blade, thin lips. His right eye was partially hidden behind an abnormally drooping lid, a disfigurement I hadn't noticed at the party. The lid's lashes were short and bristly as if cut with scissors.

I tried to ignore the drooping eye and to talk only to the good one, but I knew I was doing what everyone who met him did. He graciously pretended not to notice my discomfort, as I'm sure he did with everyone who pretended not to notice his affliction.

"It's a handy room," he said. The smile, amicable and relaxed, seemed genuine. He appeared far less threatening here than he had at the party.

"I guess not too much gets out of here that you don't want out," I said.

He was dressed in a gray seersucker suit and blue-and-gold-striped tie.

"It's a good place to come when you're annoyed. You can yell your head off and call your boss anything you want to call him and you have half a million dollars of technology protecting your privacy."

"That's better than the First Amendment."

"It is, almost. Yes."

He leaned back and studied me, the amenities over. "You want to write something about Peter Harley."

"Yes." How he found out, I didn't know. Possibly Sandra had said something.

"I know the promise that's been made to you by Senator Ehrlich and I'm not here to try to withdraw cooperation, but I am going to try to convince you that Peter Harley isn't the best man for your purposes.''

I wanted to ask him how he knew what my purposes were. Instead I said, ''Who are you?''

''I work with personnel.''

I smiled and he smiled back. He must have been close to sixty, and he had an unaffected warmth that would have made it difficult to dislike him.

''Are you based in Bangkok?'' I asked.

''Let's talk about Harley. The ambassador's waiting to use the room. I want to help you, and if you can manage not to disbelieve that for a minute or two you might gain in the process.''

''Okay. I'll try.''

''Once upon a time,'' he said, ''a special agent for the Bureau of Alcohol, Tobacco and Firearms was killed while working undercover. A man he had arrested three years earlier recognized him. That sort of thing had happened before— men working undercover for years in the same field, then getting hurt when an old acquaintance spotted them. So some genius decided that all the federal enforcement agencies ought to form a pool of undercover agents, people who would switch from case to case between agencies, handle everything— counterfeiting, drugs, firearms, aliens—in the belief that a criminal who encountered an agent in, say, a drug investigation would not be so likely to pop up later when the agent was involved in, say, an immigration case. Okay?''

''I understand.''

''Well, in the event, this pool, so-called, turned out not to be a pool at all.''

He squinted at me. I felt that all this was terribly routine for him and when it was over he was going to hurry out to eighteen holes of golf.

''There were three men in this group, but they never met each other and they had no administrative connection at all. It was just known that they were around and could be used. Then the novelty of the idea wore off and people started to forget them. They came to be thought of, by those who thought of them at all, as more or less a leftover from what had been a grand idea everyone had lost interest in.''

''Did they have a name?''

''No. Their real names were obscured administratively, and

they were referred to simply as A-1, A-2, and A-3.'' He looked amused. ''Not very glamorous, is it? Not dramatic.''

''Not very.''

''Anyway, Harley was one of these and he's the last. The problem—''

''What happened to the others?''

''I beg your pardon?''

''What happened to the others?''

''They were killed. But listen to me. Your interest will increase. The problem was that eventually the availability of these men became known in higher areas of authority and ultimately the inevitable occurred.''

I began to suspect that he was not simply relaying second-hand information but had been part of this project and spoke from experience.

''What was that?''

''They became employed in noninvestigative functions.''

He stared straight at me, his face now absolutely without expression. The good eye skewered right through to the back of my head.

''What's that mean?''

''The thing is that one of the men was Harley, and he made a mistake and now, very soon, questions are going to be asked, and answered, and if you write a story about Harley that presents him the way I think you would like to present him—as a highly admirable sort of person?—you might find yourself embarrassed. Embarrassed when it's too late to do anything about it.''

''What did he do?''

''That I can't tell you directly. I'm just trying to help you avoid a problem for your magazine. You see how it could be embarrassing?''

''If I wrote something favorable about Harley and said he was a marvelous, wonderful person, made a hero of him, and then when the story was on the stands it came out publicly somewhere else that he was in fact an ax murderer, that might be embarrassing. But you haven't told me he's an ax murderer.''

He sat forward, put his hand on the attaché case, and fixed me again with his good eye. ''When you do what men like Harley do, when you have put yourself where you want to be and are going to do what you are there for, you can't think. You have to do all your thinking in the morning and then not stop to think again for the rest of the day.''

"Not *think*? I'm not sure I understand that. What do you mean, 'not stop to think'?"

He removed his hand from the attaché case, leaned back in his chair, and the warm obliging smile returned to his face. He seemed now to have all the time in the world. He was almost fatherly, professorial, ready to instruct.

"Some things," he said, "are too important to be left to the brain."

"Such as?"

He watched closely to see how I would swallow the next line.

"Courage and loyalty. Love."

I thought he must be playing with me. I also thought maybe I could tell him something about the deleterious effect of love on the brain.

"And Harley stopped to think," I said.

He nodded slowly.

"And someone got killed."

"On the contrary."

"Oh."

"That's all I can tell you."

I thought for a moment, watching Knowles. "And on the strength of that, what you've just said, you expect me to give up the idea of writing about Harley?"

"Don't you believe me?"

He seemed unable to understand why I didn't consent to abandon Harley as a story subject, and I was beginning to feel that maybe I had failed to understand some important detail, something spoken in code that I was too naïve to grasp.

"You haven't told me anything to believe or disbelieve. You've just said that Harley did something wrong and that it might come out into the open and embarrass my magazine. That's too vague. I don't know what you're talking about."

"Have you heard of the House Committee on Assassinations?"

"Yes."

That was all. He did not go on.

"Are you telling me Harley's an assassin?"

"I am certainly telling you no such thing."

He pulled a pack of cigarettes from his jacket pocket, his patience nearly exhausted. "I am saying that certain questions will be asked and as much as some people have tried to avoid it, the questions will have to be answered. Somewhere. If not in committee, then in the press. You could do yourself a favor, and Harley, and your country, if you forgot about him. There are a lot of other agents for you to write about."

He put a cigarette in his mouth and lighted it, his thin fingers moving swiftly around the pack and matches. He inhaled, then looked back at me, and his expression was once again full of good nature. He put the cigarette in the ashtray and, using both hands, snapped open the catches on the attaché case. He did not open it, but left his hands poised on the lid.

He said, "I have come prepared to bribe you."

My heart jumped. If he opened that case and it was full of neatly stacked hundred-dollar bills, and if I refused to take them, what then?

He read my mind, of course, and was amused. "I have here a file of material that may become public. If you go through it you'll see what I mean about how you could be embarrassed. If you promise not to write about Harley, I'll let you see it. I promise you that you'll be convinced you did the right thing."

"But if I'm not convinced, I've already promised not to write about Harley."

"You'll be convinced."

"Maybe not."

We stared at each other. I really wanted to see that file.

"Look," I said. "Let me try something on you. Let me make a guess, and you just react to it any way you think's appropriate, okay?"

He nodded, dropped his hands from the lid of the case, and sat back, ready to listen. It was what he wanted. He'd rather have me do the talking.

"Someone found three men, recruited them as killers, trained them as killers, but one of them—Harley—decided he didn't like to kill."

"You are jumping to a conclusion."

"You know," I said, the thought just occurring to me, "there can't be any worse job to do than killing, if you don't like the work."

"I imagine not. Excuse me for interrupting. Please go ahead."

"So anyway, Harley was supposed to do something. And he blew it. That upset some people. They didn't like him then because he blew it, and now they don't like him because they're afraid he'll have to testify about it. They'd be happy just to lose him. They don't want people talking about him. They don't want someone writing about him. Just let him go about a regular routine sort of job someplace at the end of the earth and maybe he'll never come to anyone's attention.''

I stopped and waited for a reaction. There was none. No word, no movement of the head, not a twitch of a finger. He was admitting nothing, denying nothing.

"What if I promised," I said finally, "that if you let me see the file, and if I still want to write about Harley, I'll let you see what I write before it's published. And maybe it won't even be an article. Maybe I'll decide to write it as fiction. I don't promise to change anything, I won't let you censor it, but I'll listen to reason. If you can show me—''

Before I had finished the last sentence, he leaned forward and flipped up the top of the case and pushed it toward me.

"All right?" I said.

He still did not speak, but waved a hand at the case as if to say, "Be my guest.''

11

I ENJOY READING other people's mail—the collected letters of famous people, even the letters of unfamous people. There is something seductive about any document that was never intended to be seen by outsiders. The papers in the attaché case were color photocopies. Most of them were red-bordered classifed telegrams containing rows of, to me, meaningless numbers followed by a very few words of cryptic text:

DELTA BACKUP

or

SAYS NOT OTHERWISE

or

ONLY PRIOR TARGET

They meant nothing, but they intrigued me. There was a suggestion of action, of problems, decisions, hidden events. Even the numbers held my interest. I pored over them, trying to pick out dates, times, repetitions.

I was still scrutinizing the first telegram when I sensed the impatience of Knowles across from me. I asked him what all the numbers meant.

"Nothing, nothing, you aren't interested in any of that."

I went on to the second telegram. It was pink. The first had been white. I asked what the difference was.

"Pink is outgoing. White is incoming."

I was taking too much time.

I came to one with a rubber stamp at the top:

SECRET—NO FOREIGN DISSEMINATION

I read it carefully, studying all the codes and numbers, and stole a glance at Knowles. He had the paperback out of his pocket and had settled down for a good read while I examined the papers. I could see the title now: *The Common Sense Book of Baby and Child Care.* This was a strange man.

Several pages later I came across a document, not a telegram, the coded preamble of which included the words "Athens Station" and two lines of text that seemed to concern an individual referred to as "Alfa Two." Top and bottom of the page were stamped:

FLASH OVERRIDE

Another stamp, smaller and at the top only, said:

NIACT

I asked what these meant.

Knowles looked at me over the top of his book.

"They're transmission priority codes. Niact means night action. Flash override is the fastest priority."

"Really? How fast?"

"If you send something flash override—and you don't very often—it's supposed to be available for placement before the President in seven minutes."

"From anywhere?" I said. "Coded, sent, uncoded, carried around, everything, in seven minutes?"

He smiled tolerantly. "I think they use computers."

"Yes, I guess they do. Who's this Alfa Two person?"

"It's not significant."

"He must have been significant if what he did had to be seen by the President in seven minutes."

He was silent.

"This person who didn't get killed, whom Harley didn't kill," I said, "did he have any political significance?"

"There were no politically significant people involved in Harley's case at all."

"What about the other cases?"

He said nothing for a moment, then changed his mind. "What other cases?"

"The ones involving the other two special undercover people."

He looked at me silently, then dropped his eyes back to the book. I could see the left eye moving back and forth over the lines, reading, or pretending to.

Toward the bottom of the stack of papers I found a green page, marked "Top Secret" at the top and bottom, that was obviously not a communication but rather some kind of administrative document. It contained nine boxes filled with computer-style numbers and letters. One of the boxes had been filled in with the words "Alfa Three" and the letters PLH. A fourth box contained the letters NOK followed by a long number. Recognizing Harley's initials, I said to Knowles, "So Peter Harley is Alfa Three."

He glanced up from his book but did not speak.

"Alfa Two did something important in Athens. Who was Alfa One?"

No answer.

"But they *were* the three special undercovers?"

For that obvious conclusion I received a slow nod.

"What happened to Alfa One? Who'd he kill?"

When I said that, I wasn't even looking at Knowles. Whether he glanced up or not I couldn't say. Of course he said nothing.

"Alfa One and Two are both dead now," I said.

"I told you Harley was the last of the three men in this group of undercover agents."

"They were both killed? Neither of them survived?"

"These were difficult missions and in each case there was

an urgent need to do surely and immediately what had to be done. The agents knew that.''

"Tell me," I said, "why are the investigators after Harley if *he* never killed anyone?"

"Because he's the only Alfa left. They think maybe he can tell them something about the others.''

"Can he?"

"I hope not. I hope he'll never be asked.''

I continued through the documents and came to the one Knowles had been waiting for me to find. It was green, stamped "Top Secret," and provided a brief synopsis of a case concerning a group of counterfeiters in Tel Aviv. Most of it was in the form of an informant's report. Obviously a man involved in the crime himself, the informant told of names and places, bill denominations, serial numbers, associates of his confederates. At the bottom of the page, hand-printed in ink, were the words "Termination. Alfa Three.''

"Why did they want him killed?" I asked.

Knowles put the book back in his pocket and straightened himself in the chair. "I haven't shown you all that so you can put together the pieces," he said. "The idea is simply to indicate a picture and convince you that Harley would be dangerous for you. Would you agree with me that what you have read is enough to cause people to wonder who these Alfa people were, and precisely what they did, and to want very badly to get their claws into Harley?"

"I'd have to agree with that," I said.

"So if you write about him, make him a hero, and your story appears before all this comes out, you and your magazine could be embarrassed.''

"Maybe it won't come out.''

"If I weren't pretty damned sure, would I be showing it to you?"

That made me wonder what Washington reporter, or what congressman, had his own set of these photocopies, and what steps were presently under way to recover them discreetly. I didn't know the half of this story, I was sure of that. I'd been shown a thin film of scum from the top of a very deep bureaucratic swamp.

I straightened the pile of documents and closed the top of the case.

"That's not what I call much of a bribe," I said.

"You're not impressed?" His eyebrows went up.

"I haven't seen or heard anything that convinces me I shouldn't write about Harley."

"What do you want?"

"Why Harley? Why was he picked for this team?"

"He was an undercover for the federal drug people and it looked as if it might be safer for him if he were rotated from one type of case to another. I told you that."

"Yes, but still—why Harley? There must have been quite a lot of checking before he was sent off to kill someone in the name of the United States government."

"Without commenting on the second half of that assertion, I can tell you that he was indeed checked very thoroughly."

"Well?"

"Well what?"

"*How* was he checked? What made *him* so attractive?"

"There were two others."

"All right, so there were two others. But we're talking about Peter Harley. What made *him* so attractive?"

"He had a good record with his employers. He had a lot of street experience. He had a high IQ. He knew how to handle himself. Also he had a convenient background."

"What background? He's a foundling. He doesn't *have* any background."

"Exactly. He tried to locate his parents and had failed. Government investigators, to their pleasure and relief, failed just as completely. When they took Harley they knew they were getting only Harley. There would be no nosy relatives. On the other side of Harley's birth there was only a comforting wall of anonymity."

"Well, now you're candid," I said. "But I still don't think I've been given much."

"You made a promise."

"And I'll keep it. You can see the manuscript, but even if Harley does end up in the news, I don't think anything that comes out will conflict with whatever I write."

He retrieved the case and snapped it shut.

"Let's hope not."

Again I had the impression that I'd missed something. He gave me the feeling that I had not extracted as much as I might have from what I had been told and shown, and that he was disappointed with me.

"Tell me something," I said.

"Yes?"

"Is there some chance that as a result of this investigation you might go to jail?"

Just the faintest grin. "It's possible."

"And Harley?"

"Also possible."

"I see."

He waited patiently for my next question. Our business was over, but he was considerately granting me a brief interview on my subject, Peter Harley.

"What do you think of Harley?" I said. "Yourself, personally."

"I admire him."

"Why?"

"This will sound peculiar to you, but I admire him because he has the capacity for failure. It's nothing these days to have what it takes to win. I admire the losers."

"You don't look like a loser."

"No." He was once more the wise professor, indulgent and unhurried. "You might say I have failed to lose."

"That *does* sound peculiar."

He shrugged, one eye bright and clear, the other partially concealed behind the bristly, nictitated lid. When it was clear that I had nothing more to say, he leaned forward and wrote on a sheet of paper. As he did so he said, "Well, I guess that finishes it, then. I've enjoyed meeting you, Mr. Deniset. When you've finished your story and have something to show me I can be reached through the State Department in Washington. They'll have my number. Bryan Knowles."

He pushed the sheet of paper toward me across the desk, but he did not take his fingers off it. I looked down and read, "He will be a very dangerous man to be around." Then he took the paper back and put it in his pocket. He got up and knocked on the door for the guard.

I was astonished and didn't know what to say. Trying to cover my feelings, I said, "Do they have these rooms everywhere? All the embassies?"

"Oh, yes. They have two here. There's another on the third floor."

We shook hands, and the uniformed marine escorted me downstairs.

I walked out into the sunshine, crossed the lawn to the front gate, and stood on the curb waiting for a taxi. I wanted to go back to the hotel and write it all down. I didn't know what to make of Knowles. Somehow, I wasn't sure why, I had a good feeling about him. There had been in his one good eye a directness, a lack of guile, a readiness to smile that was difficult to associate with wickedness. I had a picture of a good man involved in a dirty undertaking. Dirty, that is, to me. Perhaps if I knew everything about it, it would not seem so dirty.

A taxi stopped and I got in. As we drove up Wireless Road past the ambassador's residence I remembered my first week at United Press International in New York after I graduated from Yale. I had learned something then about the pursuit of certainty, about what you can know and what you can't know. A plane had crashed at Idlewild and all the reporters got together at the airport, compared conflicting reports on the number of dead and injured, and picked a number. It wouldn't do for different papers to have a different number of casualties. Readers might begin to lose faith in the absolute knowability of everything. And then the next shift of reporters came on and got another set of conflicting facts and settled on the new, second-edition truth. And the truth continued to change as long as the papers continued to carry the story. I learned that when a story was so big that it went on indefinitely, the so-called facts continued to change indefinitely. It was almost enough to convince you that there *was* no bedrock, impenetrable, final Fact.

So what about Knowles? What would he turn out to be if one could dig down a few layers? Good or bad?

12

"**Y**OU GOT kidnapped," Harley said that night. "What happened?"

I told him about Knowles and the plastic room but very little of what I'd learned.

"So you got to see the bubble," he said.

"Is that what they call it?"

We were in a place called the Marine House, a building with upstairs dormitories, a downstairs bar, and a swimming pool outside in the garden. The marines who guarded the embassy, all single men, lived there and invited anyone they liked to share their cut-rate bar in the evenings.

"Spooky place," Harley said, meaning the bubble.

Sandra had come in with us but another woman pulled her off into a side room to watch a poker game. Harley and I sat alone at a table.

"I saw a piece of paper with your initials on it," I said. "It also had several other initials. OEY, NOK—I don't remember all of them. And a long number. There was something about Tel Aviv and counterfeiting and some men called Alfa. What was that all about?"

"He showed you that?"

"Yes. I got the impression they were"—I didn't want to use the word *assassins*—"that they had killed people."

"If anyone ever deserved to be killed it was the men those agents killed."

"You knew them? The agents?"

"Yes." His voice was hard.

"What were—"

"Listen, Tony, you ask a lot of questions about other people, but you never give anything yourself. No one knows anything about you."

He sounded as if he'd been worrying over those words for a long time, at least since the night of his beating when he'd asked the same question.

"What do you want to know?" I said, realizing it would be useless now to question him further about what I had learned from Knowles.

He shrugged and hunched closer over his beer, curling his fingers around the glass.

"I'm from Baltimore," I said, "my father manages a department store, I have one brother two years older than I am, I went to Yale, I was married for two years, and my wife was killed in an accident for which I was almost totally responsible. That's my life. I'm open to questions if you have any."

"Don't get pissed off."

"I'm not pissed off. You said you wanted to know about me, so I told you."

I had spoken about responsibility for my wife's death only once before, to her father, and was half expecting the world to crumble at the sound of the words. When it didn't, I felt a sudden unanticipated relief.

"I'm sorry about your wife," Harley said.

"It was a skiing accident . . ."

I paused, testing the atmosphere. Harley stared straight at me, listening. I didn't know when I might again feel ready to talk about it, so in the next five or ten minutes I told Harley what had happened.

We had been staying at Klosters, in the Swiss Alps, and my wife had said, "Tony, do you think I could handle the Derby run?"

The Parsenn Derby course is one of the most beautiful and difficult runs in Europe. It starts above Davos, about ten kilometers from Klosters, and drops six thousand feet to a finish in Kublis. Patricia had skiied only once before this vacation, but after she'd had a few classes and negotiated one of the intermediate slopes she wouldn't stop talking about the Derby course. Other people encouraged her. "Tony, stop holding the poor girl back, if she wants to try it let her try it." So finally I gave in. I thought, who am I to tell her what she can't do? We took the shuttle train over to Davos and started down the Derby. It was much too dangerous for her, and I knew it. We pushed off on steep ice, and in less than two minutes she hit a mogul and went flying. When I got to her she was conscious but she couldn't move. She had no feeling anywhere. She said, "Help me, Tony, I can't move. Help me up." But when I tried to help her up, she was like rubber. She couldn't stand. She kept saying, "Help me, Tony, help me up." After ten minutes another skier saw us, stopped for a minute, then went like hell for the *pisteurs*. Finally they came with the bloodwagon, lifted her in, covered her like a corpse, and shot down the mountain so fast they already had her in the clinic by the time I hit the bottom. She was paralyzed from the neck down. The doctor said he'd call in a neurosurgeon from Zurich.

Late that afternoon she had convulsions and went into a coma. She cried out and groaned and her head tossed back and forth. She was soaked with perspiration. I sat by the bed holding her hand and praying. She opened her eyes once and screamed and I rang for the nurse and asked if she couldn't give her a shot of something. She said she'd already given her as much as she could and the scream wasn't from pain. I didn't believe that. I sat there talking to her, praying that maybe she could hear me, and then at eight o'clock she stopped making any sounds at all, her face relaxed, and I called the nurse again and the nurse took her pulse and examined her and said she was dead. An hour later the surgeon arrived from Zurich and the next morning they found a hemorrhage on her brain. The surgeon said that even if she had lived she would have been paralyzed for the rest of her life. He tried to make me take some pills. I walked back to my hotel and called her father in New York. He was a powerful man, professionally and physically—well over six feet, strong-willed. He had started and still controlled his own investment banking firm. If he objected to his only child marrying a lowly journalist, he had never let me know it. We had gotten on well. But now, I thought and hoped, he would want to kill me. His own wife had died of Hodgkin's disease when Patricia was five, and when the doctors told him he threw a hospital intern through a plate-glass window. A few years after that he turned down a presidential appointment to head a winter trade delegation to West Germany. When a reporter asked him for his reason he said, "My daughter and I have plans for Christmas."

He flew to Zurich, chartered a helicopter, and was in Klosters that night. He walked into my room in the hotel and sat on the bed and didn't say anything. He just asked me what had happened. I told him. I told him it was my fault, that I had known the run was too dangerous for her, that I had let people talk me into letting her try it, that I had failed to protect her. He was very kind. We talked for an hour and then he said I looked as if I needed sleep. When we were back in New York I had dinner at his house and I told him again that I knew it was my fault, that I felt as if I'd killed her.

He got up and walked across the room, angry, tyring to control himself. He said, "You're embarrassing me, Tony."

I asked why.

"Because that kind of grief isn't for her at all. It's for yourself, for how you think you're going to be haunted by this the rest of your life. Think about Patricia. *She* didn't

think it was your fault. She would never have believed that.
Stop feeling guilty. Feel all the grief you want, but the
guilt—that's just—''

Before I could get any further, Sandra came back. I stopped
talking, and to cover the silence Harley said, ''Someone had
Tony in the bubble.''

''Really, who?''

''A guy named Bryan Knowles,'' I said, trying to recover.
If I'd only been able to finish the story, hear Harley's
reaction. . .

''Don't know him,'' she said. ''What's he look like?''

I described Knowles.

Sandra shook her head and looked at Harley.

Harley said, ''Doesn't sound familiar. They must have
brought him in. You sure there isn't something you haven't
told us, Tony? You're not a foreign agent, anything like
that?''

I tried to laugh, and for a moment considered telling them
that I had seen Knowles earlier at the Christmas party. I
decided against it.

When the pitcher of beer we had on the table was empty,
Harley took it to the bar for a refill. He came back with a
young Marine sergeant. The sergeant shook hands with me
and then with Sandra. She barely nodded at him, and when he
sat down she caught my eye and I felt she would have been
happier having the sergeant at our table if he'd been a lieutenant.

I asked him how long he'd been in Bangkok. He said five
months. Before that he'd been assigned to the embassy on
Cyprus, had been there when the ambassador was killed
during a riot. I was interested in how marines go about
defending an embassy.

''The uniformed marine in the booth,'' he said, ''who you
probably noticed when you went upstairs today''—everyone
seemed to be aware of everything I did—''has a sidearm and
a shotgun. There's a little room—''

Sandra interrupted. A marine in a white apron was making
hamburgers on a grill next to the bar, and Sandra said she'd
like one. All the junior men took turns at the grill and behind
the bar.

''I'll order some,'' Harley said, and left the table.

''There's a little room,'' the sergeant continued, ''next to
him with two or three other marines in it and they've got

several shotguns and tear gas and automatic weapons. There's a button back there—''

Harley returned and Sandra said, ''I hope you told him not to squeeze them.''

''—a button back there that closes and locks the steel gate to the upper floors. The third floor then has—''

''He's squeezing them, Peter,'' Sandra said, watching the marine at the grill. ''He's squeezing out all the juice. He presses them down like that and all the juice goes out. All the flavor's in the juice. If he—''

Harley gave her a look and she shut up.

''The third floor what?'' Harley said to the sergeant.

''The third floor then has about ten minutes to destroy whatever has to be destroyed. Any American embassy in the world can be occupied in ten minutes.''

''What happens to the marines in those ten minutes?'' I said.

''We're in the entrance hall.''

Harley went to the grill and brought back the hamburgers. Sandra took a bite of hers and put it back on the plate. ''It's like cardboard,'' she said. ''There's no juice at all, no flavor, it tastes like—''

Harley reached over and calmly removed the top of her hamburger. Then he picked up his own, bun and all, held it above Sandra's, and squeezed it until the juice ran out. He put the mangled remains back on his plate and wiped his hand. He said, ''Now you have a juicy hamburger. Is that all right?''

Sandra left the table.

We talked for another four or five minutes and then the sergeant went to the bar to see some friends. I said to Harley, ''I think you hurt her feelings.''

''She ought to know these guys don't get paid to make her hamburgers. That guy who was just with us took two rounds in the stomach on Cyprus. And she's bitching in front of him about no juice in her hamburger. Sometimes . . .''

He sat there quietly, thinking, drinking beer. Then he said, ''We've got to get out of here in a couple of minutes anyway. I've got a meeting.'' He stood up. ''Excuse me a second while I get rid of some beer.''

He went to the men's room and I sat alone. I recognized a few other agents from the embassy, and a couple of secretaries. Four marines were playing darts. I didn't see Sandra.

When Harley came out of the men's room, he stopped to talk to a Marine master sergeant. He was the biggest man I'd ever seen off a football field, close to six foot six, three hundred pounds. He had a crew cut, red face, and he was laughing. He was a little drunk. Two or three other men were in the group. Harley started to leave them to return to the table, but the marine grabbed his arm and pulled him back. Harley listened to a story the marine told, then laughed and started away again. The marine took hold of Harley's arms, pinning them to his sides, lifted him like a sack of wheat, and put him back down at the center of the group.

I saw Sandra come out of the ladies' room and watch this. She walked over and stood near Harley, just outside the group.

The big marine and Harley were talking, and the marine suddenly put his hands forward, cupping them around Harley's chin. He turned the chin right, then left, then back center. He let go and moved back a step and squinted at Harley's face. He reached forward with one hand and tilted the chin just slightly to the right. All of this was done in the manner of a golfer arranging his ball on the tee. Harley kept his hands at his sides and played along. Sandra moved next to him, looking worried.

The big marine made several more setting-up gestures with Harley's head, then stepped back, squinted, cocked his shoulder, and was clearly preparing to knock Harley's head into the next room.

Harley did not move and did not alter his expression of mild amusement. His arms were loose at his sides and he took no notice of Sandra.

The drunk marine and Harley looked into each other's eyes, the marine's arm now drawn back for the blow. Then the marine brought the arm forward slowly, and the other one with it, and again cupped Harley's chin, affectionately, like a child's, and roared with laughter. Harley reached an arm around Sandra's shoulders, as if that had been on his mind since she arrived. He put his other arm around the marine, shook him playfully—this was like shaking an oak—and laughed and then let him go and walked with Sandra back to the table.

"I thought he was going to kill you," I said.

"He's a wonderful man," Harley said. "He's got eight kids,

three adopted, and they all love him. He was Santa Claus last night at the Christmas party here.''

''He drinks too much,'' Sandra said.

''Not like all those sober, gentlemanly FSOs, right?''

''That's right.''

''You know what an FSO is, Tony?'' Harley said.

''Foreign Service officer,'' I said.

''Wrong. Faggot serving overseas.''

''Peter loves that little joke,'' Sandra said. ''That's why he tells it so often.''

''I shouldn't be so fucking crude,'' Harley said, teasing her. ''I should have gone to Vassar. I should have lived in Beverly Hills.''

''Oh no!'' Sandra said. ''Don't start that again. I've already heard all about your seventeen different homes, or twenty-seven, or whatever it was.''

''Twelve, actually,'' Harley said, ''if you don't count all the kindly faggots and other one-night stands.''

She looked at me, pretending to be distressed by Harley's vulgarity.

''Tony and I have to go,'' Harley said suddenly. ''Time to see a stool.''

''Asset,'' Sandra corrected.

''Stool, asset, what's the difference? Sandra doesn't like the word 'stool' because it sounds unrefined. Cops have stools, Aim has assets. Also she doesn't like it because it sounds like a pile of shit. Right, baby?''

''Don't call me baby.''

''You want to stay here or you want a ride home?''

''I think I'll go home.''

After we had dropped her off I asked Harley where we were going.

''The Oriental Hotel. I lied when I said I had to see a stool. I'm seeing Miki.''

''Oh. You want to drop me at the hotel?''

''No. Come along if you want to. Listen, I hope you won't think I'm too far out of line, but your wife, getting back—''

''What.'' I was pleased he had brought the subject up again.

''You don't mind?''

''No.''

''I think her old man was right.''

''I know he was.''

"You've got to hang on. Otherwise you cave in. You fall into yourself."

"I know."

For some reason I decided at that moment to tell him the rest of the story (the whole story, really), something I had not had the courage to confess even to Patricia's father. I said, "It's not really so easy."

"No. I guess it isn't."

"I mean, it was worse than what I told you. When we were at the top of the run, just before she started down, she looked ahead of her and set her poles and said, 'Do you think this is really wise?' She was smiling, like it was a joke. I hesitated for a second, and then before I could answer she was gone. Later I realized that she'd changed her mind. She wanted me to stop her. But she was too proud to wait around and ask me again. If I'd reached out then and taken her hand she'd have come back to the hotel with me and she'd still be alive."

Harley thought about that for a minute, and then he said, "Yes, that makes it different."

I was not prepared for such a brutal gift of friendship. I had expected him to be polite, to argue with me, tell me I had misinterpreted her remark. It was almost worth hearing the unpleasant truth confirmed to know that we were no longer strangers.

We drove in silence until we were near the hotel and then Harley, perhaps sensing that I would welcome a change of subject, said, "When Jaran told you about me and Miki, what else did he say?"

"Just that you knew her. He seemed to think it was dangerous."

"Because of her father and the embassy?"

"Yes."

"He didn't say anything else?"

"What do you mean?"

"About the morality of it? Seeing Miki while I'm living with Sandra?"

"No."

"He's very big on honor. He likes to lecture me. I agree with him. I hate this kind of shit. They both trust me and I lie to them. I feel like a fucking traitor. Every time I see Miki I tell myself I'll never do it again."

We walked across a dark terrace covered with candlelit

tables and sat at one nearest the river. I could see the outlines of rice barges moving on the water.

We had just ordered gins and tonic when Miki appeared silently and sat down. She was wearing a dark green silk dress and seemed much more subdued than she had been at the Sports Club.

Harley increased the drink order by one and for ten minutes we talked pleasantly about the loveliness of the hotel, the charm of the boats on the river, the ugliness of Bangkok's new buildings, the outrageous way developers filled in klongs to make roads, the spiciness of Thai food, the high price of wine, the excellence of the fish—and then, finally, the small talk ran its course and we coasted to silence.

"You were late," Miki said.

Her voice was soft. In the candlelight and silk, on the edge of that river, she seemed beautiful and helpless—helpless, but not harmless. The schools in Switzerland and America, the travel and money and people, had not completely overcome all the frailties of youth. She was experienced but not hard. She had many things Sandra had not yet thought to hope for.

"I'm sorry," Harley said. "I had to do some work."

"Are you staying with Peter?" she said to me.

"No. I'm at the Siam Inter."

"Have you been to his house?"

A sixth sense, and Harley's frightened glance, told me to lie. "No."

A Thai waiter in a white jacket arrived with the drinks.

"I haven't either," she said.

Harley raised his glass. "To a happy evening."

We all drank.

"Peter and I have known each other for over a month," Miki said faintly, "but I have never seen his house. Why were you late, Peter?"

"I told you."

"You promised."

"Miki, I couldn't . . ."

"Tony, do you think it's wrong for a man to have two girls at the same time?"

"Well, I don't know."

"I don't think it's wrong," she said, looking straight into my eyes with a tenderness that was just now beginning to burn away. "Unless the man lies about it. Because that's insulting, isn't it? Don't you think so?"

"Miki," Harley said, "it isn't—"

"What does she look like, Peter?"

He touched her hand.

"Is she Asian? American? Blond? Dark?"

She kept her voice low. Nothing in her tone or expression could have alerted the tourists at the next table.

"Miki, there is no one else. How can I tell you what she looks like?"

"Or maybe she is *not* beautiful. Maybe she is smart instead, or rich. Yes, I think that's it. She is brilliant and rich, but a little . . ." She waited until she had forced Harley to meet her eyes. "A little—blemished?"

Harley reached nervously for his drink. "What do you—"

"A mole?"

She rose suddenly and shook my hand. "It has been nice seeing you again, Tony. I hope you have a pleasant stay in Thailand."

She walked out.

Harley's hand had not made it to the drink. He looked at the table. Then he looked at the river. Finally he said, "I think I'd better go home and talk to Sandra."

Harley drove me back to the hotel. I saw Knowles again. He was sitting in the bar with a Chinese girl. I thought he might be embarrassed to have me see him there so I left and went to my room and ordered a drink from room service. I drank it and went to bed and tried to sleep. Patricia came into my thoughts, and the days at Klosters. I tried to think instead about what was going on at Harley's, what Sandra and he were saying to each other. I could hear music outside by the pool, and the peacocks screaming.

Songkhla

13

HARLEY CALLED at 3 A.M.

"Do you save all your calls for the middle of the night, Peter?"

"I'm sorry if I woke you."

"It doesn't matter."

"A few things have happened. I'm leaving for Songkhla in a few hours."

"The truck came through?" Then I had another idea. "The girl, the stool you—"

"The plane leaves Don Muang at three o'clock."

"Can I go with you?"

"It's Air Siam. I don't know the flight number."

"I see. What happened at home?"

"Get back to sleep."

He hung up.

I got to the airport early, checked in, and sat down in one of the plastic chairs. Peter walked in with Jaran. Jaran saw me, said something to Peter, and they went to the check-in counter. Neither gave any indication that he knew me.

On the plane I took a window seat and put my typewriter in the empty place next to me, hoping to discourage neighbors. As soon as the seat belt sign went off, Peter came back and put the typewriter under the seat and sat down.

"I'm sorry for all this cloak and dagger horseshit. I didn't want it to look like I was asking you to come down here. If anyone ever accuses me of encouraging your curiosity I want to be able to deny it."

"What happened with Sandra?"

"I'll tell you about Sandra later. The stool, the one you met Friday night, says the truck we were after passed through Bangkok two nights ago and was definitely headed for a lab in the south. So if our Intel's right and the opium belongs to

Lichai, it's worth going down and trying to hook him up with it."

I suspected from his tone, and from what I already knew about his low regard for the reliability of that stool, that there were other reasons for Peter's and Jaran's sudden rush south. I said, "Is that the only reason you're going south?"

"Also the girl. The thirteen-year-old whore- I told you about. There's been a threat against Niekro. The embassy thinks Niekro's not pursuing the girl strongly enough because of his fear about his family getting hurt. They don't want to give up on her until we find her again and see what she's got to offer."

He stood up to return to his seat by Jaran. "We'll give you a lift from the airport."

They were met by a short, nervous American about Peter's age, who shook hands timidly, his eyes never meeting their own. I stood at a distance by the baggage claim counter, ignored by the three of them, wondering what I would do if they left without me.

They picked up their bags, and when mine arrived and I had it in hand, we all walked out together.

Peter put everything in the back of a black Range Rover and introduced the thin man, who got behind the wheel. He was Tom Niekro. We pulled out onto a four-lane blacktop lined with palm trees, banana trees, and heavy brush. The Range Rover had tinted windows, like the embassy cars Harley had used in Bangkok, but in the bright sunshine there was no difficulty seeing.

"That's the last flight," Niekro said. "They'll shut down the field till tomorrow. In twenty minutes it'll be deserted."

Peter stared off into the brush. "It's hard to believe they could be in there," he said.

"Oh, they're there," Niekro said. "The Border Patrol controls this area during the day, but at night the CTs take it."

We passed an armored personnel carrier with two Border Patrol police sitting on top, automatic rifles across their laps. In a few minutes we had passed through Hatyai and were headed for Songkhla on a thirty-kilometer stretch of road that Niekro called "Bandits' Road." It was narrow, winding, and cut back and forth five times across a local railroad line. Each of the five crossings had an automatic barrier to halt traffic for the train. The train stopped running at 5 P.M. because of the CTs and bandits. Anytime you were on the road after that hour and saw one of the barriers down it meant you were about to be robbed or murdered and your best bet was to ram the barrier, or try to get past it in the ditches, or spin around and head back. The safest tactic, of course, was never to use the road at night. But that was impossible if you were working on cases between the two towns.

We unloaded our bags at a hotel called the Sawadi near a beach. The building was modern but decaying, patches of the white paint gone from the concrete walls, grass uncut, the water in a half-filled swimming pool motionless beneath a carpet of green slime. In five minutes, after depositing the bags in the lobby, we were back in the Range Rover, driving through the sunny, dusty streets of Songkhla, steering carefully to avoid water buffalo. We turned left into a heavily rutted dirt road and slowed to keep from flying out of our seats. In a moment we were hit by a stench of rotting fish.

"Damn," Peter shouted, "where the hell do you live anyway, in a fish factory?"

"Exactly," Niekro said. "That place on the right there's a canning factory."

He pulled the car into the backyard of a one-story wooden house. Before we had climbed out, a young woman, about twenty-five years old, came into the yard with a baby in her arms. Standing with the child at the back of the house, her thin face looking worried and fatigued, she reminded me of a pioneer wife in some movie Western. In a second she was joined by a young Thai maid carrying a shotgun. We stood around the Range Rover, dust swirling at our feet, struggling not to inhale the fish fumes, and were introduced. Suddenly another man appeared, a short, stocky Thai, scary-looking, clad only in torn, dirty shorts. I had not seen or heard him approach. He smiled, revealing rotted tooth stumps blood-red with betel nut stains, a man to inspire enormous assurance if he was on your side, and terror if he was not. A two-foot machete hung as loosely and naturally from his right hand as if he'd been born with it there.

The yard was filled with a half-dozen pigs who had wandered over from a nearby group of shacks (the machete man's village, I learned later) and about the same number of *kamoy* dogs. *Kamoy* is Thai for thief or burglar and almost every house I had seen in Bangkok had been surrounded by half-wild dogs kept as protection against them. One of the dogs in

Niekro's yard—a pet, not a watchdog—was a small round fluffy black puppy named Coconut. Niekro had bought him for some cigarettes in a Karen village in the mountains near Burma. It nipped around his wife's feet and she stooped to play with it and let the child touch its fur.

We went inside—all of us except the machete man, who vanished as noiselessly as he had appeared—and Peter, Jaran, and I stood on one side of a waist-high bar while Niekro mixed drinks on the other. The wife, maid, and child withdrew to the kitchen, taking with them Coconut, the only dog permitted in the house.

When we all had scotches in our hands, Niekro raised his glass and, with more feeling than would have been required by a merely social geeting, said, "Thanks for coming."

Jaran said, "I'm seeing Samak tonight. It'll be straightened out. Don't worry."

"I *am* worried. I'm worried as hell."

He waved his drink in the direction of the kitchen. "I'm not going to be some kind of hero with them around."

"It's okay," Peter said. "It's been taken care of. It really has." He looked hard at Niekro, and Niekro looked back hard, his eyes for the first time steadying themselves, trying to measure the truth of Peter's words.

"Really," Peter said. His lips, entire face tightened with the effort to drive the word through Niekro's disbelief.

There was a moment of silence, broken finally when Niekro reached for the bottle, topped up our glasses, and said to me, "Are you with the embassy?"

I knew he had made that assumption when Peter introduced us. Now I waited for Peter to say something, and when he didn't I assumed I was expected to tell the truth.

"No," I said, "I'm a writer. I'm doing a story about smuggling."

"He's been to Washington and Bangkok," Peter said. "Everbody's cleared him."

The news that I was a writer did nothing to reduce Niekro's willingness to talk. Whatever trouble he was in, he evidently felt he needed all the help he could get.

"Well, if you want a helluva story," he said to me, "you've come to the right place."

Jaran wandered off to the other side of the room.

"Nobody in Songkhla or Hatyai," Peter said, still standing at the bar, facing me, "was very happy when Washington decided to open a drug office down here. They'd killed a stool on a previous operation—I told you about that, the guy with the machete in his neck—and they didn't like the idea of American agents stationed here, operational, right out there in their jeans and sandals with guns and stools and the whole thing. So they—''

''Tell him who 'they' is,'' Niekro said.

''The traffickers, the CTs, the bandits, cops, hotel owners, massage parlor owners, whores, pimps—everybody. American agents down here are a threat to everyone, to the way things have always been run. So, for example, a week ago Tom here and some Sno cops fell over—excuse me, Special Narcotics Organization, it's a unit of the national police force, corrupt like all the other cops—they fell over a heroin lab in a rubber plantation. They had word of a stock of heroin and when they went in they found the lab. Well, labs around here are protected by the CTs. The CTs take a cut of the profits and in return provide protection. The cops wouldn't go near one of these labs because they won't tangle with the CTs, and anyway they get their cut, too. And the guy who owns the plantation where the lab is, he makes no beef because he gets a piece of it, too, and anyway he doesn't want any trouble with the CTs, who could burn down the whole damn plantation if they felt like it. So when Tom and the Sno guys, the Thai drug cops, stumbled over the lab it made a big problem. The Sno cops took off, wouldn't have anything to do with it. But Tom got some men and burned the lab down. Now that caused all kinds of loss of face for the CTs because they're supposed to be guarding it. Very humiliating. And naturally the guy who owned the lab, and everyone getting a cut from it, they were pissed off at the CTs for not protecting it and at Tom here for burning it down. So two days ago the embassy got word that Tom was going to be killed. We get a lot of threats like that and you don't listen to them because if you did you'd never get out of bed in the morning, but this one came from a stool who'd been hired as one of the hit men. He knew everything. He said, 'You don't believe me? Let me tell you. His wife's name is Barbara. They get up every morning at six. He leaves at seven. They have a nine-month-old son and when she takes him out she wraps him in a blue blanket. Twice a week he drives a brown jeep to Hatyai and buys food. They've got six *kamoy* dogs. There's a sixteen-year-old maid, the local headman keeps guard . . .' The guy gave us so much Intel you *had* to believe it. He even told us the names of the other hit men and what weapons they had and where they were gonna do it and when and every other damn thing you'd want to know. So the embassy talked with the Thais in Bangkok, and now Jaran's down here to deliver a message. And you know who he's going to deliver it to? The guy responsible for the hit? The guy who set it up and can put it down?''

"Samak?" I said.

"Right. The local head of the Provincial Police in Songkhla province. The fucking chief of police. How about that?''

I shook my head, knowing that nothing I said would sound adequate.

"And I told you who *he* belongs to."

"Lichai. So why don't the people who sent Jaran down here with a message for Samak just deliver the message to Lichai instead?"

"Tell Lichai to tell Samak to lay off?"

"Right."

"Because no one in Bangkok's going to tell a man with Lichai's money and connections, a man who used to be a member of parliament and could just possibly be a top man in the government someday, that he's a murdering drug trafficker and to lay off our agents. That kind of balls they don't have."

"So they deal a couple of levels down," Neikro said. "They try to throw a scare into Samak."

"I see."

When we sat down to dinner Barbara kept the baby in her lap. The meal—curried shrimp and broiled steak—was prepared and served by the maid, a young girl who for some reason never stopped giggling. A bottle of Heinz ketchup was on the table. Geckos crawled on the walls and ceiling.

Tom described with admiration the proficiency of the machete man, whose name was Boonchai, in killing cobras he found in the yard.

"He has a way of flicking them into the air with the point of the machete and then whacking them in two before they hit the ground." He said an apparent ability to whack people in two, as well, had secured him the role of headman in the village behind the house. Boonchai knew everyone and Tom had hired him as a house guard. Strangers who approached the house found themselves suddenly confronted by his betel

nut grin and slowly pendulating machete. Both the maid and
Tom's wife were trained in the use of the family arsenal,
which included a .38 Smith and Wesson Detectives' Special,
a .45 army issue automatic, a shotgun loaded with double-
ought buck, and for serious emergencies an M-16. Once a
week the family held target practice in the backyard, less as
practice, Tom explained, than as an admonitory demonstra-
tion of firepower. (He later confided out of his wife's presence that he had hidden a box of grenades in the room with
the freezer and hot water tank.)

The house had no telephone and Tom communicated with
the consulate, when anyone there was listening, by a small
field radio. Tom told me that things weren't really so bad
because at least he was eligible for a 25 percent pay differen-
tial awarded to agents in posts deemed ''dangerous or isolated.'' Barbara shot him a glance dripping irony and said,
''Which are we?''

After dinner a Thai corporal picked Jaran up and Tom
drove Peter and me to the hotel. We made plans to meet in
the morning; then Tom left and Peter and I had a drink in the
bar.

I didn't want to ask again about Sandra, and he didn't seem
ready to talk about her. He got on the subject of the hotel and
said it had been managed by a Frenchman for the first three
years. Then the Frenchman returned to Europe with his sav-
ings, and that was the end of the good food, clean rooms, and
sparkling pool. The only lingering benefit of his influence
was a Saturday night poolside buffet to which every Westerner in Songkhla, about forty people, came without fail.

''Tom's been here just over a month,'' Harley said. ''His
office is in the hotel, one of the corner suites. Steve Lowell,
the consul, wouldn't let him in the consulate. He said there
wasn't room. There is room, but he didn't want Tom around.
The FSOs think we're animals. Wait'll you meet Lowell. Just
imagine the biggest pompous asshole you ever met and multi-
ply that by a hundred. And lazy as hell. He could get movies
and anything else anyone wanted down from Bangkok but he
won't take the trouble. I'll tell you a story about how inte-
grated Lowell is with the local culture. Before he came over
here he went to language school for five months, like everyone else, learning Thai, and his wife went with him. They
speak a little, to the servants. So they were in Bangkok for a
while, before they came down here, and an agent who was

there at the time told me Lowell and his wife were real snobs, wouldn't go near a drug agent, wouldn't have anything to do with any Thai below the rank of colonel. One day the agent's in a short-time hotel, one of those dirty second-story places with the mirrors on the ceiling, and he hears groaning on the other side of the wall, and some guy's screaming Thai at a broad. 'Fuck me, baby, fuck me good.' That kind of shit, and all in Thai. So he listens and in a minute he recognizes the voice. It's Lowell. He can't believe it. Not Lowell. With a whore in a dump like that? He goes outside and waits in the street to make sure. And who comes out? Not just Lowell. *Mrs*. Lowell. *Both* of them. They'd gone to a whore's hotel and fucked and yelled Thai at each other. How's that for a little cultural schizophrenia?''

It was ten o'clock and the room was empty. The bartender had disappeared. Harley went behind the bar and brought a bottle of Dewar's to the table. Before I could mention Sandra, he said, ''Don't think the wrong thing about Tom. He's a helluva good agent. I worked with him in New York. He's got a lot of balls. We hit a flat full of guinea dealers out in Queens and he took out three of the bastards before anyone even had time to show a piece. But they haven't given him any support here. Valdez sent him down with a suitcase and a handful of dimes. He had no house, no office, no stools, nothing. And he got a lab. That's really a remarkable thing. They've got an office full of agents up in Chiang Mai and they go six months sometimes between labs. Then all this threat shit started and he's going a little crazy because of his wife and kid. You can't blame him for that. Jaran will fix that up and Tom'll get back to normal. He'll be okay. When they finally get off their asses in Bangkok and send him a partner he'll be able to move, he'll have some time to develop his stools and he'll roll.''

''Listen . . .'' I said.

''Yeah.''

He had run out of things to talk about.

''What about Sandra?''

As much as I wanted to know, the look that came to his face made me sorry I'd asked. He twisted his body in the chair and looked down at the table.

''I'm sorry,'' I said. ''Forget it. It's none of my business.''

''Miki had already called her. She was waiting for me when I got home. She asked me how it had gone with the stool. I told her I hadn't been with a stool. I said I'd been with an asset. Because by then I had it figured out, who Sandra really was and who Miki was. Sandra started talking and she didn't stop until she was crying so hard I couldn't understand her anymore. She was more shaken up than I was."

"Because you were seeing Miki?"

"Because she works for Aim, Tony. She already knew all about Miki. She'd been living with that since it started. She works for Aim. Miki's her asset."

He poured himself a drink.

"She never worked for the political section at all. She came over here as Aim. She was trained, she was on the farm, she's been CIA since she got out of Vassar. She recruited Miki long before I ever met either one of them. Every time I went out with Miki it was all part of a report."

He raised the glass and drank till it was empty. He set the glass lightly on the table and raised his eyes to mine.

"Logical, right? Lichai's daughter? She was educated in the States, her mother's American, she likes Americans, she moves in the right circles. A perfect asset."

"But why did Miki—"

"Because they'd had a fight. That's natural, I suppose. Even the third-floor people have feelings. Miki's reports never said anything about sleeping with me, because we hadn't, but Sandra didn't believe that, she thought Miki was lying. So they had a fight."

He stopped talking and sat staring into his empty glass. When he looked up, his face had the dry, self-deprecating smile of a man who's been duped and isn't trying to deny it.

"She's the only girl I've ever lived with, Tony. She's actually the only *person* I've ever lived with that I picked out for myself."

"Was that why you decided to come down here?"

"To get away from her? No. It was just the threat to Tom, and the truck coming down, and the girl. Jaran'll take care of the threat and after I take care of Lichai I'll be out of this fucking hole."

We had another drink, said good night, and walked upstairs. When I turned on the light in my room I saw that I was not alone. Cockroaches as big as mice scampered across the bare wood floor. I killed five with a shoe and went to bed and lay there watching a fat bloated gecko climbing the wall opposite me, stalking insects. Two smaller ones were on the ceiling. I knew they were harmless, but I was afraid one might fall on my face. The air was filled with mosquitoes, and they turned out to be more aggressive and less easily killed than the cockroaches. I supposed I was fortunate that I had no cobras to deal with.

14

AT SEVEN o'clock the next morning I got out of bed, dumped a cockroach out of the toe of one of my slippers, and walked to the window. The pool was down there, its opaque surface a radiant green in the morning light, and beyond it a beach littered with kelp and driftwood. A man on horseback moved slowly down the beach away from the hotel.

I telephoned Peter and asked him if he'd like some breakfast before we met Tom. He agreed, and as soon as we were seated in the dining room and had given our order to a sleepy, sullen waitress, he began to tell me his day's plan, rapidly and with excitement, as if it had been on his mind all night.

"I want to find that girl stool today, Tony, see if she's really got something to give us. This isn't the sort of town to hang around in. Get in, get out—that's the thing. I've got—"

Tom walked in and pulled up a chair.

"So what's the schedule?" Harley said, breaking off his words about the stool.

"I called the consulate from the office upstairs. I tried to get them on the radio from home but naturally no one answered."

"You want some breakfast?" Harley said.

"No, thanks, I had some at home. Jaran left a message at the consulate that he'd meet us at the Satellite Café at noon. Maybe I'll just have a cup of coffee." He waved at the waitress. "I wonder how he made out."

"I don't," Harley said. "You don't understand Jaran. He

always makes out. He sees to it. You knew guys like that in New York. With Jaran, you've got nothing at all to worry about.''

The waitress brought coffee and some overcooked scrambled eggs for Harley and me.

''Aside from the threat,'' Harley said, ''how're things going? You got any stools?''

''I've been here thirty-three days,'' Tom said, ''and I've spent about thirty-two of those fighting with Lowell, fighting with Bangkok, trying to find an office, trying to find a house, and trying to keep alive. Just getting the office set up in the hotel here took a week. They sent me down with nothing, Peter, absolutely nothing, like a tourist I came down here, and after one week Valdez is yelling when am I gonna make a case. I said, lemme find a desk, lemme find a bed for my wife and kid to sleep in. He's never been down here. He thinks you just move in, snap, like that, and set up your stools and you're in business.''

''How're the Sno guys?''

Tom looked at the waitress leaning on a table about twenty feet away. ''Let's not talk here. There's a nice beach.''

We went out the back door of the dining room and walked past the swimming pool to the beach and turned right. We left our shoes in a pile—Tom and Harley both wore sandals made from automobile tires—and rolled up the cuffs of our jeans. The beach extended in a straight line several hundred yards ahead, then curved sharply off to the right into a grove of casuarina trees and a village of fishermen's stilted huts. The sun was up to our left over the Gulf of Siam and the smooth dark water, free of whitecaps, glistened brightly. A trawler sent up a thin wisp of white smoke about two miles offshore.

''Don't take any walks out here at night,'' Tom said to me. ''They found three bodies by the fence up there two weeks ago.''

Harley stopped to look at the trawler. We all watched it for a moment, moving slowly south under the column of smoke.

''Guns, dope, or rice?'' Harley said.

''Probably one of those,'' Tom said. ''Maybe all three.''

''What about the Sno cops?'' Harley asked again as we resumed walking.

''Better than the Provincial Police but not as good as the Border Patrol. I'm talking about corruption. The head Sno guy here is Captain Thanon. He seems like a good man. You want to trust him, you want to *believe* you can trust him—but, you know, he's a Thai cop and . . ."

He turned to Harley, as if about to make an appeal. "You want so damn bad to have *someone* you can trust, and you try not to let that cloud your judgment, not to let your defenses down. When I first got here I think Thanon wanted to show off, prove he could catch traffickers, and he came in with half a unit of number four. He said he took it off a train. I sent some up to Bangkok and it tested out at ten percent. You know, you *never* get anything around here under ninety, ninety-five. I think he put it together himself, trying to impress me."

Harley laughed.

"I know what you're thinking," Tom said. "It was the first thing I thought. Where'd he get the stuff in the first place? This good honest cop I'm trying to trust. You'll probably meet him when we go to the Satellite."

"What's the Satellite?" I said.

"It's some toilet of a restaurant the Sno cops use for a hangout. There's a broken pay phone in the back that works without money."

"They don't have an office?" I said.

"They do, but they live there, too—it's small and full of bunks and a little out of the center of town. The Satellite's more convenient."

"In Bangkok," Harley said, "they told me you had a stool, a girl."

Before Tom could answer, he heard hoofbeats and turned to see the man on horseback I had noticed from my window. He trotted up and stopped next to us. He was about sixty years old, riding bareback, dressed in army fatigues with a belt and holster. His face—long, dark, bone-lean, tough as bark—was stretched into a smile.

"*Sawadi*," he said, bringing the reins to his chin as he joined his palms and *wai*ed us.

We *wai*ed him back and repeated the greeting. Then Harley, matching the man's smile, talked to him for a minute in Thai.

"I told him we're American cops," Harley said. "He says he's a corporal in the Provincial Police." Harley spoke to him again, then translated. "He lives in the village up there. He's been a cop for thirty-two years, twenty-eight of it patrolling this beach. He says he's outlasted four horses and he thinks he'll outlast this one too.''

Harley spoke again in Thai and the rider reached for his holster, took out a .38 revolver, and handed it to Harley. Harley looked at it, turning it in his hand, and nodded approvingly to the old man. Then Harley broke the gun and emptied the cartridges into his palm. He pulled his own .38 from behind his belt buckle, shook out the hollow-point cartridges, and put them into the old man's gun. He handed the gun back. The man took it, beaming with delight, *wai*ed Harley to the forehead, and returned the gun to its holster. He was so happy he almost fell off the horse.

We said good-bye and the old man trotted off up the beach.

Harley watched him go. ''He's out here patrolling this beach for twenty-eight years, stealing from no one, taking bribes from no one, happy as hell to ride the beach and do his job. He's a good old guy. Tom, why do we have to work with all these lying, thieving bastards? Why can't we work with him?''

''You work with Jaran.''

''Yeah, that's right.''

Tom looked at his watch. ''It's ten o'clock, we'd better head back.''

We strolled slowly toward the hotel.

''So what about this girl stool I heard about?'' Harley said.

''I was leaving the Satellite after a talk with Thanon and some other Sno cops and she came up to me on the street. She said she wanted to talk to me about drugs and she worked at the Paradise massage parlor and could I come and see her.''

''Did she know who you were?''

''She must have. I figured she'd seen me with the Sno cops. I'm an American, so I had to be either a missionary or a tin or rubber merchant or some kind of agent, and talking to the Sno cops it wasn't hard to make a good guess.''

''Did you see her again?''

''I went to the massage parlor the next day but she wasn't there. She'd said her number was 37, but there wasn't any 37. I never saw her again. I was trying to set up the office and then the threats started and I had a lot of other things on my mind. You know it's been—''

''I know, I wouldn't have had the time either. You should've told Bangkok to shove it.''

"I wanted to."

We walked in silence for a minute.

"I don't know if Valdez told you or not," Tom said. "I asked him to take me out of here. Because of my family. I told him I'd do an extra year in-country if he'd move me to Bangkok or Chiang Mai."

"What'd he say?"

"He said it wasn't possible. He was pissed off. I shouldn't have asked."

"Bastard," Harley said.

We were about a hundred yards from the hotel now and I saw a girl in orange trousers walking quickly past the pool. She came out to the beach and when she saw us she started running. I'd seen her that morning behind the reception desk.

When she was a few yards away she stumbled in the sand and fell. Harley ran forward and took her arm and helped her up. She was out of breath.

"The consulate . . ." she said. "They called for Mr. Niekro . . ."

"Yes," Tom said. "What did they say?"

"They said for you to go home. They said it was important. To go home right now."

Before she'd finished, Tom was running.

We followed him to the Range Rover. He had it started and was already moving when we jumped in.

15

WE DROVE very fast, hot dry dust swirling in through the open windows. A half-dozen water buffalo, mud caked on their black bodies, blocked the road at the turnoff leading to Tom's house. The animals, higher than the Range Rover, had lumbered to a halt in front of us and refused to move. A bare-chested Thai man whacked away at them with a stick, and a boy tugged at ropes tied to rings in their noses. In a moment I noticed a girl, almost hidden behind one of the animals, beating furiously at its rump with her fists. She was the Niekros' maid who had served us dinner, and her face was covered with tears. Her blows, which had no effect on the animal, were hysterical. Recognizing Tom, she rushed at our car, sobbing, and I heard the word "Dead . . . dead . . . dead . . ."

Tom jumped from the car and we followed him on the run toward the house. In three minutes, out of breath, we charged in through the front door and found Barbara stretched on the sofa, a large man kneeling next to her with a hypodermic syringe in his hand.

The man said, "It's all right, Tom. She's all right."

He stuck the needle in her arm and pressed the plunger. Barbara looked up for a moment, her eyes closed, and she passed out.

Tom ran to the bedroom and stood frozen in the doorway. Over his shoulder I could see the child's empty crib. The pillow and sheets were crimson with blood and above them, hanging perfectly still, was the carcass of the small black puppy, strung up by the neck, its belly slit. The rope was tied to a ceiling beam. The baby itself was on the Niekros' double bed, awake and peaceful, its dress splattered with blood.

The tall man came up behind us, took Tom's arm, and led him back to the living room.

"It's all right, Tom," he said softly. "Barbara's fine and so is the baby. Someone just wanted to scare you. Everything's all right."

Tom sat in a chair and the man reached into a bag, took out some pills, and handed two to Tom.

Tom knocked the pills away. "I'll take fucking nothing."

He looked up at Harley. "You tell your friend Jaran to go fuck himself. I'm gonna cut Samak's throat. You understand that?"

"Take it easy, Tom," Harley said. "No one's hurt. Everyone's all right. Calm down."

"Calm down! I'll calm fucking down. You with me or not, Harley? You with me or not?"

He was sweating and had started to breathe in long, difficult gasps.

"Here," the tall man said, holding out the pills again. "Take these. They won't put you to sleep. Just take them."

"Get the fuck away from me with that shit," Tom yelled.

The tall man and Harley exchanged glances.

Tom sat quietly, breathing hard, shooting quick looks around the room.

"Where's Boonchai? Where the hell's Boonchai?"

He stood up, looking for the machete man, but Harley put his hand on his shoulder and he sank back into the chair. He put his head in his hands. "Bastards! Cocksuckers! What kind of fucking . . ."

He looked up then and tears ran down his cheeks.

Peter handed him the pills and said, "Take them." Tom took them.

Harley walked to the side of the room and spoke with the tall man. The man nodded.

"Listen, Tom," Harley said. "Take it easy here for a while. I've got something I have to do, but I'll be back in an hour. Just take it easy. Everything's okay. Do what the doc here says, okay?"

"Yeah. Okay. I'm sorry, Peter. But I meant what I said. I'm gonna kill him, Peter."

"But just take it easy for now, for about an hour, and then I'll be back and we'll talk about it, all right?"

"Yeah, right. You go ahead. I'm okay."

Harley and I walked to the Range Rover and Harley spun it around and headed back to the hotel. He was furious. Every few moments he said, "Bastard! Son of a *bitch*!"

When we were just outside the hotel he said, "Ever since I got to this damned fucking country I've felt like someone was pulling a net in around me. They drop you in the top of the funnel and you don't even see the walls and then before you know it you're in a fucking *pit*."

He slammed on the brakes and jumped out of the Range Rover. As soon as my feet touched the ground I felt a sudden chill and wave of faintness. The Niekros' bedroom, the bloody dog and baby, had connected with another death room in my life.

I followed Harley into the lobby and said, "I'll wait here for you." I wanted to sit down.

"No, come up. If you want to."

I walked with him to the desk and waited while he gave the girl the telephone number of the embassy in Bangkok.

In his room he stood at the window staring out at the sky and the beach and the slimy green swimming pool. I sat in a chair behind him by the door, feeling less faint, my strength coming back.

"Was that Samak?" I said.

He turned and looked at me. His shirt was soaked with perspiration and his face was flushed. "I should have known this would happen, Tony. I'm so fucking stupid, you know that?"

"Was it Samak?"

"For sure."

The phone rang and Harley picked it up.

"Yes. Right. Okay." A long pause. "Mr. Valdez, please. Right. Helen? Is he there? Harley in Songkhla. Mr. Valdez? This is Harley in Songkhla. Yes, sir. Well, not so good, sir. We've had a problem. Yes, sir, he's here and I have an appointment with him but I haven't talked to him yet, but even so we have a problem, sir."

I could hear Valdez's voice shouting questions.

"Yes, sir, I'll find that out when I see Jaran, but we have something else now, sir. Somebody got into Tom's house this morning after he'd left and they took one of his dogs and hanged it over the baby's crib. They—"

Muffled shouts. I tasted a sudden sweetness in my mouth and felt a whiff of returning nausea. This time the cause had nothing to do with my wife. It was simply fear, a realization, as if I'd leaned out of a high hotel room, looked down, and felt what it would be like to fall. The danger of Samak and his threats, discussed yesterday at Niekro's house, was no longer an abstraction.

"Yes, sir, they tied a rope around its neck and strung it up right over the crib and—yes, sir, it was dead. They slit its belly open. And the reason I called, I think it would be a good idea if Tom and his family got out of here."

Harley was sitting on the bed and as he listened to Valdez the anger in his voice turned to desperation.

"Mr. Valdez, the dog's *guts* were hanging down on the crib. The baby had blood all over it. That would be enough to upset anyone, Mr. Valdez. They've got to get out of here, they've got—"

Harley listened, his lips moving silently.

"Mr. Valdez, with all respect, sir, I'm here and you aren't. Tom has *got* to be removed. You should have some respect for my opinion, sir. I've been— Yes, sir. What? Sir, my agreement—"

Harley took the phone from his ear and looked at it with such fury I thought he would throw it through the window. Then he put it back to his ear and listened and finally the anger drained away and his expression became one of fatigue and resignation.

"All right, sir. All right. This afternoon or tomorrow. Yes, sir. Thank you. You, too, sir. Good-bye."

He put the phone down slowly and sat quietly on the edge of the bed. He appeared stricken. I knew Valdez had told him that if Tom left he would have to stay. In a minute he stood and put his back to me and faced the window. He was perfectly still. There was not a sound. When he turned around again, his face was hard and the determination in the eyes was steady and without anger. He looked dangerous.

"Let's go," he said, moving toward the door.

16

WE WALKED into complete darkness and paralyzing cold. My eyes, in a panic to adjust from the blazing sun, displayed bright floating after-images of the street outside. Perspiration on my back turned to ice water. I sensed people around me and heard low voices and gently splashing water. At the far end of the room the wall had been replaced with glass, like the display window of a large department store, and through it, bathed in light as pure as the darkness around me, I saw a series of rising, curved tiers, covered in heavy red carpeting, surrounded by gold silk draperies. Expensive watches and jewelry might have been exhibited there, but lounging and sitting on those steps were twenty girls in evening dresses. They read magazines, knitted, and stared blankly at a television set, its screen facing into the display, toward the girls. Though the girls themselves were of every description, their expressions were all the same: quiet, bored, resigned, not quite sullen. All of them had round numbered badges pinned like corsages to the shoulders of their dresses.

As my eyes adjusted to the dark I saw that the splashing sound came from a fountain in the center of the room. Small round tables lined the walls, two or three of them occupied by customers with drinks. Two young men who had preceded us through the door stood in front of the glass examining the girls, and from the lack of reaction on the other side of the window I realized the glass was one-way. The girls saw only reflections of themselves.

"Let's sit down," Harley said, and we took a table. A number was called on the other side of the window, and a girl got up lazily, left behind a huge orange spread she had been crocheting, and vanished through the gold draperies.

A waitress came to our table and we ordered chicken sandwiches and beer.

When the waitess left, Harley said, "What do you think?"

"Well, it's cool."

We waited for the drinks and food, and stared at the window. In a minute I realized that my face had gone as blank and bored as the girls' faces. I looked at Harley. His eyes were aimed at the window, but the thoughts behind them were impossible to read.

The waitress returned and we began to eat.

"I don't see any number 37," I said.

"No. She may be upstairs. We'll hang around a little. How do you like them?"

"Number 9 isn't so bad."

Number 9 was more slender than the others and lighter-skinned. If she had smiled or moved or taken her eyes off the TV set for half a second she might have been appealing.

"You'll like them more when you've been here awhile," Harley said. "After a couple of months you begin to adjust. You stop brushing the flies off your food and you stop thinking about Western girls. When I first got to Bangkok I went out with another agent and I thought he acted like an animal. Flies were all over his food and his face and he didn't even notice them. He was *eating* flies. He was after every fat ugly whore in the place. He called them LBFMs—little brown fuck machines. I told myself I'd never get like that. But if I hang around a few more weeks you'll be writing about Harley the animal."

A tall, elegant-looking woman in a blue silk trouser suit walked out of the darkness and sat down at our table.

"Who you like?" she said.

"All of them," Harley said, smiling. "Half for me, half for my friend."

She laughed and touched Harley's arm. Her long fingers were covered with rings. She sat with us for fifteen minutes, and despite her elegant appearance she was jovial and loud and did a lot of friendly reaching and touching. If her role as Asian madam were cast in a movie, I thought, they'd pick an actress who was fat and amusingly grotesque. But the reality, the slender arms and long neck, the hair pulled back behind her narrow face, was far more interesting. She had the boisterous personality of a fat mama-san but none of the sadness that fat people often reveal in moments of repose. I wished that I could speak Thai. I suspected she would speak her own language well and with style, but her English was that of the miners, smugglers, and rubber dealers she had learned it from.

When Harley asked what her name was, she said, "Everybody call me Mama-san. Have nice light-skin girls here. Like me. European granddaddies. When I young I have blond pussy hair." She held up a finger covered in jewels. "I get these." She laughed.

"Are those all the girls you have?" Harley said.

"You don't like? More girls upstairs. Come back soon. More come later."

"How much later?"

"Four o'clock. All new girls. You wait, maybe you see something nice. Many girls upstairs. You see 22? Very, very nice." She grinned confidentially, as if she knew things about 22 that would make your hair curl.

I looked closely and picked out number 22. She had the face and body of a forty-year-old professional wrestler.

"Try her, Peter," I said.

"We'll just drink a little more beer and think about it," Harley said to the Mama-san in English. Then they spoke in Thai and I could see her open up, delighted to be telling her stories, gesturing with her long brown arms, her face laughing one moment, mock-serious the next, eyes flashing. I knew she was telling tales too good to miss, so I asked Harley to change to English. She immediately apologized for having used a language I didn't understand, and with no reserve or embarrassment switched to an inventive, richly obscene English. I asked her about the rings and she told us how extraordinary men—warriors, millionaires, spies— had smuggled them down from Burma just for her. I didn't care if she was lying or not.

When she left, encouraging us to try her girls ("They give you damned good bath, massage, fucking good for health"), Harley said, "How much of her is true, do you think?"

"I don't know. I guess it doesn't make any difference. She tells some good stories."

"And if the price was right she'd cut your balls off."

I looked at the dreary faces behind the window and thought that possibly he was right.

"How old do you think she is?" I said.

"She told me sixty. Born in Shanghai to a Chinese mother and White Russian father."

"And ended up in Hatyai."

"She's lucky. She might not get along too well in her hometown right now."

"How was her Thai?"

"Good enough so I couldn't understand a lot of it. If you guess what she's been through in her life, you have to hand it to her for guts. You can't beat a Chinese for survival."

"She didn't seem surprised to see us," I said. "Not even curious." We were the only Western men in the room.

"But she came to the table. She'll have a background on both of us before we're back in the hotel."

She was at another table now, telling her stories. Suddenly her laughter stopped in mid-roar. She leaped up and moved quickly to the center of the room to intercept two men who had just come through the door.

"Son of a bitch," Harley said.

One of the men was in uniform.

Harley leaned close to me and whispered: "Samak."

He was not at all what I had expected. My mental image was of a fat, brutish man with a flattened nose, wide nostrils, and evil, slitted eyes—a Japanese prison camp commander from a 1940s movie. Even in the darkness I could see that Samak was slightly built, slender, not tall, and his manner and gestures as he spoke with his companion and the Mama-san seemed excessively deferential, suggesting a spurious refinement. The man with him was in his mid-thirties and wore a white suit and dark glasses.

Samak had deliberately put his back to the display window, and I wondered if he was demonstrating to whoever might be in the room's dark corners that he had not come to select a girl, that his resources did not have to include public massage parlors.

The man in white took off his glasses, gave Harley and me a heavy gaze for about one second, then turned away.

"I think we've been made," Harley said.

"How could he know who we are?"

"Word travels fast. Maybe someone at the hotel."

Samak and his friend left. As the Mama-san walked back past our table, she paused for an instant and with a look of disgust extended the little finger of her right hand, letting us know her opinion of the colonel's physical qualifications.

Several numbers had been called, removing girls from the display, and they had been replaced by other girls returning from the rooms upstairs. One of the new girls wore number 37.

She was between twelve and fifteen years old with waist-long black hair pushed back behind her ears. As she sat down she said something to another girl, who raised a hand limply, shrugged, but did not take her eyes from the television set. Number 37 then looked around at the other girls, evidently seeking conversation, but found no takers. She smoothed out her long yellow dress and sat quietly with her hands in her lap, staring straight ahead at what was for her a mirror. She was pretty and appeared intelligent, and I liked the way she preferred her own image to that on the TV screen. I watched her closely, looking for an answer to the question in my mind: Could a man as cruel and well protected as Lichai possibly be vulnerable to that little girl?

"Let's take a walk," Harley said.

We went out and got in the Range Rover.

"You don't think you ought to talk to her now?"

"Jaran's waiting. We'll come back."

As we pulled away from the curb, I said, "Who was the tall guy at Tom's house? The one with the hypodermic."

"John Nostrand, a missionary doctor. He's tight with the CTs and the Thais and the Americans. When Aim wants to know what's really going on around here, without any bull-shit, they go to him. He doesn't suck, he gives it to them straight whether it's what they want to hear or not."

We were in the center of Hatyai, driving through narrow

paved streets lined with two-story open-fronted concrete shops. I could smell the stink from slabs of rubber brought in from the plantations and spread across the sidewalks. The sun was blistering, and clouds of black exhaust from motorcycles helped push the temperature into the high nineties.

"What did Valdez say?"

"Tom goes, I stay. And Tom'll never come back, once he's out. They'll have to look around for another agent, and that'll take forever. The easiest thing'll be to leave old Harley down here. And I'm alone. I don't even have a partner. The consul's some kid fart with his ass on backwards, and that just leaves the Aim guy."

I hadn't known Aim had a man in Songkhla, but it seemed reasonable that they would keep someone there to watch the insurgents. "What's he like?"

"He's okay except he's got an invisibility complex. That's an occupational disease with Aim agents. His name's Dick Kessick. He was in my office once in Bangkok and a reporter I knew walked in. Just for the hell of it I turned around to Kessick to introduce the reporter, and Kessick was gone. Vanished. He got from one end of that office out the door without passing through intervening space. Tom says he's the same way here. So how much help is he gonna be? He won't even be seen in public."

Harley was thoughtful for a moment, maneuvering the Range Rover through motorcycles and pedestrians.

"The thing to do," he said, "is just get Lichai and wrap his ass up and then go to Bangkok and fucking *refuse* to come back. Man, if you want to see an agent work, hang around, because I am gonna get Lichai so fucking fast you won't even see my hands move. And they can throw all the dog guts at me they want. They don't have *enough* dogs."

Harley parked the Range Rover on Thamonoonvithi Road and we walked across the street to the Satellite, where Jaran had said he would meet us. It was a small open café-bar next to a Chinese hemorrhoid surgeon. You took one glance at the window photographs advertising the Chinaman's work, and tried never to look in that direction again.

Jaran was at a table with an officer and three young enlisted men. The enlisted men moved to another table when we walked in. Jaran introduced the officer as Captain Thanon, head of the local Sno detachment. A chubby little girl about ten years old came over and we ordered Singha beer. The chairs and tables were brown plastic, chipped and cracking. Dirty, dented brass spittoons overflowed onto a concrete floor littered with cigarette butts, wadded napkins, beer bottles, chicken bones, and scraps of food. Shelves of stacked Ovaltine cans concealed the back wall. The sides of the room were striped with a dark horizontal stain left by customers who pushed the chairs back and leaned their heads against the wall. Above the stain hung rows of beer posters and old calendars, their designs fading beneath layers of dust and grime. A portrait of the king and queen was tacked over the cash register next to a shelf of joss sticks and wilting jasmine blossoms. The air smelled of sweat and stale beer.

Harley, Jaran, and Captain Thanon chatted for a few moments and then the captain—a young, very dark-skinned man with a serious, earnest look and manner—perhaps guessing that Jaran and Harley had other things to discuss, said goodbye and left, followed by the enlisted men.

"So," Harley said.

"I saw Samak," Jaran said. "And I told him what I was instructed to tell him."

We waited silently.

"I told him about the threat, and that the embassy's Intelligence was such that it was taken very seriously. I talked as if I thought he was hearing it all for the first time from me, as if he was completely ignorant of the whole thing . . ."

"Of course," Harley said. "Then what?"

"I told him the embassy had very good Intelligence about who the people were behind the threat, and that if anything happened to harm Niekro or any member of his family, the man who gave the order would be killed and every member of his family who could be located, back as far as three generations, would be killed. I let him understand that he should believe this part, about who would be killed, because it did not come from the Americans but from Special Branch in Bangkok. I'm sure he knew that I would not have been sent down here with a message like that unless it came from a high command level."

"What did he say?"

Jaran's eyes sparkled with pleasure. "He almost fell out of his chair. I was afraid he would have a heart attack and I would have to call an ambulance. He couldn't talk. He didn't know what to say. He started something about who had sent me and how could they think that anything like that could happen here. I said, well I didn't know anything about something like that happening here because I hadn't seen the Intel, but I knew it was very hard Intel because of the way everyone in Bangkok was reacting to it, and that it would be a terrible thing for anyone mixed up in it if any physical harm came to Niekro or his family.''

"Well, let me tell you something, Jaran, and then you'll know maybe why Samak was as shaken as he was.''

"What.'' Jaran's face tightened.

"Don't worry. No one's hurt. But they took one of Tom's dogs, a puppy, and they slit its belly and hung it up by the neck over the baby's crib. Barbara went hysterical. Tom's out at the house now with John Nostrand, and he's in bad shape himself.''

"What are you going to do?''

"I called Valdez. Tom and his family are leaving either this afternoon or tomorrow, as soon as they can make it.''

"Then they won't have an agent here anymore?''

Harley did not answer this with a word, but stared back blankly at Jaran.

"You?'' Jaran said.

Harley nodded. "They think so, anyway. But as soon as I get Lichai I'm out. I guarantee you. Bet on it.''

"Lichai could take a long time.''

"Maybe not. The first problem is Samak. If I can clear Samak out of my way, Lichai may not be so hard. And I've found the girl.''

"The stool?''

"We just saw her at the Paradise. She gets off at four.''

Jaran shook his head. "Take it easy, Peter. Don't be too fast.''

Harley ignored that and glanced at his watch. "We'd better continue this in the car. Nostrand may have other things to do today than hang around at Tom's.''

"I don't think I'll go,'' Jaran said. "I can't help and there's no point in being a spectator. I've got a case in Bangkok tonight. I'll get the one o'clock plane.''

Harley was taken by surprise. "I thought you'd stay around for a day,'' he said.

"I'd like to, but I can't.''

We had stood up and Jaran put his hand out to Harley. "Tell Tom I'm sorry.''

"Any chance you'll get down again?''

"Not with a message like this last one, I hope. Watch out for these bastards. If you need me, give a call."

Jaran had stayed at a hotel in Hatyai called the Rama. It was new and modern and cheaper than the Sawadi. We dropped him off there. In the car no one spoke.

Jaran got out and he and Harley shook hands through the window. "Good luck with that girl. And take it easy."

"You too, Jaran."

When we were on the road to Tom's house Harley said, "I hate to see that man go. I feel like I've just been disarmed."

Barbara was still sleeping, the baby was in a basket on the sofa, and Tom and John Nostrand were having a drink at the bar. Tom had settled down. Harley told him he'd talked to Valdez and that Valdez had ordered Tom and his family to fly to Bangkok as soon as possible. Harley made it sound as if the return had been Valdez's idea. He didn't mention the girl.

Tom let out a long sigh and all the muscles in his face relaxed. "Barbara's going to be very happy to hear that. I am, too. Thanks, Peter."

Harley didn't say anything.

"I don't think we can make it today," Tom said. "We'll get the late plane tomorrow. What about you? I hate to leave you here. When will you—"

"Soon," Harley said. "I'll be out of here in a couple of days. I'll see you in Bangkok."

Nostrand left his jeep at Tom's and rode back to Hatyai with us in the Range Rover. He said he was going to try to find the maid.

"She and Boonchai lost a lot of face," he said. "I doubt if you'll ever see either one of them near that house again. Have you met Boonchai?"

"The man with the machete?" I said.

"Yes. He's frightening, isn't he? Actually he's a very gentle guy. He'll have a hard time getting over this. The house was his responsibility."

Nostrand was friendly and gave me the immediate impression that he liked me. Maybe he made everyone feel that way. He must have been at least forty-five, but thick black hair, a dark tan, and smooth unlined face made him look in his mid-thirties. When he found out I was a writer and new in Thailand, he was eager to help me understand what was going on.

"You probably know already how the Thais feel about

dogs,'' he said. ''So you can understand the double meaning of what they did at Tom's. It wasn't just a threat. It was a cultural and racial statement. The Thais would never have a dog in the house. It would defile the house. But Tom did. By taking that puppy inside and killing it like that they weren't only scaring and warning Tom—they were letting him, and all of us, know that they don't like Americans and the way they live.''

''Why do you stay?'' I said. I knew he must have religious reasons, but I wondered if there was anything else.

''There are a lot of differences between me and the people here. I'll always be a Christian and an American. They'll always be Buddhists and Thais. But there are similarities, too, if you search for them. You can adjust to the differences. You can even learn to eat frogs.''

''John has a hospital here,'' Harley said.

''I *wish* I did,'' Nostrand said. ''Maybe I wouldn't be lying if I called it a clinic. And a sort of home, a shelter. A lot of young refugees come in from the mountains and the villages. We have a place where the girls can live so they don't have to be whores. Right now I've got to try to find Tom's maid. When I got to the house she ran away.''

''We saw her on the road,'' I said.

''She may be back at the clinic or at the whorehouse she used to live in.''

''She was a whore?''

''Before she worked for Tom. It's a long story. When we have time I'll tell you.''

Thinking about the dead puppy, I said, ''I don't understand how they could do it without being seen, with that machete guy around and the maid and Barbara.''

''They probably got Boonchai away on some kind of pretense. They could have had someone from the village call him. And the maid and Barbara could have been in the kitchen. It didn't take them more than ten seconds. These are jungle people. You wouldn't believe the speed and the silence—if you blink your eyes you miss everything.''

''Do you have a church here?'' I said.

''I conduct services in my house. Not very successfully, I'm afraid.''

''How long have you been here?''

''Eight years. Now you're going to ask how many converts I've had.''

"How many?"

"Six. Two of them died and two others moved away. Buddhism's a difficult religion to convert from. They're very tolerant of other religions but they don't get too influenced by them. They just don't seem to see the point."

We took him to his house and clinic, an old two-story teak building on stilts near a klong on the edge of town. The first floor had two large rooms surrounded by a screened veranda. One room was Nostrand's bedroom and the other contained an examining table and medical equipment. The upstairs was partitioned into cubicles, each with a bunk, bureau, chair, and table. Three young girls surrounded the jeep when we drove up, chattering happily to Nostrand. Tom's maid had not been seen.

At the side of the clinic I noticed an old jeep motor being used as a generator.

"Where did that come from?" I asked.

"Oh," he said, smiling, "it just arrived. You have to get along with what you can manage." I was pleased for his sake that his principles did not forbid a little benign larceny.

He made us come inside and sit on the veranda while one of the girls brought tea. I heard excited female whispers in the other room, and when a girl, all smiles, came in with the cups and a teapot I realized they had been quarreling over who would have that honor.

I wondered why Harley, who might have preferred to be back at the Paradise keeping an eye on number 37, had agreed so readily to spend this time chatting socially over a cup of tea. I had the answer when he said, "Do you know Colonel Samak?"

"Samak. Oh yes. Delightful man."

"That's what I hear," Harley said.

"I really can't hate him," Nostrand said, pouring the tea. "He's part of the environment. He's an affliction that has to be endured, like the heat or the monsoon. You know he calls himself blackjack?"

"I hadn't heard that."

"It's his radio code. He has a blackjack—not the weapon, the playing card—painted on his car. A girl came in here one night about three months ago, in the middle of the night, no clothes, hysterical, and there was blood all over her buttocks. I cleaned it off and she had a wound as if someone had torn the flesh off. I put her to bed and the next day she told me

Samak had had a man try to carve a blackjack on her. His men had picked her up on the road from Sadao and took her to him. He raped her and called in the tattooist. If you go to the Paradise you'll probably find girls with tattoos of blackjacks.''

I sipped my tea and waited for Harley to say something, but he didn't. Nostrand did not speak either. Something in their silence made me certain they had exchanged a thought. I wished I knew, or had done or seen, whatever it was that gave one the ability to be understood so completely without saying a word.

After a minute Nostrand said, ''She left here and moved over to a whorehouse I call the packing crate whorehouse because that's what it is, it's made from packing crates. She met some guy who told her she'd get a lot of money. She was from the jungle in the south and she didn't know a damn thing about anything. Two days later she was back here and I got her a job at Tom's.''

''She was Tom's maid?'' I said. He knew how to tell a story.

''Things were just starting to look up for her. Some of these people have hard lives.''

''We'd better get going,'' Harley said, putting his cup down. ''If you have some time later, come over to the hotel and have a drink with us.''

''Thanks.''

In the car I said, ''The Mama-san said they change at four.'' It was only three.

''We'll go now anyway. People don't always tell the exact truth.''

Harley parked around a corner half a block from the Paradise. We could just barely see the entrance.

''How do you feel about this girl?'' I said.

''After the threat against Tom and the thing with the dog, I've *got* to feel good about her. Samak's not going to give me enough time to develop anyone else.''

He rolled the tinted window to an inch of the top and said, ''It's hot, but if you can stand it there's no point in letting everyone know we're inside.''

After two minutes you could have grilled a steak on the seat covers. The air was still, damp with sweat.

She came out at 4:25, still wearing the yellow evening dress, its hem trailing threads as she held it up from the dirt and dust. It was a worn-out whoring gown, much too large for her, bought no doubt from one of the older girls. It hung in loose folds across her bony shoulder blades, thin buttocks, and almost breastless child's chest. She walked rapidly with a pathetic self-assurance. In the bright light of outdoors she seemed even younger than she had in the Paradise, an under-nourished jungle nymphet. She was a little girl dressed in her mother's old clothes, an apparition, a gullible child on whom a trick had been played.

Harley waited until she was almost out of sight, then started the Range Rover and drove to within a few yards of her. He parked, waited until she was again almost out of sight, then moved forward again. When she was a good six blocks from the Paradise and entering an uncrowded neighborhood of automobile garages and bicycle repair shops, he stopped the car, told me to wait, and got out. He walked up behind her and they spoke. Then she came back with him and I got out and climbed in the rear seat. She stood for a moment by the open front door, reluctant to get in. When she finally did get in, she sat up straight and looked anxiously around, observing everything. I thought she must be worried about getting in a car with strangers, or possibly about soiling her dress. Then Harley, who had been talking with her, turned toward me from the driver's seat and said in English, "She says this is only the third time in her life she's been in a car."

She reached forward and touched the dashboard, then slowly, like a child permitted to sit for a moment in a great man's chair, relaxed back into the seat.

We drove toward the country and they talked. After about ten minutes she said in English, "Yes, I do, very good." Then they went back to Thai. When we were well out of town, headed south toward Malaysia on a road lined with rubber trees, she sat up nervously and said something to Harley. He answered and turned the car around. We drove back to the garages and repair shops. Harley parked and said to her in English, "Two hours from now, near the brewery. You'll see us. Don't look around, just get in. Don't worry about Samak. Tell your brother to trust us. And make sure he comes."

"He come. I make sure."

"Good."

Harley reached over and opened the door. She got out and we watched her walk up the street toward the corner.

For almost thirty minutes I'd been sweating in the backseat unable to understand a word they spoke.

"Well?" I said.

"She's the right girl. She remembered Tom."

He was so excited he was pumping the gas pedal, racing the engine. He had his eyes on the girl.

"If you keep that up you'll boil over the radiator."

He took his foot off the gas. The girl was turning the corner. He eased the Range Rover away from the curb and started slowly up the block.

"I want to see where she lives. Then if she stands me up I'll know where to start looking."

"What did she say?"

"Her name's Anuraj. She's from Betong. That's a little town on the southern border, a CT strongpoint. Her father owns a restaurant and the CTs were taking three thousand baht a month in taxes. Six months ago her father couldn't pay it anymore. She said business got bad because the government closed the border, trying to stop CTs infiltrating back and forth from Malaysia, and they don't get any more travelers. When her father told the CT tax collector he couldn't get up the baht, a squad of CTs came around and said he'd have to give them his kids. That's this girl and her twin brother. She said the CTs told her father they'd take them to a camp in the jungle and train them to be guerrillas."

Harley reached the corner, made the turn, and parked. We could see Anuraj walking away from us a few yards up the street.

"When she and her brother heard the CTs were going to take them, they split. She said it took four weeks to get here. They walked, and hid in the jungle from the CTs and bandits. Now she does what she does and her brother's got a job at the Singha brewery. She says he's just a laborer but they promised to teach him to be a chemist because he's so smart. Try to believe that."

"And you're meeting him?"

"She's going home now, change her clothes, find him outside the brewery when he gets off at seven o'clock, and we'll pick them up."

"How come she speaks English?"

"She said she and her brother went to an English Methodist missionary school. Before the CT trouble they used to get English tourists stopping in the restaurant on their way north, from Penang mostly. She says she picked up a little French, too, from the Vietnamese cook.''

''And Lichai?''

The girl had reached the far corner and was crossing the street.

''I didn't say anything about him. But she's heard of Samak. She's scared to death of him. She says all the girls know him. I promised if she helped me I'd protect her. She says she hears about drug deals at the Paradise. A lot of traffickers go there. And her brother hears things from men at the brewery. She was nervous about her brother. I think that's the real reason she wants to talk—her brother's into something.''

Two Thai men in sport shirts stepped out of a green panel truck at the end of the block and crossed the street toward Anuraj. Harley jerked the wheel to the left, started to move away from the curb, then stopped.

Anuraj saw the men and put out an arm. Harley started the car forward again, and stopped again. He was holding himself back.

One of the men grabbed Anuraj's outstretched arm, yanked it, and sent her sprawling to the sidewalk. The other man stepped up as if to kick her. I opened the door and had one foot out when Harley reached for my shoulder and pulled me back. His eyes were on Anuraj and the men.

The one who had grabbed her arm reached down with one hand and tried to lift her by her hair. She scrambled up and when she had her balance, she swung at him.

''Damn, Harley, they'll beat her up.''

Harley let go of my shoulder and clutched the wheel with both hands. The man ducked under Anuraj's feeble punch, put an arm around her waist, and carried her to the panel truck. The other man opened the back door and Anuraj was thrown in headfirst. Then the two men went around to the front, got in, and drove off.

Harley did not move.

''Aren't you going to *follow* them?'' I was astonished at Harley's refusal to interfere.

''I already know where they're going. It's a PP truck.''

''Provincial Police?''

''Right.''

''Samak's men?''

''Right.''

I couldn't believe his cold-bloodedness. "Are we just going to sit here?"

The truck had turned the corner and was out of sight.

"Shut the door," Harley said.

I did as I was told and Harley let the clutch out and we drove up the street.

"If we'd stepped in they'd've known she was with us and they'd've guessed she was stooling for me. Then she or her brother might get killed. It's better to let her get roughed up."

"How would they've known she was with us? We might just have been driving by."

"People like that don't believe in coincidences. I don't either."

"So you're not going to do anything?"

"Shut up, Tony."

We drove in silence. Then Harley said, "I know one thing. If I lose her now, I've lost her for good. And I've lost Lichai. I know that. I *know* it."

We turned a corner. He seemed to be driving at random. After another minute he said, more to himself than to me, "If I just lay back there's no telling what the hell Samak'll do to her. Maybe he's been told she ran away from the CTs and he wants to send her back. Or maybe he's just horny and sent his men out to grab a piece of ass. If I run over and try to get her out Samak'll know she's working for me and that'll be the end."

He made another turn. We'd been around the same block twice. Suddenly he put his foot down hard on the brake pedal, the car screeched to a halt, and we sat there in the middle of the street, Harley clutching the wheel, staring straight ahead out the window. In a few seconds, just as suddenly as he'd hit the brake, he stepped on the gas, accelerated to the corner, and turned right toward the Satellite Café.

"Maybe I can use Thanon."

We parked in front of the Satellite, and as we got out Harley said, "Look pissed off."

We found Thanon inside at a table drinking Singha with another cop. Harley talked fast and loud.

"Damn, Thanon, what the fuck kind of town you got here? *I* understand, but Tony—"

Thanon rose quickly to his feet. The other cop disappeared,

evidently wanting no part of an angry American drug agent. Thanon started to speak. ''What—''

''I don't really give a shit myself,'' Harley interrupted, ''but it makes it hard for us at the embassy. You know what I mean? It looks so fucking—''

''What happen? What happen?'' Thanon put his hands out toward Harley, as if ready to offer assistance or fend off a blow.

Harley picked up a chair, banged it down at the table, and dropped into it. Thanon sat down quickly, eager to listen.

''This man here,'' Harley said, pointing to me, ''is an American journalist, right? You met him.''

Thanon nodded.

''He is a very important American writer, Thanon. He came all the way over here from New York to write about Thailand and its police and how hard you're working to stamp out dope. He was in Washington before he came here. He's been cleared by the top people, Thanon—the *top* people. You understand me? They are all waiting to read his report.''

Thanon looked quickly at me and nodded several times.

''So what the fuck happens? Tony and I are on the street and we see two cops get out of a PP truck and grab some old lady—a fuckin' old *lady*, Thanon, a little old lady in some raggedy old yellow dress—and knock her down and beat her up and throw her in the back of the truck.''

Thanon shook his head rapidly and moaned, ''Oh no, Mr. Peter, oh no, not happen, mistake, Mr. Peter, not happen, oh never—''

''But it *did* happen, Thanon, it *did*. We saw it, and Tony here—well, he had a lot of questions, Thanon, you know what I mean? Like in the United States cops don't normally go around kidnapping little old ladies off the street.''

Thanon's face was now a mixture of shock and agony. He turned to me, as if for confirmation.

I nodded.

Thanon shook his head again. ''I find out, Mr. Peter. I find out.'' He turned back to me. ''You wait? You have time?''

''Of course,'' I said.

He got up and ran into the back to the telephone. Harley yelled to the little girl for three Singhas. Under his breath he said to me, ''Look indignant. Outraged. *Seethe*, man.''

The girl brought the beer and we sat there with it, looking furious. In five minutes Thanon came back.

"I talk Colonel Samak. He not know anything. He—"

Harley waved a hand in disgust. "I don't know what the hell the ambassador's gonna do when he reads—"

"Mr. Peter, Samak say he don't know now, but he check all his men. He very angry, Mr. Peter. He say if he find his men do this he kill them." He looked at me. "He find out what happen. He fix. He very very angry. He say he kill men do what you say."

Thanon returned his attention to Harley. "Samak say he invite you and writer have dinner. He tell you then what happen. He say he sorry for back look. Want have dinner, meet writer, meet you, be good friends."

Harley allowed a look of mild conciliation to cross his face. "That's very nice, Captain Thanon. I don't care myself, you understand, but the politicians in Bangkok and Washington, they jump on something like this to use against us and the assistance programs we have over here."

"I understand. I know. I know. No problem. I very sorry. Colonel Samak, he very sorry. You come dinner?"

Harley smiled. "Did he invite you too?"

Thanon nodded. "I come too."

"Then we accept." Harley looked at me. "Okay?"

"Fine," I said. "Maybe we'll find out what really happened."

"You find out," Thanon said. "I promise. Colonel Samak find out. He tell you."

"Good," Harley said.

Thanon stood. "We meet Lotus Restaurant. Three hours. Okay?"

"Okay, Captain. We'll be there."

Thanon *wai*ed us, we *wai*ed him back, and he left.

"I hope that works," Harley said, sitting back down at the table. "After his talk with Jaran this morning Samak shouldn't want too much more trouble with the Americans."

"A little old lady?" I said.

"We don't want him to think we saw her close. From a distance she could've been an old lady."

We relaxed and drank our beer.

"I think she'll be safe now, Tony. At least until dinner. I'm looking forward to meeting that bastard. When a man's trying to waste me I like to get to know him, find out where the soft spots are."

"How much effect do you think Jaran's warning will really have on him?"

"Well, it certainly has to give him something to think about. But truthfully—not enough, I'm afraid. He may be scared of whatever unknown people in Bangkok sent Jaran down here with that message, but he's got to be even more scared of Lichai."

The girl came over and asked if we wanted more beer. Harley told her we did.

"Samak knows Lichai. He's probably seen what's happened to other people who didn't follow orders. There's no uncertainty there, no room for doubt. If Lichai says kill, Samak'll kill. It's Samak's job to get to me before I get to Lichai."

We finished our beer and Harley paid the young girl. Before we got up to leave he said, "Anyway, we'll find out tonight if Samak just grabbed Anuraj for a fuck or if it had something to do with Lichai or the CTs. Because if it did have something to do with them, if it was serious, Samak's not going to say anything. It'll just be, 'Little old lady? *What* little old lady?' "

The minute we walked into the restaurant I felt my morale lift. It was the most civilized thing I'd seen in Hatyai—round tables in a walled garden, flowering orchids, myna birds in wicker cages, a fountain, a small stage and dance floor, a star-filled sky, and a cool, gentle, blissfully dust-free breeze. As we walked past the tables I saw piles of crayfish and lobster and bottles of scotch and Hennessy.

Thanon and two of his men were waiting for us at the back. Samak wasn't with them. Thanon opened a door and we entered a bare hall with serving tables. My spirits dropped. We were not going to eat in that garden after all. Across the hall were three more doors, and it was behind one of them, in a small, concrete-floored private room, that we would have our meal. The walls of the room were bare except for a small shelf supporting glass jars of live colored fish. We sat at a low round table with a hole under it for our feet. We were to have what Thai men regard as a great treat and which they often employ to impress and honor Western visitors: a "no hands" dinner.

Captain Thanon seated us around the table. Harley, with an edge to his voice, said, "Colonel Samak joining us later?"

Thanon grinned broadly, trying to conceal his fear and embarrassment. "Colonel Samak say he very very sorry—" He stopped. Harley shot him a glance.

"He's not coming?"

"He say he very sorry, he want come, but he very busy." The smile was growing broader and broader.

"Very *busy!* What about the old lady?"

"He say he make big investigation, ask everyone, not find anything. He say maybe come later. He say mistake. No old lady."

Harley glared into Thanon's face.

"I sorry, Mr. Peter. Not my fault. Colonel Samak try find out what happen. He still try find out. Maybe come later. He say maybe tomorrow he find out more."

Harley, apparently making a decision, put a hand lightly on Thanon's arm. "It's not your fault, Captain. Nothing to do with you at all. Everything's okay. Let's have dinner."

"We have very good dinner. Very fine restaurant. Samak say everyone his guest, eat good, have good time."

"That's very kind of the colonel."

Harley leaned across me to reach for a glass and as our heads came together he whispered, "He's coming. War of nerves." I didn't know whether to believe that or not. I was trying to concentrate on the restaurant and not think about what might be happening to Anuraj.

Thanon ordered dinner, and the first dishes arrived accompanied by two of the ugliest Thai women I had ever seen. Thanon directed one to my side, the other to Harley. They smiled toothlessly and proceeded to insert bits of food into our mouths with chopsticks. The pieces of meat could be neither identified nor refused. We chewed them with polite expressions of relish and aimed delighted nods of approval in the direction of Thanon. I asked Harley what the hell we were eating.

"Pig intestines. But don't worry. They're bringing frogs." His manner now was relaxed and jovial, as if the matter of the little old lady had been completely forgotten. I was finding it difficult to be so cool. My mind kept going back to Anuraj.

More plates arrived, and with them a girl for Thanon. His two men, a sergeant and a corporal, sat at the opposite edge of the table from the three of us, not speaking, and of course without girls. They kept our glasses filled with Mekhong and picked timidly at a plate of peanuts and ginger. Occasionally, when everything but scraps of bone and fat had been cleared from a plate, Thanon nodded and they went for the leftovers.

I watched the girls. I guessed, and Harley later confirmed, that they were rejects from the massage parlors and go-go bars, available for whatever activities their customers might like to pursue after, or during, the meal. The next step down—and they seemed precariously close to it—would be one of the cheap, illegal workingmen's brothels.

Waitresses brought plate after plate of food. Harley identified chicken, beef, and fish, all of it either unchewably tough or suspiciously squishy. I kept swallowing the Mekhong, trying to get drunk as swiftly as possible.

Though Thanon spoke only broken English, his good manners required him to talk to me anyway, in Thai if necessary, and I responded with monosyllables and emphatic nods of the head. I was exhausted after an hour.

If Harley shared my distress, he was doing an excellent job of concealing it. He ate ravenously of everything stuck into his mouth, hugged the girl who fed him as if she were the loveliest thing in the world, told jokes to Thanon, and laughed loudly and convincingly at every joke Thanon told. Boredom, fatigue, and Mekhong had almost anesthetized me when the door opened and Samak strutted in.

He bowed, *wai*ed us all, and poured out his apologies. He explained in Thai, translated for me by Harley, that he had been so overcome with disappointment at the thought of missing this opportunity to meet the distinguished Americans that he had finally decided to abandon his work and come anyway. Also, he said, he had finally discovered some news of "the old lady."

Everyone expressed delight at Samak's presence and he was given a seat next to me. Another woman immediately appeared at Samak's other side and begun thrusting chopsticks into his mouth. His own servant-bodyguard—a corporal, shorter than Samak, with a thin, demonic smile—took his place by the other enlisted men. I could not be certain, but his corporal looked very much like the man who had held the door of the truck while the other man threw Anuraj in the back.

I looked at Harley, trying to catch his eye, but he gave no indication he had recognized the corporal, or that he was in any particular hurry to hear Samak's news of the old lady.

Samak appeared as polished in this strong light as he had in the massage parlor. His uniform was crisp. He had the same air of false refinement. But after a couple of minutes, when I turned to look at him directly and had his face no more than one foot from my own, I was shocked by his eyes. They were a deep black and unnaturally moist, as if from some illness.

"Like?" he said to me.

I wasn't sure if he was referring to Thailand, Hatyai, the restaurant, the food, or the girls. I looked at Harley.

"He wants to know what you think of the girls," he said.

"Oh yes," I said. "Very much. Thai girls are very beautiful."

Everyone at the table laughed and nodded and took a swig of Mekhong—though I was positive only Harley had understood what I had said. I was wondering when, if ever, Samak would get around to telling us what we wanted to know.

Samak tried more English on me. He believed he spoke the language, and though at times he spoke words that sounded vaguely like other words that were English, he rarely managed to put together an entire sentence that made much sense. I was beginning to feel like a fool, trying to react properly to what I thought he thought he had said.

In a weary attempt to take the conversational initiative myself, I asked him about the gold chains around his neck. He immediately took them off and handed them to me. They were long and heavy; one had to be looped twice around his neck. From each hung a large gold Buddha called a *prah*, a charm worn by many police and other Thais who hope to be protected from violence and evil.

I examined the chains and Buddhas and handed them back to Samak, immediately regretting the pleasure my interest had given him. He took them from me with a damp-eyed grin and I was sure he was thinking, Here we have another man who cannot resist the touch of gold.

By this time I was almost unendurably tired. I envied Harley his endurance. He had drunk as much as I had, eaten more, and he was going full tilt. In addition, he was putting on a flawless performance. Anyone watching him chatting with Samak, laughing with him as he had laughed with Thanon, would not have believed that here was an officer who had tried to kill Harley's fellow agent, would very probably try to kill Harley, and had kidnapped the best chance—perhaps the only chance—Harley now had to complete his

mission and get out of Hatyai. If Samak had hoped at this
dinner to discover Harley's true feelings and character, he
was disappointed.

"How long?" Samak said to me.

"How long will I be here?"

"Yes."

"I don't know. Several weeks perhaps."

"Weeks?"

"Yes."

He nodded enthusiastically. "Good. Good. You hunt? Sail?"

"Yes." I sailed, but had never been hunting in my life.

"We hunt. Sail. You, me."

"Fine. I'd like that."

"Mr. Peter. How long?"

"Two years," Harley said. "I've been assigned to the
consulate here."

Samak drew in his breath. "You and Mr. Tom?"

"Yes."

"Good. All sail. Hunt."

Harley raised his glass. "Very good. Like to very much."
Everyone laughed and drank.

"You write for magazine about Harley?"

I was surprised he knew about that. "Yes."

"Good. He best agent. Best New York. Best Bangkok."

I glanced at Harley. His face did not betray the smallest
surprise at Samak's knowledge.

The job of keeping the glasses filled had been taken over
by Samak's corporal. He bustled obsequiously around the
table, nodding and grinning. When I reached for one of the
small squares of tissue that served as napkins, his hand shot
ahead of mine, plucked one up, and gave it to me. I turned to
thank him and found his grinning, thin-lipped face almost
touching mine. I remembered Jaran's men in Bangkok, a
different breed.

Samak had been talking quietly with Thanon and now
turned abruptly to me and said, "I tell you."

"Tell me?" Finally I was going to hear about Anuraj.

"Come office . . . ." He stopped talking and stared toward
the ceiling, struggling for the correct words. Then he put
together the longest complete sentence I heard him utter in
English that night. He said, "You come office I tell everything you need know."

He beamed, proud of his accomplishment. Harley applauded.

Everyone laughed. Everyone but me. I'd had enough. I was tired, bored, drunk, and didn't care if I made Harley angry or not. I said to Samak, "Will you tell me about the old lady your men attacked?"

Samak laughed and waved a hand to cover his displeasure at my bad manners. "Eat now. Business talk bad. Do later."

Bad to talk business during the meal? Or the business he had to talk was bad? Either way, I was fed up. Harley was still doing his act, flirting with the girls and eating everything in sight. I could hear music outside in the garden and excused myself and I went to look for the men's room.

I found it in the hall. When I came out, Samak's corporal, smiling, was there to hold the door for me. I found it hard to smile back at him, and wondered what else he would have considered it part of his job to do for me.

I walked into the garden for some fresh air and to look at whatever was providing the music. The stage was occupied by an eight-piece Filipino orchestra and enough electronics for a space shot. The dance floor was filled. I bet myself that when I turned around to go back to the party the corporal would be behind me. He was. He walked like a man with ingrown toenails, daintily, bowing slightly, groveling on ahead. It struck me then, through my drunkenness, that in addition to abducting Anuraj, he might have been the man who cut that dog open.

As soon as I sat down, my girl put something in my mouth and I bit down on a piece of gristle. I spat it out on my plate and she gave me another piece. That was gristle too. I chewed for a moment, looking for some identifiable flavor. I could find none. What I had in my mouth was simply a thin, elongated piece of cartilage. I looked at the dish it had come from and saw other thin, elongated objects.

"What the hell is it?" I said to Harley.

"Chicken feet. You like them?"

"They taste exactly the way I would have expected them to taste."

"Wonderful. Surprises are always bad."

Samak had risen from his chair and was taking two jars off the wall shelf. He brought them to the table and sat down. Each jar contained a fish about one and a half inches long.

"You bet?" he said to Harley.

Harley looked at the fish swimming in the jars—not swimming, really, because there wasn't enough room for that, but floating listlessly, looking as tired as I felt.

"I'll bet you a drink," Harley said, holding his glass.

"Good. Bet drink."

Thanon and the enlisted men laughed, as they did unaccountably at unpredictable moments during the English phases of the conversation.

Samak held up one jar and said, "American." Then he held up the other jar and said, "Thai."

He poured the Thai candidate into the American's jar. Instantly they were fighting.

Harley said to me, "It's over when one fish tears off the other's mouth so it can't bite anymore."

That event occurred before he had finished the explanation. The American was thrashing furiously but its lower jaw had been ripped completely free of the head. The other fish continued to bite at it, but the American could only strike back harmlessly with the top of its head.

"Thai win," Samak said, delighted. He raised his glass but made a point of not putting it to his lips until both Harley and I had drunk.

When the meal had finally ended and we were sitting around drinking Mekhong, Samak said something to one of the girls, then spoke to Harley. There were ominous smiles, nods, and glances in my direction. I felt threatened.

"Colonel Samak wants to know if you would like to take your girl with you," Harley said.

She was smiling at me. Her teeth were rotted and she could have passed for the machete man's twin—for his twin brother in fact.

"Oh, I'd like to very much," I said. "She's beautiful, but I'm really tired and I've had a lot to drink. Maybe some other time."

Samak, barely getting the gist of this, looked at Harley, who translated. Offended by the rejection, Samak smiled. The enlisted men smiled too.

Harley excused himself from the table and took me outside.

"She's not so bad," he said.

"Forget her. What about Anuraj? Do you recognize the corporal? He's one of the—"

"Don't worry about that. Samak thinks you're sore as hell about the old lady. He'll talk when he's ready. Right now, you've got to go with the girl."

"*Go* with her. Are you kidding? She's a monster."

"Not to them. They think she's lovely."

"Then let Samak go with her."

"He's honoring you by giving her to you."

"I reject the honor."

"He's testing you."

"I fail."

"You'll make him lose face."

"Good."

"Be nice to him, Tony. Keep him off balance. That's important."

"Peter, there is no force on earth that could drag me into bed with that woman. I'd catch everything from syphilis to tooth decay."

"You don't have to screw her. Just thank Samak and take her with you in a taxi and give her a hundred-baht note and let her out."

"I don't even want him *thinking* I slept with her. I resent him giving me girls. I can go to the Paradise and get my own."

He was smiling.

"This is a joke, right? You're all putting me on."

"I'll tell Samak something. I'll try to get you out of it without insulting him too much."

We went back in the room and Harley leaned over Samak and spoke in his ear. I was angry. They looked like buddies, co-conspirators. Samak nodded energetically and seemed distressed. He raised his glass at me and said, "Sorry. Sorry. No understand. You forgive."

Harley encouraged me with his eyes.

I said, "Yes, of course," and raised my glass and drank. I had no idea what the hell had been said, but evidently I was no longer expected to take the girl.

Suddenly Samak, still wearing his expression of distress, said to me, "You make mistake."

"I did?"

Harley watched him intently.

"Not old lady."

"Oh?"

He smiled. "Look very hard old lady. Not find." He sounded just a little annoyed at having been made to waste his time looking for someone who did not exist.

"But I find girl—maybe you see girl?"

I hesitated. Harley answered for me. "She was wearing a yellow dress."

"Yes. Yes." As if to say, "That's right, stupid, *now* you've got it."

"She wearing yellow dress, but she young girl. You make mistake."

"We only saw her for a moment," Harley said, "and she was a couple of blocks away."

"She bad girl," Samak said, shaking his head solemnly. "She run from home. Father very worried. Father think she get trouble. We send back."

"You sent her back?" Harley's tone was casual, just making conversation. He seemed to have no great interest in whether the girl went home or not.

Samak said to me, "I sorry you think not right. You try understand. Father worried. She bad girl. Try to fight."

"I understand," I said, working hard not to show my feelings. "I guess I was too far away to see what really happened. Has she gone back already?"

"Go back tomorrow."

It must have been only a few more minutes before I passed out. After I'd finally heard what Samak had to say, exhaustion and drunkenness overcame me. The next thing I knew I had woken up in the front seat of the Range Rover, a railroad barrier was lowered ahead of us, and I realized it was the middle of the night and we were on the Bandits' Road to Songkhla.

17

HARLEY WAS yelling at me.

"Are you fucking awake over there? Get on the floor and keep your head down!"

Suddenly I was sober. The wooden crossing barrier was brilliant white in our headlights and coming at us fast. Two men with rifles stood next to it. Harley stepped on the gas and switched off the lights, and the barrier and road vanished in darkness. I slipped to the floor and pressed my face against the rubber mat six inches from Harley's right sandal.

I heard and felt a jolting crash, followed by another bang as something struck the side. Harley's foot slammed down hard on the gas pedal and we lurched heavily, slowed, bounced, rocked, and speeded up again, fishtailing violently. When we had straightened out and were back in control, I climbed up onto the seat. Harley was bent forward over the wheel, straining to see the curving road. In a moment he put the lights back on but did not slow down. The hood had a three-foot-long crease in it.

"What happened?" I said.

"I think Samak just answered your question about how seriously he took Jaran's warning. You okay?"

"I'm fine. Did they shoot?"

"No. Probably they thought we'd stop. I think it broke their concentration a little when we hit the barrier."

He was perfectly cool.

"Samak knew we'd be using this road," he said. "You can't give a man like him that much edge and expect to stay alive. We ought to be dead now."

"He doesn't waste any time."

"You'd better be more careful who you ride in cars with. You'd've been better off with the whore."

"I was thinking the same thing."

We passed two more crossings, no barriers down.

"What the hell did you tell Samak anyway?"

"I said you had your cock shot off in Vietnam."

"That's nice."

"Look at that fucking hood. Lowell's gonna have a baby when he sees that. More work for our overburdened consul."

"What do you think's become of Anuraj?"

"I don't even want to think about it. I'll call Jaran when I get to the room and see if he can use a little more of his muscle."

We had slowed down and were approaching the hotel. It was 3 A.M. The only light was a single bulb behind the reception desk. As we headed for the stairs a voice called from the darkness of the lobby. We turned and saw Anuraj walking toward us. Harley smiled, and I thought he'd throw his arms around her. They spoke in Thai. She had a bruise on her left temple but seemed otherwise unharmed. She was a lot prettier in a white shirt and blue jeans than she had been in the yellow dress.

Harley and I followed her back into the dark lobby and saw a boy sitting on a sofa. He was wearing a blue denim shirt and trousers and looked too old to be the girl's twin. His round chubby face had large eyes and a lot of shiny straight hair falling over the forehead. He stood up quickly as we approached, and Anuraj introduced us. His name was Prasong.

"Her brother," Harley said to me.

They spoke for several minutes, then Harley glanced in the direction of the desk. He said to me, "We'd better do this upstairs."

Harley had no key to Tom's office. We went to his own room and he and I sat on the bed and gave the only two chairs to the boy and girl. The chairs were on each side of a small wooden table.

Harley and the boy and girl talked for a minute in Thai, then Harley looked over at me and switched to English.

"You escaped?"

Anuraj nodded.

"Tell me again."

"When we got to police house they open door and I run."

"They didn't stop you?"

"I run fast."

That didn't seem like a very full explanation, but for some reason Harley let the subject drop.

"I see. How did you know I was staying here?"

"People say other man, your friend, have office here. So I think maybe you here too."

"What people?"

"Where I work."

"The girls?"

Anuraj didn't answer.

"The girls know everything, is that it, Anuraj?"

"Your friend never go there," she said. "I not mean that."

"Then how do they know?"

"They know lots of things. Talk all time. Everybody know."

"The cops who go there told them?"

She shrugged.

"So after you escaped, you found your brother, and then how did you get out here?"

"We went bus station, hitched ride."

"With who?"

"A man."

"What time?"

"About eleven."

"You've been here four hours?"

They nodded.

"And your brother has something he wants to tell me."

She looked at the boy. He brushed hair from his eyes. "I meet people sell heroin."

"What do you do at the brewery, Prasong?"

"I carry sacks. Unload trucks. They teach me chemistry."

"Sacks of what?"

"Sacks off trucks."

"What's in them?"

He shrugged and looked uncomfortable. Harley got up from the bed and took two steps to the boy's chair. He picked up the boy's hands, smelled them, and turned to me. "Take a smell. Smell his hands."

I did.

"What do you smell?"

"Vinegar?"

"Right." To the boy: "You ever heard of acetic anhydride?"

The boy looked puzzled. "What?"

"Acetic anhydride."

He shook his head.

"Tell me more about the beer, how they make the beer."

He shrugged again, and wiped the hair back. "I don't know. I only—"

"Carry sacks. You know what you are, Prasong?"

He shook his head. The girl's thin, almost hairless eyebrows came together in a frown. She was nervous and frightened.

"You're a lying motherfucker," Harley said.

"No. I not lie. I work—"

"You work at a number four lab, you lying little prick."

Harley's voice was calm and low.

"He work at brewery. Why you call my brother names? You just a—"

"Shut up," Harley said.

"I don't—"

"Your brother's hands are stinking of acetic anhydride," Harley said to the girl. "He's been working in a heroin lab.

You brought him here because you thought he had something to tell us. Well, you were right. So tell him to stop jerking us off and say what he has to say. If he doesn't want to talk, then get the hell out of here and let us go to bed. This country is stinking with heroin labs and I don't have time to listen to a lot of horseshit about beer, you understand that?''

The boy and girl looked at each other, talking with their eyes.

The girl said, "How much we get?"

"Depends on what he tells us and how good it is and what happens. The Thai government gives six thousand baht per kilo of number four seized, and the American government matches that. If we seize the lab and get some people with it, you'll get more, depending on how many people we get and who they are. Frankly, if we get the right people you can collect a very large amount of baht.''

They exchanged looks again. Finally the boy said, "I go to jail?"

"No. Definitely not. I can promise you that. If it works out you'll have enough money for both of you to get away, you can disappear, go somewhere and buy a farm.''

"Go to America?" the boy said.

"That's something else. I can't promise that.''

The boy said, "You right. I work at lab. I give you lab, all the people, many kilos number four, if I go to States.''

"Why the States? I can't promise you that. But I can promise you plenty of money if we get what you say.''

"I want to go to school in States.''

"Your sister too?''

"I make money, bring her myself.''

Harley looked at me. I was afraid that if I even breathed I might cause an interruption that would bring everything to failure.

"Where's the lab?" Harley said.

The boy and girl did not answer.

"You know," Harley said, "maybe I was too hasty. I think I'm beginning to believe what you said before.''

"What?" the boy said.

"You really *do* work in a brewery. You just rubbed some acetic anhydride on your hands so I'd think you worked in a lab and you could con me out of some money. Right?''

"No! I work at lab. I tell truth.''

"What do you do there?''

"Help chemist."

"Who's he?"

"Chinese. Old Chinese."

"What do you do?"

"Break blocks."

"What blocks?"

"Morphine."

"Then what?"

"Put pieces in big drum, add chemicals, light fire."

"What else do you do?"

"Bicycle pump. I pump to get air out of bottle."

"What other chemicals does the Chinaman use?"

"Don't know names. Black powder, like when wood burns. Acid. White powder. Many things. Don't know names."

"The morphine base, the blocks you break up, how does it get to the lab?"

"Truck."

"From where?"

"Don't know."

"When was the last one, the last truck?"

"Last week."

"How do you know?"

"Because I go there and work three days last week."

"How often do the trucks come, how often do you work there?"

"Two, three times a month."

"How'd you get this wonderful job, Prasong?"

The boy looked at Anuraj and she nodded.

"When we first get to Hatyai . . ." He leaned back slightly in his chair, happy to be off the subject of the lab itself, relaxing for the first time since he entered the room. "First day, we very tired. Go to little restaurant and ask if we can sleep there. They say okay and we sleep in back. A man comes and wakes us up and asks Anuraj if she want a job. She says yes and she start working at Paradise."

"Right then?"

"Next day."

"Who was the man?"

"Don't know. He take Anuraj to Paradise and she don't see him again."

Anuraj nodded.

"Woman at Paradise give Anuraj money and send her to hotel and we stay there. After a few days I leave, go to another hotel. Anuraj talk to old lady about me and she talk to man who takes care of Crown Hotel and he give me job."

"What's his name?"

"People call him Mr. Kuk."

"What kind of job did he give you?"

"Working kitchen. But when he find out I speak English he give me job at desk, reception desk. Hotel gets American customers and Mr. Kuk only man speak English."

"What kind of Americans they get?"

"Merchants."

"Of course. Rubber? Tin?"

"Yes."

"And dope."

"Yes."

"Then what?"

"One day he tell me go to room and go in with key and take package off bed and take to Chinese hotel and give to man behind desk. When I get back he give me ten baht."

"What was your salary?"

"Two hundred baht a week. After that many times I carry packages for him, sometimes from Crown Hotel to other hotels, or go places and get packages and leave in rooms at Crown. One day—"

"When?"

"Three month ago. He take me in his car and we drive to—we drive someplace and we pick up five packages and he tell me where to take two and let me out and he keep other three. He start doing that a lot, taking me to this place in his car, maybe once a week. Then he ask me one day if I want special job for three days at place where we drive to. He say someone there sick and they need man and he'll give me hundred baht extra on my pay if I stay there three days, sleep there, and work. I say okay. That was first time I work at lab. After that I work there two or three days every couple weeks."

. "What happened to the heroin? Did Mr. Kuk still pick it up?"

"After two or three days, when we finish, Mr. Kuk come and both of us take bags and deliver."

"Sometimes to the Crown, sometimes other hotels?"

"Yes."

Harley thought for a moment. The room was dead still. I

pretended to be completely occupied with the movement of a gecko on the wall above the table.

"Do you have a gun, Prasong?"

Harley's voice was gentle now, the interrogation over.

Prasong nodded and pushed back his hair.

"Where?"

He reached down and hiked up his trouser leg. A thin piece of metal was attached to the side of his calf with white adhesive tape.

"A Cobra," Harley said. "Let's see it."

Prasong pulled off the tape and handed the piece of steel to Harley. Harley turned it over in his hand, shook out three .22 caliber bullets and gave it to me.

"They call that a Cobra," he said. "It's probably the most dangerous handgun ever made—to the guy who's using it."

It was a flat slab of steel about four inches long, two inches wide, less than half an inch thick. Three holes large enough for the bullets had been drilled in one end. The firing pins were three screws pulled back against springs, the screw heads hooked over notches cut in the steel body. If you slipped a screw off its notch, the spring shot it forward into the back of a cartridge, firing the bullet. There was no safety catch. Any light blow against a screw head would fire it.

I handed the gun back to Harley and he reloaded it and returned it to Prasong. Prasong started to tape it back to his leg.

"Not like that," Harley said. "Aim it down. Then when it goes off it'll blow your foot away instead of your balls."

To me Harley said, "You wouldn't believe some of the weapons they turn out in this country.

Harley looked at his watch. "Okay, Prasong, tell me something. When do you think's the next time you might work at the lab or deliver some heroin or anything like that?"

"Tomorrow."

"What's going to happen?"

"Yesterday I come back from lab with five packages. Mr. Kuk tell me leave them in hotel with him, tomorrow deliver to Chinaman, collect money, take back to Mr. Kuk at hotel."

"What time?"

"Anytime after five o'clock, Chinaman not work till five o'clock."

"And you'll just pick up the stuff at the Crown, where you work, and carry it to the Chinaman and bring the money back, at any time you want after five o'clock? Have I got it right?''

"That right.''

Harley thought for a minute. "How are you getting back to Hatyai now?''

They shrugged.

"You can both stay here tonight and I'm going to think about this, and tomorrow, Prasong, I'm going to have something I want you to do for me, okay?''

"Okay.''

Anuraj smiled and took hold of Prasong's hand.

Harley said, "Prasong, I'm going to tell all this to my people and find out what they can do for you.'' He moved closer to the edge of the bed and leaned toward the boy and girl. "I don't want you to worry about anything. You both did the right thing telling me all this, and I believe you. I'm on your side. You have very strong people on your side now. Don't worry. We'll help you as long as you stay honest with us, you understand?''

They nodded vigorously.

"I'll be right back.''

Harley walked out into the hall with me.

"What do you think of all that?'' he said.

"Sounds good. But her story about escaping was a little incomplete.''

"Exactly.''

He opened the door to the room and said, "Anuraj? Come here a minute.''

She stepped out into the hall and Harley closed the door.

"Is there anything else you want to tell us about your escape, Anuraj?''

She shook her head.

"Why do you think Samak's men picked you up?''

"I not know.''

"No idea?''

She shook her head again.

"You told me how you and Prasong ran away from Betong. Did you tell anyone else?''

"No.''

"Anuraj, you've got to trust me. I can understand that maybe something happened with Samak you don't want Prasong to know. That's okay. But *I've* got to know, you understand?''

She stared at him, silent.

"Did you tell anyone else, Anuraj? About running away from the CTs?"

"I tell girl at Paradise."

"And Samak told you he knew the CTs wanted you but he'd let you go if you told him things you heard at the Paradise. Is that right, Anuraj?"

She looked down and nodded. Then her eyes came up and looked at Harley straight in the face. "But I no tell him anything. I promise him because he say if I not good he send me back to Betong. But I never going tell him nothing."

"I know you aren't, Anuraj. Did he make you have sex with him?"

She shook her head.

"If he did and you told me, I wouldn't tell your brother. You know that?"

"If Prasong think Samak do that he try kill Samak."

"I know that, Anuraj, so I won't say anything about any of this to Prasong. But next time don't lie to me, okay? Because I can't look out for you and your brother unless I know what's really happening, you understand?"

She nodded.

"Now go back inside and I'll see you in a minute."

She went inside, closed the door, and Harley said to me, "Samak told her if she fucked him and informs on her customers he won't send her back. He's probably got half the girls at the Paradise helping him shake down customers."

"Do you think he'll bother her again?"

"Not as long as he thinks she's keeping her ears open for him."

"What about the lab Prasong works at—is it Lichai's?"

"I'll have to check out Mr. Kuk. I've got an idea. I'll baby-sit with these two and give you a ring in the morning."

"What happens then?"

"I'm not sure yet, but when Prasong goes to do whatever he's going to do, we'll be there."

I started for the stairs. As an afterthought, Harley said, "You know, it *could* have been vinegar. Do they use vinegar in breweries?"

18

I WENT TO bed that night wondering if it had ever occurred to Harley to murder Lichai. I thought about the hanged dog and the lowered railroad barrier, about Samak and Lichai, and wondered if Harley ever thought of arranging an accident. I didn't know what his orders were in Songkhla, exactly. I had not thought to ask Knowles if Harley at the moment was under instructions to kill anyone.

I lay there with the lights on, thinking these troublesome thoughts, while a fly the size of a bumblebee slammed annoyingly into the mirror across from my bed. He was amazingly resistant to impact. He'd fly headlong into the mirror, bounce off, loop around, and smash into it again, over and over, trying to get through to the other side. When I turned out the light I could hear him buzzing around, lost. I wondered if the fat gecko would get him.

The next morning I got up, looked out the window, and saw Harley and the twins running together on the beach. They were tumbling and laughing, playing like children. The old corporal was there, too, watching from his horse, trotting along the beach to keep up with them. He slid off the horse and Harley mounted it and trotted a distance down the sand and came back. He tried to get Anuraj, and then her brother, to take a ride, but they refused. The four of them sat together on the sand for several minutes, facing the gulf, and then the old man climbed back on his horse and Harley, leaving the twins on the beach, headed toward the hotel. Five minutes later my phone rang.

"You're very cheerful this morning," I said. "Running around playing grab-ass with little girls."

There was a silence on the phone. I hadn't meant the accusation literally, but it had evidently embarrassed Harley or made him angry. Finally he said, "You're a fucking spy, you know that?"

"How are they?"

"They're nice kids. I've got to bring you up to date. Do you mind missing breakfast? I'd like to get them back as soon as possible."

"Five minutes?"

"See you at the car."

When I got downstairs Harley was not at the car, and I walked out to the beach looking for him. He was sitting on the sand, watching the twins and the horseman playing a hundred yards up the beach.

"I thought you were in a hurry," I said.

"I was, but fuck it. We've got a few minutes. They really hit it off with the corporal."

I sat down. "What was the idea you said you had last night?"

He reached down between his knees and drew a line in the sand. "If I can show a connection between Kuk and Lichai—any kind of half-assed connection at all—then I'll be convinced that Prasong's lab belongs to Lichai and I can sell it that way to Bangkok. I'm nine-tenths convinced already. I can't see Lichai standing still for too many labs around here that aren't his. The problem's going to be connecting Lichai to the lab legally. They don't have conspiracy laws here—you've got to grab a guy with the drugs actually in his personal possession. That's impossible with a man like Lichai, but I've got an idea we could maybe catch him with the money instead—make the case with the payoff cash instead of the dope. If I can control the payoff every inch from the lab to Lichai and prove that the money paid to Kuk for the dope ends up with Lichai, we'll have a case."

"You said on the telephone you had to bring me up to date on the twins."

Prasong and Anuraj had waved good-bye to the horseman and were headed back toward the hotel, walking slowly, holding hands.

"Out here on the beach, playing around, I made a deal with Prasong. I told him I'd do my best to make Bangkok agree to send him to the States to school if meanwhile he'd go along with me and trust me a little and let me get a look at the money he picks up this afternoon. So he told me where to park the Range Rover and he's going to wander by after he's got the money and if no one's with him he'll jump in. He doesn't know it, but we're going to tail him from the time he comes out of the Crown Hotel with the package."

"You think he's telling the truth—about the delivery to the Chinaman and collecting the money for Kuk?"

"I'm trying *hard* to believe him, Tony. What I'd really like to do is put a Kel on him and catch some of the talk when he hands the money to Kuk. Then if the right things got said we could squeeze Kuk. But maybe that's too risky. I don't want to burn Prasong. We'd lose everything."

"Including Prasong."

"Yeah, probably."

"I think you might be in danger of acquiring a couple of dependents, Peter."

"Every stool has to be handled differently. But I don't really think of these two as stools. One thing I like a lot, they didn't ask for both of them to go to the States. You'd expect them to. As long as you're shooting for the moon you might as well go all the way. But they only ask for what's essential. They take care of themselves."

"You think he'd bring her over if he got there?"

"Damn straight. He'd work his ass off. And she knows it, too."

Anuraj and Prasong stopped six feet away and *wai*ed us.

Harley said, "Let's get you kids back to Hatyai."

Prasong was living in a small Chinese hotel occupying two stories above a pharmacy on Niyomrat Road. We dropped him off and drove Anuraj to her hotel. I asked her how she liked it there.

She made a face.

"You don't like it?"

"Not nice people like Paradise. Too many dirty girl. Too many boyfriend. Make fuck all time."

"Make love, Anuraj," Harley said. "It may not be the case, exactly, but it sounds better."

"Make love," she said.

When we got to the building she said she lived in, Harley insisted on walking in with her. We went through a door on the street and along a narrow corridor, partially blocked by three motorcycles parked along the wall, to a court in the back. The court was covered by a skylight and surrounded by small cubicles built from old pieces of discarded plywood.

The cubicles had makeshift doors fastened with nailed-on hasps and padlocks. Water leaking out under the door of a wooden toilet stall in the back formed a large puddle on the concrete floor. There was a heavy stench of urine. Around the puddle girls and men—one with a gun in his belt—sat on a straw mat drinking beer and Coca-Cola and playing cards. Towels and underwear hung from wires strung above their heads. Through a door in the back of the court, next to the toilet, I could see a yard of sun-baked clay littered with empty milk cartons, beer bottles, two old motorcycle tires, and a half-starved hen.

One of the men playing cards on the mat was John Nostrand.

"Well," Harley said, "recruiting inmates?"

"You could call it that," Nostrand said, excusing himself from the game and standing to talk to us. "Just letting them know there's an alternative."

An old woman appeared through the back door with a bowl and a block of ice. She set the ice down on the concrete, just happening to put it in the puddle since most of the dry surface was occupied by mats, and proceeded to chip the block into small pieces. She collected these, along with whatever toilet leakage adhered to them, into the bowl, and placed it in the center of the floor handy to the Coca-Cola drinkers.

Anuraj had printed her name in pencil on the unpainted door of her cubicle. She unlocked the padlock and swung the hasp open. We removed our shoes and entered. It was seven feet square, the walls rising to within four feet of the ceiling, the remaining space screened with chicken wire. It contained a double bed, a green plastic clothes bag (yellow gown within), a narrow table with mirror, cosmetics jars, Buddha, joss sticks, and wilted jasmine blossoms. A thin brown towel covered the cement floor next to the bed. Electrical wires ran everywhere, branching from multiple plugs, hanging from a light socket tied to the clothes bag, disappearing over the walls into neighboring cubicles. I could see why Nostrand called it "the packing crate whorehouse."

Two small cotton balls lay on the pillow.

"What are they?" I asked Anuraj.

She made the face again. "Too much noise all time. Put in ears. All time everyone make fuck."

"Make love," Harley said.

"Make love."

I began to notice other evidence that a child's attempts to

get along in this scary world had failed. The base of a light bulb broken off in the socket had not been removed. A wire clothesline, attached to one wall, had proved too short to reach to the opposite partition. It was pathetic and hopeless. I didn't see how Anuraj was going to survive. Then I watched her talking in Thai with Harley, and my feelings reversed. Her face was so animated and alive, she was so full of confidence, so childishly ignorant of how impossible her position was, that I thought maybe she stood a better chance of survival than I did.

I turned to Nostrand. "Are they all prostitutes?"

I was sure that Anuraj, though she did what was necessary at the Paradise, did not pick up extra money here.

"Almost," he said. "One or two just live here because it's cheap."

We went back to the courtyard and left Anuraj alone in her cell. I asked Nostrand about two of the girls he'd been playing cards with on the mat. They looked even younger than Anuraj.

"They're sisters," he told me, "twelve and thirteen. They just got here from a village in the mountains, and Samak's after them already. He wants to have them together and he's going crazy because the Mama-san at the Paradise where they work—you've been there?"

"Yes," Harley said, "we met the Mama-san."

"She's keeping them away from him. Trying to, anyway. I don't know how long she can hold out. She's sending them up to Bangkok in a few days, to another place up there."

"How well do you know Anuraj?" Harley said.

"Not well. She's not here often. I think this is only the second time I've seen her."

"Would you let her live at your place?"

"Certainly. That's why it's there. Anyone I can get out of here . . ."

"She works at the Paradise."

"Doesn't matter. Getting them out of here's the important thing."

Harley and I walked back to Anuraj's room and knocked on the door. When she let us in she was wearing the yellow dress.

"Time to go to work?" Harley said.

"Yes."

Harley closed the door. "Listen, Anuraj, your brother's got a gun. How about you? Do you have anything?"

She locked the door with a hook-and-eye latch. Then she reached into the bottom of the clothes bag and pulled out what in her tiny hands looked like a cannon. It had a muzzle a half-inch wide, big enough to fire large ball bearings.

Harley held it and grinned. "Now that," he said, "is what we call an alley sweeper."

It was in fact a sawed-off, six-inch length of shotgun barrel fitted to the body and grip of a .38 pistol. It was loaded with double-ought buck. Harley asked Anuraj if she knew what that meant. She shook her head.

"That means that when you pull the trigger, this thing, in addition to breaking your hand, sprays a pattern of nine slugs, each one about the width of a .38 caliber bullet. So whoever catches the whole load, it's like getting hit with nine .38 slugs simultaneously."

Her expression, which had been awed to begin with (awed by Harley, not by the gun), did not change.

"That may be hard for you to understand," Harley said, "but anyway if you're close to your target and aim it straight, whoever it was who was bothering you won't bother you anymore."

She put the gun back in the clothes bag.

"Be careful of that thing," Harley said.

"Oh yes," she said solemnly, her eyebrows coming together as they had last night. "I very careful."

"Where'd you get it?"

"I buy from friend."

"Well, look, Anuraj, let me ask you something. Do you like it here?"

Her bony shoulders jumped up around her ears in a shrug of acceptance.

"Wouldn't you like to live someplace where you had a nicer room and there were not so many people all the time?"

"Very expensive," she said.

"No."

"Where?"

"You know Mr. Nostrand?"

"Man with you now, outside?"

"Yes."

"I just see him once."

"Well, you ask the other girls about him. He has a place

where you can stay. You ask them and see if you think you might like it there. Okay?''

Her eyes brightened and she gave Harley a smile that could have melted rocks. ''Okay.''

She had to go to work. She said good-bye to us and walked quickly through the courtyard, past the people playing cards, and down the hallway filled with motorcycles. She didn't speak to anyone.

Harley told Nostrand he might have another tenant and asked him to talk to Anuraj.

''See if you can get her out of here, John, will you?''

''Don't worry. Today if I can.''

Then to me Harley said, ''We'd better get out of here ourselves. I've got to get the Range Rover over to the consulate and ruin Lowell's day. And we've got to get set up for Prasong.''

19

WHEN WE were outside, walking toward the Range Rover, I noticed something drawn in the dust on the driver's door.

It was a heart.

I was moved by that, certain Anuraj had done it, and wondered what Harley's reaction would be. I said, ''It looks like you've won a friend, or something.''

''It needs a wash.''

''I wonder who could have done that?''

''She's playing around.''

''With that shotgun pistol? She doesn't strike me as the kind of person who plays around.''

He started to reach for the ignition, dismissing the subject, and I said, ''I was thinking about something last night.''

The hand dropped. ''What's that?''

''I was wondering if you ever thought about killing Lichai.''

He laughed. ''I never think of anything else.''

"Really?"

"For a while I thought you had a lot of balls, Tony, coming down here with me, hanging around, taking the chance of getting hurt, and then I decided it was because you just didn't know what the hell you were doing. Now I see you've started to think. Maybe Knowles did that for you? You could be killed here, you know that? And it would be a shame if it happened without your having any idea what the hell was going on."

"So what's going on? Tell me."

He slumped in the seat and I could feel his reluctance. There was something he would like me to know if he didn't have to be the one to tell me.

"You said Knowles told you about the Israeli counterfeiting operation, about the Alfa people."

"Yes."

"Did he tell you I'd been in a hospital?"

"No."

Nostrand came out of the building and saw us and waved. We waved back and he got in his jeep and drove off.

"I had some personal problems before that operation. I was upset about the Alfa—about what the Alfa people were doing. We'd been in training together and we kept in touch. We weren't supposed to, but we did. They weren't bad guys, Tony. Just because whatever you might have heard about them from Knowles and what you might think, maybe that they were assassins, murderers—but the people they went after, any sane man would have seen the justice in what they did if he could have known it all. But you see—I'm still trying to convince myself, you can tell that, right? Even now. I was upset about it. Killing people as a profession, in cold blood, on order. And that counterfeit operation, my operation, had something different about it. I wasn't sure about it. It had a bad smell. It didn't *feel* right. Going out on the ledge after that guy in New York—you remember that story?—*that* felt right, I knew that was the right thing to do. But this counterfeiting thing, I couldn't make myself believe it. You know—let me explain something to you and you do anything you want with it. If you're going to get hurt here you ought to know a couple of things. On an operation like that counterfeiting one, like any of the Alfa operations, the agent doesn't know everything, he just knows a little that he has to know, and he's aware that even that little bit may not be true. But he

has to make himself *believe* that it's true. There's something called Operational Truth. Operational Truth is what you're told and what you have to believe so you'll do the right thing, do what they want you to do. You *must* believe it. Because what you're *told* is what will motivate you properly, and if you don't believe it you won't make the right moves. If you stop for a second to disbelieve it, to doubt it—well, then your next step is 'What *is* the real truth?' And then you're lost. The operation is lost. Because your actions in response to that question won't be the actions that the total operation requires. You see what I mean?''

''Of course.''

''You really want to hear all this?''

''Very much.''

He shifted in his seat, turning to face me.

''They told me there was a guy, and they gave me a name, a description, and an address in Tel Aviv. He was an American and he'd been to Dartmouth, thirty-three years old. He and some other people were counterfeiting Israeli hundred-pound notes and buying arms with them for the Palestinians. We had good, hard Intel about a deal involving large quantities of plastic explosives and some new solid-state detonating devices that were very sophisticated and versatile. You could set them to trigger on a radio wave, a light beam, sunlight, sound, motion, even moisture. They told me this guy whose name they gave me had been blowing things up all over the place, and they wanted him taken out fast. He was an American, the detonators were American, his contacts were supposed to be American, so the Americans said they'd take care of it. I had a pack of Dunhills with two .45 rounds built in. The problem was that I knew about the earlier Alfa operations, that was two killings, Tony, one right after the other, and I was a little tight. But I didn't say anything, and I went to Tel Aviv. I got into the guy's apartment and I found what I was supposed to find. It was full of notes. I scooped up a couple of stacks and took them back to the hotel and I weighed them. I'd brought a Dobson with me, an electronic balance made for checking things like bank notes. It's small and so sensitive it'll spot the difference in a postage stamp before and after the glue's gone on. You can counterfeit engraving perfectly with optical printing, but you'll have a helluva time getting the weight consistently exact. An uncirculated Israeli hundred-pound note weighs .983 grams. I

made it my business to find that out before I left the States. And I took the Dobson. Well, I counted out two hundred notes and I weighed them. They weighed 196 grams plus a fraction—in other words, that's exactly what they should have weighed. They weren't counterfeit. They were real, Tony. Okay, so they told me they had hard Intel the notes were counterfeit. And they weren't. So what about the rest of the Intel? Was that wrong too? Who the hell *was* this American I was supposed to smoke? What were the *real* reasons they sent me out there? For all I knew someone fucked up and he's a good guy, one of us. So I didn't use the Dunhills. I sent a telegram instead. 'The bills aren't counterfeit, what should I do?' It was a stall. I wanted something to break to give me more information. And something did break. The morning after I took the notes out of his apartment, the morning after I should have wasted him, a school bus blew up in Bat Yam and killed thirty-seven children. I was there thirty minutes after it went up. It was still burning. The front end was fifty feet from the back end. There were pieces of bodies all over the street. Children's bodies. An Israeli cop was crying. He said what he'd like to do to whoever was responsible for that. And it was *me* he was talking about. *I* was responsible. That was the reward for my righteousness. The Israelis picked up my American friend, from Dartmouth, that afternoon. I went back to Washington and checked into a hospital and I stayed there three weeks. Knowles was very sympathetic.''

''You didn't get in trouble?''

Harley put his hands on the wheel and pushed himself back into the seat.

''In that world, Tony, you never get in trouble. You're either there or you're not there. The only kind of trouble you get in is the trouble inside yourself. I'd been wrong not to do what I was sent there to do. Thirty-seven children died. How much wronger can you be than that? But was I *wrong* not to just say, 'Oh, sure, someone you want killed? I'll get on it right away.' What do you do?''

The windows of the Range Rover were open, and flies buzzed in and out. Harley relaxed a bit and draped his left elbow out the window.

''It's so easy if it's not really you, Tony. Newspapers, television, all they do is comment, they never have to decide. No one at the *New York Times* went into the hospital when that bus blew up. I know this sounds dumb to you. There're probably a dozen reasons why it doesn't make sense. But it doesn't *have* to make sense. Not for the man with the gun. That's something I liked about Knowles when he came to the hospital to see me. He didn't say anything about it at all. It wasn't something he wanted to talk about. You know what he told me? He said, 'Anyone who sees moral questions not abstractly but at the point of a gun always ends up with the same problem.' I said, 'What problem?' He said he had an agent once who quit, and the reason he gave for quitting, he said, 'The things I have to do to stay alive make me wish I was dead.' I told him maybe I was getting to feel the same way.''

''*Do* you feel that way?''

''Yes. I can understand what the other Alfas did, as I don't hold it against them. Maybe they were right. I know they saved a lot of lives by killing the men they killed. But I'm not going to do it. So that answers the question you asked me, if I'd ever thought about murdering Lichai. That's the real reason Knowles was in Bangkok.''

He looked over at me and smiled. ''Sorry to have to tell you this, Tony. You were only an afterthought.''

''I thought he'd come all that way just to talk to me.''

''Well, you're the only one who's been told, the only one who knows. Even Valdez doesn't know what my orders are with Lichai, and he's sure as hell never heard of the Alfa people. He doesn't have to know. Knowles told you because you worry him. You fell into this and he doesn't know how to get you out. He couldn't get rid of you from Washington, so he wanted to see you and get a make on what you might be up to, or good for. Contingency is the name of the game.''

He looked out the front of the car and his smile disappeared. ''Knowles is a good man. He looks after his people. He doesn't let them down. That's one reason why I'm determined to make this operation work. I owe him something. He never said one word to me about the Tel Aviv case. When I left the hospital I told him I wanted out of the Alfa group. So he got me a job back with the Drug Enforcement Administration and I ended up out here, with Lichai. When I first saw it, it looked routine. Drug traffickers. All that same old shit. Then I found out what a big shot Lichai is politically, I found out about his CT connections, and I thought this *can't* just be coincidence. I began to see Knowles involved some way, and then finally he showed up in Bangkok and he told me he knew I'd get Lichai through the normal procedures but just in case I didn't, I ought to think about getting him any way I could. He told me all over again who and what Lichai is, what it will mean if he's allowed to keep operating. You listen to Knowles and he practically gives you the names and addresses of the thousands of teenagers who'll die from Lichai's dope, and all the people who'll be killed in the explosions and the riots, and what will happen if the Communists he's supporting take power in Thailand. He really makes you *feel* it. It's like someone's giving you a chance to kill Hitler. How the hell can you say no?''

"But you said no?"

"I said no. I'll get Lichai my way. I am not going to kill him, Tony. Because I am not going to *have* to kill him. I've promised myself that. I will not kill Lichai. I will get him legally."

"I hope so."

"Meanwhile, though, things could get a little rough. Have you ever been in a fight?"

"Not really. I mean, in the eighth grade, but not a real fight."

"The secret is not to wait to find out how the other guy's going to fight. Set the level yourself. Kick him in the balls immediately. If you've got something hard, like a bottle or an ashtray, hit where skin touches bone—knees, collarbones, shins, elbows. It'll hurt like hell and while he's thinking about the pain you can get another good shot at his balls."

"You're a dirty fighter, Peter."

"If you're not fighting dirty, you're not fighting. I'm not talking about grammar school recess. I'm talking about someone who wants to kill you. If a man wants to kill me, and I don't want to kill him—I'm dead. The man who wants to kill, kills, and the other guy dies. To stay alive, you've got to want to kill."

"Do you want to kill?"

He laughed, an ironic little chuckle.

"Definitely not. That's one of my problems."

"But the other Alfa agents, you said you knew them—I mean professional assassins generally, they . . ."

"Want to kill?"

"Don't they?"

"I suppose so."

"Why?"

"Because they think they're doing right."

"Never just—just because they like it? The excitement?"

"Yes. But they still think they're doing right. They're working for a country. They may know they're near the line between soldiers and murderers, but they also know they haven't crossed it. It's the moral and professional distinction between men who gamble secretly in doorways and men who gamble on Wall Street. It's definitions. You can make yourself believe anything."

He looked at me to see if I was satisfied. I nodded silently, and this time he turned the key and pressed the starter.

20

WE PULLED away from the packing crate whorehouse, made a left turn past the bus station, and Harley said, "Before we go to the consulate I want to dig up Thanon and see what I can make him tell me about Mr. Kuk."

He was brisk now, on the move, chin tilted up in the breeze from the window. He appeared to have put our conversation completely out of mind, but I had the idea he was only trying to conceal his own fear and diminish mine.

Thanon was not at the Satellite, so we drove over to Sno headquarters. His car was parked in a small yard overgrown with tall grass and weeds. We found him behind a desk. An old woman with bare feet brought us tea in metal cups.

"We just came by to thank you for the dinner," Harley said. "Not that we exactly remember all of it."

"We do again," Thanon said. "Colonel Samak say he want invite everyone next week."

"No, next time we're the hosts."

"We do many times."

"Good. Listen, maybe you can tell me something."

"What you like know?"

"Kuk."

"Oh, Mr. Kuk. You meet him?"

"No. I just wondered who he is around here."

"Businessman. Runs Crown Hotel, had restaurant, many things."

"And?"

"He nice man. Never make trouble. Crown good hotel."

"What's he look like?"

"Always wear white."

"How old?"

Thanon shrugged. "Thirty-five maybe."

He was the man we'd seen with Samak at the Paradise.

"Who's he work for?"

"I not sure."

"You ever hear the name Lichai?"

"Oh, yes. Very big man here."

"How big?"

"He own plantation, have big house, businesses in Bangkok."

"He come here often?"

"I don't know. Probably. He have business here."

"You never had any dealings with him?"

"No. Mr. Peter, if he have anything to do with drugs, maybe he do, but not—" He waved a hand, taking in the small office and the barracks-like dormitory that was the only other room in the house. "He not anyone we see."

"I understand. But if he owns the Crown, and Kuk manages the Crown, then obviously Kuk is his employee."

"I think Kuk take care of things for him in town, you know? He look after things."

"You know where his house is?"

"I never see it. He don't like people coming unless he invite them. I wouldn't—"

"It wouldn't be good to barge in—just walk up and knock on the door?"

Thanon grinned. "Not good idea."

"Even for the cops."

"Maybe Colonel Samak. I don't know. But Lichai not my business."

"Not mine either, Thanon. We're driving Tom to the airport later. I know he'd want to see you and say good-bye, but after what happened he's staying home with his family."

"Sure, of course. Tell him I sorry. I hope everything go good for him."

"I'll tell him, Thanon. See you later at the Satellite maybe."

Outside, Harley said to me, "We'll see if Kessick, the local Aim guy, has a background on this Kuk."

The whitewashed consulate burned in the sun. Even looking at it through dark glasses, I had to squint. A young man in beige linen trousers and a blue button-down shirt came out the front door and waited while we parked. When we were out of the Range Rover he took off his sunglasses—pink-tinted lenses in round colorless plastic frames—and looked at the hood and the grille.

"What the hell's that?"

"A dent, Lowell," Harley said. "Several dents."

"It's not the consulate's responsibility, you know."

"I hit a water buffalo."

"Harley, not even—"

"I had to run a railroad crossing coming back from Hatyai. We'd been—"

"I don't want to hear about it. As far as I'm concerned you're not even here. You can get yourself in whatever trouble you like, but don't expect me—"

"Shut up, Lowell, and say hello to Tony Deniset. Tony, our consul."

We shook hands. "I'd heard you were here. A writer, aren't you?"

"That's right."

He put the glasses back on and smiled thinly. "I hope you understand about this. Agents like Harley are not officially my responsibility, though we try to do everything we can to assist them. Within legitimate limits, of course."

"What about the Range Rover?" Harley said. "It's got to be fixed."

"There's a consulate car that's been in the garage for three weeks," Lowell said. "As soon as I get it back I'll try to see what I can do."

Harley made very little effort to conceal his contempt. "Thank you very much. You're really too cooperative, you know that?"

"I do."

Wisps of Lowell's blond hair, very fine and thinning back from his forehead, waved gently in the still air. Driving up the street we had passed an old Sino-Portuguese house, its upper floor overhanging the quiet tree-lined street. As Lowell and Harley talked I found myself examining the lawn around their feet and remembering what Sandra had told me about the informant who was found there with a machete through his neck.

"Let's go inside," Lowell said. "I hope you'll excuse us for a moment, Harley. I'd like to talk to Mr. Deniset."

"Go ahead," Harley said. "I've got to see Kessick."

We went upstairs to Lowell's air-conditioned office. I felt perspiration chilling on my skin.

"It's a peculiar kind of problem," Lowell said, moving behind a large teak desk. "These drug agents are in the business of catching dealers, some of them Americans. Then I have to go and try to get them out. It's ridiculous, one government representative trying to put American citizens into jail and another one trying to get them out."

He had a mild speech defect, a problem with his *r*'s, that might have been embarrassing if it had been more pronounced. In fact, it was not unattractive and seemed therefore slightly suspect.

"Who's Kessick?" I asked. I wondered how Lowell would react to the question, if it would fluster him.

"He's my vice-consul," he said evenly.

"What's he do?"

"He assists me. You're writing an article, I understand." He named the magazine.

"That's right."

On a table behind the desk I could see a stack of six folded blue shirts, identical to the one he wore. They must have been his day's supply.

Lowell had replaced the sunglasses with another pair having identical rims but clear glass. A double silver frame on his desk displayed a photograph of himself shaking hands with Henry Kissinger and another picture of a girl, presumably his wife, in a long dress. She was posed in front of a wall of leather-bound books, her hand resting on a table amid various silver and china objects. For some reason it was not at all difficult to imagine the two of them in a whores' hotel screwing and yelling Thai at each other.

Lowell reached behind his desk for a pipe and proceeded to fill it slowly as he spoke. He could not have been more than thirty years old.

"I hope that if there's anything I can help you with while you're here, you'll feel quite free to ask me. Strictly between us, confidentially, I wouldn't be too careless around Harley. These people sometimes get involved in rather unpleasant scrapes.''

I was a little surprised that he had not asked Harley how Tom was, and wondered now if he even knew about the slaughtered dog.

"My wife and I," he said, drawing on the pipe, "are having a few people by for dinner Friday, and we'd be very happy if you'd join us." He blew the smoke out. "The ambassador will be there. He's coming down for a day or two and—have you met him?"

"No, I haven't."

"Well, this would be a nice opportunity for you, then. I'm certain he'd like to talk to you."

"Thanks very much. I'd like to come. I'll have to talk to Harley. He may have to work and not be able to—I'm not sure what his plans are."

Lowell put the pipe down. "Actually, I'm afraid Harley won't be able to join us. There are a lot of people who have to be invited, you understand, other consulates and missions and people from the town. It's a small house, and we just can't fit in everyone. The next time the ambassador's here, of course—he makes a number of trips during the year."

"I see," I said. "Maybe I can let you know tomorrow."

"That would be fine."

He stood up. My audience was at an end.

Harley was waiting in the Range Rover. We pulled away from the consulate and he said, "We'll stop by and see how Tom is. I promised to take him to the airport. What'd you think of Lowell?"

"I tend to agree with you. Does he know about Tom and the dog? He didn't say anything."

"I'm sure he knows Tom's leaving. He can't be that out of touch. But he might not know about the dog. He wouldn't care. You saw how eager he is to be kept informed. He figures we're animals because we wear jeans and sandals and carry guns and actually talk to the savages. He tries to protect himself with ignorance. If something goes wrong he can always say he didn't know about it, that we didn't keep him informed."

"Did you see Kessick?"

"Kessick," Harley said, his almost beardless face igniting with the uncontained delight of a six-year-old, "is so excited he almost wet his pants. It's probably the first time in ten years he's raised his voice. First I told him I had a line into one of Lichai's labs and I was going to tie him to it with a payoff. That didn't even wake him up. He's a sharp guy, but sometimes he can really convince you he's dead. He's so fucking cool. But when I told him about Prasong and Kuk it knocked his socks off. I think he's going to be more help than I thought. He's letting Bangkok know, pressuring for the States thing, and I sent a message to Valdez. They've never been this close to Lichai before. We're gonna tear that cocksucker a new asshole.''

"Colorful.''

"Kessick's not too happy about you, by the way.''

"What do you mean?''

"He's a little hinky, afraid you might get in the way. I told him it was all right. I said you were cleared all the way up to the White House. You are, aren't you?''

"At least.''

We had reached the place in the road where the water buffalo stopped us yesterday.

I said, "Did you know the ambassador's coming down?''

"To *Songkhla?*'' He almost ran off the road.

"Yes.''

"Lowell said that?''

"Yes.''

"That son of a bitch. When's he coming?''

"Lowell said he's having a party for him Friday.''

Harley jerked his foot off the gas and let the car slow down. He turned to me. "He invited you to a party for the ambassador?''

"Yes.''

He sat for a moment, the car now slowed almost to a halt, then turned back to the wheel and put his foot on the gas. "Can you believe that bastard? What did he say?''

"That's all. The ambassador's coming for a day or two and he and his wife are having a dinner party for him. He said he couldn't ask you because there were too many other people he had to ask and there wasn't room.''

Harley was stunned. "There are only six Americans assigned to the United States consulate in Songkhla, and the United States ambassador is coming, and the consul is not inviting all six. Beyond fucking belief.''

We found Tom and Barbara inside sitting calmly on a sofa

with the baby beside them in its basket. Eight large suitcases were lined up on the back porch.

"Hey," Harley said, "the plane doesn't leave for six hours. You guys aren't anxious to get out of here or anything?"

"We're ready," Barbara said. "We've been ready since six o'clock this morning."

Several bottles of whiskey were lined up on the bar. "I assume you're willing that to the poor bastards left behind," Harley said.

"It's yours all right," Tom said. "I guess you'll need it."

"Thanks a lot."

"I'm really sorry to be leaving you in a situation like this, Peter."

"Sure you are. Don't worry about it. I'll be out of here myself in a few days."

"Something develop?"

"It will. You really all ready? Everything set to go?"

"Completely," Barbara said. "Tom's been holding me back. I wanted to go out and wait at the airport."

No one said anything about the dog.

"Just for a going-away present," Harley said, "I'll give you something else on Lowell. You know the ambassador's coming here tomorrow?"

"No. What for?" Tom said, surprised.

"I don't know. Checking up on the branch office, I guess. Lowell's having a party for him Friday night. He invited Tony but he said he didn't have room for me."

"Are you going?" Barbara said. The question had a sharpness to it and the three of them looked at me. I was being asked to choose sides.

"No," I said.

There was a moment's silence. Then Barbara said to Harley, "It's so stupid of him. The ambassador must know you're here. He'll think Lowell's crazy."

"What's happening to your house now?" Harley said.

"That's the landlady's problem," Tom said. "It's paid till the end of the month."

"Could I borrow it?"

"You shouldn't live here, Peter," Tom said. "Don't make it easy for them. Look how easily they got in before. You'd be out of your mind."

"I don't mean that. Just for Friday night."

"Why?"

"I thought I might have a party myself, for some of my most intimate friends and associates."

We all looked at him.

"I figure there're probably a lot of other animals in town didn't get invited to Lowell's and maybe we could all get together and have some fun of our own. Why not?"

"Harley, are you in *love* with trouble?" Barbara said.

Tom went to the bar and refilled his glass. "You're dangerous, Peter. I'm glad I'm getting out. If Samak didn't get me you would."

"What's wrong with a party? I'm allowed to have a party. Even agents need some relaxation."

"Yeah, right. Of course." Tom looked at his wife. "You want to cancel the tickets, Barbara? Hang around another day and help Peter celebrate?"

"I don't think so. Thanks very much all the same."

"Who'll you invite?" I said.

"I don't know. We can dig up a few people. Those kids we saw at the packing crate whorehouse. The Mama-san, some of her girls, maybe that old guy we met on the beach. We'll find people. They'll enjoy it. And maybe there's a couple of people, if someone paid some attention to them they might step forward and—" He stopped, obviously not wanting to sound as if he were getting at Tom for not developing stools.

Tom pretended not to notice. "You'll end up adopting the whole town, Peter. You and Nostrand can start an orphanage for stools."

Harley laughed. "Well, that's not too bad an idea."

"Anyway," Tom said, "you're welcome to the house. And the booze."

By the time we left for the airport there wasn't that much whiskey left. The plane didn't take off until five, but at three we already had the bags checked in and were settled at a table in the small terrace café next to the field. It had been Harley who insisted on arriving early. We talked and drank, and Harley told jokes and worked to keep the atmosphere from growing solemn. We spoke some more about his party and finally he agreed that it might not be a good idea.

"Give it up," Niekro said. "You'll have all the trouble you need without it."

"Maybe you're right. I shouldn't get carried away. But people like Lowell really piss me off. You *have* to let men like Lowell know where you stand, Tom. Otherwise they start taking neat little bites out of your ass and then bigger bites and before you know it they're chewing on your balls.''

"No party," Tom said. "Do me a favor."

"Okay, no party."

I was disappointed. I had wanted to see Harley and all those people together.

When the plane landed Harley pulled his chair from the table, faced it toward the field, and watched anxiously as the stairs were rolled out. The doors opened and passengers appeared at the hatch. A moment later I realized why he had wanted to be there early for the arrival. Sandra, fresh and beautiful in rose-colored slacks and blouse, strolled briskly across the tarmac and into the airport building.

Harley turned his chair back to the table.

"We'd better get to the gate," Tom said.

"We've still got time," Harley said, sipping his drink. "Wait'll they announce it."

Harley and I stayed at the airport until the plane took off. Harley didn't want to leave. We leaned against a waist-high chain link fence at the edge of the field, and the minute Tom and Barbara were out of sight through the hatch, his farewell smile vanished and he was the saddest man I'd ever seen.

"Look at that," he said. "There it goes. They'll never have to see this place again."

"So Sandra's here," I said, thinking that might cheer him up.

"Yeah. And why? Tell me that."

21

SEVERAL PEOPLE had told me Harley was tough, "a good man on the street," and in the next hour I saw first hand how he had gained his reputation. After we left the airport we stopped in Hatyai at the Rama Hotel, where Jaran had stayed, because it seemed likely that Sandra would be either there or at the Sawadi, our hotel in Songkhla. When we were parking the car Harley said, "There's Kessick."

A tall, lanky, rather awkward-looking man, very much as I had imagined him, was hurrying across the parking lot.

"That's not like him," Harley said, "seeing her where she's staying. He must be losing his touch."

The man behind the desk told us no American girl had checked in since he came on duty at noon. Harley did not give him a name, and in fact did not know what name she had used.

We were just outside the hotel's sliding glass doors, about to step off the curb, when I realized that a man was standing next to Harley, so close that their bodies touched. I thought they had bumped into each other. When we started across the driveway to the car the man walked with us, still very close to Harley. The man's face was tightened in pain, and in the middle of his forehead was a tattoo of a downward-pointing dagger.

Harley spoke to him in Thai, softly but fiercely. As we approached the Range Rover I realized that Harley's arm was around the man.

"You drive," Harley said to me, "and roll the windows up."

Harley pushed the man into the backseat and climbed in after him. I turned around and saw Harley hit the man three short hard blows in the stomach, then shove him to the floor and put his gun in the man's face. With his other hand he dropped a small revolver onto the front seat next to me and said, "This is our day for guns."

The man said something and moved his arms. Harley hit him on the cheek with his gun. He put one foot on the man's stomach, the other on his neck, and reached his free hand into his jeans pocket for the keys.

"Drive back the way we came from the airport," he said, and I started the car.

I looked in the rearview mirror and saw Harley staring absently out the window. He looked like a bored tourist.

When we were out of town, Harley said, "Slow down to twenty-five. I'm gonna have a talk with my friend."

He bent over and I heard short Thai sentences, muffled blows, grunts. There were moans of denial, defiant at first, then increasingly pleading.

"Stop the car," Harley said.

He got out on the road side, walked around, opened the door and reached in and dragged the man to the ground. He lifted him to his feet, held his chin in his hand, steadied him, looked straight into his eyes, and hit him in the stomach. The man doubled. As his knees buckled Harley hit him again, throwing him backwards into the brush.

The man lay there. Harley watched until a leg moved, then got in the front seat.

"Let's go back."

He took a cloth from the glove compartment and wiped his hands. "Something else for Lowell to yell about. The backseat's full of blood."

He put his hand under his buttocks and pulled out the man's gun. I turned and looked at it. It was a small .45 with no barrel at all. The bullets fired directly from the cylinders. Each protruding slug, wide as my little finger, was polished to a golden brilliance.

"That was like staring into six brass basketballs," Harley said, putting the gun back on the seat.

"Why all the rubber?" I said. The grip was wrapped in rubber bands.

"So it won't fall down his pants leg. The rubber helps it stick under the waistband. He's the motherfucker who sly-rapped me in Bangkok. I tried to make him tell me he worked for Lichai, but he never heard of him. I believe him. He'd've told me if he did."

"Who does he work for?" I said.

"I don't know." Harley looked at his watch. "And now I've fucking missed Prasong. I wasted all this time trying to find out something and I don't know any more than I did in the beginning. He gave me a name at the end there, but it didn't mean anything. Could be one of Lichai's men, or anyone."

"It's too late for Prasong?"

"By the time we get back it will be. He's already left the Crown and I can't really expect him to hang around the street with a package full of money under his arm."

"How is this guy?" I said, meaning the man Harley had left in the brush.

"He's okay. He'll just have a long walk back."

"What about the CTs?" It was almost dark out.

"He's probably a CT himself. If not, tough shit."

The rest of the way back to Hatyai, Harley was sullen, looking straight ahead out the window. As we entered the edge of town he said, "I just figured it out. You know who that cocksucker works for?"

"Who?"

"Who did we see leaving the Rama? Kessick wasn't there to see Sandra. Because Sandra's not there. He was seeing that fuck we just had in the car. Aim had me taken apart in Bangkok. It was Aim—fucking *Aim*."

He fell back into silence, angry and brooding.

"Where now?" I said. I was positive Harley was wrong. Aim would not have done that.

"Songkhla. The Sawadi. How the hell am I gonna find Prasong?"

We drove for another ten minutes through brush and palm trees.

"I hope no one decides to take *you* out," Harley said. "If I was paranoid I'd say there was a conspiracy to cut me off from the whole fucking world."

When we pulled into the hotel drive, Harley said, "I can't believe it. Why would they do that to me in Bangkok? And Sandra—she's Aim. Did *she* know?"

He twisted toward me and grinned weakly, apologetic for some reason, as if ashamed at a situation he should have been clever enough to avoid, for both our sakes.

"Will you do something for me?" he said.

"Of course."

"I can't risk losing contact with Prasong. If he thinks I'm

not serious enough to keep an appointment he might think I'm not serious enough to keep my agreement about what he'll get for helping me. On the other hand, I can't go hanging around his hotel looking for him, and I want to try to see Sandra tonight. I have to know what brought her down here."

"So?"

"Go to Nostrand's tonight, see if Anuraj has moved in yet, get her aside, and tell her I missed Prasong. Don't tell her any more than that. Just ask her to talk to her brother and see if he can meet me at Nostrand's around ten tomorrow morning. If not, when can he meet me. Okay?"

"Okay, but why don't I just go to Prasong's hotel and find him myself, or leave a message?"

"No good. I don't want those people over there wondering why some *farang* is sniffling around Prasong."

He put a hand on the door handle, then hesitated. "I can give you a piece if you want one."

"No, thanks."

"It might not be a bad idea."

"No."

"Sure?"

"I'm sure."

22

AT EIGHT o'clock I looked in the hotel bar, bought a fifth of Johnnie Walker, and asked the man behind the reception desk to call me a taxi. Earlier he had told Harley and me that an American girl dressed in slacks had checked in "under the name of Jenkins." He said it as if fully aware that that was not her right name. Right names were not the rule at the Sawadi Hotel.

The taxi driver had thought I would be going to another address in Songkhla. When he heard the word "Hatyai" he put his Toyota in park and set the emergency brake. I pulled out a wad of hundred-baht notes, and for the equivalent of thirty dollars he agreed to drive me to Hatyai, wait for an hour, and bring me back.

I was too preoccupied with Harley and Prasong and the dagger man to worry about the railroad crossings. Would Aim really have had him beaten up in Bangkok? I could not believe that. What reason would they have had? The dagger man's warning, *Tell him not see girl*, could have referred to Sandra as well as Miki; but Fred Stewart, the station chief in charge of Aim, the man who had lived with Sandra before she went to Harley, was certainly not the jealous lover type. Questions concerning Aim's motives were, in any case, a waste of time because only facts could answer them, and the facts I would never have. Nor would Harley. How could anyone ever know what was really going on inside Aim, or inside a man like Knowles? The uncertainty, the mystery, was part of the atmosphere in which Harley worked. It was, in Nostrand's words, an affliction one had to endure as one endures the heat and the monsoon. No wonder Harley's grin as we pulled up to the hotel had been weak and apologetic. He had to accept the "Operational Truth." He had to behave as if everyone on his side were behind him. Otherwise how could he work at all? But he knew that at any moment he might be betrayed, beaten up or killed, by a fragment of the operation surfacing, through intention or error, from a level of which he was entirely unaware. Paranoia became a mark of Harley's trade.

Harley had failed in Tel Aviv and had suffered for it ever since. He could not survive another failure here. He would never leave Thailand until he had defeated Lichai or been killed trying. In a certain way, I was caught with him. For I could not leave either. And I wanted to leave. I was frightened. The wise thing would have been to take the next plane out. But unfortunately I had acquired a feeling of loyalty to Harley. I could not just say good-bye and take off and check back later to see how it all came out.

At Nostrand's I paid the driver and watched him park the taxi. A woman and a young child, a girl, were sitting in the dark on the veranda. I sat beside them and listened to the insects in the jasmine bushes and banana trees that surrounded the house.

Nostrand came out with a man who had his arm in a sling. He said good-bye to the man, turned to the woman, and saw me. His face brightened and any apprehensions I had had about intruding disappeared.

"This is a nice surprise," he said. "Can you stay for a while? I've just got about ten more minutes and I'm free."

When he had finished with the woman's daughter, he sat down with me on the veranda and I brought out my bottle and offered him a drink.

"No, thanks. I'd like to but you never know what might walk in in the middle of the night." He handed me a glass and apologized for the absence of ice. "I won't try to tell you I don't have any, but I have damned little and I need to save it."

I asked him if he'd seen Anuraj.

"She's moving over. She said she'd get someone to bring her tonight. What'd you think of that place?"

"Not too nice."

"But to them it's a palace. Just to have a bed—some of them have never even *seen* a bed before."

There was no light, but in the almost total silence, broken only by the insects, I could hear the deep, slow breathing of Nostrand immersing himself in the first relaxed moments of his day. I let him alone for a couple of minutes, drank my scotch, and then said, "Do you mind if I ask you how you happened to pick Hatyai?"

"I didn't. It was picked for me. They needed a doctor to send here, so I came."

"Who's they?"

"The Christian Missionary Union. I didn't know anything about Thailand, but when I found out they only had one doctor for every 6,500 people that was all I needed."

"Where was your practice in the States?"

"Boston. I'll tell you what happened. A taxi came around a corner on Boylston Street, jumped the curb and knocked me into a plate-glass window. One of the shards went through my liver. I was in the hospital two months. I was cut off from the world, in pain, and very suddenly aware of what a thin fabric my daily life was. My practice, my work, didn't mean anything to me anymore, nothing at all—a lot of people who weren't really sick, who had things that'd go away anyway, things that could be handled by any other doctor around the corner. I made up my mind that when I got out I'd go someplace where there weren't *any* doctors, where if you got hurt you just fell down and died in your agony."

"But there's a hospital here."

"It's not enough, not nearly enough. The poor people, the people in the villages you never see, they don't even know it's here. And there was also something else . . ."

He stopped talking and waited to see if I would head him off. I had no intention of doing that.

"I won't bore you with it—you can see why I've had only six converts—but I was worried that maybe I never should have gone into a scientific profession in the first place. I didn't agree that truth exists in the form of facts that can be rationally determined. The most important truths are specifically those that *can't* be known, but only believed. As a doctor I had all this scientific *knowledge*, but I didn't have any real understanding."

He noticed my bottle on the floor and dragged a small table around next to my chair.

"I talked about that with a friend of mine once, and he asked me this, he said, 'Which is better, to have absolute knowledge that your wife's not cheating on you, or to have absolute faith that she's not? Both produce certitude, but only one involves love.' I knew a lot scientifically, but I wanted more than that, I wanted to see into another world where facts couldn't admit me. So I decided to spend some time at a seminary and become a medical missionary. And here I am, boring the hell out of you."

"You're not boring me at all. I think I know what you mean. My wife was killed two months ago. I'd never had anything bad happen to me and then suddenly I wanted to die."

"I'm sorry." He was looking straight at me.

"It's all right now."

"Is that why you came to Thailand?"

"I had to come to do a story."

He kept his eyes on mine for another second, then looked away, too polite to tell me he knew I was lying.

A girl upstairs shouted something and another girl shouted back. Nostrand glanced at the ceiling of the veranda and listened for sounds of an enlarging quarrel. After a few moments of silence, I refilled my glass and we sat quietly. The darkness, peace, and silence seemed to extend from the veranda endlessly in all directions. I wondered how Harley was doing, if he'd found Sandra and taken her off to dinner.

"If you listen carefully," Nostrand said, "you can hear monkeys in the trees over on Sanaruk Road."

I listened, but it was not the monkeys I heard. A car stopped in the street, doors slammed, and the thin, authoritative voice of Anuraj came to us through the trees and bushes. In a moment she was climbing the steps of the veranda, followed by a man carrying her clothes bag.

She *waied* John and they spoke in Thai. A string of jasmine blossoms was pinned in her hair.

"Be back in a second," Nostrand said to me, and led her inside. The man with the clothes bag followed, and as he stepped into the light of the doorway I recognized him—the skinny, obsequious little corporal who'd come to dinner with Samak. I was stunned. In a minute the corporal came out, bowed to me, *waied*, muttered something in Thai, and disappeared into the bushes. I heard the car drive off.

Nostrand came back and sat down.

"Mission accomplished," he said cheerfully. "I put her in a room with another girl from a village near where she comes from. She'll be fine. She's a pretty girl, isn't she?"

"Samak must think so. That was his corporal who brought her."

Nostrand shook his head. "That's too bad, but it doesn't surprise me. When it comes to girls, Samak takes his pick. It's a matter of pride with him."

I wondered if I should tell Nostrand about the abduction of Anuraj and the role the corporal had played. I decided not to. There might be things going on I didn't know about—there were for damned *sure* things going on I didn't know about. In any case, my real worry was not what to tell Nostrand but what to tell Anuraj. If she was friendly with the corporal— and with Samak? —would Harley want her to know when he was seeing Prasong? But that kind of thinking was ridiculous— Anuraj had brought Harley and Prasong together in the first place. Prasong was her brother, after all.

"Do you think I could talk to Anuraj for a minute?" I said. "I have something Harley wanted me to tell her."

"Sure. Go on up."

I left Nostrand on the veranda and went inside. Anuraj was just coming down the stairs with an empty glass in her hand. When she saw me she smiled. I didn't say anything about the corporal, deciding to let Harley handle that himself. I put my hand lightly on her arm and said, "Peter has something he wants you to tell Prasong."

Her smile vanished. "Prasong very very unhappy. He tell me find Mr. Peter, say he very sorry."

"Prasong's very sorry?"

"He go hotel get package but Mr. Kuk say Chinaman not want till tomorrow. Not have money yet. He tell Prasong stay hotel, work at desk, so Prasong not able meet Mr. Peter. He very very unhappy, say he lose face with Mr. Peter. He say Mr. Kuk tell him take package tomorrow. He tell me find Mr. Peter, tell him very sorry, meet same place eight o'clock tomorrow."

"Prasong's going to meet Peter the same place at eight o'clock in the morning?"

"You tell him?"

"I'll tell him, Anuraj."

She smiled again and ran off toward the kitchen with the glass.

I walked out to the veranda, eager now to get back to the hotel and leave a message for Harley.

"It's getting late," I said. "I'd better get out of here."

"How're you going back? It's not that safe a ride, you know."

"I've got a taxi waiting."

"You'd better make sure he's still there."

We walked out to the street, and of course the taxi was gone. I felt foolish having expected him to wait. I had to let Peter know about his new appointment with Prasong, but I couldn't go wandering around at night looking for a taxi, and Nostrand had no telephone.

"Don't worry about it," Nostrand said. "There's a cot in my surgery, you can sleep there. No difficulty at all."

I didn't want to impose on Nostrand, but there was no way back to Songkhla. I would have to sleep on the cot, get up early, and make it back to the hotel by seven.

Nostrand put a blanket on the cot for me, sprayed the room with bug killer, and said good night. I lay down with my clothes on. I heard Nostrand brushing his teeth, walking around, then silence. I turned the light out and the room filled with shadows. I don't know how long I had been lying there, worrying about getting the message to Harley in time, when I heard a noise in the garden. I ignored it, telling myself the strange surroundings had made me apprehensive. I heard it again, something moving among the bushes, and tried to believe it was either my imagination or one of the monkeys from Sanaruk Road.

After five more minutes spent rigidly still on the cot, my ears reaching into the darkness, I finally convinced myself that whatever it was had gone. I was about to fall asleep when the door opened and Nostrand rushed in.

"I'm sorry, Tony, but I have to ask you to move. You'll have to go upstairs. Take the blanket."

His hand was on my arm, pulling me to my feet.

I started to put on my shoes.

"Carry them," he said impatiently. "Hurry. It's an emergency."

I grabbed my shoes and followed him out the door and ran up the stairs. At the top, trying to see around me in the dark, I heard harsh, urgent voices downstairs—Nostrand and two other men. They went into the surgery and the door closed. I spread the blanket on the floor and lay down. After thirty minutes the surgery door reopened and I heard Nostrand leading the men to the front door, their voices low and calm.

The front door closed. Nostrand returned to his room. I lay down on the floor, suddenly very tired. It had been a long day, and I had had a lot to drink on the veranda before Anuraj arrived.

When I woke it was already twenty minutes past eight.

23

I RAN ALL the way into the center of Hatyai and got a taxi back to the hotel. When I picked up my key the desk man handed me a message. It said simply: "Call me now." That had to be Harley.

"Where are you?" he said when I phoned from the desk.

"In the hotel. I've got a message for you. Prasong—"

"Come to the room right away." He hung up before I could answer.

Harley opened the door with a gun in his hand. The floor was covered with money—two neat rectangles of five-hundred baht notes, each rectangle ten notes long and five wide. Prasong was sitting on the unmade bed, which had been pushed against the wall to provide more floor space. Next to him was a small suitcase filled with stacks of notes bound in rubber bands. Sandra was standing in a corner by the window.

I edged along the wall, trying not to step on the money, and sat on the bed beside Prasong. Sandra nodded at me. She looked as if she'd dressed in a hurry, and probably in the same clothes she'd worn at dinner.

Harley didn't speak. He was astride one of the rectangles, focusing down on it with a small camera. He took a picture, then moved to the other rectangle and photographed it. He gathered up the bills, added them to a pile on the floor next to Sandra, and set out others taken from the suitcase.

I looked at the rumpled bed, and felt Sandra's presence behind me against the wall. Evidently love—or sex at least—had managed to survive betrayal.

"They make a nice picture," I said, looking at the notes on the floor.

"I'll be finished in a minute." Harley snapped the pictures, scooped up the bills, and laid out two more rectangles.

"What happened?" I said.

"We'll get all the numbers on film and then we can talk."

One more rectangle, plus a few odd bills, and Harley was finished. He arranged the money back in the case, and handed it to Prasong.

"When you get it to Kuk," he said, "if everything's all right call me here. When I answer tell me it's a wrong number, apologize, and hang up. If something's wrong, give me an address, but don't wait for me at that address, you understand? Be where you can see it, that's all, and when the Range Rover drives by come out on the street. I'll see you and pick you up. Okay?"

Prasong nodded, took the case, and left.

Harley turned back from the door, and clapped his hands.

"We've got the fucker, Tony. We've got his ass, man."

"How much money is that?" I said.

"About twenty thousand dollars. Prasong missed the meet too."

"I know. I saw Anuraj. She said Prasong was going to meet you this morning at eight, but I couldn't get here in time to—"

"It's okay. When I didn't show up this morning Prasong decided to bring the money over here. He just walked up and knocked on the door. He's got balls, that kid."

"So what happens now?"

Sandra, saying nothing, came around and sat on the bed next to me. Harley ignored her. I was aware of a tightness in the room.

"Now it's easy," Harley said. "We just wait. Kessick's got people in the banks who let him monitor accounts. He told Sandra last night that the Crown Hotel's held by something called Siam Enterprises with an account in the National Bank of Thailand on Montri Road. Kessick got photocopies of the deposit and withdrawal records. Two or three times a month somebody puts 100,000 to 500,000 baht into the account. The next deposit, Kessick's asset'll call him, and all I have to do is go over and take another set of pictures of the bills. If the numbers match the ones I just photographed here, then we've got Prasong exchanging junk for cash and the cash entering the Siam Enterprises account."

"It won't be hard to find out who owns Siam Enterprises."

"Lichai owns it, Kessick already checked."

"So you've done it. You've got him."

"Not quite. Lichai will say he didn't know anything. He'll say he thought all the deposits were from the hotel. He didn't know Kuk was running a drug operation. Kuk could have been skimming money from the hotel and making up the difference with drug payoffs."

He walked over to the window, looked out at the beach and stretched, reaching long stiff arms toward the ceiling. "But Sandra thinks that doesn't matter. Tell him, Sandra."

"Peter . . ."

"Oh, fuck, Sandra, tell him. He knows who you are and he doesn't work for Lichai."

She studied my face, uncertain. "You're not going to write this, are you?"

"Sandra," Harley said, impatient, "he's not some kind of idiot. By the time he write it, if he writes it at all, this whole case will be ancient history. Tell him."

Sandra looked at Harley, glared, then turned back to me. "Miki makes a lot of trips to Europe. She went to school in

Switzerland, she has friends there. We checked the departure dates on her passport and . . .''

She stopped. She had decided she really didn't like this at all. I think relating information to an outsider made it difficult for her to maintain her self-image as some kind of Jane Bond.

Harley came away from the window. ''Miki's here now,'' he said to me. ''Aim thinks maybe she's been a little naughty. Maybe she hasn't been a completely candid asset for them. They got the idea she might be carrying dope out in her baggage, so Sandra came down to buddy around with her, try to find out when her next trip is and where's she's going. Then Aim could put surveillance on her when she lands in Europe. But now that theory's changed. It turns out that four out of five of the withdrawals, *big* withdrawals, from the Siam Enterprises account were made the day before Miki left the country. So she isn't smuggling dope out. She's smuggling cash. Next time there's a withdrawal and she leaves here the day after, we hit her bags at the airport. First, it's illegal exportation of funds, for which she can do five years. After that, all kinds of possibilities open up. Maybe when we show her the pictures of the bills and tell her where they came from, she'll have something to say about her old man she hasn't mentioned before. She's not the type to get along well in the slammer. Or maybe the old man won't want his daughter going to jail. And won't want the Bangkok papers to hear about the drug deposits in his bank account. Maybe he'd rather work for Aim. Before Aim just wanted him out of the way—but *working* for them, man, that they hadn't even dreamed of. Kessick can't sleep nights, just thinking about it.''

I said to Harley, ''Why would Miki have been helping Aim if she was really working for Lichai?''

''Sometimes people try to work both sides of the street.''

''Did Aim say anything about Prasong?''

''If we get Lichai, Prasong goes to the States. I just told him that and he was so happy he almost shit. He wanted it in writing. I gave him a piece of paper, nice and vague so it won't hurt him if someone finds it. Now he feels like he's got a contract. He is one happy kid, Tony. Kessick said the third floor went for it in a flash. They're ready to put him through Harvard.''

''That's terrific.''

"You know, with a little luck we could be out of here by the end of next week."

"But you've got to wait for Miki to make a trip."

"She's due now. She hasn't left the country for five months."

"When do you think she'll go?"

Harley turned to Sandra, who had stretched out on the bed. "What's your guess?"

"Tomorrow morning."

The tightness in the room quadrupled.

"*Tomorrow* morning?"

"Yes. Tomorrow." She was staring at the ceiling, pleased with herself.

"You know that?"

"She's leaving on the 11 A.M. flight to Singapore."

"Reservations?"

Sandra raised her head from the pillow and nodded. Harley looked sharply at me, then back at Sandra. He couldn't believe it. She swung her legs over the edge of the bed and sat up.

"You didn't tell me she was leaving tomorrow," Harley said.

"I hadn't had a chance."

"She *can't* leave tomorrow, Sandra. If she takes the morning flight . . . Where's she going?"

"She has a connection in Singapore to Rome and Geneva."

"She'll make a withdrawal in the morning and Kuk won't have made this deposit by then."

"It's all right, Peter. Don't get all stirred up. She'll still be smuggling currency, whether she has this last payment or not."

Harley took a step toward the bed and stood over her. "But she won't have any currency from an account we've identified with drug money. We won't have proved the account's dirty until Kuk makes this deposit. It won't work at all, Sandra. The money I just photographed is the only cash we can positively identify. It's got to go into the account, then we can prove the account's dirty, and when she makes a withdrawal we'll have her and her father linked to a drug operation. If we do it your way all we'll have is Miki illegally exporting currency. That's not going to make Lichai work for Aim."

"Aim thinks differently."

"But he's a *trafficker*, Sandra. He deals in *heroin*. We can prove that now. Aim will *own* him. All you have to do is prevent Miki from leaving until Kuk has put this money in the account, and then when she goes she'll have money taken from an account we can *prove* contained a drug payoff."

"We can't keep her from leaving, Tony. If she wants to leave—"

"Oh, come on, Sandra, don't play with my brains. Aim can do anything it wants. Have the airline tell her they lost her reservation. Close the bank tomorrow so she can't make the withdrawal."

"Peter, you can't always have cases all wrapped up as elegantly and neatly as you'd like, you have—"

"You're telling *me* about cases?" He was furious. "Sandra, it's not a matter of elegance, it's a matter of getting Lichai. He is *not* going to throw himself into Aim's arms just because you caught his daughter smuggling currency. Probably half the population of Thailand smuggles currency."

She got up from the bed. "Lichai is a very proud man, Peter, and he won't want his daughter going to jail, not for anything. And maybe she *will* have this last payment with her. Maybe she'll take it directly from Kuk. Maybe she'll pick up the money from the bank and add this new money to it."

She and Harley were facing each other, almost nose to nose.

"Right from Kuk's safe," Harley said.

"Why not?"

Harley didn't have an answer for that. He hesitated, reluctant. "I don't think she'd do that, Sandra."

"Why won't she?"

Harley walked back to the window.

"She's leaving tomorrow, Peter. Whatever you do. So you might as well—"

"Take what I can get. Okay, I'll grab her at the airport. Where will you be?"

"I'm going back to Bangkok this afternoon."

"That figures."

Sandra straightened her skirt and walked to the door. "I'd better get going. I'm supposed to have lunch with Miki. If I find out anything more I'll call you."

"Do that."

When she had left, Harley looked as if he didn't know

whether to laugh or cry. Tomorrow morning, if all went as Sandra said it would, he'd have Lichai.

"If this works," he said, a tone of hopeful enthusiasm creeping into his voice, "I could be back in Bangkok in two days. I could be in New York in a week."

Then I told him about Anuraj, that she had arrived at Nostrand's with the corporal carrying her clothes.

24

WE PULLED into the airport parking lot and looked around for Thanon, who'd been briefed the night before. I knew Harley hadn't spoken to Miki since she walked away from our table at the Oriental Hotel, and I asked him if he looked forward to the reunion. He said, "I just hope she doesn't have a gun."

Thanon and two of his men were waiting for us in a Toyota. They were wearing civilian clothes and each had a walkie-talkie hidden in a folded newspaper. Thanon slipped into the backseat of the Range Rover, and Harley said, "I don't want her to see any of us till we make the collar. But I'd like for you to talk to the check-in people and make sure they have her identify her luggage—actually ask her, 'Are these yours?' and get an answer from her. I don't want her saying she never saw the bags before. We've got to wait till she's checked in on the flight so she won't claim she was waiting for a plane to Bangkok. It's got to be exportation—out of the country. You understand?"

Thanon nodded.

"As soon as she's left her bags at the check-in counter and she's well out of sight I'd like the bags taken to the airport manager's office and I'll open them there. I don't want anyone else opening them. Okay?"

"I understand."

"Then if we find what I think we'll find, I'll wait for her to board the plane—I want her actually on the plane— and then you and I will board the plane and take her. I'm going to keep out of sight now and I'll see you in the manager's office.''

Thanon went back to the Toyota and Harley parked the Range Rover behind the terminal. We got out and stood at the building corner, watching the entrance. After about an hour a black Mercedes pulled up and Miki got out, followed by the chauffeur with four suitcases.

We went in a back door to the manager's office and found Thanon sitting behind the desk smoking a cigarette. Through the cracked door we had a view of the check-in counter.

''I talk to check-in people,'' Thanon said. ''They okay.''

''Good,'' Harley said. ''That's fine. There she is now.''

Standing on tiptoes to see over Harley's head, I watched the chauffeur put the bags on the scale. The check-in man took the ticket, said something to Miki, and she nodded and spoke. Then she retrieved one of the bags, a large overnight case, and the check-in man removed the others from the scale and handed her a boarding card. She moved off out of sight toward the boarding gate.

In a moment one of Thanon's men arrived with the checked suitcases and laid them on the floor. Harley said, ''Well, there's no point in breaking them open. It'll be in the one she's carrying.'' He looked at Thanon. ''Where is she now?''

Thanon spoke into his walkie talkie and in a moment we heard a muffled answer.

''Tell your man to let us know as soon as she's on the tarmac.''

''She going now,'' Thanon said.

Harley and I hurried with Thanon to the runway and saw Miki climbing the gangway to the plane. When she was through the door, Harley broke into a run. He was well ahead of me and by the time I reached the top of the gangway and looked forward into the passenger compartment, he was already talking to Miki. She was about to sit down in an aisle seat. Harley reached across her for the bag on the seat by the window. She grabbed his arm and yelled, ''Stop that!''

Other passengers were staring and a stewardess started up the aisle. Thanon held her back.

Harley took the bag and gripped Miki's arm. He turned to Thanon. ''Tell her she's under arrest.''

Thanon spoke to her in Thai and immediately she dropped into the seat and gripped the armrests.

Harley gave her a gentle tug, but she sat rigidly, braced in the seat. Again Thanon spoke to her in Thai. She looked straight up into his face, and spat. The spittle hit under his right eye and ran down his cheek.

Harley handed the bag to Thanon and pulled a pair of handcuffs from the waistband under his shirt. He wrenched one of her hands from the seat, cuffed it, twisted it behind her back, pulled the other hand free, and cuffed it. He took her by the upper arms, lifted her from the seat, and standing behind her, holding the cuffs in one hand and pushing gently with the other, propelled her, kicking and yelling, up the aisle toward the door. Thanon followed with the bag.

Back in the manager's office, Harley refastened the handcuffs around the arm of a heavy metal chair and told Miki to sit down. Her face was crimson with rage, her teeth clenched, and she watched Harley through eyes that were struggling not to cry.

"My father will have you killed for this," she said softly, but with more venom than could have been put into a shout.

"Killed?" Harley said with feigned surprise.

"He'll get you fired."

"Oh, fired only. You had me worried for a moment."

He put the suitcase on the desk and extended a hand toward Miki for the key.

She spat on his hand.

Harley wiped his hand on his jeans and asked Thanon if he had a knife. One of his men, who until then had been backed against a wall, pulled a knife from his pocket, opened it, and gave it to Harley. Harley sprung the locks and lifted the top of the suitcase.

We saw white trousers folded trimly next to a red knit sweater. Harley lifted these carefully with both hands and looked underneath. He shook his head, smiled at Miki, and said, "Naughty, naughty."

He took away the layer of clothes. The bag was filled with rubber-banded stacks of five-hundred-baht notes.

Harley put his hands into the suitcase and took out several stacks of bills and examined them. Then he glanced at me, smiled, and winked, and I knew he had found what he wanted— bills whose numbers matched the series on the bills he had photographed in the bedroom. Miki had taken the last payoff directly from Kuk. Harley was about to return these stacks to the bag when he hesitated and put them aside and removed the rest of the money. He riffled through the bills, as if checking the number series, then returned them to the bag.

Harley closed the suitcase and said to Miki, "Is there anything you'd like to tell us?"

In one movement she stood up, gripped the chair arm where the cuffs encircled it, and swung. The chair flew about five feet, pulling her with it, missed Harley, and struck one of Thanon's men on the thigh. He yelled and collapsed, the chair and Miki going down with him. They lay in a heap, the man holding his leg, Miki screaming hysterically.

Harley pulled Miki to her feet, righted the chair, and sat her in it. He unlocked one of the cuffs and reattached it free of the chair.

"I'll meet you at Samak's," he said to Thanon and struggled with Miki out to the parking lot. He put her in the back of the Range Rover and sat beside her. One of Thanon's men drove and I sat next to him. Thanon went ahead in his own car with the suitcases.

When we arrived at the provincial police headquarters, Thanon was already there and the suitcases, still closed, were on the floor of Samak's office.

Harley put Miki in a leather chair.

"Well," Samak said, smiling and cordial, "you make arrest."

"Thanon has himself a good collar, I think," Harley said, cordial right back. "The young lady here appears to be in the export business, not altogether legally, I'm afraid."

Samak looked startled.

"Drugs?"

"Not that bad. Money. But quite a lot."

The room was silent. No one moved. Everyone stared at Harley.

Harley lifted the overnight bag, felt its weight—and panicked. He swung it furiously to the top of Samak's desk and threw back the top. The bag contained white trousers, a red knit sweater, a hairbrush, and a carton of Marlboro cigarettes. Nothing else.

Harley's eyes jumped to Thanon, who stood stony-faced in a shaft of sunlight by the window. Miki, legs crossed, gently kicking her foot, looked at Harley with an arrogant, pitying grin. Samak's smile had not changed.

Harley waited until the flush had left his face and his

breathing was back to normal. Then he shrugged, forced a grin, and flipped the top of the suitcase closed.

"Funny thing," he said. "I could have sworn."

No one else spoke. Harley stood for a moment by the desk, the target of everyone's eyes, then took the handcuff key from his pocket, handed it to Thanon, and walked out.

Not until we had pulled away from the headquarters building and were well out of sight did Harley's grin vanish. He beat his hand on the steering wheel and yelled, "Oh—my *own fucking fault!* I was an asshole. *What* a fucking asshole. I should've made Thanon fight with the cunt and taken the bag myself. What a fucking dumb shit I am!"

I kept my mouth shut and looked straight ahead.

"The payoff money was *there*. The same bills I photographed. I fucking *had* Lichai, and I blew it. That's a deadly mistake in Thailand, Tony, thinking you know what's going on. They turn the page on you and you've got a whole new lesson to learn. Why should Thanon be loyal to me for free when he can be loyal to Samak and make money at it?"

"That's not really loyalty."

"Of course it isn't. That's why Jaran's still a lieutenant. Nonnegotiable loyalty. Very fucking rare."

Harley was driving fast, still pounding the wheel.

"How much will Thanon get?" I asked.

"A fortune—to him it'll be a fortune. Samak'll return the money to Lichai like a hero, and they'll have a drink and a laugh and go for a sail and Lichai'll give him back half. Samak will lie to Thanon and give him a few thousand baht, maybe half a year's salary."

"Samak won't just give it right back to Miki?"

"No way. He'll keep the glory for himself. And the reward. He'll wait till he has a chance to hand it over personally to Lichai."

He drove in silent fury, headed for Songkhla—then suddenly he hit the brake, spun the wheel, and skidded us violently back in the direction of Hatyai.

I peeled myself off the door. "What the hell are you doing?"

"The payoff money was there. But it wasn't *all* there."

I remembered how he had riffled through the bills. "What's that mean?"

We were doing eighty.

"It means we're going to have that party after all."

"Why?"

"Because I'm through fucking around. The time has come to kick ass and take names."

25

HARLEY DROVE to the Paradise and ran inside and told the Mama-san he was having a party.

"Tonight? Why you have party tonight?"

"It's short notice, Mama-san, but you've gotta come."

I think she'd heard of Lowell's party for the ambassador and thought Harley was asking her to that. She was delighted—tall and proud, flourishing her fan, black hair pulled back behind her beaming, mischievous face.

She asked why we'd not been to the Paradise, what we were doing. I asked her if Samak had been back.

"Pig! He rape all my fucking girls and he never pay one shitty baht. I kill that cocksucker some day, I going to tear—"

Harley interrupted. "We'd like to invite some of the girls, too."

She raised a hand and bowed her head. Say no more. It was taken care of.

When we were back on the street, speeding off in the Range Rover, I said, "Give me a clue. Why the party?"

"Stop asking questions. When this party's over, you'll be able to walk Samak on a leash."

I had a flash mental picture of Harley going out on that ledge in New York. If I'd been writing about him then, would I have followed him out? So why was I with him now?

We found Boonchai, the machete man, in his hut by a canal, sitting cross-legged in the door. We approached precariously on narrow rotting duckboards over a swamp of discarded beer cartons, bottles, eggshells, banana peels, chicken bones, and fish heads. Asking directions of naked children who stuck their heads from open doorways, Harley led the way through a maze of thatched and plywood huts. The machete man stood and *wai*ed and backed timidly into his home, inviting us to enter. He must have thought we had come to humiliate him over his failure to protect Tom's family. Harley and I kicked off our sandals at the door (I'd bought a pair from a street vendor in front of the Satellite) and walked in. It was hardly larger than Anuraj's cell at the packing crate whorehouse, but it was clean. A color magazine photograph of Mark Spitz swimming at the '72 Olympics in Munich was tacked up next to a picture of the king and queen. Harley told him why we'd come, but the man did not understand. Harley had to repeat the invitation several times. It was as if some mechanism in the man's brain kept rejecting what it heard as impossible, and looked for other meanings.

When he finally grasped Harley's intent, he accepted with an excited display of appreciation, fingers raised to the top of his head in an extravagant *wai* properly reserved for kings.

"You think he'll come?" I said, back in the Range Rover.

"I don't know. It threw him into shock just being asked."

The horseman was not on the beach, but we found him in his village, his horse wandering among the huts and drying nets. *He* understood Harley's invitation immediately and when we left was already half drunk in anticipation.

At the packing crate whorehouse, Harley invited everyone in sight—the girls, their boyfriends, the old lady who'd come in with the bowl of ice. We went to Nostrand's and asked him and all his tenants. The girls leaped and giggled. They had never before been unpaid guests at a Western party. Anuraj put her arms around our necks, Harley's first, and kissed us.

When we were standing on the veranda getting ready to leave, Harley took Anuraj by the arm and led her back inside. I could tell by the worried look on her face that she had guessed I'd told Harley about her arrival with the corporal.

Later, pulling away in the Range Rover, I said, "Did you ask her about the other night?"

"Yeah."

"And?"

"Let's have a beer first. It's been a shitty day, and we've only got a few hours before the party starts."

We went to the Satellite, and when we had two bottles of

Singha on the table, Harley tilted his chair back, stretched his legs, and gazed up at the smoke-blackened ceiling. Then he fell forward over the table and picked up his beer.

"She's fucking Samak. She says he raped her three days ago when she was grabbed off the street and if she doesn't do what he wants she'll get beat up and sent home. She says Prasong doesn't know—if he knew he'd try to kill Samak. She says you can't stay in town unless you fuck Samak. She doesn't really seem to care that much, except she's afraid for her brother. You love who it's necessary to love. That's what she said."

"She *loves* Samak?"

"I don't think she's as sentimental about that sort of thing as some people."

"I guess she can't afford to be."

"She's not from the States, Tony, she's from Betong. She walked here, she's trying to stay alive. And to keep her brother alive. She says Samak's got so many girls she'll almost never have to see him anyway. Also, she's a Buddhist. She takes what comes, rolls with the punches, hopes for a better life next time around."

"That doesn't sound like her brother."

"Anyway, she swears there's no way Samak could know she and her brother are stooling for me. I hope she's right."

"So you don't think she's doubling on you?"

"No. Knowles told me once, behave as if everyone's doubling on you—half the time it'll be true and the other half it won't hurt to believe it anyway. But Anuraj? No, I don't believe it. Samak would kill her brother. And she loves her brother. I think she'd do anything to get him what he wants."

"Get him to the States."

"Yes."

The chubby little ten-year-old waitress we'd had before came over and asked if we wanted more beer. Harley smiled and said something that sent her away giggling behind her hand. He told me he'd asked her if she wanted to go to a party with him tonight. She returned, still giggling, with two more bottles. Four Thais who had been eating chicken at another table got up and left. In a moment an old man in rags came in from the street, sat down at their table, finished the leftovers, then came to us and held out his hand. Harley gave him some coins and he left.

"Have you said anything to Kessick about the guy with the dagger tattoo?"

"Yeah. I saw him the other night with Sandra. He was pissed off. That really got to me. *He* was pissed off. He said I'd compromised one of his assets. I said, 'Hey, asshole, he tried to beat the shit out of me in Bangkok, and if I ever find out what third-floor motherfucker put him on me I'll kick the shit out of him.' He tried to tell me the guy's a free-lance, does informal little hits for the Thai government. I said, 'Hey, this is one of those informal little hits right here you're talking to. And he's a friend of yours? You're talking for him?' I was so fucking pissed off I almost hit him. He wanted me to believe it wasn't the third floor who told him to rough me around."

"Maybe it wasn't."

"Yeah, maybe. Probably. I'm getting paranoid, Tony. I *know* it had to be Lichai who did that, but——these third-floor secret squirrels, they never go in the street, they don't do their own work, and then they get pissed off when you wrinkle someone's shirt."

We were silent for a minute. I was thinking about the man with the dagger tattoo. Informal little hits. In a way, he and Harley were in the same line of work. A couple of Cains, wanderers and fugitives on the earth. Well, the dagger man had his mark, but what about Harley, what saved him from the slayer's hand?

Finally I said, "A couple of men came to Nostrand's when I was there. I think they'd been hurt."

He didn't seem surprised.

"Probably CTs. He treats their wounded sometimes, then Kessick debriefs him. He's such a straight guy no one seems to mind his keeping friends on both sides. They know exactly where he stands, he doesn't play games, so they don't worry about him. Kessick gets a little Intel and the CTs get medical treatment. You should ask John about it, the CTs."

"Will he tell me anything?"

"I think he might. It's no big secret."

We finished our beer and Harley sat there for a moment, distracted, his mind going back. "Anuraj wasn't lying to *me*, but maybe she was lying to herself. Maybe Samak knows more than she thinks. Do you know what could happen if Samak got pissed off at her, Tony, what the hell that bastard might do?"

He slumped in the chair and looked down at the spittoon near his foot. A wet cigarette butt was stuck to the side and he knocked it loose with his sandal. Then he sat up.

"Well—if we're really going to have a party tonight we'd better lay in some food and booze."

"You're really sure this party's a good idea, Peter?"

"It's *not* a good idea. It's the *only* idea."

26

HARLEY COULDN'T keep himself away from Lowell's party. An hour before his own was to start he parked the Range Rover up the street from the consul's house and watched the guests arrive. The house was large, with a garden in front and a low wooden fence. Two uniformed Thai police patrolled near the fence gate, and a young crew-cut American in civilian clothes, a Marine guard traveling with the ambassador, stood on the corner with his hands behind his back.

"Do we need the windows closed?" I said. "They'll recognize the Range Rover anyway."

"They don't have to know we're inside."

The windows stayed closed, and we sweated. Harley had stopped by the consulate and picked up a black attaché case which now rested, somewhat ominously, on the backseat. When I'd asked him what it contained, he'd said, "You'll find out later."

Lowell and his wife—heavier and older than she looked in the photograph—talked in the garden to several early arrivals. A Thai in a white jacket brought out a silver tray with drinks on it.

"I know you probably think I'm sick for doing this," Harley said, "but I really think there might be something to be gained by seeing who's here and who comes with who."

What surprised me was the number of well-dressed, educated-looking people who poured in through the gate. I had spent so much time in the packing crate whorehouse, the Paradise, and Satellite Café that I had forgotten another class of resident might exist. I saw how different—and how much easier— Lowell's life was than Tom's had been, than any agent's could be. Even a charade of refinement supported by garden-party props helped to conceal the violence of a place like Songkhla, to preserve illusions of gentility shipped in with the American sheets and silver. I understood the hatred between Harley, peering from the darkened windows of the Range Rover, immersed constantly in the filth of Hatyai, and Stephen Lowell, Foreign Service officer, determined to insulate himself from Hatyai and fearing and resenting Harley's threats to penetrate that insulation.

"Look at that," Harley said.

Samak and Kuk had arrived together, Samak with a block of colored decorations above the pocket of his tunic, Kuk in white as we had seen him at the Paradise. He was taller than Samak, a wispy, twiglike man with a round, Eurasian face that seemed the only fully nourished part of his body.

A woman, evidently Samak's wife, stayed one or two paces behind him and slightly to the right. Dressed simply, almost shabbily, in black, she seemed out of place. She was squat, rather dumpy, but wiggled in a pleasant, jolly way as if just tickled from behind. A giggle seemed to be struggling to break through the solemn expression she had adopted for this party. How could a woman like that put up with Samak? Harley should have invited her to his own party.

The three of them entered the gate and immediately fell into conversation with Lowell's wife.

Harley started the Range Rover and put it in gear.

"Well, you can see how exclusive a party that is. Every fucking bum in—"

His hand froze on the gear shift. A black Mercedes sedan had stopped at the gate.

"Can you fucking *believe* that?"

Miki stepped out of the Mercedes, its door held by the chauffeur. She stood on the sidewalk and waited while a man emerged from the other side and walked around to join her. The man was warily eyeing the Range Rover.

"Is that her father?" I said. The Range Rover was suddenly hotter than ever.

Harley spoke without moving his lips—*Lichai!*—the word no louder than a breath.

We watched the two cross the sidewalk, Lichai a smallish man, well filled out, his beige linen jacket following perfectly every movement of his body. I reached for a pen, but could not take my eyes off him long enough to make notes.

At the gate Lichai turned again toward the Range Rover and hesitated, staring straight at us as if he could see right through the tinted glass.

Harley stared back and whispered, *"Yes, you fucker. Here I am."*

Lichai's face looked as I had expected Samak's to look— flat-nosed, heavy, cruel. The skin was dark brown and creased, like a sheet of copper foil wadded into a ball. He continued to stare at the Range Rover.

Lowell's wife spotted Lichai and his daughter through the gate, and hurried to greet them. Lichai turned from us and shook hands with his hostess. He did not smile. She led him and Miki toward the center of the garden. They passed Samak and Kuk, and Lichai stopped to say hello. The three men *wai*ed each other and spoke. Then Lichai saw Samak's wife. He took a deep breath through his nose, as if clearing his sinuses, and, with his face still contorted by that effort, looked contemptuously at the woman. For a moment I thought he was going to spit on her. She took a step forward and her hands came up to *wai* him. Lichai turned from her, spat on the lawn, and spoke to Samak. Samak looked as if he knew what was coming. I think perhaps he had been warned before about presenting his wife in polite society. Lichai may have considered it a loss of face to be in the same room with her. For just an instant a protest flickered in Samak's eyes, and then he took his wife by the arm and led her out to the street. He put her in the back of the car they had come in with Kuk and returned to the party, a broad smile of shame and embarrassment covering his face.

"Oh," Harley said, softly as if in prayer, "to walk in there right now and put the cuffs on Lichai and haul him out in front of Lowell and the ambassador and take him back to Bangkok on the five o'clock plane and toss him in Klong Prem and keep right on going to New York. That's what heaven is, Tony."

He turned the wheel and pulled out from the curb. As we passed the crew-cut American guard on the corner, I recognized him as the Marine sergeant who'd sat at our table in Bangkok. Harley waved at him, despite the dark glass, and we drove in silence to Tom's house.

27

THE HORSEMAN came on his horse, the girls came in evening gowns, and the machete man taught the Mama-san how to kill snakes. Everyone got drunk.

Nostrand brought his Sony and waltzed with the Mama-san. They held each other at arm's length, spinning, dipping, flying around the room, laughing their heads off, breezing past the girls and boyfriends who watched from the edges, amazed by the sight of it. Everyone took turns falling off the horse. Anuraj went up on one side, came down on the other, then gathered her yellow dress around her tiny waist and approached the problem seriously. The horseman held her hand and the horse's mane and ran alongside, encouraging both. When everyone had had a ride—including of course the Mama-san, whose skirts-over-ass header provided, I am willing to bet, one of the most joyous moments yet in the lives of her flabbergasted subjects—the old man tried to lead the horse inside, was discouraged by Nostrand, and instead brought out two cases of Singha, which he shared with his mount the rest of the evening.

Remembering that Anuraj had said her first ride in the Range Rover was only the third time she'd ever been in a car, Harley asked around and found three girls and a boy who had *never* ridden in a car. He packed them into the Range Rover, along with quite a few others, and raced them out the rutted path from the house to the main road. He was gone for ten minutes, then reappeared at the main road, put the car in four-wheel drive and came tearing back across the open field. When they pulled up behind the house and got out, Harley's passengers pushed around him, shaking his hand. He was laughing, joking, patting them on the shoulders—apparently happier than any of them.

Harley walked over and stood next to me on the back porch.

"They really *loved* that," he said.

"I know," I said. "I know they did."

"Can you imagine that? Thirteen, fourteen years old and never rode in a car? One of them asked me how long it would take to drive to New York. I told her about a week and she said, 'Let's *go!*' She was ready, man. I had to tell her you can't drive to New York. She'd always thought you could drive anywhere. There's roads all over the place, right?"

Anuraj came rushing out of the house, begging Harley to take her for a ride on a friend's motorcycle. She had her own bicycle, or rather shared one with Prasong, and the idea of a motorcycle excited her. It was an enormous 1000 cc Honda Gold Wing, fire-engine red. The boy had been trying for an hour to get her on it. She had refused at first, frightened by the machine's size and explosiveness, but finally promised to go on it if Harley took her. The boy was with her now, encouraging Harley, pushing the keys at him, believing that if Harley once got her on the machine she would stop refusing to ride with him.

"Look at that monster," Harley said, "wouldn't you love to have something like that?"

I said, "Where do you think he got it? It's got Malaysian plates."

"He probably stole it. Or he's doing something wrong for somebody."

Harley let them talk him into it, and climbed aboard. Anuraj looked at the immense forbidding mass of steel, chrome, and machinery with far more apprehension than she had displayed toward the horse. I could see that she was genuinely scared, and I felt sorry for her. Everyone was watching.

She gathered up her dress, and the bike's owner stepped forward to help her. She pushed him away, lifted her leg, and jumped on. She placed her hands lightly on Harley's back, but when he pressed the starter and the machine roared, her arms shot around his waist in a death grip. Harley let the bike idle for a moment and asked Anuraj if she was all right. Her mouth smiled, but the eyes stayed scared. Harley let the clutch out and rolled the bike slowly forward, moving it in a tight arc around the backyard. After the third slow circle, her frightened eyes and smiling mouth gave her the look of a child at a horror show, happily scared out of her wits.

When Harley stopped the machine after the fourth circle, she leaped off quickly and refused to get back on. It was as if 'Well, I've *done* it, and that's that.' No one, not Harley or the owner or the Mama-san or Prasong or any of her friends, could get her near the bike again.

"What'd I do wrong?" Harley asked me. "She's scared shitless of that thing."

"She's just embarrassed by the spectators," I said. "A little proper coaxing and less of an audience, she'd learn to love it."

Later in the evening when it was almost dark, Anuraj and Prasong, holding hands, danced and sang a folk song from their native Betong. After they had finished, I took Anuraj and led her outside to cool off. I wanted to do some work before beer and Mekhong put everything out of hand.

"Are you looking forward to going to the States?" I said.

"No. Prasong want to go but not me. I go if he want me, but—" She shrugged and made a face. "I rather stay here."

"Why?"

"I like it here. States too far. I get scared in States. It dangerous in States."

"Not always."

"I not need all these things they got. Prasong go to movies all time, say, 'I see this, I see this, I see this.' It good he go to States, get education, get rich, be happy . . ."

"But you're already happy."

"I very happy. Why not?"

Nostrand appeared, panting and sweating. "Look out for her, Tony, she's one of mine."

"How's it going in there?"

"Harley ought to do this all the time. I'm exhausted." He wiped his face with a handkerchief. "That woman's really got a filthy mouth, you know that?"

Anuraj, who had been regarding Nostrand with something like reverence, smiled delightedly at this bit of grown-up gossip about her boss.

"Did you tell her you're a missionary?" I asked.

"She already knew. I think that's why she talked so dirty."

"She talks like that to everyone. I think it's her only English vocabulary. Why don't you try her in Thai?"

"Maybe I will."

Harley waved to Anuraj from the house and she left us to go inside and dance.

"Peter's very discreet sometimes," Nostrand said, watching Anuraj leave. "He told me you might be interested in hearing about the CTs. I'm sorry you had such an unpleasant night's sleep."

took off, leaving behind a fleet of bicycles, several motorcycles, and one drunken horse tied to a tree.

I sat in the front next to Harley, a girl on the floor under my feet, two more on my lap, and assorted arms and legs of both sexes draped around and over my head. Harley was angry. I didn't know why he was so upset at having other people along, but the look on his face kept me from asking questions.

"You back there, too, John?" Harley yelled.

"I'm here," Nostrand called. "I can't move, but I'm here."

We got out in front of the Paradise and the Mama-san met us, silencing gigglers in the group, shushing everyone. She herded us into the lounge, darker than ever now that there was no light even in the glassed display room.

Everyone sat around on the floor, bumping knees, whispering, wondering what all the silence and mystery were about. Harley had the black attaché case with him.

I saw Anuraj and Prasong, obviously sober, sitting next to each other, holding hands. As I watched them they pushed closer together, and Anuraj, hunching her bony shoulders, gripped Prasong's hand in both of her own. She looked up at him and he gave her a quick smile of reassurance. I imagined them on their flight from Betong, walking at night, sleeping in the jungle, hiding out from the CTs and bandits.

After several minutes we heard a door slam and the whole room went silent. For perhaps thirty seconds there was not a sound, and then a sharp angry cry, as if someone had stumbled in the dark, shot from the display room. The voice was Samak's. Next we heard female cries and giggles, Samak's laughter, another door slamming, more giggles, and loud whispers.

For what was probably three or four minutes but seemed like a week, we sat there listening to the giggles on the other side of the glass. Then with a suddenness that blinded and startled me, the lights went on in the display room. In the middle of the room, sprawled on one of the red-carpeted steps, Samak and two girls—the sisters I'd just seen dancing, whom Nostrand had said Samak wanted so badly—lay in their underwear, tangled in each other's arms and legs. The girls leaped to their feet, grabbed armfuls of clothes, and scrambled for the door at the front of the room. Before Samak

closed and locked.

Samak jumped up. Orange and white tiger-striped jockey shorts were pulled down around his thighs, his erection aimed out over the top like a toy cannon. He took an abrupt step forward, still blinded by the blazing light, his cannon melting rapidly, the confusion on his face changing to rage. Suddenly he grabbed for those shorts—then hesitated. Which made him more ridiculous, his nudity or those jungle-beast shorts? He yanked them off and crumpled them furiously in his fist. That left him completely naked except for brown shoes and white ankle socks.

The audience of girls and boyfriends, after a moment of shock, exploded in laughter. When I realized that Samak, facing us on the other side of the glass, was looking at himself in a mirror, was seeing his own tiny spindly body planted in those shoes and socks, was hearing the muffled laughter, recognizing himself as a clown, I fell sideways with laughter, blinded by tears now instead of light.

When I looked again, Samak was at the door, pounding and kicking. It held fast, and he turned again toward the mirror and the laughter. He looked around desperately, cornered. He pounded on the glass, the laughter rose to thunder, and he turned and ran up the carpeted steps to the back of the room. He looked left and right, and finally sat down, knees together, arms crossed, and remained still and angry, a caged bundle of rage with nowhere to run to, no place to hide, no one to turn to for help.

I looked around for Harley and spotted him standing in the dark at the back of the room next to the open attaché case. He was holding a camera with a telephoto lens and was taking pictures through the glass.

I turned back to the display room. Samak had decided not to move, to do nothing now that might increase the pleasure of his invisible audience.

The laughter began to subside. After several minutes, when it became clear that the best was over, that Samak was not going to move, Mama-san stood up near me and went to the bar. She broke out a case of beer, opened the bottles, and handed them around.

The girls and boyfriends began to drink and talk and everyone repeated to each other his favorite part of the performance. It was all in Thai, but I had no trouble interpreting the

looks and gestures. "Did you see that tiny little hard-on, the way it just went—boomp?" Renewed laughter. "And the way he banged on the door—banging and banging . . ." Still more laughter, but silly now, and less and less spontaneous. I twisted around and saw Anuraj and Prasong behind me, exhausted with laughter, cheeks streaked with tears. She was clutching his arm, her face flushed.

Ten minutes and another few cases of beer later, with Samak still stationary on the top step, an impotent statue of resignation promising no further merriment, the girls and boyfriends turned to each other, and before I knew it they were pairing off, moving to the corners and sides, wiggling into each other's arms, peeling off each other's clothes. I saw the horseman stretched out along a wall, sound asleep behind a reef of empty beer bottles. I searched for Nostrand, but he wasn't there. I wondered how early he had left, and recognized in myself a faint uneasiness, something like guilt.

I stood up and walked back to where Harley was standing. He had returned the camera to its case. I was relieved to know finally what his plan had been. It had happened, and so far no one was hurt.

"That must be the worst fucking thing in the world," he said. "I'd rather get shot in the gut than have that happen to me."

The Mama-san came over, covered with smiles. "I *get* him," she said, snapping her fingers. "For two years I tell myself, I get that little no-cock son bitch. Now I *got* him."

Harley said, "It might've been better, Mama-san, if it'd just been us here. You didn't have to bring the whole crowd."

"Why not? They have good time, have good joke. Everyone laugh good."

"That's fine, but what's he going to do tomorrow?"

"He no do nothing. He hear laughing but he not see who here. Anyway, tomorrow he just hide. I not worry about tomorrow. He don't dare come out now for long time. Everyone laugh at him. Everyone in Hatyai going to know about this."

"But he'll do something someday," I said.

She shrugged. "Sisters in Bangkok. They go tomorrow. He not hurt them. Not hurt me either. Mama-san got one or two friends."

The party was turning into an orgy. The floor was covered with naked squirming bodies.

"Let's split," Harley said to me. Then, to the Mama-san: "What are you going to do?"

"I get everybody out, then I unlock door and turn off lights and go home and Samak, after a while he try door again and come out. Tomorrow we all come back to work like nothing happen."

We said good-bye and got in the Range Rover and drove back to the hotel. On the way Harley said, "Well, you can't control everything, can you, Tony. But I really wish she hadn't brought in all those other people."

"What really happened? One of the sisters called Samak . . ."

"Right. She told him she and her sister had seen him, heard about him from the other girls, hot for his body. But they were leaving tomorrow, so it had to be now, at the Paradise, they had a key. He fell for it. He thinks he's irresistible. Also, I guess he was pretty loaded on Lowell's scotch."

"Samak seemed to take it pretty stoically, at the end, I mean."

"Yeah, but it's hard for us to realize what it meant to him. Losing face in private before one other man would be painful to any Asian. But losing it in public, at the hands of a couple of girls, witnessed by a crowd of laughing people, and the way he lost it, naked, and not just an Asian, but Samak, an arrogant cop bastard like that—I don't think any American could possibly understand what happened to him tonight. From now on he'll live for revenge. We've got to get this thing over with, Tony. Get Lichai and get out."

I said, "What do you think he'll do? Samak, I mean."

"I don't know. But I hope we're not around. And I hope Anuraj and Prasong aren't around. I wanted to go over with just the sisters and the Mama-san. I'd figured I'd have to get her in a pretty jolly, juiced-up mood to make her do it, but I was wrong. She went for it strong. All those other people. That was . . . It upset me, Tony. I looked around at that room full of kids laughing their heads off at Samak, and what I saw was another school bus full of children."

I didn't know how to respond to that. When we were almost back to the hotel I said, "What are you going to do with the pictures?"

"You probably think I'm some kind of creep, right? Taking pictures like that? You hear about intelligence agents getting people into situations and taking pictures and black-mailing them.''

"In Samak's case I don't see anything wrong with it. What are you going to do now?''

"I'll drop the film off with Kessick in the morning.''

"And then?''

"His wife'll develop it. She does all his technical work.''

"I mean—''

"Then I'll hit Samak.''

29

SAMAK'S OFFICE, large but simple, had only two personal touches. One was the head of a wild boar, three-inch tusks thrusting ferociously from a long, twisted snout. I decided to ignore it and deny Samak the satisfaction of telling me he shot it himself. The head was mounted on a wall above the other item of interest, an immense teak desk, the largest desk I had seen outside Hollywood. When Harley and I entered, Samak was seated behind this expanse, almost out of sight, his head and neck sticking up like a jack-in-the-box.

"You very nice come,'' he said, waving us into a pair of black leather chairs, nothing in his tone suggesting the humiliation he had suffered the night before. "Happy accept invitation.'' That threw me for a moment, until I remembered his invitation to me the night of our dinner. He thought this was a social call.

"You like Hatyai?'' he said, looking from me to Harley and back again. The broken English seemed out of place with his studied, meticulously achieved refinement, as if everything had been possible but the learning of a language.

"Very much,'' I said. "The country is beautiful.''

The heavy gold *prahs* he had displayed at dinner formed lumps beneath his freshly pressed khaki shirt.

"Any time you want see something, I give you man. Not good go alone."

His eyes fixed on the brown manila envelope in Harley's lap.

"You want anything," he said to Harley, "you tell me. Want to hunt, sail boat, I fix. Many important friends."

He couldn't take his eyes from the envelope. I think it was dawning then on Samak that Harley would not have brought that envelope along unless it contained something he intended to discuss. So this was not a social call after all.

"I'll do that," Harley said, crossing his legs and letting the envelope balance on one knee.

Samak was thinking fast. His hand went to his shirt front and he began to fidget nervously through the cloth with the *prahs*.

"Sorry about the mix-up yesterday with the suitcase," Harley said. "I didn't mean to waste your time."

"Oh, that all right, I . . ."

He stood abruptly and hurried around from behind his desk, as if in response to a sudden decision.

"You like I show you office? You like see?"

Before we could answer he was out the door, waving to us to follow. Three enlisted men leaped from their desks and *wai*ed us. "Very fine men," Samak called back, and led the way upstairs to a barracks. I don't know if the performance we were about to witness was some kind of impromptu defense against the threat of that envelope, or if it was a bit of routine intimidation planned since the no-hands dinner. In any case, he showed us the barracks, then took us back downstairs to the entrance of the building, past a sergeant at a desk, and into the cells, which I realized at that moment were what he had really wanted us to see.

There were two. One was a large barred chamber with a concrete floor and a raised center platform of wood on which three men reclined on straw mats. The other, much smaller, had a wooden door with a barred window. Samak looked through the window, then called to the sergeant. The sergeant unlocked the door and opened it. The cell was about six feet square and contained no windows or furniture or mats or anything at all, except an emaciated naked man.

The sergeant yelled at the man, who looked about fifty years old. He struggled slowly to his feet, frightened and in pain. Samak pushed the sergeant aside and spoke to the man softly. The man then came out of the cell, walking slowly with a crablike sidling motion.

Samak put his hand lightly on the man's shoulder and gently turned him around. Wide, heavy scars cut across the man's buttocks.

"Cane," Samak said. "He not walk good now."

He asked the man a question and said to us, "Happen ten years before. He still no walk good." He spoke again to the man. "Kuala Lumpur they do it. He rob store. Six stroke."

He looked at us with his slender, sharp features, his black moist eyes. "Very tough. Look—"

A wooden waist-high table and chair were set behind us against the wall. We moved aside and Samak brought the table to the center of the narrow corridor. The three prisoners in the larger cell had come to the bars to stare at the naked crippled man, who himself gazed absently at the dusty gray floor, revealing no interest in anything.

"I show you," Samak said and took the man by the arm. He led him to the edge of the table—slowly, gently, not hurrying. Then he put his hand on the back of the prisoner's neck, pushed lightly, and bent him forward over the top of the table. The man's body tensed suddenly and he let out a deep-chested groan. The other prisoners moved closer to the bars and watched with fascination, it not yet having occurred to them to be afraid.

I do not know if the man groaned because of the pain of bending or because the position recalled the experience that had crippled him. Whatever their cause, the groans, though they diminished, did not stop. Samak appeared deaf to them. Pushing the man's chest down flat on the table, he reached down and took hold of his legs. He did this tenderly, as if not wishing to cause the man unnecessary discomfort. Samak raised the legs to table level, then pivoted the man—moaning all this time—so that his body from neck to knees was stretched across the top of the table.

Then he turned to us.

"You see," he said, "put man on table. Guards hold legs. Other guards hold arms. Hit with cane. Cane very hard, one inch thick. Soak in oil two days."

The prisoner's groans had slackened now to whimpers. Samak left him on the table and backed up several paces toward a garbage can in a corner of the corridor next to the sergeant's office. A broom rested against the wall. When I saw the broom I was frightened.

"Man with cane," Samak went on, watching me closely, "take three step. Not allow take more. He trained. Caning very difficult art."

He picked up the broom and held it in both hands. The sleeves of his khaki shirt had sharp creases. He raised the broom above his head.

The three prisoners watched spellbound, eyes wide. Even the sergeant, who had withdrawn some steps to the door of his office, appeared ready to turn and run.

Samak crouched—and sprang. He took three leaping steps toward the naked man on the table, swung the broom in a wide arc above his head, and brought it down hard, stopping just six inches above the man's buttocks. He froze in that position, his face rigid with emotion. The naked man was sobbing with fear and the other three prisoners had scrambled away from the bars to a far corner of their cell.

After about four seconds, Samak dropped his arms, exhaled loudly, and looked at Harley.

"Always have doctor," he said. "Give one blow, doctor look. Unconscious, not go on. Man go hospital. When okay, give next stroke. Very tough punishment. Very cruel."

Holding the man's legs, Samak tenderly helped him from the table and walked with him to the cell. He had never been the least bit harsh in his physical contact with the prisoner; he had appeared solicitous of the man's physical comfort, and utterly indifferent to his terror.

Samak, Harley, and I walked outside into the sunny, well-tended yard surrounded by a barbed-wire fence hidden among banana trees and flowering shrubs. I tripped on a large stone dislodged from the border of the path, and Samak took my arm to steady me. His touch, as gentle as it had been on the legs of the prisoner, made me recoil. Everything he had wanted me to know and feel about his power and capacity for cruelty was transmitted in that instant of contact between his fingers and my arm. Suddenly I did not want him to think I had anything to do with the contents of Harley's envelope.

Samak walked us to the Range Rover and shook my hand, no doubt delighting to find it limp. He smiled, his black eyes in the bright sunlight more moist than ever.

"Thank you to come," he said.

"Yes," I said weakly, "thank you." I was thinking about that crippled prisoner.

He shook hands with Harley. "Good see you."

"Thanks," Harley said, his face blank. He opened the driver's door and put one foot into the car. I thought, with relief, that he had decided to delay, for the moment at least, showing the pictures to Samak. Then Harley pulled his foot back and turned and faced Samak. He was smiling.

"I almost forgot," he said, but with such vengeful delight that you knew it was a lie. He had forgotten nothing. He opened the flap of the envelope, slipped out one photograph, and held it two inches in front of Samak's nose.

Samak had to pull back to focus on the picture. Harley continued to hold it, giving Samak as long a look as he wanted. Samak's jaw muscles tightened and his lips set in a thin hard line. When his eyes left the picture, and looked over at the building, Harley said, "I have others."

Samak stared at the building, silent.

Harley put his hand into the envelope and began to draw out another photograph.

"What you want?" Samak said, his voice brittle with anger.

"I want the money back in the bank where it belongs."

"What money?" His eyes had not left the building.

Harley withdrew the second photograph and held it in front of Samak's face. Samak knocked the picture from Harley's hand.

"When?"

"Right now. We'll give you a lift."

Samak started for the building.

"Colonel . . ."

Samak turned.

"You want to leave that there?"

Samak bent down and picked up the picture and took it with him into the building. In about three minutes he was back with a canvas duffel bag. We drove him to the bank, and when the money had been deposited, Samak left.

Harley, working under the eyes of the bank manager, Kessick's asset, photographed the bills. He did so swiftly with no show of emotion.

When he had finished he walked out and got back in the Range Rover.

"Now Kuk," Harley said.

30

"YOU SURE he's coming?" I said.

"He'll come."

It was ten hours after our visit to Samak's office and we were at a table by the hotel pool, eating curried shrimp and fried vegetable patties picked from a buffet table. The photographs Harley had taken at the bank, developed now, were in an envelope next to his plate.

"Kessick says he's been here every Saturday night for the past six months. Everyone comes to this thing."

Harley picked at his shrimp.

"Dogs and cripples," he said. "Proxy victims. See why I'm so worried about my stools? Samak can do anything he wants in that building. Throw someone in a cell and tell the other prisoners what he wants done. Come back in an hour and there's nothing left but a bloody lump."

Around us I recognized many of the faces I had seen entering Lowell's party. Up the beach a group of local Thais sat around a bonfire chanting atonal, discordant folk songs. The moon was full and bright, casting a straight white ribbon across the dark waters of the gulf.

After a pause Harley said, "There's Kessick."

The tall, lanky man I'd seen in the parking lot was picking up plates at the beginning of the buffet table and passing them back to his wife and three children. They were an attractive family, the wife pretty and well dressed, but solemn. The children followed along quietly and unsmiling, as if recently punished. When they had reached the end of the line, their plates full, Kessick looked around at the tables. Finally, with I thought just the smallest expression of disappointment from his wife, he turned and led them back inside to the deserted dining room.

"Poor bastard," Harley said. "He looked around and saw

you and me and probably a few local assets and figured it was safer inside.''

"You mean he can't even go out to dinner?''

"He's afraid someone might come up and talk to him and then someone else will see it and say, 'Hey, he knows that guy, how does he know that guy, is he an asset?' You're writing something, so maybe you go up and talk to him, or maybe I introduce you, and then he has to go in tomorrow and write a report. Every time he talks to someone in public he has to write it up. It's easier and safer to eat inside. I'm surprised he even came in the first place.''

"Maybe his wife likes it. I suppose he can't keep them locked in a cave.''

"She goes out with the kids. You see them in town. I was with Kessick in Hatyai once and Nancy and the kids walked right by us on the street. He didn't bat an eye. No one recognized anyone. Even the kids acted like they didn't know him. Well trained. He's afraid if people know who his family is they might hurt them. If you thought Tom had an arsenal over there, you ought to see Kessick's house. He's ready to fight a fucking war. His oldest kid, a girl, eight years old, could kill you with her hands.''

"Not really.''

"Yeah, she could. I'm not kidding. She's fluent in Thai, knows how to handle all his weapons. He told me he wants to send her back to the States, all the kids. He says she'll be an old lady by the time she's twelve.''

Harley's eyes fixed on someone coming up behind me. Then I heard Lowell's mock-friendly voice, trying hard to conceal anger and resentment. "How's the food?''

"Delicious, Stephen,'' Harley said. "Like to join us?''

"No, thanks, we already have a table. How's the article?''

"Fine, thanks,'' I said.

He stood for a moment, afraid to speak.

"You seem to have something on your mind,'' Harley said.

"The ambassador's not too happy with you.''

"The ambassador isn't or you aren't?''

"Well, I'm not too happy either. That was a—that was a damned stupid thing you pulled last night.''

"What thing is that? I have trouble keeping track.''

"Your party, inviting all those people to embarrass the ambassador.''

"Come on, Stephen, if he wasn't embarrassed by the people you invited I don't know why he should care about my party."

"He took it very badly."

"Stephen, your inability to lie well is very annoying. I hear Samak is out to get you. Did you know that? I was going to warn you. Someone used your party as an opportunity to set him up for something."

"Don't try to bullshit me, Harley. I'm not stupid, whatever you think."

"Seriously. He did leave early, didn't he? Someone suckered him out and set him up. I hear he's out for your guts."

"Set him up for what?"

"I don't know. I was going to ask you. You weren't involved in any way?"

"You're full of shit, Harley."

He left us and walked to the buffet table.

Harley was grinning. "You know, maybe Samak really *will* connect him with it in some way."

"That would be terrible," I said.

"There's Kuk," Harley said.

"And—"

I didn't finish the sentence. Harley had looked quickly away, and now slowly returned his gaze to Kuk and the two men who stood with him around a table. One of them, dressed in brown trousers and a black sport shirt, was the man with the dagger tattoo. He looked toward us, then maneuvered around his own table until he had his back to Harley. The three men sat down and ordered drinks. Kuk was wearing a white suit and a vest, the only vest I had seen in Thailand.

"Isn't that *interesting*?" Harley said.

He watched the table out of the corner of his eye. Kuk was doing all the talking.

"Did Kessick say he would be here?" I asked.

"No. I have an idea he'd not working for Kessick right now. Tonight he's working for Kuk."

"So what do you think Kuk's up to?"

"I don't know. Some kind of fucked-up deal that'll get someone hurt. Kessick calls him Sadim, Midas spelled backwards. Everything he touches turns to shit."

"Kessick knows a lot about him?"

"Yeah. Kessick sits on his ass over there in the consulate but he gets good stuff."

"How can he meet people if he never goes out? Does he have a safehouse where he sees them?"

I hated to ask questions about Kessick because I felt it was putting Harley on the spot.

"No. A safehouse is only safe until you take someone there. It's better to use hotels. He says Kuk's problem is that he's stupid and doesn't know it. He keeps having delusions of grandeur. He opened up an Italian restaurant in Hatyai and bragged about the fortune he was making. Then someone caught the Chinese cook making veal scallopini with dog meat, and the restaurant folded. Not even Thais like dog scallopini. So he sold the place and took the money and went to Italy. His father had been an Italian married to a Singaporean. About a year later he was back in Hatyai telling everyone how the Mafia wanted him to set up an Asian connection for heroin. He was going around like a big man, trying to get money, talking about all his Mafia friends, dropping little threats on a lot of businessmen and showing off to the girls. Then one day a couple of three-hundred-percent guineas showed up, dark suits and thirty-inch necks, and Kuk took a fast walk. No one saw him for six months. When he showed up again he was at the Crown."

"As manager?"

"Yeah."

"So Lichai has some Mafia connection?"

"No, not at all. Lichai doesn't need the Mafia. He wanted someone to look after things in town and he knew a guy like Kuk would be easy to control. Dumb and no balls. He wants to be taken seriously, probably all he ever wanted, so Lichai lets him think he's hot shit, keeps him scared, and knocks him around every once in a while. Knocks him around in private, of course—lets him give the world whatever front he wants, but in private Lichai makes sure he knows who the boss is."

"Who's the guy he's with now, other than the dagger?"

"I don't know. Probably a rubber merchant and he's buying him dinner so everyone will see him and think he's got some big deal going down. What kind of asshole would wear a vest in this weather?"

Something made me look over at the door by the buffet table. Samak had just walked through it and was picking up a plate. He filled the plate with food and went straight to Kuk's table. He sat down and Kuk leaned toward him and began to speak. Samak listened for a moment, answered briefly, then sat quietly while the other men spoke.

Harley stopped eating. He stared openly at Kuk and the other men, his eyes as intense as they had been in Jaran's office questioning the stool. He said, "For a bug under that table I would give one year of my life."

31

"**H**ERE'S YOUR big chance, Kuk. Grab it, man. Be the big man you always knew you were destined to be— the biggest thing in dope, they'll make a movie about you, the Asian connection."

Harley had a threat in one hand and charm in the other, beating Kuk back and forth with both. We had followed him back from dinner to the Crown Hotel and he was sitting now in an office next to his bedroom, wearing black silk pajamas and staring at a pile of photographs scattered across his desk. Taken by surprise, scared and confused, Kuk looked like a man who'd just been told he had terminal cancer. Ten minutes ago everything was bright and happy, and now stone walls were cutting out the light.

"You *see* the pictures, man," Harley said, pointing with his finger, running through it again. "*Those* are the bills you got for the dope and *those* are the bills you gave to Miki before she went to the airport. The *problem* is that there's 100,000 baht missing. You were *skimming*, man. What's Lichai gonna say when he sees these photographs?"

Kuk stared, sweat trickling from his sideburns.

"He's gonna kill you, man. Right? You *know* that. I'm here to help you stay alive."

Kuk looked from one set of pictures to the other, trying hard to make them go away.

"It's not as bad as it looks, Kuk," Harley went on,

cheerful and reassuring as a doctor promising two more years of life despite those horrifying X-rays.

"You'll be the General Motors of dope," Harley said. "Why be Lichai's flunky when you can get rid of him, take over yourself?"

"I can't hurt Lichai," Kuk said miserably. "He helped me too much."

"I know. Been like a father to you."

"He saved my life," Kuk said, wanting to challenge the sarcasm, his eyes straining to squeeze one last drop of sincerity from a supply long since exhausted.

"So why do you steal from him?"

"You don't know my problems. You don't know what my life is like here."

"I'm sure it's hell, Kuk. So why feel any loyalty to Lichai? He's been using you. He gets all the money and you have to steal. I don't *blame* you for stealing from him, like it's really your money anyway, isn't it. You're just getting what's yours."

"You know how hard I worked for this? To be manager of this place? To make a few baht out of this hotel?"

"I know you worked like hell for it, Kuk, but that's not the point. The point is that it's over now. Lichai won't fire you when he sees these pictures. He'll kill you. What we're talking about now is your life. I'm offering you a chance to stay alive, Kuk, and to have a better life than this thieving hole you've got yourself stuck in now. You could really be a big man, Kuk. And it's the only chance you've got. Frankly, I can't see why it's taking you all this time to make up your mind."

I remembered what Harley had said of Kuk—was it his own insight or had it come from Kessick's file?—that he wanted simply to be taken seriously, to have someone else believe in his ambition as he did. Kuk must have spent a lot of time trying to convince himself that the people who used him were telling the truth, that they really did believe in him and were on his side. This time Kuk found the choice an easy one. If he refused Harley, and the pictures got to Lichai, Lichai would surely kill him, immediately and without difficulty or even much reflection. If he went along with Harley, Lichai would probably still find a way to kill him. Lichai would be very busy for a while, scrambling to defend himself, but in the end he'd almost certainly have him killed. So it was a choice of certain death now or probable death later.

"If I do what you want," Kuk said, "and maybe I can get some of Lichai's operation, how long will I keep it? The Americans will come after me, the way you did Lichai."

"That's a whole different problem," Harley said, dismissing it with a wave of the hand. "That's for the *future*, not to worry about now. Worry about today's problem today, Kuk. You do this now, you'll be a winner, you'll be on top. And what do you care what happens after that? What more can any man ask than to win for a while?"

Kuk shook his head despairingly.

"Life is roles, Kuk. You've got to decide who you are and play that role and after a while if you play it long enough and good enough you *become* that role. You understand? Lichai was a cheap Chinaman with nothing until he started acting big, started dreaming, Kuk, playing like a big man, and now he *is* a big man. You see that?"

Harley himself didn't believe a word of it, of course. He was talking to Kuk the way others talked to him—offering images, visions, making magic. Kuk picked up the pictures and examined them slowly one by one. Then he dropped them back on the desk.

"What can I do?"

"It's easy, Kuk. You hardly have to do anything at all. It'll be painless, completely painless."

32

HARLEY STAYED at the Crown talking to Kuk for another half hour, and by the time we got back to our own rooms at the Sawadi it was two in the morning. He put in a call to Jaran at home in Bangkok. It took forty minutes for the call to come through, and when it did the connection kept breaking. Finally Harley managed to get it across to Jaran that he wanted him to come to Songkhla in the morning. He refused to tell him on the phone exactly why, only that since the Miki disaster there were no local police he could trust and that he needed Jaran for what was to be a final all-or-nothing assault on Lichai.

"This is it, Jaran. Now or never. I need you."

Jaran agreed to come, but it took some talking. I think he might have sensed in Harley's tone an unhealthy desperation, as if Harley were pushing something along faster than it wanted to go. When he did finally say yes, I had the impression it was more to protect Harley than to get Lichai. And he refused to come before Monday. Harley argued, yelling into the phone, but then the connection broke for the third time and he hung up.

"He says he's got a case going down this morning and his kid's got mumps. He can't come till Monday. So how do I keep everyone alive till Monday?"

Later that morning, Sunday, we drove to the Paradise and found Samak's corporal parked in front with the dagger man in the seat beside him. I was half afraid Harley would pull them both out into the street right then and there. He put the Range Rover out of sight behind the building and we went inside.

"You here very early," Mama-san said.

"Nothing else to do today, Mama-san. Thought we'd hang out with you for a while."

"You not have to come look out for Mama-san," she said. "That car out there don't worry me none."

"Doesn't worry us either, Mama-san. You got any beer this early?"

The day before Miki was arrested at the airport, and on one or two other occasions, Harley and I had spent a little time at the Paradise, chatting with the Mama-san, eating fried shrimp, drinking beer, running upstairs with the girls. I had been celibate since my wife's death, but I knew I couldn't stay that way forever. When I was sixteen I lost my virginity honestly to a whore, and at the Paradise, feeling the same desire and guilt, I lost it again the same way.

The rooms at the Paradise were small—bathtub, bed, mirror on the ceiling, a telephone for ordering drinks. The tubs contained hairs from previous customers, and the massages were as violent and haphazard as a mugging. You learned to skip the preliminaries.

Two or three of the girls were older than the others, not so pretty, and judging by the piles of knitting at their feet, not so popular either. Harley had insisted on paying as much attention to these girls as to the more desirable ones, out of a sense of social justice, he claimed, but more likely in support of his determination to prove that nothing in Hatyai could exceed his endurance.

Today Anuraj cornered me at a table while Harley was busy watching the street through the window curtains. There was no shyness now, no drawing hearts on the sides of Range Rovers. She came right out with it.

"Why you and Peter no make love with me ever?"

"I don't know, Anuraj. Maybe Peter thinks . . . I don't know."

She had included me in her question only to avoid hurting my feelings.

"Other girls all have Peter, they all say he my friend, why he doesn't take me."

"You're very pretty, Anuraj. You're the prettiest girl here. But you're very young, too, and Peter likes you. He's thirty-two years old. You're only thirteen."

"Other men not think I too young."

"Maybe they don't care about you."

"They care enough make love."

She spotted Harley coming toward the table and got up and ran.

At about eleven o'clock Harley was back at the front curtains, keeping watch on the street, when he pulled suddenly away and came back to the cashier's counter where I was standing with the Mama-san.

"He's coming in."

The dagger man came through the door, took a table in the darkness, and sat watching the girls in the display room.

Anuraj was upstairs.

Harley was silent for a half minute, then to the Mama-san he said, "I want to take Anuraj out of here, Mama-san, but I don't like to leave you with that scumbag there."

She smiled slowly, her face filling with menace and delight. She reached under the counter and brought up a bone-handled knife with a blade about a foot long. She laid it on the counter, reached down again, and came up with an Army .45 automatic and put that next to the knife. She said, "You no worry about Mama-san. Mama-san take care Mama-san, have very good time."

She rang the telephone in Anuraj's room and told her to come down. We left through the back door and got in the Range Rover and headed for Songkhla.

"Why you make me leave?" Anuraj said. "I working. Why I have to leave?" She was still wearing her yellow evening dress.

"We talked the Mama-san into giving you a day off, Anuraj. Thought we'd take you to lunch. It's too nice a day to spend indoors."

She brightened. "Where we go?"

We drove to a small restaurant in a grove of casuarina trees up the beach from our hotel. There was nothing there but a half-dozen old wooden chairs and tables and a makeshift wooden covering on poles sunk in the sand. It would all fall down with the first breath of the monsoon, and the family would rebuild it next season. The old man and woman who ran the place cooked prawns and sea bass on a brick grill and served them with beer.

It seemed like a safe place, not many people and good visibility in all directions. I was relieved to be away from the Paradise and the corporal and the dagger man. We had been there only a few minutes when Harley, who was wearing jeans cut off at mid-thigh, kicked off his sandals and ran down into the water. A large family of Thais at another table stared with disbelief as the crazy *farang* swam in the gulf, ran around in the sun, then came panting back into the shade and sat down soaking wet next to a thirteen-year-old girl in an evening dress.

We drank beer for about five minutes, Harley staring thoughtfully out to sea, and then he said, "Maybe I shouldn't have left the Paradise."

"Mama-san looked as if she had things in hand," I said.

"She did, didn't she."

"You said you had to get Anuraj out. You can't worry about everyone, Peter."

Hearing her name, Anuraj said, "What you say?"

"Nothing, Anuraj," Harley said.

"There's only a few more hours," I said. "Jaran'll be here in the morning. Nothing's going to happen."

"Yeah. Let's believe that."

Harley got up and trotted off again toward the water. Anuraj stayed beside me, watching him as he strode out into the gulf, then dived beneath a wave. Her lips parted and her eyes opened wide in an expression of envy, daring, and adventure. Suddenly she reached for the zipper at the side of her dress, opened it, wriggled free of the shoulder straps, and let the dress fall down around her ankles. She was wearing white bikini panties and a small white bra. She left the dress in a heap on the sand and ran toward the water. The family of Thais stopped talking abruptly, their chopsticks frozen between plate and mouth.

For several minutes I watched Anuraj and Harley swim, then decided that I didn't want to drink beer with all that good fish. I jogged back to the hotel and bought two bottles of Chablis and borrowed an ice bucket and corkscrew. While Anuraj and Harley played on the beach, I moved our table and chairs into the sun. The Thais watched with curiosity.

I opened one of the bottles, and when Harley and Anuraj returned we all sat baking in the sun, our bare feet digging into the sand, and drank chilled wine and ate plate after plate of fresh prawns and sea bass.

After several minutes Anuraj, still in her underwear, looked up from her plate, her mouth covered with butter and flakes of charcoaled fish. Harley reached across and wiped her mouth. As his hand came away it left behind a wide happy smile. She said, "This nicest place I been since two years."

"Where were you two years ago?" I said.

"My father take me to Penang. He have to do business in Butterworth and we take ferry and have lunch on top of Penang Hill. There big hotel there and we have big lunch. But we not have wine."

"Did you spend the night there?" I said.

"One night." She said it quickly, as if something had disturbed her, and went back to the fish on her plate.

Harley glanced at me, and I think we had the same nasty thought—that when Anuraj left home she might have been running away from something more than CTs.

She finished everything on her plate except a fish head, and started to eat that. I said, "You don't have to eat that, Anuraj. Have another fish."

She looked at our plates and saw that we had left the heads. "You not eat head?" she said.

"No," I said.

"Why?"

"It's not good," I said.

She looked at Harley. His face was neutral.

"I like head," she said finally, and cut into it.

"It's the best part," Harley said. He dug out a piece of meat behind the eyes and ate it.

We finished both bottles of wine and Harley sent the owner's grandson back to the hotel for more. We were getting a little drunk. Anuraj, finishing a plate of rice and shrimp, pushed suddenly back from the table with a movement that dislodged her bra. The right side pulled up almost to her shoulder, revealing a large pink nipple rising plumply from the white skin.

Harley looked away.

Anuraj saw the movement of his eyes, and was angry. She left her bra where it was and said, "You don't like?"

Harley, his eyes still avoiding her breast, said, "You're very beautiful, Anuraj, and Tony and I like you a lot."

She looked away sharply and yanked the bra into place. No one said anything for a couple of minutes and then Harley, taking another long drink of wine, leaned back, stretched out his arms, and said, "Let's have a swim."

Anuraj watched him enter the water, swim a few strokes, and come out. He started walking up the beach away from us, and she jumped up and ran after him. When she was about four feet behind him, she took a flying leap and landed on his back, arms around his neck, legs gripping his waist. His knees buckled but held. While he recovered from the shock, she slid around to the front and kissed his face.

Harley dumped her onto the sand and ran back into the water. She got up and chased him but he went deeper than she was willing to follow. In five minutes they were both back at the table and we had opened another bottle.

Sitting in the chair with his legs extended to dry in the sun, Harley had another couple of glasses and I realized how really drunk he was getting. Anuraj watched him, then looked at me and giggled.

"Man, ain't it fine . . ." Harley said, his words slurring. "Drinkin' wine. . . . In the sunshine . . ."

Then he fell sideways off the chair, cried out, and lay in the sand, tangled with the chair, helpless and laughing. In a moment he was asleep. He lay very still, breathing evenly, the corners of his mouth turned up in a drunken grin. Anuraj walked around and kneeled next to him and took his hand as if to help him up. The hand was limp. She held it briefly and then placed it gently back on the sand. She stared at his face.

"You know what I think?" she said.

"What?"

"I think it not the wine that make him drunk."

"Why do you think that, Anuraj?"

"I think he just happy to be here."

33

I AWOKE AT seven o'clock the next morning and from my window saw Harley with Jaran on the beach. I watched them walk slowly in the direction of the fishing village, Harley taking shorter, quicker steps than Jaran, twisting toward him, hands raised. He was selling, Jaran didn't want to buy.

I dressed and found the two of them in the dining room having breakfast. I did not sense the thickness of the emotional atmosphere between them until I had sat down and it was too late to leave. Jaran greeted me pleasantly but with a certain distance. He'd have been happier if I weren't there.

"Jaran says it won't work," Harley said with a tone intended to challenge Jaran, to accuse him.

"Yes?" I said, not wanting to make any response myself that would involve me in the dispute.

"He says I'm desperate, grasping at straws."

Jaran had a cup of coffee in front of him, black and cold. He said nothing.

Harley's urgency had affected me almost physically. I knew he could not tell Jaran that if this plan failed he would have to murder Lichai.

After a minute, breaking the silence, Harley pushed violently away from the table, knocking over his water glass. He grabbed for it and set it back slowly with a show of steadiness.

"If you want out, Jaran, I'll go ahead and do it alone."

"I'm here, Peter. I'll do what you want. But you asked me what I think and I think you're making a mistake. If you send Kuk into Lichai's home with a bag full of money, trying to get him to say incriminating things, he'll smell it, he'll act like he doesn't know anything and throw Kuk out. It's a waste of time, Peter. All it can do is get someone hurt."

"Kuk says he's been over there a lot of times, taking money. Prasong backs that up. He went with him once."

"Drug money?"

"Drug money, hotel money, what's the difference? Kuk'll say the bank's closed, he'll say he's being followed, he's afraid of getting robbed and shot, so he takes the money to Lichai. What's wrong with that?"

"Why doesn't he leave it in the hotel safe?"

"Because Lichai told him never to keep more than two million baht in the safe. He *did* tell him that, Jaran, I'm not making it up. Kuk told me."

Jaran looked down at the table and shook his head.

"I know about Kuk, Peter. Once he believes you can do something for him, he'll tell you anything he thinks you want to hear."

"You really just don't want to be involved in this, do you, Jaran? That's it, right? You just don't want to be involved."

"I'm here, Peter. But I don't want to see someone get hurt for nothing."

"For nothing."

"Tell me, Peter—if the thing with Miki had never happened, if you weren't feeling pressed, would you do this?"

"Damn straight. I thought of it in the airport as soon as I saw some of the notes were missing. I just didn't need it then—not until an hour later when the money got lost."

"But you're feeling the heat now. When you failed with Miki, you knew—"

"Right. I'm anxious. But so what. It's still a good idea."

Jaran shrugged. "If you want, Peter, I'm here."

"Well, I want."

34

A NARROW, ALMOST invisible dirt road led from the airport highway into the brush. We were parked on the shoulder a hundred yards from the turnoff, listening to the static from the Kel strapped to Kuk's waist as he walked toward Lichai's house.

"How far is it?" Harley said.

"Not far," Prasong said, "two, three minutes."

He'd come to the Satellite on his bicycle and we'd met him there and explained the plan. He hadn't liked it any better than Jaran had.

Jaran was up ahead of us, out of sight, parked with eight men in a Border Patrol truck. If everything went well, they would make the arrest.

Harley spoke into a walkie-talkie. "Okay? You in position?"

"In position." It was Jaran's voice.

We sat—hearing only the Kel static and the rhythmic crunch of Kuk's footsteps.

Prasong was next to me in the back seat, feeling the tension but afraid to ask questions. After two or three minutes of silence he said, "You get him, Mr. Peter."

"Better had, Prasong. This is it."

Prasong looked at me. "You go back when?"

Harley answered. "Tonight or tomorrow."

A revelation exploded behind Prasong's eyes. He had not guessed that this was it—all or nothing. I thought, He is wondering what his piece of paper will be worth if Harley fails and flies away to Bangkok.

The windows were open and a hot breeze blew dust in from the road. Harley, facing sideways toward the tape recorder on the seat beside him, had one hand on the steering wheel. He stared hard at the white sky, eyes squinting against the glare.

Louder sounds came in on the Kel now, scrapings and

bangings. Harley pushed a button on the recorder and the reels began to turn. We heard voices speaking Thai.

Prasong leaned forward over the recorder and listened.

"You know that voice?" Harley said.

Prasong shook his head.

More banging, another voice.

"Lichai!" Prasong said.

Silence. Voices again.

"Someone's getting tea," Harley said. He stared at the sky and listened.

We were getting steady conversation now, two voices, Kuk and Lichai.

Jaran's voice came over the walkie-talkie. "Is he there?"

"They're talking now," Harley answered.

Prasong was hanging over the tape recorder, straining for every word.

Harley saw the look on his face. "Relax, Prasong. It's gonna be okay."

Kuk and Lichai were speaking very rapidly, their voices raised.

"You get what you need?" Prasong said.

Harley raised a hand to silence him.

"You get enough?"

"Shut up, Prasong."

The voices stopped.

"Is he going for it?" I said.

"Sounds like it. They're talking about the money."

Lichai shouted something and Kuk answered.

Prasong looked anxiously at Harley.

Harley's face was blank.

Suddenly the back door flew open and Prasong was out of the Range Rover, running into the brush.

Harley threw the walkie-talkie at me. "Tell Jaran!"

He jumped out of the car and took off after Prasong. I pushed the button on the radio and said, "Jaran!"

"Go ahead."

"Prasong's run into the brush. Harley's gone after him."

"Okay. Stay in the car."

One of the men from Jaran's truck came running up the road. He was wearing jungle fatigues and carried an M-16.

I heard shots not far off and got out of the car and ran toward them. The man in fatigues yelled and came after me.

I followed a narrow trail to a dirt road, ran along that for about a hundred yards and came to a high wire fence and an open gate. I went through the gate and after another fifty yards saw the house—dark teak, hugging the ground, almost invisible against the scorched brown of the forest. A half-dozen Border Patrol police were already around the house. None of them moved to stop me.

I ran inside and found Jaran talking to a uniformed officer. The room was carpeted in white. The furniture, chromium and white leather, could have been stolen from an airline ticket office.

Prasong's body lay face down, an arm supporting his head as if in sleep. Lichai, clothed only in white undershorts, was dead beside him. Someone had stepped in a patch of blood next to the bodies, and faint red footprints led across the white carpet to the back of the room where Kuk, his hand still gripping a revolver, lay dead under a window.

When Patricia had died, I sat beside her for half an hour without really understanding what had happened. Her face had been calm, relaxed, and as beautiful as ever. Then suddenly I became aware of what for all that time had been a horrible stillness. Death showed itself to me then, and I left the room and never looked at the body again.

That had been my only experience with death when I walked into Lichai's house, and it did not prepare me for what I saw. Lichai was on his back, blood from a chest wound running down and across his stomach. His head was twisted to one side, the lips parted, spittle dribbling onto the carpet. His eyes were open, and their expression, intense yet lifeless, was even more horrifying than its counterfeit always appears in movies.

Harley knelt next to Prasong, examining something on the carpet. Then he stood and I saw that he had the Cobra, Prasong's gun, in his hand. He walked over to Kuk's body, turned it slightly on its side, and for a moment studied the chest. Then he walked back to Jaran and the uniformed officer.

"When I came in, Kuk and Prasong were throwing shots at each other," Harley said. "Prasong must have come in with the Cobra drawn and Kuk panicked and opened fire. Kuk's got two rounds in his chest. It looks like Prasong's got one of Kuk's in his head and Lichai caught a stray in the heart."

Harley stopped talking and the only sounds were the police

moving around outside the house. Finally Jaran said, "What was happening? Could you hear it on the Kel?"

"I really believe Lichai was taking the money, Jaran. It was working. We would have had him."

"Do you think Prasong knew that?"

"It doesn't look like it, does it?"

"No, it doesn't. He must have wanted to make sure Lichai got put away."

Jaran took the Cobra from Harley's hand. He examined the top of it, then turned it on end and looked down into the three empty shell cases. He removed the cases and held them in his fist. "Stupid. He should have known he wouldn't have the only gun in here."

"I'd better get back," Harley said. "I want her to hear it from me."

35

HARLEY TOLD Anuraj that Prasong was dead. He said he'd been shot to death at Lichai's house and that Kuk and Lichai were dead too. She stood in her yellow dress in the darkness next to the Mama-san's cash register and listened. She did not speak. The Mama-san and Harley and I watched her, and then Harley reached out and touched her arm. She turned and walked away down the corridor. The Mama-san went after her.

We left the Paradise and after twenty minutes of aimless driving Harley went by the Satellite Café and asked me to go inside and buy a fifth of Mekhong. "I'd do it myself if I thought I could stand seeing any of Thanon's men."

We drove back to the hotel, and when we had reached the end of the driveway at the front entrance, Harley shifted into four-wheel drive and went up over the curb, across the narrow lawn to the beach. We drove up the beach a few hundred yards and parked on the sand facing the gulf.

We were there five minutes, passing the bottle back and forth, and it began to look as if Harley had no intention of doing anything except get drunk. To break the silence, as much as to find out what had happened, I said, "I don't understand why he did that?"

"Did what?"

"Ran in the house."

Harley raised his eyebrows and shrugged.

"I mean it was working, wasn't it? You said Lichai was talking about the money."

"It's all there," Harley said, nodding at the tape recorder on the floor next to my feet.

I handed the recorder to him and he held it on his lap. "You want to hear it?"

"If it's okay."

Not too eagerly, he rewound the tape and pressed a button.

"What's he saying," I asked.

"Lichai's asking him why he brought the money. Kuk says because he was afraid to leave it in the safe and someone was following him for two days. Lichai says he should've left in in the safe anyway. Kuk says, but you told me not to."

Harley punched the stop button. "That's when I knew I'd get him, Tony—as soon as Lichai didn't deny outright that the money was his. A little more talk like what you just heard, plus Kuk's testimony, and Lichai would've been headed for jail, or for the border."

He tossed the recorder into the backseat, took a drink from the bottle, and sat quietly for a minute. Then he said, "But nobody's going to give a shit about that now. Lichai's dead, so who gives a fuck if my little scheme was working or not? They'll bury his body and they'll bury Prasong and no one will ask any academic questions about precisely how it all happened. There was an exchange of fire and the mission was accomplished. The operation was a huge success."

He looked at me. His eyes were red and unfocused. "We're the only two people alive who know Lichai was going for the money, Tony—and believe me, we're the only two people who give a shit."

"I guess Prasong didn't understand," I said. "He must have thought it was going wrong."

"And he ran in to do the job himself, kill Lichai, and guarantee his move to the States."

"Right."

Harley tipped up the bottle.

"But I don't see why Kuk shot at Prasong when he saw him come in the house. He would have thought Prasong had come to help him."

"Yeah," Harley said. "Unless Prasong shot first?"

"Why would he do that?"

"I'm paranoid, Tony. I'm a nasty cynic. I always look for the worst in everybody. And I have a terrible, sick suspicion that Prasong turned. Maybe he couldn't believe me, that I'd get him to the States. Maybe he had an idea how much Lichai would pay someone who pulled him out of the soup. Maybe right there at the last minute he figured Lichai was a better gamble than I was. What do you think of that?"

I was surprised. I thought maybe Harley was getting too drunk to think straight.

"It sounds pretty far-fetched. In fact, I think it's kind of a brutal way to look at things. Prasong wouldn't have done that."

He raised the bottle and drank.

Neither of us said anything.

After about ten minutes I broke the silence. "Anuraj didn't seem very upset."

"You don't think so? You don't know her very well. She's holding it in in front of the *farangs*."

At that moment I remembered something I'd seen at the Satellite when I bought the Mekhong, or rather something I had not seen.

"Peter . . ."

"Yeah."

"When we stopped at the Satellite, Prasong's bicycle wasn't there."

He was silent. I thought he hadn't heard me.

"Maybe . . ."

He turned the ignition key. "We'd better look around."

She was not at Nostrand's and she was not at the packing crate whorehouse. We tried the Sno headquarters, thinking she might have gone there to ask about Prasong. Finally we went to the Provincial Police. A sergeant there told us Anuraj had come by asking for Samak. When we got back in the Range Rover, Harley's face was pale and his hands trembled on the wheel.

We drove to Samak's home and I followed Harley across the yard. We were at the front door when we heard an explosion. We ran inside and found Samak's body on a bed, the chest and stomach a wet crimson mess of torn flesh. The wall behind the bed looked as if someone had thrown a bag full of blood at it. Blood had soaked the sheets and was dripping onto the teak floor. The gold *prahs* Samak wore for protection around his neck lay shining in the wounds. His face, unmarked, wore an almost arrogant expression of complete confidence. Death must have come as a great surprise.

Anuraj stood near the bed with the shotgun pistol in her hand.

Harley looked at this scene for perhaps three seconds, then quickly took his gun from under his belt and handed it to me. "Keep this. I gave it to you in case you needed it for the operation. Don't change that story no matter what anyone tells you."

He took the shotgun pistol from Anuraj, wiped it on his shirt, removed the empty shell, and wiped that. He put the shell back in the chamber, handled the gun back and forth from hand to hand, and put it in his belt.

A door slammed.

We all looked at the open bedroom door and listened.

Harley turned back to Anuraj.

"Anuraj, listen to me."

She was sobbing.

He put his hands on her shoulders. "Listen to me, Anuraj."

She looked up at him. Footsteps were approaching the room, but Harley did not take his eyes from Anuraj. "You came here to make love to Samak. I followed you. When I saw you here with Samak I got crazy and I pulled out the gun and shot him. Just that. That's all."

The footsteps were louder now, and Harley glanced at the door.

"Do you think you can remember that, Anuraj?"

She turned her head and looked at Samak's body. There was a window by the bed and the late afternoon sun gave a dark richness to the blood-soaked sheets and wall.

Harley squeezed her shoulders and she jerked her eyes back to his face. "Can you remember that, Anuraj?"

She nodded.

Harley looked desperately at the door. The footsteps sounded padded, someone in slippers.

Harley looked back at Anuraj. "Tell me!"

"I come make love Samak. You follow me and shoot him."

"Right. Just like that. Don't make anything else up, Anuraj. Don't try to make it sound better. Leave it short. No matter what happens. Don't—"

An old woman stood in the doorway. She was Samak's wife, the chubby little woman he had had with him at Lowell's party. She was wearing white pajamas, her hair uncombed, and as she stared at us now with the same restrained giggle she had had at the party, I realized she must be either retarded or insane.

Anuraj fixed her eyes on the woman and said, "What will happen to you, Peter?"

The woman now looked away from us and for the first time comprehended what was in the room. Her lips parted and she made a soft, barely audible sound, a rising note of pure grief. She took a slow, disbelieving step toward the bed and then with a mournful, death-filled cry threw herself at her husband. I had never heard a sound like that before, but I knew the pain at its source.

"Nothing," Harley said. His face was colorless, exhausted, and he could not take his eyes from the woman. He put his arm around Anuraj. "Nothing," he repeated. "Nothing will happen to anyone. I have immunity."

36

ANURAJ TOLD me the rest. She said the first time the CTs came to her father's restaurant in Betong, she had known it was the end of Prasong. He was stupid, she said. Even before that he had wanted to run away and go to Kuala Lumpur and get rich. He had thought you could get rich in the cities—the bigger the city, the richer you got. When the Communists came he headed north for Bangkok and she went with him. In

Hatyai the man they met in the restaurant, the man who told her about the Paradise, said the Americans had drug agents in town, and from then on Prasong had talked about going to America. He was so stupid and helpless. When he'd said today was the day, the day he'd earn his trip to America, she hadn't answered him. "I just look at him like it last time I ever see him."

She was upstairs at the Paradise in a room with the fourteen-year-old son of a businessman from Penang. His father was down the hall with a friend of hers, and she had the boy in the bath. He didn't like the bath. He said he had lots of baths at home. He wanted to get on with it. She'd been working hard and wanted the relaxation of having him in the bath for a few minutes. When the telephone rang she thought it was his father calling him, but when she heard the Mama-san's voice telling her to come down, only the second time ever that she'd been interrupted during a job, she knew Prasong was dead.

She left the boy in the bath and went downstairs. "When I see Peter's face I know the truth. When he tell me Prasong is dead he tell me something I already know. It like he tell me my mother is dead, and my mother been dead already four years."

She found Samak alone at his home. He thought she had come to make love. His wife was sleeping in another room and he took off his clothes and got on the bed. She went to the shelf next to the bed and lighted the ends of the joss sticks in front of the Buddha. She took a jasmine blossom from her hair and laid it next to the joss sticks. Then she went to the foot of the bed and laid the rest of the jasmine flowers from her hair at Samak's feet. He looked back at her, saying nothing, excited by the delay. She *wai*ed him, bringing her fingertips only to her chest as one would to insult an enemy. He frowned and raised a hand. She took the shotgun pistol from under her dress and fired, aiming it at an angle from his feet.

The recoil knocked her backward. She felt chilled and sick to her stomach. She began to shake. Then she heard Harley's voice and saw him standing in the doorway.

37

THE NEXT evening a man came to the door of my room at the hotel. I had spent the day looking for Harley, and thinking about him. I wondered if I would have been as swift as he had been to see and execute the one move that could save Anuraj's life. Or would I have taken some seconds to consider the penalties to myself? Would I have stood there thinking it all over while the footsteps came on into the room and settled the problem for me? Testimony from Samak's wife that she saw Anuraj with a smoking shotgun in her hand would have assured trial, conviction, and execution. I recalled what Knowles had said about some things that are too important to be left to the brain.

I could not find Harley. I put his gun in a dirty sock and wrapped that in dirty underwear and shirts and hid the bundle in the bottom of my suitcase. If anyone found out Harley had been carrying that gun, and *not* the shotgun pistol, it would be the end of Anuraj.

Harley had checked out of the hotel without leaving a message or address. Lowell told me he didn't know where he was. Nostrand said he didn't know either, but that two American men had come to the clinic asking about him. They wanted to know how long Nostrand had known Harley, how long Harley had known Anuraj, why Anuraj had moved there, had Harley had anything to do with Samak's death. They showed embassy credentials. Nostrand said one of them was dressed in a linen suit, "sort of a young-FSO-on-the-make uniform," and the other one "looked like he'd just fallen off the back of a turnip truck."

The man who came to my door must have been the second one. He was about forty, with a heavy, creased face that smiled while he spoke. He had on a dark crumpled suit bought for a colder climate. He said his name was Ed Reine, he was staying in room 352 up the hall from me, maybe we could have dinner together.

We went downstairs to the dining room. He said he'd come from Washington. "I guess you know what about."

I said I guessed I did. He was relaxed, down to earth, unaffected, a nice guy. Under the circumstances, that scared me. I'd have much preferred someone like Lowell, whom you recognized as a fool, or a harsh tough interrogator who let you know exactly where you stood. Reine was too likable.

He asked questions about Thai food (did they really eat rat?), commented on the music (were its origins Chinese?), told me all about his family (a wife and two children, both girls), talked about a friend of his from college who was a writer in New York (did I know him?). Never once did he mention Peter Harley or Anuraj or anyone else in Thailand. When I was back upstairs I sat down on my bed and wondered why he had taken me to dinner and what the hell it was he had wanted to know.

Evidently he had simply wanted to know me. Was he a psychiatrist, one of those CIA people who do personality evaluations? I left my room and walked up the hall and stood outside his door. I heard typing. He was writing up a report of our evening. What was he saying? Where would those pages finally come to rest? I went back to my room and lay on the bed with the lights on, sweating, watching the fat gecko stalk a spider.

38

I SPENT THE next day at the hotel trying to figure out how to go about locating Harley, what I ought to do. I went to bed early but awoke suddenly in the middle of the night. I lay still for a second and heard a quiet knock at the door. I looked at my watch. It was four o'clock. The knocking came again, softly. I put on my bathrobe and went to the door and said, "Who is it?"

"Me."

I opened the door and Harley was standing there with a suitcase:

"Where the hell have you been?" I said.

"I just came to say good-bye."

"Come in."

I opened the door farther and stood aside, but he didn't move.

"I didn't want to leave and have you think I just walked out on you," he said.

"Well, come inside a second. You can't be in that big a rush. Where the hell have you been?"

He came in but did not put the bag down. I closed the door.

"I've been answering a lot of questions," he said.

"I'll bet you have. What the hell happened?"

"I've been in a safehouse. You remember I told you Kessick didn't have a safehouse? Well, he does."

"Sit down for a second. Talk to me. Where're you going?"

He put the suitcase down and sat in the chair.

"Well, I'm PNG'ed, of course. I'm supposed to go back to Bangkok tomorrow and then the States. But I decided to leave early. It's finished with my job, so I thought I'd take a little vacation."

"Where are you going?"

"Maybe Malaysia first. I don't really know. Did they bother you at all?"

"No. I got a free dinner. What'd they do to you?"

"Nothing. They're so fucking sympathetic—about all the wrong things, of course. They said it was too bad the way I had to get mixed up with the whore and why the hell wasn't I more careful. Fucking around with an LBFM is okay, but I must have been a really dumb fuck to get mixed up *emotionally*, throw my career away for her. If I loved her, well, that was stupid, she's not worth it, how could I marry her, how could I take her back to the States, what would my friends think of her, what would my family think. My *family*. I felt like some hillbilly private who wants to marry a gook and his commanding officer has to talk him out of it, save his future for him."

"Then they really bought it, that it was you who killed him and not Anuraj?"

"Oh, yeah. Easy. They're just happy Lichai's gone. And sympathetic with me for blowing my career on a whore. They figure I'm disgraced. Fuck the disgrace. I haven't done anything I'm ashamed of, so why should I care about disgrace? That's other people, not me."

"Where's Knowles in all this?"

"Nowhere at all. The men I've been with are all federal narcotics types, internal security. Knowles doesn't come into it at all. He's just someone I used to work for."

"And Anuraj? How is she?"

"Not so good. The Thais who worked on her weren't as sympathetic as the Americans who worked on me."

"Did they hurt her?"

"Not physically. But they gave her head a good scrambling. They're good at that, you know. They didn't believe her story. They know I never carried a shotgun pistol. That's a Thai's weapon. They sweated her good. They kept her awake for forty-eight hours and scared the living shit out of her. I saw her for the first time a couple of hours ago. She looked like hell but she'd stuck to her story. She said she just kept saying it over and over, telling them like some kind of prayer, and they got mad and said she was a CT, that's why she lived at Nostrand's, because he was a CT sympathizer and if she didn't tell the truth she'd be shot. But she stuck to her story. They were afraid to hit her because of all the embassy people down here. So they let her go. What she needs now is a rest. They didn't sweat you at all? I was afraid you might have a sudden attack of honesty and tell the truth."

"They never even asked me. Some guy named Ed Reine took me to dinner and talked about everything except you and Anuraj. I think he was just feeling me out."

"Because you're a writer. What would you have said if they'd leaned on you a little?"

"I'd've said what you and Anuraj said. It's the truth, isn't it?"

"It is for me."

He picked up his bag.

"What'll she do now?" I said.

"Anything she wants—stay here, leave, whatever she wants. I guess it'll take her a good long time to get her head back together. I wish like hell it'd been the other way around—her with the Americans, me with the Thais.''

He went to the door. We shook hands and he walked quickly up the hall toward the stairs.

I lay down on the bed and turned out the light. I thought about Harley, his sudden departure, and things I wished I had thought to ask him. It was a hell of an ending to my story. It was no ending at all. I had no idea where Harley was really going or for how long or what he would do next. What was going to become of him? I hadn't even given him my address. I knew what an editor would say when he read this story. ''Well, how did he finally end up?''

I was brooding about this when I heard shouts outside, followed by pistol shots and a short burst of automatic fire. When I got to my window I saw a man in a sport shirt running toward the beach.

I dressed as fast as I could and ran downstairs. The man in the sport shirt had returned and was out of breath, talking to another man who held a small submachine gun. They were both Americans.

They saw me and the man with the gun said, ''He was with you?''

''Who?''

''*Harley* who, stupid—'' He started toward me, angry, the gun held out to one side as if he intended to slap it across my face.

The other man caught his arm. He was the marine who'd sat with Harley and Sandra and me in Bangkok, the sergeant we'd seen outside Lowell's home.

''Do you know where he went?'' the sergeant said.

''No.''

They started toward a car parked at the entrance and I said, ''Can I come with you?''

They ignored me, so I followed them and got in the backseat.

''Where would he go?'' the sergeant said. The other man was driving.

''I don't know.'' Then, afraid they'd put me out of the car if I couldn't help them, I added, ''Hatyai probably.''

We drove slowly to Hatyai, both men watching the brush along the side of the road. I wondered if they knew about the barriers, what to do if one of them was down.

When we got to town the driver stopped the car and said, "You got any ideas?"

I said, "No. He could be anywhere."

They looked at each other and then the sergeant said, "We've got some things to do."

"I can get a taxi," I said, and got out.

They drove off.

I was on Pridarom Road, about two streets away from the Satellite Café. I walked until I came to an alley, turned into it, and spent a moment looking back at the street, wondering if the sergeant and his partner had decided to follow me. I didn't see anyone, so I continued up the alley until I came out by a movie theater. I stood there for about five minutes, but no cars went by and I saw nothing of the two men. I walked across the street to the theater and got in a taxi and told the driver how to get to Nostrand's house.

39

HARLEY WAS there, in Nostrand's surgery, changing into camouflaged fatigues like those the Border Patrol wear. His suitcase was open on the floor, and Nostrand was repacking its contents into a backpack. Three young Thais, also in Border Patrol fatigues, watched nervously, anxious to be on their way.

No one was very happy to see me. They had no time to speak, and I had intruded on a secret.

"Some men are after you," I said to Harley. "One of them's the Marine sergeant we saw outside Lowell's."

"I know."

Nostrand helped him on with the backpack. Dressed in fatigues and boots, hunching his shoulders to work the pack into place, his sandals and jeans in a heap on the floor, Harley was no longer the street-wise drug agent.

I had been asking myself questions about the three Thais.

Now Harley said, "These aren't Thais, if that's what you're thinking. They're Burmese, Karen tribesmen fighting CTs and the Burmese government . . ."

"Where are you going?"

"They've got a camp just over the border."

"Can I go with you?"

He looked at me and his face softened into a grin. "Why the hell would you want to do that?"

"Because I won't have any story otherwise."

"In a week or so," Harley said, "you'll be glad you didn't come."

"What the hell does that mean?"

The three Burmese guerrillas were at the door, worried and impatient.

Harley took a step toward them, stopped, and turned to me. "I'm sorry. I don't want to fuck up your story."

"That's all right," I said, ashamed that I had brought up such a minor problem.

He pulled a piece of paper from his pocket and wrote on it.

"Here's a number where you might be able to reach me in a couple of months."

He gave me the paper and looked at Nostrand and the Burmese.

"Go on out," he said, "I'll be there in ten seconds."

When they were through the door, he said to me, "Those initials you asked me about, NOK. Remember? They're not a person. They stand for next of kin. That long number after them, the last seven digits of it are the same as the phone number I just gave you."

He seemed not at all rushed now, suddenly the street agent again, his fatigues more a costume than a uniform.

"I hope you can get some kind of ending out of that," he said.

"Where do you go after Burma?"

"Who the hell knows?"

He smiled, and then the smile went away and his face for an instant was naked, in a way I had never seen it before, and terribly frightened.

He turned and went out through the door.

40

I PROMISED MYSELF I would stay in Songkhla at least as long as the investigators. The magazine I was working for had given me three thousand dollars' expense money, from which I had had to pay air travel, and it was almost gone. Paying my bill at the Sawadi would wipe out the expenses and start me on the five hundred dollars I had brought of my own money.

Still, I was determined not to leave before the investigators. For three days I saw them in the mornings having breakfast in the hotel dining room, the Marine sergeant and his partner, the man named Reine who had taken me to dinner, and two other middle-aged men in dark trousers and short-sleeved sport shirts. In the evenings they were in the bar. Always they pretended not to recognize me.

Each day I went to Lowell and Nostrand, hoping for news of what had become of Harley. Lowell patronized me, delighted to be able to take the position that Harley had let me down, had let everybody down.

"He behaved very badly, Mr. Deniset, very badly indeed."

His peculiar accent-impediment annoyed me even more than it had the first time I met him. It was a handicap, I knew, but I couldn't help believing that he was pleased to have it, as Sandra was pleased with her mole.

Lowell confided to me, in a tone that managed to be at once condescending and conspiratorial, that "we" had heard nothing of Harley. It was obviously his hope that I would interpret the pronoun to include all the most secret intelligence services of the United States and Thailand reporting directly to himself. In fact, I was certain he would be the last man in either government to learn any news about anything.

I asked him about Anuraj.

"That little whore. I know you liked Harley, Mr. Deniset,

and I don't like to speak against him. But how's that for judgment? I saw the danger of that a mile off. I saw it coming. Even if she had been a different kind of person, from a good family, she was still a Thai."

He made it sound like a disease.

"And only sixteen. There's something—"

"Thirteen."

"—sick about a man his age falling in love with a child. I've seen so many of these Thai-American affairs before, Mr. Deniset. It's *always* the American who gets hurt. The Thai has nothing to lose. Harley should have known that. For all his so-called street sense he was really very naïve. If he had talked to me . . ."

"Do you know where she is?"

"Where she is?"

"Where she is."

"I assumed—well, naturally she would be . . . I suppose she's at home."

"Thanks."

After Lowell, I went to Nostrand. When I asked about Anuraj, he repeated what Harley had said, that she was safe. That was all I cared about, really, so I did not embarrass him by pressing for details. The second day I visited him he said he had heard a rumor—no more than a rumor—that Harley and the three Burmese, dressed as tourists, had taken a boat from Phuket, a Thai resort on the Andaman Sea, and landed in Burma up the coast near Mergui. They were now safe in a Karen camp.

"Did that come from Aim?" I hoped it had come from Aim because if it had, it was probably true.

"It's just a rumor," he said.

The next morning when I asked Lowell if he'd heard anything about Harley he said, "We don't have anything. He seems to have abandoned everyone."

"You didn't hear anything about Phuket?"

"He's in Phuket?"

"No, he's not in Phuket. I just wondered—"

"That's correct, he's not in Phuket. If he were in Phuket we'd know it."

The fourth day I came down to breakfast and the investigators were gone. I spoke with the girl at the desk and was told they had checked out two hours earlier.

I went to the consulate and asked Lowell how much longer

he thought the investigators might be in Songkhla. I thought that if he knew they had left, he might also know why. Perhaps they had left because they knew Harley was no longer in the country.

"They'll be here at least until Monday," he told me. "Why do you ask?"

"No reason. Just wondering."

I took the five o'clock plane to Bangkok.

New York

41

SIX UNIFORMED men with submachine guns stood behind the exit gate at the Bangkok airport. Two other men in civilian clothes checked passports and opened luggage, unusual for a domestic flight.

When I reached the front of the line I opened my bag and said, "What's the problem?"

A man I hadn't noticed stepped forward and said, "You come from where?"

"The United States."

He smiled, just perceptibly, and I had the impression that he was not so convinced as his superiors of the need for this inspection.

"I mean on this flight," he said.

"Hatyai."

He slipped his hands through the layers of clothes.

"What's the problem?" I said.

He nodded for me to close the bag, and stepped back. When I looked up again he was behind the row of uniformed men, quietly scrutinizing the disembarking passengers.

Traffic was unusually light on the highway into Bangkok, and when we passed the television station north of Victory Monument I noticed three jeeps parked outside. The monument itself, an obelisk surrounded by immense bronze soldiers in battle dress, was guarded by two tanks and an armored personnel carrier. We raced through the open square, normally choked with traffic, and encountered only police cars, military jeeps, and a dozen taxis. Coming out the other side into Phya Thai Road, I took a chance the driver might know some English and said, "Why the tanks?"

He waved an arm at the almost empty street. "Queer foo."

I leaned forward. "What?"

We were passing Chulalongkorn University and I saw more tanks and APCs.

"Queer foo," the driver said, waving his hand at the tanks.

"*Curfew*," I said.

He nodded. "Queer foo."

We were into Silom Road, almost to the river, and he stopped the cab and let me out. My hotel was narrow, four stories, wedged between an Indian restaurant and a pharmacy. I had very little money left and didn't want to squander it at the Siam Intercontinental.

I checked in and asked the Thai desk clerk what had happened.

"What happened?"

It was not his job to alarm nervous tourists.

"Yes. What happened? There are tanks in the streets."

He shrugged and smiled, as if I had called his attention to a small and harmless insect in the bathtub.

"Oh, nothing. Some kind of exercise."

"I see," I said, and went up to the room.

The bed, rickety and concave, was made of wrought-iron tubing and looked as if it belonged in a whorehouse, where for all I knew it was. The bathroom, smelling of damp plaster, had a drain in the middle of the floor and a shower head in the middle of the ceiling. When you turned on the shower, water sprayed on the sink, toilet, door, and window. The window looked across four feet of rancid air to the brick wall of the Indian restaurant. The ground below was paved with garbage.

I picked up the phone and asked the man downstairs to connect me with the American embassy.

"Very well." He sounded tired.

It was past eight o'clock, but I thought there might be a chance Valdez would still be in his office. He was not.

I went out, defying whatever sort of curfew there was, and walked five blocks past the nightclubs and restaurants to the Oriental Hotel. I had a gin and tonic by the river, at the same table I had shared with Miki and Harley, then went up to the Normandy restaurant on the roof and ate sea bass with a bottle of Chablis and thought about the lunch Harley and Anuraj and I had had on the beach in Songkhla. I looked down at the dark shapes of rice barges and longtail boats and pretended that the other side of the river was Burma. I wondered where Harley was and what had become of him.

42

"**I** WARNED YOU," Valdez said.

They were his first words to me, looking up from behind his desk as I came through the door.

"What do you mean?"

"I told you Harley wasn't the man you wanted."

I sat down in one of the chairs and tried not to let him see that the words had made me angry. I didn't like Valdez thinking he knew my business better than I did.

"I'm not so sure he wasn't," I said.

Valdez moved some papers around on his desk, too busy to argue about it.

"Well, he ran out anyway," he said.

"Ran out on what?"

"The disgrace. Getting tied up with some fucking jungle whore."

"Why should he worry about disgrace if he wasn't ashamed?"

Valdez ignored that and finished shuffling the papers and leaned back, ready to get rid of me.

"What can I do for you?"

"What have you heard about him? Where is he?"

"I don't know. Some guy came in here yesterday and told me he'd seen him last Wednesday at the airport in Kuala Lumpur. If you want rumors you might as well make up your own."

"But factually, for sure, you don't know?"

"I have no idea. He's a fugitive. He's PNG, on the run. We're looking for him."

"Who is 'we'?"

Valdez was impatient. This interrogation insulted him.

"The government," he said.

"Would there be any point in my asking Aim?"

241

For a moment he seemed about to say, "What's Aim?"

"None whatsoever."

"That's what I thought," I said.

We stared at each other, his eyes trying to kick me out of the office.

"What's the reason for all the tanks and the curfew?" I said, just to annoy him.

Without a word he picked up a newspaper and handed it to me across the desk.

I took the paper and walked out.

It was the Bangkok *Post*. I read it in the hallway outside Valdez's office. It said the government yesterday afternoon had arrested a small group of "disgruntled" army officers, namely two generals and a half-dozen colonels, who had been plotting a coup against the government. The government had learned of the intended coup from documents found in the home of a Thai businessman murdered last week in Hatyai. Certain "precautionary measures," including a brief curfew, had been discontinued this morning, although further arrests were expected as the government's investigation continued. One of the generals was known to have connections in Songkhla Province in the south and, according to a government spokesman, had been in communication with Communist insurgents there and in Phitsanulok Province in the north. Two tons of opium found nine miles east of Mai Sai near the Thai-Burma-Laos border, as well as a large cache of explosives and weapons found in a textiles warehouse in Thonburi, had been linked to the rebellious officers.

There was no mention of Lichai by name, of how the opium and explosives and guns were discovered, or of the particular American agent without whom Thailand might this morning have awakened to a different and, it was fair to say, less tolerant government.

Well—no wonder Valdez had been so hostile. What a *loss* he had suffered! Harley's triumph would have ennobled everyone around him, and the idiot had thrown it away. For the love of a whore! An LBFM—little brown fuck machine. Harley, triumphant, on the very verge of spewing glory all over every superior in sight, had shot a cop and fled into the jungle. Valdez had been robbed.

I put the paper under my arm and walked out of the

building, across the embassy lawn, past the shrubs trimmed in the shapes of elephants and peacocks. I stopped at the fountain and watched the thin columns of water shooting into the clear sunlit air, arching, hanging for an instant, then shattering into spray. I smiled. Here's to you, Harley, wherever you are.

43

HE WAS killed in an attack by Border Patrol police near the town of Sikao about 140 kilometers northwest of Hatyai. He and the three Burmese were hiding in a complex of caves in a rocky island rising from the Andaman Sea 250 meters off a beach called Pak Mong. They returned Border Patrol fire and were killed four hours later by flamethrowers helicoptered in from a camp in Trang. They had been waiting for a boat to take them up the coast to Burma.

Sandra told me all about it.

After leaving the embassy Friday, I'd gone back to the hotel and called Jaran. He was up-country in Chiang Mai on a case. I called Sandra, then hung up before she could answer. I decided to wait for a while. She was my last hope in Bangkok for any real news of Harley. If anyone in the embassy knew anything, Sandra was the only person who might be willing to tell me.

I spent the day thinking, resting, and typing notes. I was down to $203 and a return ticket to New York. I decided that on Monday I would talk to Sandra. I had enough money to spend Monday, Tuesday, and Wednesday exhausting every last possible means of finding out what had happened to Harley. Then I would have to go home. I called Pan Am and made a reservation for Thursday on flight 2.

I had a weekend to kill, and I did not want to spend it brooding about what had happened to Harley. During almost two months in Thailand I had seen none of the things everyone else goes there for. I had not seen the Grand Palace, the Emerald Buddha, the National Museum, the Sleeping Buddha, the Giant Swing, the Weekend Market.

So Sunday morning I started at the Weekend Market. An immense labyrinth of tents and stalls had been thrown up in the Sanam Luang, a wide park that had once been the royal funeral grounds, and the canvas-covered pathways smelled of spices, incense, and cooking food. You could buy anything there: roasted cockroaches, to be ground for soup flavoring; thrushlike birds charcoal-broiled on hibachis; wild honeycombs on sticks; sugarcane juice from stalks run through a hand-cranked mop wringer; hundred-year-old eggs with black yolks; live geese; fighting fish; cobras; tiger cubs.

In the center of this park, just inside a row of makeshift noodle stands, children flew kites and rode bicycles. They rode endlessly in huge figure eights, laughing, going nowhere. I pushed through a mob of spectators to find a magician waving a cobra over the motionless body of a female assistant. I watched for ten minutes but never learned what he was trying to accomplish.

Sitting at a dilapidated wooden table by one of the noodle stands, I ordered a bowl of chicken curry. I watched the shoppers, the strollers, the kite flyers, the bicyclists. Surrounded by all the commotion and noise, my mind turned inward and I found myself thinking that if I left Thailand without learning what had happened to Harley, I would never know.

I paid for the curry and returned the *wai* of the smiling girl who had served me. I walked out from under the canvas coverings of the market, stepped off the curb, and fought my way through buses and motorcycles to the Grand Palace complex on the other side of Na Phralan Road. When I reached the sidewalk outside the palace wall, four crippled beggars scrambled up from the pavement, grabbed their crutches, and hobbled quickly onto the grass separating the wall from the pavement. A slender young policeman walked disinterestedly up the pavement for fifty feet, turned around, walked back, and then, without having glanced at the beggars, crossed the street to the front of the Defense Ministry and got into a car. When he had driven off, the beggars returned to their positions on the sidewalk. I was wondering about the good intentions of civic-minded lawmakers who thought a simple ordinance could remove beggars from the sidewalk in front of Bangkok's number one tourist attraction, about whom you could blame for useless laws enacted in good faith and necessarily ignored by both obedient enforcers and helpless violators—when suddenly I saw Sandra.

She had stepped out of a taxi with two other women and was walking toward the palace entrance. I called to her and she turned. Her face brightened.

"I've been *looking* for you," she said, taking a few steps away from her companions. "I called the hotel in Songkhla and they said you'd checked out. Then I called the Siam Inter and you weren't there either. Where the hell have you been? I've got—"

Her face became abruptly serious.

"I've changed hotels," I said—waiting, knowing from the look on her face, a heavy weight of dread growing in my stomach.

"I've got terrible news, Tony."

Why the hell didn't she just say it?

"What's happened?"

"Harley's been killed."

"How?"

She told me about the caves and the flamethrowers. The bodies were charred. An embassy dentist had gone down with Harley's X rays. Of course they would keep the X rays handy.

"If you want to go," she said, "you'll have to call the press section immediately in the morning."

"Go?"

"There's a press tour flying down tomorrow."

"A *tour*?"

"Some reporters wanted to go to the scene, so the embassy's flying them down."

"That's nice," I said.

She touched my arm and looked into my face with eyes that had the same pleading intensity I had seen in Kuk's eyes, struggling to counterfeit an emotion that could no longer be felt.

"I'm sorry," she said.

I turned away from her and walked quickly into the middle of the street, waving my arms for a taxi. Someone on a motorcycle screamed at me and then a *samlor* slowed down and I jumped in. The old man didn't ask where I was going and I didn't tell him. I bounced along, feeling the growth in my stomach swell up through my lungs and throat.

44

AFTER FIVE minutes we were in the middle of Chinatown and I leaned forward and told the driver the name of my hotel. He waved a hand. I sat back, then changed my mind and yelled out, "Hotel Oriental!" I could not have stood that sad, squalid room. He waved again. The gesture contained a touching element of reassurance. Something— maybe the way I had walked out into the middle of traffic— must have given him the idea I was in trouble.

He let me out and I walked across the Oriental's terrace and sat at a table by the river. I ordered Mekhong. The more I drank and stared at the river, the more unsettled I became. The sensation I felt of abandonment and grief was too familiar. To escape, I forced myself to think only of facts, not of my feelings, as one tries to ignore the early twinges of approaching nausea. I pushed my brain back to the beginning, to the first sight I had had of Harley at the Christmas party, to the warning from Knowles, to the hanged dog, the crippled prisoner, Lichai's death, Samak's murder, Harley's flight. As if drawn by a subconscious gravity my thoughts came finally to rest on the half hour Harley and I sat together in the Range Rover on the beach after Lichai and Prasong were killed. Something jogged loose from my memory what Harley had said there—a hint he had tried to give me—and his words struck with an impact they had not had before. I realized suddenly that his *suspicion* that Prasong had run from the car to help Lichai had in fact not been a suspicion at all. It had been a confession.

I left some money on the table and ran the five blocks back to my hotel. I grabbed the key from the man at the desk, waited a second for the elevator, then gave up and took the stairs. Breathing hard from the climb and from the knowledge of what I knew I would find, I went in my room, locked the door, and sat on the bed. I told myself to calm down—there was no desperate need to have the answer in the next five seconds. When my breathing had settled, I kneeled on the floor, pulled my suitcase from under the bed, and opened it. I reached into the bottom and pulled out a wad of laundry. I peeled off the dirty shirts and underwear and shook Harley's gun out of the sock. I broke it open and looked at the cylinder.

Two rounds had been fired.

Lichai and Prasong.

45

I DID NOT take the tour.

I had heard Harley's own vivid description of broken, charred bodies—had seen on his face the legacy of that little treat—and did not wish to find him in a similar condition. Instead I called downstairs to the man at the desk and asked him to send up a bottle of Mekhong. I sat cross-legged on the rickety iron bed and drank, thinking of Harley. The one thing he feared most had happened. He had had to make a choice. His determination not to kill Lichai had confronted Knowles's arguments that Lichai had to be eliminated. Harley's plan had been working, until Prasong ran to Lichai's aid. Harley followed. To defend himself (and perhaps in an attempt to defend Kuk, whose testimony he hoped for), Harley had had to shoot Prasong. With Kuk and Prasong dead or dying, the plan aborted, he had had to kill Lichai.

And in the Range Rover I had failed to listen. Harley had told me of his "suspicion," and certainly he had expected me to respond with the obvious question. If Prasong went to Lichai's aid, how did Lichai end up dead? Harley's implicit request for questions, his need to *talk,* had bounced right off my arrogance. I already *knew* what had happened in Lichai's house. I'd been there, seen the bodies, heard Harley tell Jaran how Prasong had walked in with his gun out, exchanging fire with Kuk. What the hell did I need with theories? With another version of the facts? Harley had wanted to tell me the truth, but I never gave him the chance. Once again I had failed to react to the words behind words. *Do you think this is really wise?*

So he'd kept the truth sealed inside. There couldn't have been anyone else around he was willing to unburden himself to. Knowles, maybe. But he'd died before he got that far.

I was two thirds through the bottle of Mekhong and falling softly, warmly into the welcoming arms of guilt. I caught myself, put the top on the bottle, and went for a walk in the sunshine. Harley was dead, and his demons could look out for themselves. I was under no obligation to offer them a home in my conscience.

I strolled unsteadily up Silom Road to Lumpini Park. Curiously, or maybe it was not curious at all, I did not think less of Harley for having killed Lichai and Prasong. If anything, the knowledge increased my sympathy for him.

I felt sorry for Prasong. He had tried to pull himself free of his country, but his country wouldn't let go. Someone, with perhaps nothing more to go on than a hint or a suspicion, had put thoughts into Prasong's head. Had it been Samak? Kuk? The dagger man? Or had there been in fact something *more* than a hint, had there been definite knowledge of Prasong's connection to Harley, and a well-developed plot to subvert Prasong, to turn him around? Was that what Samak, Kuk, and the dagger man had been discussing at the Saturday night buffet dinner at the Sawadi Hotel?

Whatever the facts, I was certain of this: some threat or promise had been working in Prasong's mind as he sat in the Range Rover and listened to the voices from the Kel. And in the end it had been easier for him to trust Lichai than Harley.

I walked among the trees and lawns of the park and came out an hour later on Wireless Road, just a few steps from the American embassy. I decided to go in and ask if the tour was back. Maybe there would be news about Harley.

The young American secretary in the press attaché's office said the tour would not be back until evening. She asked if I would like to see the passenger list. I glanced at it: a half-dozen scrawled names, trained, professional, objective newsmen now engaged in satisfying the world's desire for reports from the scene. She smiled prettily and handed me a press release.

I thanked her and took it out into the sun and read it as I walked back to the hotel. It said that Peter Harley, an American government employee, had killed a Thai police officer, had fled the authorities of both countries, and was finally killed in an exchange of gunfire with Border Patrol police. It did not mention flamethrowers or the presence of three companions, nor did it say specifically what Harley's job had been in Thailand or why he had shot the officer. It said the case was still under investigation.

Special planes and press releases—when Harley was alive Knowles had wanted no publicity about him at all; and now that he was dead Knowles (who else?) couldn't get enough.

I changed my reservation to Tuesday, and flew out of Don Muang Airport with twenty-two dollars in my pocket.

46

FOR TWENTY-THREE hours, sitting in the same 747, emerging only briefly in New Delhi, Teheran, and London while airport crews swept out the old Kleenexes, cigarette packs, and empty scotch miniatures, my eyes grew heavier, my mind foggier, and I began to wonder—with more hope than I wanted to allow myself—if Harley might not still be alive.

I had nothing to do but think. What were the *facts*? I had not *seen* him killed. There had been no recognizable corpse. I did not *know* that the X rays the dentist took down were really Harley's X rays. I didn't even know for sure that *any* dentist had taken down *any* X rays. Given the professional duplicity of men like Knowles and of organizations like Aim, why did I accept so readily the *fact* of Harley's death?

Because I could feel it.

There was an inevitability about it.

I had had four breakfasts one after the other, each preceded by scotch and accompanied by three quarter bottles of red

Bordeaux, and I was not thinking clearly. It did occur to me, however, that the nagging optimism I felt was a considerable improvement over the bitterness that had been with me when I made the trip in the other direction.

I called the number from Kennedy Airport. A woman answered. Her voice was friendly, trusting, with a peculiar pitch and lilt that could have been the result of old age or madness. I had an immediate mental picture of the kind, insane old lady who twenty years ago had been the only soul in the city of New York willing to adopt a twelve-year-old foundling named Peter Harley.

I spent my last fifteen dollars on the taxi to Manhattan, put my bags in the apartment, showered, dressed, cashed a check in the bar across the street, and went to see her.

47

S HE WAS lovely: seventy years old, very thin, with a gentle friendly face, transparent white skin, flaming red hair, and eyes that were green, sparkling, and beautifully mad. She shook hands with me and said her name was Mrs. Spillner. I followed her through a dim hallway to the living room and noticed that her hair, fine and wispy as an infant's, was coming out of the back of her head in patches. Fiery strands of it were everywhere, on the carpets, on the heavily uphol-stered sofa and chairs, on the small end tables covered with bits of lace and porcelain and picture frames. She asked me gently to sit on the sofa, and settled purposefully across from me in one of the chairs. She was wearing blue slacks and a sheer white blouse beneath which—a more disturbing sign of madness than the eyes or voice—I could see her nipples, small and black. She crossed her legs. She watched me, saying nothing. The apartment smelled of boiling vegetables.

"I just thought I'd stop by and tell you I've seen Peter," I said.

"Oh, yes, Peter," she said.

"Peter Harley."

"Oh, I know who you mean. When you used that name on the telephone I knew immediately who you were talking about."

I looked nervously around at the picture frames. None of the photographs was of Harley.

"Did you just arrive?" she said.

"Yes. It was a very long flight. Twenty-three hours. I haven't slept yet and I'm a little groggy."

"Would you like to take a nap?"

"No, thank you."

Still glancing around, unable to settle my eyes on her, I spotted a bright red motorcycle helmet under a table in the corner.

"Is that yours?" I said.

"What?"

"The helmet."

"Oh, yes."

That was all. She saw no need for an explanation. I hesitated. Well, why *shouldn't* a skinny seventy-year-old psychotic have a red motorcycle helmet? Skinny twelve-year-old psychotics had them.

She was watching me closely now. I think she was beginning to find me a little peculiar.

"I wondered if you had heard from Harley," I said, thinking that certainly she would have been informed of his death.

"Oh, he gets in touch whenever he can. But of course I don't call him Harley."

"No, of course not. I'm sorry. I meant to say 'Peter.' "

"Harley," she said, smiling at me warmly. "That's a nice name. I like that name very much."

I didn't know how much of my confusion resulted from her madness and how much from my own fatigue. But *something* was wrong here.

"He didn't take your name, when you adopted him?"

"Oh, yes, he did, for a time, you know, and then he started going away—"

Her thin liver-specked fingers gripped the arms of the chair, digging in, and she tipped her head back and laughed, a brittle, tingling, genuinely amused, old-lady's laugh.

"I *never* knew. He was here, he was there . . ."

Her head jerked forward and she shot me a solemn stare that made me feel accused.

"*Always* came back home, though. Came *back* . . . *Every* time . . ."

Her fingers let go of the chair and her entire body sagged into repose. She was still and silent, and just when it seemed that she might stay like that all day, she leaped up and without a word left the room.

I didn't know what to do. She was crazy. She might not ever come back. If I stayed she might come back in an hour and demand to know who the hell I was and what I was doing in her apartment. How had Harley grown up with this woman? How had he handled her, taken care of her, kept her out of trouble? There must have been hundreds of times when neighbors, shopkeepers, cops, acquaintances, doctors, wanted her put away. What a time he must have had with her. She had given him a home.

She returned in a minute with a large cardboard carton in her arms. I jumped up to help her with it, but she turned quickly and said, "No. No. Don't you take this from me."

"I'm sorry. I was going—"

"Here! It belongs *here*."

She dropped it on the floor in front of the sofa.

"Sit down!"

I sat on one end of the sofa and she put herself at the other end. The box was on the floor between us. She unfolded the top and revealed stacks of letters. They were from Harley. Most of them were handwritten on Xerox paper, the universal paper, ubiquitous, untraceable. A few were on conventional airmail stationery. She lifted one of these.

"This was his last trip," she said, reading it silently.

"Why are they on different kinds of paper?" I said.

"Different paper?" It was as if she hadn't noticed before. "Who knows?"

I pointed to the ones on airmail paper. "Are those all from the last trip?"

"Yes, the last trip."

She gave me the letter in her hands. I read it.

Dear Mom,

Thanks for your letters—I just got a batch. I'm happy you're feeling better and that you finally went to see Warren. I told you it would work out. You're much more persuasive than you think.

The weekend sounds good to me, really good. I hope you'll do it, and do it the way you and the other lady worked it out, just like that.

I wish I could tell you what I'm doing but all I can say is it's nothing and don't worry. I'll be back soon and we'll check out the bikes. But not till I get back, Mom. Promise! We'll do it together. And be careful. New York's filled with nuts, and they're not all muggers.

I've got to go. But listen—don't worry. Stop trying to figure out where I am. Don't read the newspapers. Just remember what Danny used to say—"There is only one fact, and this is it." That and my love. Believe.

See you soon.

Much love,

It was signed "Pete." I had never heard anyone, Sandra or Miki, call him Pete.

"Who's Danny?" I said, handing the letter back.

"You can have that," she said, as if awarding me a treasured family heirloom.

"Thank you."

I folded the letter and put it in my pocket.

"Who's Danny?" I repeated.

"I don't know now."

"You—"

"He's dead."

"Oh. I'm sorry. Well, who *was* he?"

"My husband. He was a police officer. We used to sit in front of the TV—he was retired. Peter and Danny and I used to sit in front of the TV and watch 'Dragnet.' That's why he said that in the letter. That's what you wanted to know, isn't it? We watched 'Dragnet,' and every time Jack Webb said, 'Just the facts, ma'am,' Danny would pipe up and say, 'There is only one fact, and this is it.' It doesn't mean anything, it's just something he liked to say. He was a little touched, you know. And sometimes he didn't say it fast enough, and one of us, Peter or me, we'd say it, and then sometimes we'd race to say it and we'd all say it together at once. 'There is only one fact, and this is it.' Only Jack didn't know that, of course, so he'd always wait to hear what the witness had to say, and often as not it would be all wrong and lead them all around this way and that way on some terrible wild goose chase and then Jack and that other man who was always with him would have to start all over and they'd get some other witness, and Jack would say—''

I couldn't stand it. "Where was he a police officer?"

"On the television."

"I mean your husband."

"Danny. Lots of places. He was retired." She lowered her voice. "He wasn't quite all there, upstairs. That's why he always kept saying that. But we loved him, you know."

"Yes, of course."

She fell silent again. I waited a couple of minutes, and then I said, "After your name, Spillner, Peter started using Harley? Why did he happen to pick that name?"

"Harley?"

"Yes. What made him pick that name?"

"Harley."

"Yes."

She stared at me. "Well?"

"What?"

"Go ahead."

"I don't understand. I—"

"What is it you wish to know? I'm afraid I don't quite follow your drift."

"I'm afraid I'm not making much sense," I said, laughing, trying to make it all a joke. "I merely wondered when it was that Peter had started using the name Harley."

"Well, I'm sure *you* can tell *me* that."

Accused again.

"Why? Why are you sure?"

"You told me that was his name. I never said that was his name. When you called on the telephone and said you were a friend of Peter Harley I said to myself, 'What a nice name. I wonder where he got that name.' Where did he get that name? Did you give it to him?"

Now I was home. Finally. Home and stunned.

"No," I said, "I didn't give it to him. I don't know who did. Did you like the other names as well?"

I thought back to the initials on the green page Knowles

had shown me in the bubble, trying to pull them out of the back of my hung-over, jeg-lagged memory.

"Young was *very* nice," she said. "But there are so many Youngs."

"Yes, that's true."

Had one of the initial sets ended in *Y*? I wasn't sure. But it didn't matter. I knew now. Harley had been Alfa—*all* the Alfas. After each killing his "death" had been staged, making him unavailable for interrogation should questions be asked later. Were there others, too? Were there Bravos and Charlies? Deltas? Echoes? I remembered how frightened Harley had looked at Nostrand's the last time I saw him, and I realized how much he must have suffered from doubt, from a lack of conviction that these attacks on his life would always be false ones.

He had been an assassin. He had been an assassin *repeatedly*, and now he had the guilt—the guilt of what he had done, and of the consequences of doing it no more. He had responsibility for the men he had killed, and for all the victims of those he refused to kill; responsibility for the deaths of terrorists, and for the deaths as well of the children they blew up in buses.

And I had thought he looked trapped at the Christmas party. Trapped! Where was he now, was he finished now, or was he still in the trap, hunting someone else, hoping he wouldn't have to kill but believing there would be less guilt in killing than in letting his quarry live?

"What name did you use?" I said. "When you wrote to Peter."

"His real name, of course. Peter Spillner."

But not even that was his real name. His real name was the name of his father, and no one knew that name.

"When did you hear from him last?" I asked, going back to the beginning.

"Yesterday."

"Yesterday!"

"Yes."

"From where?"

"Oh, I don't know from where. He never says from where. He just calls. Even his letters, he can't say anything even in his letters. But I understand. Just so long as I hear from him, you know. Know he's—"

"But you had a phone call from him yesterday?"

"Of course."

It was impossible to know how much of what she said was madness and how much was truth. She was the only person I could get to in the world who knew anything about Harley, and she was insane. I wondered if that was an accident. Knowles came into my mind, the image of him sitting across from me in the bubble with that droopy eyelid and Dr. Spock in his seersucker pocket, and I thought how nice it would be to put these two together, Knowles and the mad Mrs. Spillner. Strangely, I had the feeling they would get along wonderfully, that they would understand each other perfectly. They both seemed to operate on a level of truth that was just slightly out of my reach. Journalist or no, when it came to discriminating between fact and fiction, I'd lost all confidence. The experts were people like Knowles and the madwoman— insiders, mystics, viewers of the only fact, which is that there are no facts, only points of observation.

I had told Knowles that I might write Harley's story as fiction, to conceal certain facts, and he had agreed immediately. Of course he had. He knew, in that lunatic sub-underground world of his from which even Aim was excluded, that it would *have* to be fiction. He knew that I would end up loyal to Harley and want to protect him and that to do it I would have to tell the story as fiction; and that as fiction the story could have no claim on factual truth and would be disbelieved.

"So he's *alive*," I said, shouting at this crazy woman.

"Of *course* he's alive. Certainly he's alive. Why would he not be alive?"

"I don't know," I said, exhausted. "I don't know why he would not be alive. I don't know at all."

48

I CALLED HER every week.

She said she would tell me when she heard from him. She said she would tell him to get in touch with me. After a month she became annoyed. "I *told* you. I will call when I know something. You don't have to keep telephoning me."

So I cut the calls to once every two weeks, then once a month. Finally I called Knowles. I left a message with the State Department number he had given me in Bangkok and two days later he called back. I asked him what had happened to Harley.

"He was killed. I thought you knew that."

"I know what the embassy said and what I read in the paper, but I wasn't sure it was all true."

"It's true."

His voice was cold and guarded.

"His next of kin disagrees."

He didn't answer.

"Hello?"

"I heard you."

"Well?"

"What you heard in Bangkok is correct."

"Would it be better if we talked in person, instead of over the phone?"

"No."

His directness confused me. I didn't have time to think.

"You said you'd like to see me when I finished my research and had an idea what I was going to write."

"I don't think you need worry about that now."

"I'm not worried about it. I'd like to see you and talk about it."

"That's not necessary."

"Well, may I anyway?"

"No."

"But Mrs. Spillner insists that—"

"I have to go now. I appreciate your honoring our agreement and you may now consider yourself released. Good luck to you."

He hung up.

I called Mrs. Spillner's number. There was no answer. I kept telephoning for four days, and once I let the phone ring for a steady twenty-four hours. I took a taxi and went to see her. No one answered the bell, and when I found the super on the roof drinking beer he told me she had died.

"When?"

"A few days ago, last week."

"What happened?"

"She died. People die."

"But how? What happened?"

"How should I know, I'm not a friend of the family. They came in an ambulance and took her away. She died."

"Who came?"

"An ambulance."

I reached in my pocket and handed him twenty dollars.

"Listen, fella, I'm sorry, but I don't know nothin' about it. The men in the ambulance, they take her out, half hour later a truck comes, takes out the furniture. You want to look you can look, the place's empty."

He kept the twenty in his hand until I said I'd like to look, then he slipped it into his pocket and took me downstairs.

The rooms were bare. The carpet had been taken up. The light fixtures were missing from the walls. The curtain rods had been removed and their brackets unscrewed. Nothing remained but dust.

I telephoned every ambulance service in Manhattan and every funeral parlor. None had any record of a recent call to that address. I called the State Department number for Knowles. A girl's voice said they had no Knowles. I told her I had reached him at that number just last week. She checked again, apologized very pleasantly, and said there must be some mistake, they had no Bryan Knowles.

So there you are. Harley has vanished, and Anuraj, and the madwoman. I half believe that if I returned to Thailand I would find Jaran and Nostrand gone too, disappeared without a trace. Every couple of months, as the memories grow more dim and time erases details—I can see the Mama-san's body now, her elegance and gestures, but the face is gone—I reread Harley's letter:

There is only one fact, and this is it. That and my love.

I like that.

It is Christmas again, a year since I left for Thailand, and the air is sharp and cold. But the skies are sunny and the faces on the streets are smiling and expectant. I am settled in my new apartment, and once or twice a month I have dinner with my father-in-law. We speak, painlessly, about Patricia.

In the absence of facts, one settles for faith. Harley and Anuraj and the madwoman are alive. I am certain of that now. Not in the hotel atop Penang Hill—that would be fantasy. But in America somewhere, maybe in New York. Someday I'll be walking down Third Avenue, or waiting in line for a movie on Lexington, or looking in Tiffany's window, and I'll see them, the madwoman in her red helmet clutching Harley's waist on the back of a Honda Gold Wing, and behind her, long black shiny oriental hair streaming in the wind, will be Anuraj—eyes astonished, mouth laughing, hanging on for dear life.

About the Author

James Mills is a well-known journalist-turned-novelist who has lived in St. Tropez, France, for a number of years. He is the author of the best-selling *Report to the Commissioner* as well as *The Panic in Needle Park* and *The Prosecutor* among others. Mr. Mills is currently at work on his newest novel, *Target Fourteen*.